MISS SCARLET'S
SCHOOL OF

Patternless
Sewing

ALSO FROM KATHY CANO-MURILLO

Waking Up in the Land of Glitter

MISS SCARLET'S SCHOOL OF

Patternless Sewing

A Crafty Chica Novel

KATHY CANO-MURILLO

GRAND CENTRAL
PUBLISHING

NEW YORK   BOSTON

Copyright © 2011 by Kathy Cano-Murillo

Grand Central Publishing
Hachette Book Group
237 Park Avenue
New York, NY 10017

www.HachetteBookGroup.com

Printed in the United States of America

First Edition: March 2011
10 9 8 7 6 5 4 3 2 1

Grand Central Publishing is a division of Hachette Book Group, Inc.
The Grand Central Publishing name and logo is a trademark of Hachette Book Group, Inc.

The publisher is not responsible for websites (or their content) that are not owned by the publisher.

Library of Congress Cataloging-in-Publication Data

Cano-Murillo, Kathy.
   Miss Scarlet's school of patternless sewing / by Kathy Cano-Murillo.
      p. cm.
   ISBN 978-0-446-50923-7
   1. Hispanic American women—Fiction.   2. Handicraft—Fiction.
3. Phoenix (Az.)—Fiction.   4. Domestic Fiction.   I. Title.
   PS3603.A556M57 2010
   813'.6—dc22

2010019304

*Dedicated with all my love to my dad,
David O. Cano—for showing me that anything is
possible and to always dream big. I love you.*

MISS SCARLET'S
SCHOOL OF
Patternless Sewing

PROLOGUE

Driving along one of the busiest highways in the state, the cabbie slouched, relaxed as always. With one hand on the wheel, he glanced again in his rearview mirror.

He couldn't take his eyes off them.

Three exquisite young women in sparkling, jewel-toned evening gowns. Each with a different flower—a lily, a rose, a daisy—behind her ear. Brilliant hair colors of Raquel brown, Liz black, and Lucy red. Beaming smiles of sisterhood. Even squished together in the backseat, the women's enthusiasm didn't waver.

He had picked them up in front of the Mission Hotel around midnight at the close of some fancy fashion event—the high-end, snooty kind that brought out all the socialites draped in furs and diamonds. The girls didn't notice his taxi's top light was off. One of them practically leaped in front of his car, waving, begging him to pull over. He couldn't resist; their presence intrigued him.

He wasn't one to eavesdrop on customer conversations, but their excited energy bubbled throughout the vehicle and reeled him in. They may have had similar features, but their personalities couldn't have been more diverse.

"Three cheers for the lucky buttons! We did it!" cheered

the redhead, shaking a small glass jar over her head. "I swear, I thought we'd blown our cover. But we actually pulled it off! Did you see how everyone gawked when Reese ordered the champagne in our honor?"

"*You* did it, not that old jar of buttons, and certainly not us," remarked the girl with the wavy ebony tresses as she calmly adjusted the bodice of her teal dress. "You're the one with the creativity and vision; we just helped you fine-tune the patterns and stitching. I'm happy for you—and beyond proud...but like I said before we left, don't count on me to stick around in the business. Fashion is your dream, not mine. Next week I'm signing up for the Peace Corps. Travel the world and do some good for humanity."

Next, the brunette spoke up in a high-pitched voice. "I'll still help as long as you put me on the payroll. All I want is a normal, respectable life so I can raise my son."

The redhead crossed her heart twice with her finger. "I know," she said. "I promise to honor your wishes from here on out. With all my soul, thanks for helping me. I'm sorry I hurt you when I ran away. I'm so ashamed. I was so desperate to make it; I let go of everything I loved—my best friend, all my work, even myself—and worse...almost you two..."

The brunette leaned over, kissed the redhead's cheek, and then took a stern tone. "We're sisters. We'll always be here to protect each other. And speaking of protecting—I saw you and Reese scribbling on paper. Please tell me you didn't sign anything. You need to hire a lawyer to read the fine print, get the contract notarized in front of a witness, triple-check the royalty amounts—"

The cab made a swift lane change, jostling the girls. The brunette lunged up toward the taxi driver. "Hey, mister! Slow down up there. I want to get home in one piece!"

The cabbie, startled by her abruptness, agreed with a mini-nod of his head.

The redhead raised her chin. "Don't worry, Mr. Reese is an honest businessman. Come spring, he's going to put my designs in stores all over the country. All that matters is we made the deal. A shiny one!"

"Hopefully shiny enough to polish up your reputation after that sham of a marriage," mumbled the brunette.

The redhead bowed her head. "It wasn't a sham . . . I still love him."

"No frowns tonight," said the raven-haired girl, sliding her arm across to hug her sisters. "We're celebrating a fresh start. Let's focus on the positive, our little victories—they will add up to greatness."

"I love that—'little victories'!" gasped the redhead as she attempted to sit up tall to clap, but the sturdiness of her bouffant combined with the cab's low roof prevented it. She turned to face the others. "After tonight we're all going our separate ways, but we'll always be united in spirit. Family. All of us together. Just like right here, in this taxi, smashed like sardines in a can. I *love* you girls!"

"I love you both too," the brunette said, tilting her head and smirking.

"Why the guilty grin?" asked the redhead.

"Because we're gonna be stinkin' rich!" she replied, scrunching in her seat and rubbing her hands together like a miser. "I'm going to use every penny to send my baby to the finest schools!"

"Only the best for our little nephew," agreed the redhead.

They all giggled and clumsily climbed across the seat to hug one another. Touched by the intensity of the moment, the driver spied in the rearview mirror once more. This time his eyes met with those of the redhead. He flinched. Instead of happiness, she wore an expression of five-alarm terror.

"Watch out!" the girls shouted in unison. "The road!"

Snapping his gaze forward, the driver realized he had weaved into oncoming traffic. He shouted obscenities over the women's screams and overcorrected, causing the car to veer off the side of the road and, to his horror, down the side of a steep, dark embankment.

With twists of the steering wheel, the driver tried his best to keep the car from careening into the dark waters below, but the tire struck a large rock, which sent it and its passengers end over end into a violent roll.

A slow-motion montage of flailing limbs, hair, and flying glass filled the rearview mirror as the vehicle finally came to a crashing stop at the water's edge. The deafening silence permeated the scene, only to be broken up by the faint sound of Bobby Vinton's "Fly Me to the Moon" on the radio, as petals of lilies, roses, and daisies floated away into the night.

DaisyForever.com
magical musings about love, beauty & fashion
inspired by the life of Daisy de la Flora
as told by Miss Scarlet Santana

Thursday, September 15, 11:59 p.m.

Introducing: Miss Scarlet's School of Patternless Sewing!

Hello, my dahling Daisy-ites!

Miss Scarlet at the controls to bunny up about the latest news flash from the DaisyForever.com headquarters!

Let's start with some trivia. Did you know Daisy rarely used traditional patterns in her dress designs, instead opting for unconventional methods of measuring, draping, and shaping?

Well, dolls, to celebrate DaisyForever.com's 10th birthday, I'm going to tap into that by taking on a new adventure so utterly fantabulous, Daisy would flash a wink or two.

Ready? *Drumroll, please* . . .

Miss Scarlet's School of Patternless Sewing!

Hold on, put those flappers down, chickadees, and save the questions for the end.

What is my motivation for offering this closet-brightening, self-esteem-boosting, educational series? Miss Scarlet wants each and every one of you divas-in-the-rough to not only crack the shell of your ho-hum rut, but smash it to pieces like a cascarón on New Year's Eve! I want all of you to sass up your attitude, turn some heads, drop some jaws, transform the stiffest of critics to Jell-O, and make people look at you and say, "I'll have what she's having!"

To do that, I'll share what I know best: designing and making tailored clothes. Having a petite soda-pop-bottle silhouette myself, I've never been able to find my beloved Lana Turner–inspired frocks at secondhand shops, much less the mall. What could I do? Wear a polyester tracksuit and call it a day? I think not.

My Nana Eleanor, an educated activist for all things threaded, woven, and stitched, taught me early on that every curve of a woman's body has a three-part novella to tell. And to fully appreciate the fleshy package God gave us, we must tune in—measuring tape in hand—to discover the tragedies and triumphs that exist from the top of our tresses to the edges of our toenails. I sure did. My body's secret stories made me sob as much as cheer. I empowered myself to dissect my frame and stitch my own wardrobe from scratch.

Here's the dealio, tutti-fruttis: I'm going to personally instruct you how to make custom clothes for your one-of-a-kind body. With Miss Scarlet tutorials, your gams will look longer than Betty Grable's; your waist tighter than a Victorian corset, and your décolletage juicier than Jessica Rabbit's. You'll learn to design from instinct and explore the ins and outs of clothing construction. In this 12-week program, students of all skill levels will tackle assignments to learn the art of freeform sewing applied to practical wearables and accessories.

And it is all *patternless*... well, patternless in a traditional sense. No confusing, bland tissue paper here. We'll hiss at militant guidelines of what is considered correct. In this class, your body is the head honcho to please; it is the *only* pattern that matters.

The program is $500, and I'll gladly accept weekly payments. I'll provide the sewing machines, but you'll need to spring for your own fabric. I'll throw in a gift bag from my own stash of vintage trims, plus extra one-on-one time each week if you need it. One of the shimmery highlights of my program is that it will be held at the swanky Carly Fontaine Studio in downtown Phoenix.

The atmosphere is metropolitan frou-frou and we'll have a spacious area, professional worktables, massive overhead lighting, a 60-inch plasma TV so we can watch crafty cinema while we stitch, and best of all—there's a catwalk! How did I swing this? Let's just say being Ms. Fontaine's right-hand threadmistress for the past two years has earned me a pot-o-perks. Oh, did I mention that I'll also bring baked goods from La Purisima Bakery, home to the best apple empanadas in all of Glendale, Arizona? I hope all of these are reasons enough for you to sign up!

My faithful readers, here's a nugget of personal news I'm proud to share: I am now one degree closer to Daisy de la Flora. Yours truly has finally been accepted into the Johnny Scissors Emerging Designers Program for next year!

For those of you newbies, Johnny "Scissors" Tijeras is Daisy de la Flora's nephew and only surviving relative. Every year he presents the program for ten students where they are mentored at the Casa de la Flora headquarters in New York City. The program has been known to launch the careers of its participants. Thousands of dreamy dressmakers like moi apply, but only a few are selected each year. And after being rejected five times running, my boo-hoo days are over.

The tuition is very steep, thus the Patternless Sewing fees will help pay my way. I've also set up a donation widget to the left of your screen, for any millionaires out there who care to hook a girl up. ☺

This summer, my life is about to change and I owe it all to Daisy for inspiring me to design from my heart. Every week I share light, fluffy recipes; sewing projects; and creativity exercises here, but now I want to show my gratitude to Daisy and take this blog to a deeper level. Therefore, I'm opening my treasure chest of Daisy clippings that I've accumulated throughout the past decade and I'm going to share them with you. I've kept them to myself all this time because...well, I guess the exclusivity made me feel closer to her. But Daisy, wherever she may be in the world, would not want that. Her story is golden and deserves to be told. I, Scarlet Santana, want to be the one to do it. And it's perfect timing—this coming January is the 50th anniversary of Casa de la Flora!

Miss Scarlet's School of Patternless Sewing begins soon. To enroll, ring me at the Carly Fontaine Studio, 555-796-2874.

Hop on it—limited seats!

Uh-oh, Scarlet thought.

Loose thread on the side seam of her tailored waist jacket. How could that be? She had meticulously stitched and steamed the masterpiece until four a.m. to appear pin sharp for her meeting with her boss, locally celebrated designer Carly Fontaine.

Scarlet's Nana Eleanor had a superstition that if you pulled a loose thread and it came out short, something miraculous was about to happen. But if the seam unraveled—bad news could be expected. For all practical purposes, Scarlet decided *not* to touch the thread. She planned to leave Carly's office with a promotion today and had no time to worry about the meaning of a silly piece of string.

Oh, what the heck.

She gently tugged the strand. Short!

Two years ago Scarlet Santana changed her career path to pursue fashion design and ever since, all the necessary components had fallen into place like flouncy rayon ruffles. An award-winning blog, a full-time gig at Arizona's most noted fashion house, topped off with an upcoming New York City apprenticeship with one of the country's hottest designers.

All because she loved to sew.

Running fabric through her machine without interruption brought Scarlet tranquillity. It served as her therapy when she needed to think through disagreements with her family or fantasize about walking the halls of Casa de la Flora headquarters. When Scarlet worked on her dresses, she couldn't tell the difference between the moon or the sun, coffee from tea, or even if there were shoes on her feet.

Sketching, constructing, and embellishing clothing brought her happiness, and she refused to accept anything less. One way or another, she would make it her lifelong career.

Scarlet tried to rest comfortably in Carly's reception area chair—a modern Spanish monstrosity that could pass as a bean bag with oars for arm rests. She likened it to Carly: intimidating. Once Scarlet finally found her sweet spot, she stared through the glass windows of Carly's building and beyond the two lanes of traffic on Roosevelt Street. She sat still, her hands folded on her lap as she fixed her gaze on two statuesque blondes leaving the sandwich shop across the way. Scarlet imagined reconstructing their dresses with fancier necklines. The vision felt so real, Scarlet could hear the sewing machine already, as if it were right there by her side.

"Miss Scarlet, is that your phone buzzing from your purse?" asked Carly's administrative assistant, Yoli.

Scarlet winked at her and retrieved her cell from her clutch. "Thanks, doll!" she sang out while glancing at the screen to see who was calling. She slouched just a hair and then took a deep, confident breath.

"Hi, Mom!" she answered merrily, in the hopes she could control the tone of the forthcoming conversation.

No such luck.

"If she doesn't promote you," her mother started, "it's a sign from Nana Eleanor to get rid of that tacky rhinestone sewing basket of yours and get a real job!"

"Mom, Nana Eleanor is in a retirement home, not heaven. She isn't sending me signs unless it's through snail mail," Scarlet said. To outsiders, it sounded like her mom, Jeane, had stomped all over Scarlet's flower garden of self-esteem, but really, Scarlet knew her mom meant to pump her up.

"If she doesn't promote you"...here Jeane meant it was due time that Scarlet upgraded to a more worthy position other than her current role as Carly Fontaine's underappreciated sidekick.

"...it's a sign from Nana Eleanor to get rid of that tacky rhinestone sewing basket..." Nana Eleanor had served as Scarlet's sewing mentor since childhood. She taught the girl everything from proportion to basting to pinning to even measuring bodies with finger-walking and tight bear hugs. Most important, she instructed her granddaughter on how to make impeccable gowns from scratch with little to no resources.

Every Wednesday after school, Nana Eleanor and a then eight-year-old Scarlet took a ninety-minute bus ride to Neiman Marcus at the swanky Biltmore Fashion Park. After perusing the racks, they selected contrasting dresses, took them into the fitting room, turned them inside out and applied Nana's reverse engineering method. After sketching a fabulous hybrid version, they returned home to make it. By her high school years, Scarlet was carrying out the tradition solo when she crunched inside the tiny stalls of Glendale thrift shops and designed vintage pinup-girl apparel.

Nana Eleanor loved the creative connection she shared with her granddaughter and as a gift for her eighteenth birthday, she presented an authentic 1962 Daisy de la Flora bejeweled straw handbag that had been converted into a sewing basket. The gift changed Scarlet's life. She had been obsessed with all things Daisy ever since.

"*. . . and get a real job,*" Well . . . every mother thinks her child deserves more, right?

"Scarlet, did you hear me?" her mother snipped. "Promise me you'll hot-tail it out of there if she doesn't make you partner. Tell her you want your own office so you can brag about it at Thanksgiving dinner tomorrow!"

"I'll give it my all, Mom, like I always do—the way you and Dad taught me," Scarlet said graciously, pretending her mother had told her not to worry because she would win Carly over with her talent, skills, and charm. "It'll go great. I practically run this operation. This promotion is a long time coming."

"Even if she does promote you," Jeane continued, ". . . now, don't take this the wrong way, I'm only telling you straight because I love you . . . but I think you're shortchanging yourself if you stay at that sweatshop. You deserve better. No child of mine should be sweeping the floor."

Scarlet knew her mother had her own Dr. Phil style going on, but now she had gone too far, especially at a time when she should be sending good luck to her daughter, not cut-downs. She wondered if her mom, or any of her family for that matter, would ever take her life goals seriously.

"I mean it, mija," Jeane continued. "You're thirty, you should be wearing suits, not those cartoon dresses you make. And you should have bought a home by now. And a fancy car."

Scarlet had had enough. "I *am* wearing a suit right now, and I *do* have a fancy car!" she whisper shouted so Yoli wouldn't hear.

"Nana's clunker Mercedes is fifty years old and stinks like vitamin E oil. You should sell it and put the money toward your school loans."

"I'm not selling Nana's last memento of freedom, Mom. You

know the highlight of her week is our Sunday lunch dates. It would break her heart if I sold it," Scarlet said, glancing at Yoli, who had positioned herself front and center, pretending to sort papers so she could eavesdrop. Both their heads perked up with the click of Carly's doorknob.

"Mom, my meeting is about to start. I'll call you later, OK?"

"Good luck, Scarlet. Knock 'er dead, and then pour sugar on her."

That's all it took to make Scarlet feel at ease. A sliver of a cheer from her mom always worked wonders. She knew her mom truly wanted her to be happy, even if her version of happiness, like most things, didn't suit Scarlet's taste.

"Thanks, Mom, I love you," Scarlet said. But before she hung up, she heard, "Scarlet, wait!"

"Yeah, Mom?"

"Your sister can't make the mashed potatoes for tomorrow. I told her you could—you know, since you're single and have free time. We'll need enough for forty people. By three o'clock. Thanks, mija."

*　　　*　　　*

Scarlet sat across from her boss's desk, anticipation peeking over both shoulders, as she watched Carly skim the personnel file, using a heavy gold pen to add notations. Scarlet couldn't help but admire Carly's glossy ink-black hair and how it hung straight and blunt on each side, as if someone had draped a silk scarf over her head. Even though she was full-blooded Mexicana, Scarlet thought she could pass as a taller version of a camera-ready Kimora Lee.

"You were fired from the night shift at Fabrictopia last year? Assaulting a customer? I didn't know that," Carly said, tapping her pen on the paper.

"Ha! Oh yeah...simple misunderstanding," Scarlet explained, wondering how that information had ended up in her file. "I was demonstrating an easy way to use your arms to measure a body. I gently embraced this lady's mother in a bear hug. How was I to know she had a bad case of shingles? She sorta freaked out on me and—"

"That's enough," Carly said, scribbling more notes. "You better not do that here."

"Never have. Never will," Scarlet said. With her ankles crossed and knees tilted together at the side, she kept her composure even though her heart was beating crazier than a caffeinated Chihuahua.

Carly paused halfway down the page and peered over her chunky white eyeglasses. "OK. Let's do this. What do you want to talk to me about, Scarlet?"

"Well," Scarlet began. "I originate and stitch all my ensembles, and each one is based off of fashion icons of the silver screen. This one I'm wearing is inspired by Kim Novak's suit from *Vertigo.*" Scarlet smoothed her hands down her crisp gray lapels. "My Etsy store is quite the grandstand online. I also have three boutiques outside of Arizona that carry my other dresses. And I know you've seen my fashion blog, DaisyForever.com. Its horn has been tooted in *USA Today* and the *Arizona Republic*. I guess you could say I'm a star on the rise!"

Carly tilted her head, squinted, and nodded in faux fascination, as if she'd never heard any of it before (Scarlet made sure she heard it every day). Scarlet played along because she was over-the-moon proud to be one of her thirty employees. She worked her rump off to prove it.

She'd spent the first month at Carly Fontaine Studio unrolling bolts of fabric and trims to measure them for accuracy (something she now did from sight alone). She glued hundreds of sequins and feathers to headbands, fixed stubborn sergers, threaded a gazillion bobbins in advance, and sorted thousands of crystals by size and color. By the end of her first year, Scarlet had reorganized, upgraded, and improved the efficiency of Carly's storage, production, fitting, and showcase rooms. Her second year brought on the title of Personal Assistant to Carly, which put Scarlet on call 24/7 for every crisis. Scarlet proved her value throughout the past two years and that's why she knew Carly would offer her a promotion. If not partner, at least designer. If not designer, at least a raise.

Carly replaced the lid to her pen, slipped it in her black leather pencil cup at the corner of her desk, and closed the folder. She took a generous sip from her checkerboard-patterned mug, set it down, and smiled.

"Again, what would you like to discuss? We have five minutes left."

"I want you to make me partner," Scarlet said.

"Partner?" Carly repeated. "Well. That's quite a big aspiration, seeing as I've never considered having one. I built this little empire while I went to school. And I did it all on my own. I would never bring on a partner. Even if I did, they'd have to have the gift, the experience, plus the degree to go with it. Why would I change that now?"

It was the million-dollar question Scarlet had been waiting for.

"Because...I am...a dress healer."

"Excuse me?"

Scarlet excitedly scooted her chair close to Carly's desk, hunched over, and stared her down to ensure full attention.

"Carly, I've been designing and sewing since the third grade. I *dream* about designing. I'd rather sketch than...than... breathe! I don't see fabric and thread as just fibers. To me, they are storied seasonings ready to be stitched into submission. My eyes devour colors, my mouth waters because I can practically taste them. I tune into each and every article of clothing I meet, deconstruct it in my head to create an improved version. I can apply all of this to your business and take it to a higher level." She then looked dreamily toward the ceiling and raised her hands to form a frame. "We could combine our best traits into one line and call it... *The Scarly.*"

"I'm a dress healer too." Carly shrugged, unimpressed.

Scarlet stiffened. "If that were true, you'd know that the A-line skirt you're wearing is a half size too big." The words spilled out of her mouth before she had a chance to stop it.

"Oh really," Carly replied. "Well, it appears you're coming apart at the seams. Is that a hole in your jacket or is that how Kim Novak wore it in the film?"

Scarlet clenched her teeth and grazed her hand over the side of her rib cage and, indeed, felt flesh.

Double darn! I should have never pulled that loose thread!

Carly released a sigh of boredom. "Request denied." She leaned back in her wide black leather chair as if to wrap up the meeting.

"Maybe partner is out of the question—for now," Scarlet pleaded. "But I should at least be promoted to designer. We both know my work hits a target market you haven't been able to penetrate."

"Out of the question, at least until you enroll in fashion courses," Carly stated. "If you choose that path, I'll gladly move your hours around your schedule. I'm sorry, Scarlet, that's where I stand."

Scarlet couldn't believe her ears. Desperation bubbled up. "You *know* I have two degrees, both of them in coveted areas of engineering. One is in structural, isn't that what dressmaking is? My other degree is chemical engineering, which lends itself to textile science."

Carly shook her head. "Your spin won't work on me."

"In life, you have to stray outside the lines to stand out," Scarlet said. "My engineering skills could be a secret weapon if only you opened your mind. Do you know I could be earning four times my pay right now? I gave that up for my love of the craft. I'm dedicated. I'm a valuable resource and I'm right here under your nose. I'm already considered an expert! You know the patternless sewing workshop series I'm teaching here? Well, it's sold out!"

Carly's eyes opened wider than jumbo buttons. "Workshop *series*? What do you mean, *here*?"

"*Here*, as in . . . the production room. I requested it months ago and you approved. I saved the e-mail."

"I can't allow a private workshop here," Carly said. "I can't risk the potential damage. I'd probably have to take out extra insurance. Those are lines I'm not about to cross."

Scarlet stared blankly at that flashy gold pen resting in Carly's pencil cup. Patternless Sewing began in three days. Twenty-four students and no place to put them. She wouldn't dare cancel. Her credibility would be shot. Even worse, no Johnny Scissors tuition money.

"Scarlet, I do have some good news," Carly announced. "You are doing an excellent job as my assistant. I'm giving you a ninety-five cent weekly pay increase."

"$49.40 a year? Thank you," Scarlet said as she rubbed her thumb over the hole in her jacket. One last thought came to her mind.

"What if I told you I was accepted into the Johnny Scissors Emerging Designers Program? What if I completed it and earned a fashion degree that way?" Scarlet asked.

Carly let out a mini snort, and rose to escort Scarlet out of her office. "Wouldn't we all love to be accepted into that program? I've applied every year since college. I hear Marc Jacobs and Stella McCartney are each starting rival programs. You're so cute, Scarlet. The day you bring me a diploma from Johnny Scissors is the day I make you partner. Now, get back to work."

*   *   *

Twenty-four hours later, Scarlet arrived at her parents' Peoria home with a tub of creamy mashed potatoes in tow. On the drive over she vowed, as she always did, that under no circumstances would she bring up fashion, fabric, Carly Fontaine, or Daisy. Much less Johnny Scissors.

Thanksgiving dinner went like clockwork. The house was filled with chatty aunts in the kitchen, uncles clustered in front of the big-screen TV watching the football game, kids running rampant from one door to the next, and a dozen cousins downing beers on the back patio. Above all the small talk Nana Eleanor could be heard bragging about her latest doctor's appointment. Ever since her early seventies, the only prescriptions her doctor required were a daily dose of fresh air, a multivitamin, and a weekly shopping spin with Scarlet around town in her Mercedes. Nana made up the last one, but no one dared question it.

By eight p.m., everyone had left except for immediate family. It was a Santana ritual. Scarlet's older siblings, Charles and Eliza, sat at the kitchen table and took turns explaining, in detail, their current respective work projects. The conversation always ended with rounds of accolades for one another.

Scarlet listened to all their play-by-play anecdotes, knowing her turn to discuss her accomplishments would not arise. Her life choice had become the white elephant of family talk fests. One would think she'd shaved her head and married a female unicorn instead of choosing to work in fashion. The Santana clan considered her budding profession a joke, and the otherwise upbeat discussions turned into career intervention. To avoid headaches on all parts, Scarlet muted her own professional accounts and simply tuned into everyone else's.

After her second serving of turkey, Scarlet joined her eldest brother, Charles, in an in-depth review of his latest work project: designing a solar-powered light system for a new public art sculpture that would sit atop Glendale's tallest building.

"Traditional solar panels are so bulky and sci-fi-looking, they'll distract from the beauty of the art piece," he said. "Too bad that's what we have to work with."

Scarlet shrugged. "Why limit yourself to tradition?"

"Oh, here we go, little Scarlet's going to save the day again," Charles said with a wide smile.

"I will," she replied, more confident than Donald Trump cashing a check.

"I know you will," Charles nodded. "That's why I said it."

"Substitute the panels with that new stretchable solar-cell film that comes in different colors." She winked at Charles and removed the pen from his shirt pocket. He slid a paper napkin her way so she could sketch her vision.

"See?" she said as she sketched. "Why not construct a seating area on top of the building to complement the sculpture? The solar-cell film will cover flake-shaped frames to provide the shade. The effect will cast a soft rainbow kaleidoscope of color for visitors to enjoy, plus keep the lights on at night. The best part? It will run off a brain the size of a quarter."

Scarlet snapped the cap on Charles's pen and slid it back into his pocket while everyone sat at the table in silence, amazed at her rapid-fire mash-up of creativity and critical thinking. Well, everyone except a bored Eliza, who pulled out her phone and began to text.

"Scarlet is as gifted as she is beautiful," Scarlet's father, Manny, announced. She gazed at him in appreciation. He had the same pride in his eyes as he had when she took first place at the science fair every year in middle school. She'd give anything to record this moment—and replay it whenever she felt inadequate.

"Thanks, Daddy," she said.

"Now, if only she'd make this seamstress business a hobby and get back to engineering as her real job. Scarlet, you have enough patience to juggle both. It's like I always say..."

Scarlet blew air out of the corner of her mouth and looked to the low popcorn ceiling. "'To achieve success we must strive for balance in all we do.' Yeah, Dad."

"Hey, Scar," Charles said. "My buddy at Metropolitan Advanced Systems said he'd love to hire you. He was really impressed with the freelance work you did for them last summer."

Here it comes, she thought. Time to change the subject. Scarlet waved her hands in front of her face. "Nah, I'm cool, really. OK, kiddos, I'm going to clear the table for Mom's pie. Everyone, pass plates to the right, please."

Eliza, Scarlet's older sister, shoved her plate to the left. "I'm so sure! What about me? Why are all of you always trying to help Scarlet when she doesn't want it? I hate *my* job right now, I'd give anything to get one of those gigs!"

"You already have a good job, Eliza. But Scarlet is a natural talent who is undervalued by her current employer. She could sew circles around that Carly," her father answered. "We're presenting promising alternatives for her to consider."

Scarlet didn't acknowledge his comments as she removed the paper napkin from her burgundy pencil skirt. Dusting the crumbs from her baby pink angora cardigan, she stood, picked up the stack of plates, walked a few steps into her parents' kitchen, and set them on the counter. She hoped that by the time she returned, they would have switched topics. She wiped her hands on a dishtowel and walked back into the dining room to find her mother serving huge chunks of chocolate-chip pumpkin pie on clear plastic dessert plates.

"Tell them about your big promotion, Scarlet!" she said.

Scarlet gulped.

Manny rose in his seat, appearing a smidgen impressed. "It's about damn time. What is your new title? How much of a pay increase?"

Great, Scarlet thought. She couldn't have asked for worse timing. She hated that in every other aspect of her life, she felt confident and ambitious, yet here, she couldn't even make eye contact.

"Designer!" she replied, popping up her shoulders in exaggerated delight. "It takes effect right after I come back from the Johnny Scissors Emerging Designers Program this summer."

"The what?" Eliza asked, squishing her face like a cartoon character, hamming up the scene. She took pleasure whenever Scarlet sat in the hot seat.

"I told all of you about it at Dad's birthday party," Scarlet reminded them, scooting up in her chair. "It's an exclusive design academy in New York City led by *the* Johnny Scissors. He is going to be my mentor. Thousands applied, and I was one of the few selected."

Scarlet knew she had already said too much when her father cleared his throat. Her mother continued to dish out the pie.

As always, Charles added his two cents. "Why would your boss make you go to New York just to get a promotion in Phoenix? That's illogical. And how are you paying for it? You barely make enough to pay Nana rent and cover your living expenses, your school loans..."

"Scarlet does just fine," Nana Eleanor said. "She's quite the businesswoman. Aren't you, mija?"

"Thanks, Nana, but never mind," Scarlet said, gliding her fork into the soft, gooey layer of warm chocolate chips on her dessert. She wasn't in the mood to fight, and at least she had the chocolate to soothe her spirit. A second piece would be in order. "Let's just enjoy the pie."

"I've seen your site, Scarlet," Patricia, Charles's wife, said as she lifted her fork to her lips. "It's cute."

At last, a ray of sunshine from the bleachers! "Really?"

"Yes! I searched online for a cheese ball recipe last year and DaisyForever.com came up."

Laughter broke out around the table—except for Jeane, Manny, and Nana Eleanor.

"Award-winning cheese balls! Come and get 'em!" Eliza hollered.

Scarlet bit the inside of her cheek to keep from snapping at her sister. In as calm a voice as she could muster, she began to explain. "I share recipes sometimes, but mostly I offer ideas of how to live an artful life. I also show how to translate vintage fashion into contemporary wardrobes. I recently had some national press. Look, I'll show you!" Scarlet started to rise to get her parents' laptop from the other room. She'd show them the subscriber count, the award graphics, and even links to the recent *USA Today* article. That ought to cool their heels!

"It's OK, Scar, we trust you," Charles said, leaning back to put his hand on her wrist. "Good for you. I hope it brings you all the fame and fortune you desire."

A surge of pride came over Scarlet. "Like I've been saying

for the past two years, all I want is to make a living doing what makes me happy."

Manny sighed and pushed his chair away from the table. "Have you ever heard the quote by Eleanor Roosevelt? 'Happiness is not a goal, it is a by-product.' Put that through your serger and see what comes out." He stood up and was about to leave the room when Nana Eleanor stood up too.

"*That* Eleanor is long gone," she said, wagging her crooked finger. "However, this one is still alive, and she says with or without your blessing, our Scarlet is going to find her happy."

Mary Theresa knew of eleven steps to avoid headaches. Today she'd had time to complete only ten.

She had barely inserted the key into the lock of the front door of her two-story Chandler home when her first brain throb of the evening hit. Her six-year-old twins, Rocky and Lucy, who had the ears of night bats with hearing aids, sensed her arrival. Even through the thick, white wood door, Mary Theresa heard them shriek in unison as they pounded their fists against it in excitement.

While the rest of the country enjoyed their Thanksgiving feast, for her, the evening merely marked the close of another ten-hour day in software-design hell. She would have given anything to enter her contemporary castle, slink past her family, and crawl into bed with her new issue of *PC World,* but she didn't dare. The thirty-five-year-old would instead burst into the house and express her undying gratitude to her husband and twins, because that's what devoted mothers did.

Mary Theresa didn't notice the gorgeous November air, or the glittery fall wreath her children had created for the mailbox. She was too busy clenching her teeth, pasting on a fake smile as she opened the door, just in time for a heavy whiff of pumpkin pie. She couldn't decipher if it was the gourmet candle she had asked her husband, Hadley not to light, or an actual pumpkin pie. As exhausted as she felt, either one would do.

"Mommy, Mommy, Mommy! We've been waiting for you!" the kids sang out.

She had barely loosened the grip on her rolling briefcase before they attempted to leap on her. She adored her children, but at forty-three pounds each, Mary Theresa couldn't afford to lift them and throw her back out again. She politely blocked their advances and offered kisses as a substitute.

"Mommy, we missed you," Lucy said with a heavy lisp due to two missing front teeth. "It's Thanksgiving. Everyone left already. Why didn't you come home?"

Rocky interceded. "Daddy said it's 'cause the world'll stop spinning if she doesn't work for a day."

She couldn't believe her husband had made such a rude comment about her to their children! She was also appalled at what the kids were wearing. Rocky hopped around in Lucy's Easter Bunny costume, and Lucy crawled on all fours in Rocky's red reindeer flannel pajamas, pretending to be Rudolph.

At the same time, Hadley's favorite spastic John Coltrane LP blasted throughout the house, but it was no match for Mary Theresa's vocal cords. Especially as fired up as she was.

"Oh my God, Hadley, is this how the children were dressed in front of your family today? I spent eighty-five dollars on new outfits. Didn't you see them laid out on the dresser this morning? Must I do everything?"

Hadley exited the kitchen and approached her in the foyer. A twinkle danced in his eye as he handed her a goblet of white wine. In order to keep the peace, she reluctantly accepted and sipped. For an instant, her mood shifted from annoyed to pacified. Chilled Chardonnay, her favorite, had that effect on her. The sweet, buttery tang hit her bloodstream just right—so

much so that she downed the rest of the glass in four uninter-
rupted gulps.

"I just wish you would keep to the plan," she said through a
shiver as she gave him back the glass. "I can only imagine what
your mom and dad think of us as parents."

"They think we have creative kids, sweetie," he said calmly.

Hadley had to be the kindest, gentlest man Mary Theresa
had ever met in her life. On nights like this, it grated on her
nerves. But she had to admit that after ten years of marriage, he
sure knew how to soften her up.

"Mare, it's still Thanksgiving," he said, seductively sliding
his hand behind her neck. "This day is about relaxing and making memories together. We're happy you're home. Come on, we
have a surprise for you." His stroked her arm and led her across
the entryway, through the formal seating area toward the dining
room.

"Hadley. We've been married all these years and I still have
to ask you to not call me that," she said, wondering why he
couldn't—or rather, wouldn't—respect her proper name.

She could tell he held back an eye-roll. "Sorry, honey," he
said with a hint of irritation. He sighed and stopped when they
reached the room. "Mary Theresa, this holiday is about chilling
out. We're not being graded or watched or judged. It's just us.
Let's enjoy the night."

"But Mary Theresa is a strong, Catholic name given to me
by—" She decided to stop midsentence because he wasn't listening anyway. Why waste her breath.

"Close your eyes, Mommy!" Rocky sang out. Both kids
planted their little hands on the small of her back and shoved
her into the dining room for the big reveal. A fleeting thought
popped into Mary Theresa's mind of a cleared table and a spot-
less kitchen. Tomorrow was Black Friday and the clock had just

chimed eight p.m. She wanted to get in her seven hours of sleep and wake up refreshed and in time to hit the early-bird sales.

"Open your eyes! Lookie! Mommy, we saved Thanksgiving for you!" Lucy proclaimed, gesturing her stubby arms across a fully set table. "Sit down!" Lucy could barely contain her excitement, as if she had waited all day for this very moment. Feeling a tad guilty, Mary Theresa smiled and hugged her daughter.

Hadley pulled out a chair, cleaned it with an invisible duster, and gestured for Mary Theresa to sit, as if she were a queen. She wanted to be mad at him, but how could she after this royal treatment? She nodded, sat, placed the napkin on her lap, and admired the turkey-silhouette placemat the kids had made.

"Mommy, we are celebrating today because the Native Americans stole America from the white man," Rocky announced.

Mary Theresa's son never ceased to shock her. Even when she thought she'd heard it all, he always managed to eke out a gasp from her. The kid spent an entire year yelling "Daddy!" every time he saw George Lopez on the TV or in magazines, because Hadley resembled the comedian. Therefore, the family dubbed him Rocky "Just the Wrong Facts Ma'am" Cotorro.

"No, big boy. That is inaccurate," Mary Theresa corrected. Her son may have been cuter than a newborn puppy, but she couldn't indulge his historical inaccuracies.

"Nuh-uh, Mommy. That's what I remember from school!"

Mary Theresa rose from her chair. "Well, your teacher should have taught you better. Come on, let's go to the computer and I'll show you on Wikipedia."

Hadley flashed her a hard look and swooped up both kids in his arms. "Sit back down, Mare. I'll be right back. Kiddos, let's let Mommy eat in peace; it's bedtime."

"No, Hadley," she argued. "We must correct Rocky

immediately. We can't have our son spewing out inaccurate facts like that. We'll look like inattentive parents!"

It irked her that Hadley simply shook his head and playfully jogged up the stairs with the kids, as if Rocky's words were no big deal. She wondered how he could be so casual about the education of their only son.

Mary Theresa made sure to have the final say. She raised her hand to the side of her mouth and shouted, "You must talk to the school about this first thing Monday! This is *very* important!" She paused for a split second, then added, "I'm not saying it is your fault, honey. It's the school's fault!"

Oh, whatever, she thought. She knew her husband would blow it off. His theory was that as long as Rocky straightened out his facts by middle school, he'd be fine. This is where they clashed as parents—and spouses. Hadley accused her of being a micromanaging control freak, while she lectured him daily about his happy-go-lucky attitude and how it doesn't work in real life. When they began dating, the "opposites attract" cliché seemed romantic. But after almost a decade of marriage, the appeal had thinned.

Mary Theresa told her husband many times that she would be glad to loosen up on certain issues, but only if *he* would tighten up on others.

She picked up the plastic fork from the placemat, tapped it on the table, and reflected on the past ten years. Was she happy? Shouldn't she know? Shouldn't the answer come easily? She wanted to be thankful today, but she couldn't recall a recent week when she and Hadley hadn't raised their voices. Even over small issues like what kind of movie to see or where to put the potted plants on their bedroom balcony. There had been larger battles too, like in what neighborhood to raise their kids. He wanted to live near his family in the West Valley, but the schools on the east side of town ranked higher on the national average. Why did he have to counter every suggestion of hers? Didn't he know how much thought and research she put into her findings? Winging it was adventurous for childless couples, not for parents of twins.

Mary Theresa didn't even want to think about their belongings. If it were up to Hadley, their furniture, appliances, and vehicles would all be rusty and pre-owned. She insisted on brand-new. Mary Theresa worked hard for her income and enjoyed celebrating her accomplishments with objects that brought her fresh-off-the-assembly-line joy. How could she be taken seriously as a team leader at work, driving up in a used clunker?

She shook her head to clear away the angry thoughts and decided to focus on the Thanksgiving treats. The feast Hadley and the kids had set out for her scored a strong B+. A basket of rolls, steamed veggies, mashed potatoes, mac 'n' cheese, a tray of sliced turkey, and another of ham. Chocolate pecan pie, and pumpkin pie too—definitely not the candle. She removed the cellophane from the turkey, and the rich scent hit her nose. Starving, because she hadn't eaten since her protein bar at breakfast, she chose two medium slices of the poultry, a heaping portion of broccoli, and a single tablespoon of mashed potatoes and gravy.

A faint chorus of *"Gooooood night, Mommy!"* filtered down from upstairs, her kids' voices muffled due to the John Coltrane music that still blared through the house speakers.

"Sweet dreams, I love yooooou!" she shouted back.

She lifted her knife, cut into her turkey slice, and before she took a bite she swallowed tears.

They had started marriage counseling again.

Third round, new therapist. She found the ordeal ineffective.

Last week the couple was asked to share the memory of their initial introduction, and Mary Theresa actually had to fudge. She knew they met as computer programming students at Arizona State University, probably in a class. Why were those exact details so important to remember anyway, especially with a full-time job and two kids to contend with?

Her military parents were so strict with her that, when she met Hadley, his humor and charm drew her in like nails to a magnet. Hadley was one of the few people who could make her laugh about the ordinary and live in the moment.

A simple lunch date led to a string of dinners, late-night snacks, and, ultimately, daily breakfasts at his downtown Tempe apartment. They married soon after without any hoopla. He went on to design video games for a toy company and she joined a global communications firm as a software designer. That was about it—nothing momentous or cutesy like in the movies.

It was their third Christmas as husband and wife when they both acknowledged they were meant for different paths. The sign came when she gave him a $1,500 pocket watch with his favorite Bob Marley quote engraved inside:

"Don't worry about a thing, every little thing is gonna be all right."

What did he get her? A painted cigar box filled with "honey-do" coupons and handwritten love notes. Weren't those items a given when you are married? She'd never been more offended. The couple argued about it for three days, ignored each other for two, went to therapy once, and pretended the problem was solved.

They made love that night, more as an unspoken swan song to their relationship than a commitment to fixing it. Hadley moved out the next week.

A month later, the universe delivered a message. Mary Theresa became nauseated right before a department presentation. She thought nerves had caused her queasiness, but when it happened again throughout the week, she went to the doctor and learned Rocky and Lucy were on the way. She phoned Hadley from the doctor's parking lot and by dinnertime, he had moved back in.

For all practical purposes, she should have been terrified, but all she could think of was that silly Bob Marley quote. She felt like maybe every little thing would be all right. For once, she felt relieved. Ecstatic was more like it. Those days without him were flavorless, uneventful blocks of blah. Once they reunited, they kissed and agreed to swap $100 gift cards for Christmas from then on.

Unfortunately, the arguments escalated throughout the years. It started when, because neither one wanted to send the children to day care, one of them had to resign and become a stay-at-home parent. Mary Theresa figured since she made more money, he should be the one. One afternoon, she brought up the topic and left an opening for him to volunteer, but he didn't. So . . . she suggested he quit. When he balked, she pulled out a five-year-plan diagram that showed how much money they would lose if she stayed home. He didn't take kindly to her plan, but went with it. Each day had been a challenge ever since.

But through all the fights, deep down, she knew he loved her. And he knew she loved him. At least, she thought he knew.

She put a small forkful of potatoes in her mouth and turned to see Hadley jogging into the dining room. He spun around on his tiptoes, rocked his shoulders, and bobbed his head to the spastic groove of Coltrane's free-form jazz. "All righty, los niños are tucked in; now it's time for *us*," he said, throwing out a finger-point in her direction. All of a sudden, his posture went limp.

"Aw, Mary Theresa, you didn't wait? I wanted us to eat together. It's the first night in a long time you're eating dinner at the table. I wanted to make it romantic and relaxing. Didn't you notice the two place settings?"

She was all for relaxing too, but couldn't because his music drove her bonkers. *Seriously, how long is each song?* she thought. *And why didn't he say he wanted us to eat together when he shoved me in this chair?*

"I'm sorry," she said. "I was so hungry, it all looked so good..."

"Aw, no worries," he replied. "How does it taste?"

"Everything is delicious," she said, trying for optimism. "The broccoli is excellent, but the potatoes are a bit salty. Did you stick to the recipe? Oh, darn, I just lost count of my chews!"

Out of her peripheral vision, she witnessed Hadley frown.

"According to the American Medical Association," she explained, "we're supposed to chew each bite between twenty and thirty times for proper digestion."

Hadley chuckled and reached for one of the tapestry-covered dining chairs, parked it close to her, and then stroked her chin. "I love you, Mary Theresa."

What a pleasant surprise. She didn't expect that. Her stomach tingled, and not from the aroma of the pumpkin pie.

"I love you too, honey," she whispered back, her eyes moist with happy tears. The saxophone tune in the background slowed to a smooth pace she could appreciate.

He clasped her hand. "Can I ask you something?"

She nodded. "Of course."

Hadley rested his nose on hers. It had to be the most intimate moment they had shared in months.

"I finished my class this week," he said. "I was wondering if you had a chance to enroll in yours."

Mary Theresa ripped her hand away, stood up, and began to clear the table. *How dare he ruin the night?* she thought. Set her up like that only to make her feel like she wasn't doing her part for their marriage. She marched into the kitchen and, with trembling hands, scraped the full trays of food into the trash bin. Her breathing quickened and she felt her face heat up from the anger.

At the latest session, their marriage counselor gave the fractured couple an "assignment." Hadley was to enroll in a life-coaching program to assist him with establishing goals and deadlines. Mary Theresa's task? To "foster her spontaneity" and join some kind of "rule-free" creativity class such as mixed-media collage or abstract painting. Mary Theresa did not see an ounce of value in the exercise, and she cringed at the thought of taking time away from work to create New Age woo-woo crafts. She hoped Hadley would disregard the idea, like he did with all her ideas for running a more efficient household.

However, he loved the assignment and completed his courses straightaway. *Of course,* she thought, *Hadley had every day of the week free while the kids were at school. How hard could it be to care and cook for them?* She could only imagine what he did to pass the time. Probably dance around the house, listening to his crazy jazz. She, on the other hand, pulled in sixty-hour workweeks. Not only did she have to meet her own quota at the office, but make sure her team members did as well. By the time her weary body made it home, all she wanted to do was collapse and recharge for the next day.

Mary Theresa didn't think the assignment was fair. In her mind, she didn't need a class to foster her spontaneity. If she had the time, she'd be spontaneous! She marched back to the table, loaded up her arms with stacks of serving dishes, and dumped them on the kitchen counter. She couldn't even look at him, she was so furious.

Hadley chewed on his bottom lip, slouched against the beige kitchen wall, folded his arms across his chest, and stared at the tile floor.

"I guess that means no," he deadpanned.

"Of course not!" she snapped. "I'm a horrible wife and mother, remember?" She then ripped open the dishwasher door and turned to face him. "How dare you make me feel guilty. I'm the one bringing in the income around here. If it weren't for me, we wouldn't have this beautiful house, or the means to serve this expensive, sodium-laden dinner."

She didn't only open Pandora's box, she dumped it over his head.

Hadley clenched his fists at his sides, pursed his lips, and stepped into her personal space. Now *his* face turned bright red. Mary Theresa expected him to holler, so she braced herself. But instead, he took a long, deep breath and then blew it out, as if to release as much hostility as possible.

"It wasn't my idea for you to be the breadwinner," he said slowly, accentuating every syllable. "You make up the rules and chisel them in marble. I didn't have a choice. I never have a choice." His tone sped up the more he explained his feelings. "I never asked for this house. All I ever wanted was peace of mind and most of all, love—but that isn't enough for you. Every day you get up with the roosters and leave without kissing your son and daughter good-bye. Your idea of cariños is a chore list on this overpriced refrigerator that you barely open. Or self-help books on the kitchen table for me to read. Everything with you is about lists, rules, schedules, and critiques, on and on and on. I'm sick of it. I'm ready for a change."

Mary Theresa wasn't buying it, but did agree on one thing.

"We both need change," she said. "With all we have going on, we need structure . . . you think some silly art class is supposed to help me? Come to think of it—how was *your* organization class supposed to help me?"

"It's supposed to help *us*," Hadley replied, holding back his fury, proven by the bulging veins on his forehead. "Don't you see? It's not the class itself, it's the act of taking the step, meeting halfway, making a sacrifice. Why can't you lighten up? Let go and, God forbid, have a bit of fun. Mary Theresa, we're only thirty-five, but we look forty-five from the stress. Can you honestly say you're satisfied with this life right now? Do you want our children growing up thinking this is how a normal household is? They need their mother. The way it stands now, you're more like the house warden."

They stood in silence for a few seconds, leaving only the controlled chaos of Coltrane between them. At that moment, Mary Theresa hated Hadley as much as she hated his stupid music. She covered her ears and ran out of the kitchen. Her reasoning couldn't keep up with her emotions. Her feet carried her swiftly to Hadley's prized stereo system, having no clue what she was about to do. She watched as her hands pried open the smoky gray plastic cover of the turntable and flipped it up. Her thin fingers clasped the needle and tore it from its hinges. Next, she snatched the album, snapped it in half, and pitched it across the room.

She panted so hard from anger, she worried she might be having a heart attack. But the thought vanished as soon as she heard Rocky shriek from upstairs. The argument had woken up the kids. She closed her eyes and counted to two, and as always, Lucy started up next. Together, their cries mimicked an ambulance siren.

Hadley was nowhere to be seen, but Mary Theresa heard footsteps coming down the stairs and the cries getting closer. It was him, with one kid over each shoulder.

"We're spending the night at my mom's," he said, grabbing his wallet and car keys.

More than anything in the world, Mary Theresa wished she could have rolled back the clock. She'd never, in all her life, acted out so violently before. She didn't want them to leave.

"Honey, please...stay, I'm sorry," she begged, running up behind him, reaching for his arm, or at least a pinch of his shirt. She began to sob when he brushed her hand away. "Please...I'm sorry, don't go. There's an article in my new *O Magazine* about how to handle meltdowns. I'll read it and do it so this doesn't happen again! I'll buy you a new record, I'll do my assignment, I promise, Hadley. I love you. Please stay...I'm begging you!"

His eyes filled with tears as well, but he shook his head and walked outside. The kids' sobs downgraded to sniffles, but they hung on to him for dear life. All three of them stared at her as if she were an alien with two heads.

"Happy Thanksgiving, Mary Theresa," he whispered, right before he shut the door between them.

DaisyForever.com

magical musings about love, beauty & fashion
inspired by the life of Daisy de la Flora
as told by Miss Scarlet Santana

Thursday, November 24, 2:45 a.m.

Leaving the Nest

Hi-de-ho, Daisy dillies!

It's Thanksgiving night and I'm going to share a Daisy ditty about gratitude, kindness, karma, family—and never giving up faith in your vision. I must admit, my cyber duchesses, this post is as much to help me, as you.

First I'll start with thank-yous to all of you for visiting DaisyForever.com. We're up to 100+ reader comments a day, and it feels good to know I'm channeling Daisy's spirit to do good in the world! She is the dandelion, I'm the one blowing, and all of you are carrying her artful message, one-by-one, far and wide.

Here is the question I present today: How do your personal goals contrast with what your family has in mind for you?

I come from a large, loving brood that only wants the best for me—as long as it conforms to their definition of "best." Earlier this evening, somewhere between the pumpkin pie and drying the dishes with my sister, I had a bit of a heated conversation with my parents about my Daisy daydreams and how they fit into my future. Even with the success of this website, my coveted gig at Carly Fontaine Studio, and my acceptance into the Johnny Scissors program, every time I'm around my family I feel like I'm in high school all over again. The insecure, chubby math geek with braces, wearing her handmade vintage-inspired clothes, carrying around a sewing basket and a graphing calculator.

I'm not that girl anymore.

Are you like me, and feel like you're alone in your quest for greatness? Rather than sulk and toot a cardboard horn at a one-person pity party, we must funnel the frustration into ambition. Tonight I came to the conclusion that to earn respect from my inner circle, I have to leave the nest to prove I can fly on my own.

Can you relate? If so, I have the perfect example to share.

This flamboyant flashback is from an exclusive interview that Daisy's high school best friend, Saide Gomez, gave to *Vanity Fair* in 1985. Of all the Daisy articles and press clippings I've collected over the years, this is, by far, one of my favorites. I cry every time I read it. The article ran in honor of the thirty-year anniversary of Casa de la Flora.

First of all, cue the mambo music!

The year? 1953. Daisy, sixteen, turned heads every time she stepped out of her aunt and uncle's house, which was nestled in a modest suburb in Miami's Coconut Grove area. If she wasn't on her way to school or one of her two jobs; she was headed to the movie house to soak up a flick by her idol, Carmen Miranda. But Daisy didn't go for the tropical tanginess of the star. No, she considered it practical education and went with a notepad and a sharpened pencil to sketch all of Carmen's delicious outfits and accessories.

While most other teenagers in America were obsessed with Marilyn, Daisy's mind swirled with the music, colors, and art of Carmen. The world perceived Carmen as "The lady in the tutti frutti hat," but Daisy knew she was more than that—a painter and fashion designer as much as she was a dancer, singer, and actress. (Did you know that from early in her Hollywood career to the very end, Carmen designed and even made many of her multitiered gowns, stacks of heavy beaded necklaces, and chandelier-inspired headdresses?)

After school, Daisy worked as a waitress at the corner coffee shop, and on weekends, after the movies, she attached clasps at her aunt and uncle's leather handbag factory. After almost every shift, she brought home small bags of unwanted findings, studs, and trims. On a good day, she'd leave with a few defective bags. To her, they were blank canvases to play with. Daisy spent hours each evening painting and glazing mini-strawberries, bananas, and other fake fruit she sculpted from bread dough, and let harden in the sun. She used the items, along with gems and feathers to Daisy-fy belts, shoes, hats, and clutches and then wore them with every outfit she owned.

Saide said in the interview that by the time Daisy turned seventeen, she had a steady roster of local customers who loved her flamboyant creations. They consisted mostly of circus, stage, or burlesque performers, but still, they were fans. Go, Daisy!

Daisy's dream was to give Carmen one of her treasured items. But how does a lowly Miami teenager make good with one of the highest-paid entertainers in show business? The only way Daisy could think of: fan letters.

Once a week for a year and a half, Daisy sent a package to Carmen. She shared her sketches, comments on her films, and even suggestions for new costume ideas. She decorated each package with doodles and pasted-on fashion pictures and mailed them along with a sample of her work to Carmen's fan P.O. Box address that she found in the back of a magazine.

Daisy's sisters and aunt and uncle frowned at her obsession, scolding her for wasting her money and time. Embarrassed by her flamboyant lifestyle, they criticized, but Daisy simply responded by adding extra crystals and sequins to her designs. (Now we know why her work was so sparkly.) Her uncle even tried to tell her that Carmen was nothing more than a drug addict and a Hollywood puppet. He despised the woman's act and hated that Daisy worshipped her. Little did he know, his resentment made Daisy adore Carmen even more.

Someday, Daisy thought, she would escape Coconut Grove and her stuffy family forever and find her way into Carmen's entourage.

Then one day, a small parcel arrived.

Daisy's face flushed when she read the return address, and she raced to her best friend Saide's house to open it.

The package was from the president of Carmen's fan club. She thanked Daisy for her support, and informed her that Carmen had indeed received, adored, and even wore one of her gifts—a wrist cuff featuring the outline of a parrot, accented with rows of gems, sequins, and rhinestones. Also included in the package was a small glass jar of green buttons from Carmen's personal dressmaking stash. Carmen, impressed by Daisy's devotion, had them sent as a good-luck charm for her design career. She invited the teen to attend a musical stage show and requested that Daisy bring samples of her collection. Carmen's people would introduce her to a team of national sales reps, who would also be in attendance that night. Enclosed was a set of two show tickets to a live broadcast of *The Perry Como Show* and a reservation for a hotel.

"We're going to the Big Apple to meet Carmen!" Daisy cheered. The girls hugged, and jumped up and down on the bed. Saide snatched the letter from Daisy's hands to reread it calmly, as if examining the fine print on a contract. A frown spread across her face.

"The event is the Saturday after next," Saide said, dejected.

"Exactly!" Daisy replied. "We have two whole weeks to prepare!"

"Daisy, New York City is over a thousand miles away." She asked Daisy how they could afford transportation, and reminded her that she didn't even have any products to show because Daisy had either sold them or mailed them to Carmen.

Saide and Daisy had been soul sisters ever since grade school. Out of everyone in the universe, she knew how much this meant to Daisy. Can you believe she actually tried to talk Daisy out of going? Some friend, huh? Greeby. Instead of encouraging our Daisy, she tried to break her spirit. Grrr...people like that make me growl like a cranky mama tiger.

Anyhoo, back to the story...

You might think those little obstacles would hold Daisy back, but she clocked in extra hours at her jobs, even pretended to be sick so she could stay home from school and work instead. By night the devoted designer enlisted her reluctant sister to help her build up the best samples ever. And, to add to the drama, she had to do it all under-cover because no way would her aunt or uncle let her go alone with Saide to New York City! That was unheard of for two eighteen-year-old girls from Miami in the 1950s.

On August 5, 1955, Daisy and Saide checked into the Plaza Hotel.

Daisy couldn't pinpoint why, but sadness hung in her heart. It took all her might not to cry, and that confused her. She hadn't experienced such sorrow since a tragic bus accident took the lives of her parents ten years before. Those wounds were painful, so she pushed the memory out of her head and focused instead on her love of designing and the joy of seeing Carmen.

Decked out in Daisywear from head to toe, the girls waited in the humid August evening in front of the hotel for a cab to pick them up and drive them a few blocks to the Ziegfeld Theatre. Saide paid the driver and, just as they exited the vehicle and shut the door, he leaned over and said through the open window, "You gals dressed up like that in honor of Carmen?"

They nodded and giggled.

"It's a real shame," he said, bowing his head as he drove off.

Saide and Daisy exchanged confused expressions and went on inside, still giddy. Daisy took a deep breath and clenched her heavy suitcase of decorated hats, headbands, purses, gloves, and belts. She had planned to take one of each but couldn't decide what to pick, so she brought everything to be safe. Hopefully she would be going home in the morning with good news to share with her family.

"Is it just me, or does this scene feel...I don't know... weird? This is supposed to be a lively concert, but it feels like a funeral," Saide whispered, noticing a subdued buzz among the crowd. They walked past the main entrance and into the theater in awe, amazed at the gorgeous art deco architecture and lush upholstery. They found their seats, front and center in the second row! The girls hugged each other, proud of their successful journey and excited to see Carmen perform before their very eyes. Ready to dance and celebrate, they held hands, as well as their breath, when the house lights dimmed and the red velvet curtains opened.

Silence. No band, no dancers...no Carmen.

Instead, one spotlight shined down on a large, gold-framed portrait of Carmen that rested center stage. Dozens of floral bouquets and wreaths surrounded it, and draped across the front of it all hung a black ribbon that read IN MEMORIAM.

Daisy gasped and covered her mouth with her free hand, while Saide tightened her grip on the other.

A man in a sharp black suit walked onstage, and the crowd rose and lowered their heads. Daisy's chest began to heave. She knew what he was about to say.

Carmen Miranda, the Brazilian Bombshell, had died.

Saide recalled that being the longest night of her life. Of course, Daisy went into hysterics, and Saide had to practically carry her limp, sobbing body back to the hotel. She stayed up with her all night, cradling her head, rocking her to sleep.

By the way, Saide is back in my good graces at this point.

Daisy never met with the president of Carmen's fan club, much less the Saks Fifth Avenue buyers that night. She didn't care. Her creative spirit had vanished. The next morning, she quietly packed up all her belongings and prepared for the thirty-hour train ride home.

Daisy told Saide she planned to ask her uncle for forgiveness and start fresh at his business, but not anywhere near the factory. She swore she never wanted to see another sequin as long as she lived. She would lead a quiet life and work in the office with her sisters. Carmen had been a bright shooting star in her life, and now that light was no more.

The girls walked in silence to the nearest subway that would take them to Penn Station. The brilliance of the city now appeared tarnished in their minds. Daisy allowed herself one sniffle of self-pity. Sadness consumed her, but she knew a greater destiny awaited her. She looked up to see her reflection in an empty store window. She stopped and blinked. Was that Carmen staring back at her?

Daisy pressed her face to the glass and cupped her hands around her eyes for a clearer view. A chill raced up her spine. There on the countertop sat a large picture of Carmen, her dainty hands framing her delightful chin, wearing the towering crown of fruit, smiling with a devilish grin as if she owned the world. It was an image that would later become iconic. Daisy looked into Carmen's bright eyes and felt mysteriously compelled to enter the store.

Once inside, Daisy dropped her off-brand Samsonites and picked up the photo and gazed into it as if it were a crystal ball. Saide followed, but didn't look at the photo. She was too intrigued with the merchandise of the boutique. Sleek party dresses, silky gowns, stunning tiaras, satin handbags, and the most scrumptious array of heels she had ever laid eyes on.

"Such a shame," the handsome storeowner commented to Daisy. "Carmen Miranda was so full of light and love. She'll be missed."

Daisy nodded, clenching the picture to her chest.

"You have such lovely merchandise, why isn't your store window filled up? I bet you could get a lot of business in here," Saide said.

Daisy stepped back and glanced around the glitzy shop.

"Oh, I know that," the shopkeeper chuckled. "My sister is queen of all that. We're in between displays. Window dressing is an art form; we're waiting for that flash of genius to strike, I guess you could say. Fall is right around the bend, but I'm bored with the usual autumn hues of brown and olive...."

Daisy perched up an eyebrow and approached the storeowner. "Let us decorate it. In honor of Carmen."

The man hesitated and then folded his arms. "Well, may I ask who you are? Do you live in the city?"

Daisy scrambled from one dress to another, pausing only to put her hand on her chin and intensely ponder. So much for her plan of working in her uncle's office. She'd leave that for her sisters.

The storeowner's eyes flickered about, shadowing Daisy's every move, not sure what to make of her. Saide noticed his concern.

"My friend is a designer who is...was...inspired by Carmen. She's very shaken up about the news," Saide whispered. "She's still dealing with it as you can see."

"*Is* inspired by Carmen," Daisy corrected, picking up a business card from the counter. " 'Her Madgesty's Closet.' Cute name. Let me guess. Your sister is Madge?"

He nodded. "Isn't it clever?"

"What's your name?" Saide asked, flicking her lashes like a Cuban Betty Boop.

"Javier," he said, flirting back.

"Hey, Javi," Daisy said, interrupting the love connection. "I was supposed to meet Carmen last night. It sounds farfetched, but I swear, she was a fan of my work. We're from Miami, and her fan club president paid our way out here to see her show. We came all this way, and well . . . anyway . . . it would be my honor to create the most elegant, beautiful window shrine dedicated to Carmen. I have a suitcase full of accessories, combined with your gorgeous dresses and mannequins—I think Carmen will smile down from heaven. Saide, would you do the honors?" she asked, gesturing to her friend.

Saide used the pointy tip of her leather flat to pop open the suitcase on the floor. She scooped up a black pillbox hat trimmed in a row of rhinestone swirls with a strawberry in the center of each one. "Take a gander at this. One hundred percent Daisy made," Saide said proudly as she modeled the hat. "Maybe it's something your wife would like?"

Javier removed the hat from her head, inspected it, and then stepped over to Sadie and looked into her eyes. "Actually, I don't have a wife. Or a girlfriend." He smiled at Sadie for a moment before remembering Daisy's request. "Nice work, ladies. Let's do this."

Saide put her hands behind her back and nudged her shoulder at him. "The window or a date?"

"Both," he said. Daisy, her spirits lifted, began to measure the window with her arms, while Saide and her new beau chitchatted.

The three of them worked all weekend to create a magical visual tribute to Carmen. In addition, Madge and Javier decided to carry Daisy's accessories in their store, which became so popular they had to hire a small staff to produce them. Daisy and Saide never returned to Miami. Both their families were heartbroken, but the girls paid no mind. Saide had found her soul mate, and Daisy her career. They rented the room above Her Madgesty's Closet and filled orders that came in from around the globe. Models, socialites, costume directors, photographers, movie stars, and magazine editors...everyone scrambled for Daisy originals.

Of course, the fairy tale didn't last forever. Saide married Javier, but they divorced a year and a half later, and she refused to ever speak of it. In fact, some kind of falling out took place between all of them. Daisy, estranged from Saide, became somewhat of a recluse, even after she hit the big time. Someday I hope to learn the details of this mystery!

I have several reasons for sharing this story. In spite of all the obstacles of her family, heartache, and tragedy, Daisy found a way to make her mark in the world in a big way. She took risks, raised eyebrows, and went against what everyone expected of her because she believed in her talent. She also teaches that ultimately, we don't have control of what happens. Sometimes you have to let it go and have faith that God, the universe, karma—whatever you want to call it—will bring it back in a better way.

I have a lot of opposition in my life right now, many challenges to conquer. But Daisy's story gives me hope and pumps me up. Tomorrow is a new day and I'm going to make it the best I can. Besides, you'll NEVER believe what I scored at an estate sale last weekend—the jar of Carmen's lucky buttons! They were passed on to a woman from her grandfather who used to live in Coconut Grove. I only paid $50, but we all know they are priceless. My dream is to someday meet Daisy in person and return this precious gift to her. Daisy, if you are out there, come find me!

So go out there and make the most of what you have to work with! Find your own window display to gussy up, put together your own jar of lucky buttons! Miss Scarlet, Daisy, Saide, and Carmen want you to!

Scarlet, flat on her belly like a squirrel in midflight, swept her arm under the massive, low-set armoire in search of her black-and-white saddle shoes. A decent set of ground grippers were in order today; she had a heck of a lot on deck.

At last, her middle finger felt the smooth edge of the wood heel. With one last stretch, she grabbed it and joyously hugged the long-lost footwear to her heart. She then jogged down the hallway and set the shoes on top of the dresser next to the antique radio that played Glenn Miller. Actually, it was her iPod system parked behind the radio that played Glenn Miller—all the same to Scarlet.

After an ego-deflating Thanksgiving dinner, Scarlet came home, wrote on her blog, and sewed up a storm to reconfigure her confidence levels. She started and finished a new dress that came out much different from all her others. The frustration from the dinner had filtered its way out of her system by way of satin and lace. Scarlet loved that she could process negativity and transform it into an item of beauty. However, she felt groggy from the stitch-a-thon. It was already seven thirty a.m. and she still had to dress for work.

As she combed through the racks in her walk-in closet, Scarlet practiced breathing exercises to calm her nerves that were currently more tangled than a tarantula's jump rope. She needed to find another location quickly for the sewing class, or scrap the idea and find another way to pay her Johnny Scissors tuition.

Otherwise, she'd fail miserably and prove her family right.

She took a deep breath and let her worries float away, if only for the moment, so she could focus on Glenn.

Music always got her going. Her limbs warmed from the inside out as she swayed to the peppy grooves and toe-tapped her way into the kitchen. Her trusty percolator smiled back at her as she filled it with water and added the coarse grounds to the brew basket. On went the gas flame, and she set out a pink Stetson Melmac cup.

Savoring the peaceful vibe created by the scent of fresh coffee and the sound of "Sunrise Serenade," Scarlet wondered why she let herself get so worked up in the first place. Mother Nature beckoned the girl to relax. The cool November air flowed through the open ninety-year-old kitchen window and it already smelled like Christmas. She squeezed her eyes tight and thanked the universe for what she did have going in her favor.

She may have been the ill-fitted square peg at her folks' house the previous night, but not here. Scarlet's casita measured one thousand square feet of pure palatial paradise. Formerly her Nana Eleanor's residence, the classic 1930s Craftsman bungalow was now a historical Glendale landmark in the Caitlin Court neighborhood. Scarlet had more memories of walking up the shallow steps to the triple-arch porch than she did of her parents' southwest stucco entrance. Every day in front of the rock wall fireplace, Nana conducted a type of home-ec boot camp for Scarlet. She taught her how to pin the perfect hair curls, bake foolproof piecrust, polish silver, and make tamales at Christmas and menudo at New Year's. Nana had schooled Scarlet right. And even in her adult years, Nana Eleanor proved to be her strongest ally.

When Scarlet decided to trade in a ruler for a measuring tape and do the fashion thing, it was the night of her twenty-eighth birthday celebration. Before she blew out the candles on her red velvet cake, she announced to her family, friends, and fiancé that pursuing her dream was the best present she could give herself. The crowd freaked, just as Scarlet had expected. But what made her flinch the most was when Cruz, her dapper fiancé of four years, dumped her that very night—on her birthday!

As the couple drove home from her parents' house to his Ahwatukee condo, he gave her an ultimatum: Take one of the six-figure engineering jobs that had been generously offered to her or move out. His reasoning was that even though he supposedly loved her, he had "put up" with her fascination of all things retro long enough. He assumed Scarlet would transform overnight into a business-suit-wearing corporate maven—a perfect match to his law career.

They were stopped at a red light on Chandler Boulevard when Cruz confronted her, the softness in his big brown eyes replaced by emptiness. In that moment Scarlet knew his supposed love for her came solely from her income-earning potential. She should have seen this coming, but Scarlet's downfall was that she always noticed the good in people first.

Looking back, Scarlet had no idea why she had stayed with the louse as long as she did. She preached to high heaven on her blog all the time that her readers should surround themselves with positive people. And yet there she was, being made to feel like a misfit minx by the one person who should have been holding her pincushion. There at that stoplight, Scarlet decided to take her own advice. She made Mr. Man pull over and gave him a piece of her mind. She ditched his fancy wheels, called a cab, and went straight to Nana's.

Spending the night at her grandmother's house after emotional distress was healing, thanks to the combined blast of cologne, spray starch, and vitamin E oil when Nana opened the front door; the fresh fruit pie and the pitcher of sweetened tea always ready in the fridge; and the collection of ceramic elephants in the china chest. Everything her grandmother had lingered from decades past. In any other setting it would seem odd, but in Nana Eleanor's house, it all belonged.

Scarlet and her nana nibbled that night on apple empanadas and washed them down with cups of café con leche while the music of Pepe Aguilar crooned through the record player. Nana lent Scarlet one of her frilly nightgowns from the '40s and made up the couch for her to sleep on. She promised her granddaughter that the karmic scales were tilted in her favor and told her to sleep tight. Scarlet did as she was told. She couldn't care less that she had been dumped on her birthday, had no place to live, and not a lick of a fashionable job opportunity.

The next morning, Nana asked her to drive her to see Scarlet's mom and dad. And there, over grilled burgers and potato salad, Nana informed them that she wanted to move to Thunderbird Retirement Resort and rent her house to Scarlet. Nana explained that at eighty, she was too old to tend to the property.

Fast-forward twenty-four months, and Scarlet had converted one bedroom into her sewing studio and office space, and the carport into a potting shed. She picked up where her nana had left off in the outside garden and planted flowers, vines, and veggies. Her dad even installed a bench swing in the center of the lush garden, making it her go-to sanctuary for self-reflection. Aside from that, she kept almost every doily in place. Most of her possessions were bona fide relics that ranged from the 1920s to the 1970s, but she also accumulated modern resources as needed. Miss Scarlet couldn't go without her iPhone, MacBook Air, Lean Cuisine, or local Target!

Scarlet reminisced as a jazzy piano version of "The Way You Look Tonight" piped through the house. Before she dressed, she stopped by her glass curio to admire her most-prized Daisy collectibles: autographed glossies, magazine clippings, limited-edition Daisy wallets, the jar of Carmen Miranda's buttons, even a Daisy toy doll.

Scarlet adjusted the straps on her slip and wormed her way into a polka-dot shirtwaister, but it reeked of Shalimar. Must have been the one she wore dancing last week, and she accidentally hung it back in her closet. OK, black pedal pushers and a paisley smock it was. Standing in Nana's pink-and-black tiled bathroom, Scarlet tied on a silk scarf to hold back yesterday's teased bouffant with the sprayed curl at her forehead, patted her tan skin with Pan Cake foundation, then swiped her lids with a broad line of black eyeliner, followed by two coats of mascara. Last—and most important—cherry matte lipstick.

One swoop left on the bottom lip, and pat, pat, pat on the upper. As Scarlet meticulously applied her lip color, she gave herself an internal pep talk. Even though Carly didn't promote her and her dad hurt her feelings and she had no place to hold her class…and even though she'd have to pull money from savings she swore she'd never touch in order to make her first down payment on the Johnny Scissors program…she would find the silver lining.

In this life, Scarlet told herself, people have to look at the big picture and what it takes to move forward. Sometimes sacrifice is involved. So Scarlet would make an offer to the universe and sell off a chunk of her vintage record albums.

At thirty, Scarlet had more vinyl on her wall-unit shelves than dollars in the bank. The records took up an entire wall in the living room. She carefully selected fifty titles to escort to the indie record store on Glendale Avenue, Vega's Vicious Vinyl.

Sometimes when Scarlet needed a break from the sewing machine or felt like embroidering in an abstract setting, she'd head over to the indie record store and chat with the owner—the brooding, mellow, and mysterious Mr. Marco Vega. An odd fellow, he was. His store carried hundreds of collectible recordings, and he could recite the categorical details of every one of them, but that was about it. Most indie shopowners, whether they ran scrapbook stores, vintage clothing boutiques, or record stores, considered their business a marriage. Yet Scarlet noticed that Marco treated Vicious Vinyl like a long-lost adopted cousin. He kept it going, but clearly, the love wasn't there.

Scarlet didn't know why, but he made her jumpy—perhaps because he towered two heads taller than her. Sometimes if her eyes lingered a second too long on the curvy shape of his lips, she'd lose all train of thought. She wondered what they would look like in a full smile, teeth and all. If she didn't know better, she'd swear she had a crush on him. But never in a lifetime would he take her seriously. Scarlet knew she made his head spin with all her talk about old Hollywood scandals, Daisy de la Flora, and her soft spot for Herb Alpert and the Tijuana Brass. Scarlet would yammer on, and Marco politely listened. She often wondered what crossed his mind, as he rarely spoke unless it was to complete a transaction or help a customer.

One day when she walked in, she noticed he had a ripped shirt pocket. To an addicted seamstress like her, it was like the last drink of beer to an alcoholic. She couldn't let it be, and she offered—no, *demanded*—to stitch it up for him. His face turned paler than bleached cotton. She took it as a hint to back off. But just when she thought he'd had enough of her, he invited her to choose the tunes to play in the store. She played cuts from her LP collection and told him all about her favorites. He assured her that if she ever wanted to sell any of them, she knew where to go.

She hoped his offer still stood. It wouldn't be enough to make a dent in her tuition, but Scarlet believed the action would at least kick-start her plan.

I t's Black Friday," Nadine, lead cashier for Vega's Vicious Vinyl, said to her boss. "Marco, get with it. The store is finally kinda sorta crawling with customers and you're pining over that *Gone With the Wind* chick again."

Marco, emotionless, drew a large graphic sign on the chalkboard to promote the holiday sales. "She's named after Miss Scarlet from the game Clue. Not Scarlet from *Gone With the Wind*."

Nadine snorted. "Ha! Classic. Who in the hell would name their kid after a board-game character?"

"Her brother and sister did it," Marco said. "By the time her mom had Scarlet, she ran out of ideas and let the older kids name her. Clue was their favorite game. Plus, all that red hair. Focus on the customers."

Marco continued to assist Nadine with their version of the holiday rush (ten people), but at the same time, he glanced at the framed dollar hanging on the wall and blushed a little. His first sale. Smack dab in the center of the bill was a big red lipstick smooch from Scarlet, and *x*'s and *o*'s she drew with a teal Sharpie from her keychain.

She'd become a semi-regular. From her hairdo to her makeup

and retro dresses, she could pass for a '50s movie star, but was not to be confused with the crop of baby-bang rockabilly chicks who frequented his shop. She reminded him of the girl in a formal gown who would dive into the pool at a stuffy party. Scarlet's style was as unique as her range of music. He never knew what to expect. One day it was a Weather Report jazz album, the next Laura Nyro's Greatest Hits. In his prison of mundane secondhand retail, Scarlet Santana was a blinking neon sign of living the good life.

"Hey, lover boy. Check who just crossed the threshold," Nadine grunted, jabbing Marco in the back with her elbow. "Why does she always look like she just escaped from an *Archie* comic? Saddle shoes? Really?"

Marco gulped and saw Scarlet headed his way. "Whatever. It'll never happen. If she's an *Archie* comic, I'm a boring page from the phone book. We have nothing in common," he said.

Nadine spun him around, gripped his shirt pocket with her black-polished fingertips, and ripped until the sound of snapping stitches filled Marco's ears. "What the hell? Why did you do that again?" he asked.

"Now you have something in common."

Carrying a stack of albums in her arms, Scarlet approached the counter. "Hi, Marco. Merry Christmas!" She beamed, blinking through a feathery set of black lashes and checking out the eclectic mix of customers. "Wow, you kiddos are busy today. It's like pennies from heaven in here!"

Nadine slammed the drawer to her register. "On that note, I'm going to light a new stick of incense for Michael. Whistle, scream, or set off the fire alarm if you need me."

Marco ignored Nadine. "What can I do you for?" he asked Scarlet, motioning for her to step to the end of the counter with him. She followed, sliding the albums down the way.

"You know how I told you about my records? Well, I want to

unload some of them. For starters, I will bestow upon you my entire David Bowie picture disc collection! Each one is worth more than a gold nugget, barely played. I'll show you...."

Always put together, in control, Marco thought. Never a crack in her voice or a hair out of place. Thanks to the shine of her smile, he didn't notice the postman elbowing his way up front.

Scarlet winked at Marco, removed a thick tri-fold album set from the top of the stack, and opened it in front of her. Just then the postman nudged her out of his way so he could shove a certified letter into Marco's hand. Scarlet slipped.

Nearly falling, Scarlet tossed the album case and air-clawed to grab on to the first thing she could reach, which happened to be her stack of LPs. They went flying at all angles across the concrete floor. Scarlet would have fallen too, if it weren't for a group of grade-school kids who, gliding up on wheelie sneakers, managed to catch her. The small crowd shuddered at the sounds of their four sets of wheelies crunching over vinyl, and scrambled to the point of impact to find neon shards strewn everywhere.

A teenage girl knelt down and sorted the shards into stacks. "Wow! I make collage mosaics—these will be perfect! I can make earrings, too!"

"Stop!" Scarlet said sharply, her arms stiff at her sides. She turned to the girl on the floor and glared. "Those are mine! I need to sell them!"

The girl on the floor froze while still holding the pieces. "Can I just have a few? What good are they now? Look. They're smashed."

"Fine! Take them!" Scarlet's scarf slipped down the back of her hair as she dropped her head into her hands. "What else can go wrong? What did I do to deserve this?"

"Damn," Nadine said, approaching the counter. "I've never seen this in an *Archie* comic."

Without hesitation, Marco put his arm around Scarlet's shoulder to comfort her. Flustered, she pulled back and noticed the tear in his plaid cotton shirt. She couldn't help but poke her finger in it. At least it distracted her from the mess she'd just made.

"Another one? Wow, Mr. Vega, you're really rough on your menswear. I can repair this one in a jiffy."

For the first time all week, Marco chuckled. "Come on," he said. "I'll show you the restroom so you can clean up. Don't worry about the records—consider them bought."

She stopped. "But what will you do with them? They're useless."

"I'll put the pieces in a jar and sell them as craft supplies. Maybe it'll bring me new customers. Like that girl on the floor."

*   *   *

Calm and refreshed, Scarlet exited the restroom to notice Marco in his office down the hall. She remembered the torn pocket. The least she could do was fix it after the debacle out front. She opened her bag and retrieved a small tube of EmergiSew, a chemical adhesive concoction she mixed up—"for when you're in a stitch."

"Knock-knock," she sang out, rapping her fingers on the open door before entering. "I'm here to fix that rogue pocket of yours." She unfolded a metal chair that rested against the wall and circled her finger above his head for him to turn around.

Scarlet leaned in close to examine the damage before going to work on the repair job. She slid her arm up and under the front of the shirt, to act as an anchor. He stiffened like a surfboard to allow her a flat surface to work on. When the back of her hand skimmed up his ripped abs, she told herself over and over that she was a school nurse tending to a student's playground scratch. It didn't work.

She tried not to let her nerves get in the way, but the silence between them made her tense, like she had invaded his personal space. She glanced around his desk for something to talk about while the glue dried. Next to a large seashell and a small bottle of sand, a photo of a tattooed teenager caught her eye.

"Cute picture. That's your brother, isn't it?" she asked, stretching her thin eyebrow in the direction of the black frame. She licked her finger to smooth down the raw threads on the fabric. "You guys look a lot alike."

Marco wasn't big on chitchat. He had his own idea for a conversation starter. "What happened back there? You're not the type to lose it over broken records."

Scarlet squeezed her eyes shut as if trying to hide from the memory. "I'm so embarrassed. Sorry about that," she said. "That poor little girl. . . . She only wanted to make earrings. Who am I to crush her creativity?"

"Pffft." He shrugged. "That kid is in the store every day, begging for freebies. Don't worry about her. So what's up? I've never seen you on edge. Can I help with anything?"

"No one can help but me. It's stupid," she said. "I made all these plans and they fell like dominoes. So I set them up again . . . and they tumbled again. I finally cracked. Unfortunately, on your showroom floor."

"Hey, no worries." Marco pulled his desk chair a little closer to Scarlet. "Are you OK?"

"Oh, I'll be fine. I have no choice but to bounce back up and keep going."

"Tell me about it," he said, as if he thought he might be able to help.

What did she have to lose? When the cute guy from the record store offers a life raft, a girl has to at least give him a shot.

"Well, I come from a family of engineers," she explained.

"I grew up thinking it was mandatory to follow in their footsteps even though I love making clothes. I followed their plan and graduated with two engineering degrees; I had some jobs lined up. And then I ditched it. I put that life on hold and gave myself a few years to pursue fashion. It's been more misses than hits, and my family is watching every move, waiting for me to fail so they can say 'I told you so.' But I'm going to prove them wrong." Scarlet scraped her finger up and down his pocket as if it were a scratch-n-sniff sticker. "Hey, it's dry, and as good as new!"

"I know what you mean," Marco said. "Family are the ones who should lead your fan club. A lot of times, they don't even believe you have one."

"Exactly." She wondered if his comment came from personal experience, but since he didn't elaborate, she didn't ask.

Marco stood up, grabbed a pen, licked his finger, and pulled a piece of paper from his desk printer.

"Scarlet, what would make your life easier right now?"

"I don't even know where to start!" Scarlet half-joked, then she sat up tall. "All right. I've told you about my Daisy de la Flora blog? Well, her nephew is Johnny Tijeras—you've heard of him, right?"

Marco nodded. "Yeah, go on."

"Well, he holds a mentor program for emerging artists...." She paused and tossed her hands in the air. "Oh, I'll cut to the chase. I need a space to hold a weekly sewing class to raise cash."

She watched for a frown of solidarity on Marco's face. Instead he just stared at her, as if he hadn't comprehended a word she said. Tossing down the pen, her curled his pointer finger for her to follow him. They exited the office and walked through the main floor of the store into a separate room that had a huge window facing Fifty-eighth Avenue.

"Has this room always been here?" Scarlet asked, astonished. She didn't want to jump to conclusions, but she had a feeling what he was leading up to.

"Sure has. It's where we hold our listening parties. It's nothing fancy and needs better lighting. But there are plenty of outlets and I have extension cords and tables you can use. If it'll work for your class, it's yours."

Scarlet put her hands on her hips and walked around the edges of the area. Black-and-white-checkered tiles covered the back wall. The other two were papered with concert posters, autographs, framed portraits of '80s stars, and ticket stubs.

"Are you serious?" she asked, still surveying the memorabilia on the wall and tapping her lips with her fingertip. "I can make this work. All I have to do is postpone the first class by a week and we're good to go. I'll pay you a rental fee. Oh my gosh, I'm so happy—Marco, I'm indebted forever!"

He shook his head no. "Don't worry about renting it. We'll work it out."

Scarlet scratched the big red hair-sprayed curl that sprouted from the top of her head. "Why are you doing all this?"

"Because I can tell you know exactly what you want," he said. "And I know what it's like to be the underdog of the family. This is your life, not theirs. Don't ever lose sight of that."

Scarlet meant to thank him with a polite hug, but because she was so short, and he so tall, her face landed in the center of his chest. He didn't know what to do with his hands, so he patted her shoulders.

As she felt the fabric of his shirt against her cheek, she wondered if perhaps...maybe...they had more in common than either of them thought.

5

The Monday after Thanksgiving arrived. Hadley and Mary Theresa still hadn't gotten past the trauma of the record-breaking incident.

All this grief over music, she thought. *How immature of her husband.* Sure they had a list of conflicts to resolve, but acting like a self-ish teen wouldn't help. The worst part was that the holiday season was in full swing, which meant family events at every turn. Mary Theresa refused to let on about their marital mishaps and therefore would pretend her home life was as endearing as the Cosbys'.

She had never been more grateful for her office job—a haven from the emotional carnage of home. The thirty-minute commute allowed her to peacefully separate her personal business from professional. She knew that people who mixed the two were in for a world of migraines.

Maybe Hadley didn't appreciate her qualities, but her superiors at Deltran Computronics Corporation did. Once her Easy Spirit pumps hit the carpet in her corner office, she ruled. No one dared to question or doubt her reasoning and experience. As a team leader, she squeezed the maximum amount of energy out of her staff, and to date had set the highest productivity rate in the company's history.

Her current challenge involved informing her crew that December did not translate into party month. Mary Theresa grew up as a God-fearing Catholic. She embraced the true essence of Christmas and blocked herself from insipid cover songs and tacky, dollar-store garlands like the kind that hung about the office. What really irked her were the heart-clogging snacks. She wondered who in the name of Baby Jesus thought of the idea of stuffing a Hershey's Kiss inside a peanut butter cookie? Pure gluttony.

Every day her team paraded in with green-cellophane-covered paper plates and set them at the corner of their desks. And every hour, her staff strolled from cubicle to cubicle to nibble. They knew full well it was against policy to commune outside the designated nondenominational company Holiday Hoopla, which was the third Friday of December. From her assistant to her lead programmer, they gnawed on candy canes at what seemed like every opportunity.

The disrespect appalled her. So the previous week, she kept track of who left their desks to eat holiday goodies—and then she wrote them up. Each employee who broke the rule would be greeted with a yellow insubordination slip. "Discipline is a means to an end" is what her parents always told her.

However, that morning, Mary Theresa had broken her own rule and spent her brainpower on Hadley, not work. Her conclusion was, as usual, to be the bigger person and apologize. Crediting the debit would be as simple as buying him a new record album—so she thought. After a bit of research, she learned that the Coltrane record was only available on CD. The album version had become a collectable. No wonder he stormed out that night. Frantic about the crack in her plan, she spent the morning on the phone until she hunted down an authentic copy at a small Glendale record shop.

Her lunch hour turned into a game of Beat the Clock as she weaved in and out of freeway traffic, ran yellow lights, and made it to the store. Once she stepped inside, she cringed. The hole-in-the-wall retail outlet looked like it hadn't seen Mr. Clean in decades. Dirty posters hung from the ceiling, crooked record bins were covered with glittered paper that peeled at the corners, and the tacky wall mosaics made from guitar picks were not her idea of a classy place to shop. She reminded herself she was there to save her marriage, and that involved sacrifice. Thank goodness she had a travel bottle of hand sanitizer in the car.

Ultimately, she didn't curse the hassle, because the excursion ended on an unexpected high note.

While she waited for the record to be gift-wrapped by the store's punk-rock attendant, Mary Theresa spied a mannequin in the corner of the store.

Wait, she thought, *it's a real person—a petite and exquisite one at that.* Mary Theresa marveled at her outfit from afar—a red, sparkly and swirly brocade knee-length shirtcoat, definitely vintage, over black leggings with velvet flats. Her hair was fiery red and pinned back at the crown like Rita Hayworth in one of those old black-and-white films. Before Mary Theresa could look away, the young woman noticed her, walked over, and introduced herself as if they were high school friends, finally reuniting.

"I love your hair color; it reminds me of Natalie Wood's. I have friends who would kill for that shade of chestnut. I'm Scarlet Santana, by the way. My friend owns this place," Scarlet said in full glee, admiring Mary Theresa's head.

Mary Theresa wished she had an ounce of Scarlet's radiance as she shyly ran her fingers down her own bangs and over the back of her thick ponytail. She wasn't used to being complimented out of the blue like that and had never considered her hair to be "chestnut." Just plain, old, boring dark brown. Hadley often remarked about how much he loved her wavy locks, but Mary Theresa assumed he was being polite and brushed him off. Maybe he really meant it. Why didn't she pay more attention to those moments? Maybe she would get one tonight after he opened her gift and listened to her apology.

She smiled back at Scarlet and praised her head-turning ensemble. Turns out, Scarlet had made it from scratch, without even using a pattern! They struck up a conversation about sewing. Back in high school, Mary Theresa loved to sew all her own clothes. Scarlet told her about a new "patternless sewing" class she was going to teach there at the record store. Mary Theresa concluded that patternless sewing definitely qualified as a "free-form" art workshop for her marriage counseling assignment.

Mary Theresa left the store with a copy of John Coltrane's *A Love Supreme* in one hand and a $500 receipt for the sewing class in the other. Gritty or not, she planned to revisit Vega's Vicious Vinyl once a week.

And this is going to fix my marriage. Go figure, she thought.

Mary Theresa impressed herself with her multitasking skills. Only five minutes late from lunch! If only Hadley would open his mind, he could learn a tip or two from her. She proceeded to her desk, where she released a confident sigh and placed her belongings in the bottom drawer of her desk. Just as she was about to check her e-mail, she saw it—a note from Sandra, her supervisor, asking for Mary Theresa to stop by her office ASAP. Assuming it had to with the yellow slips, Mary Theresa picked up her notepad to head over. As she walked down the gray-carpeted hall, she passed Jay, the new college intern.

"Enjoy your holiday. See you next year!" he chirped.

What an odd thing to say, Mary Theresa thought as she saluted him with two fingers to her forehead. She'd better mention it to Sandra. The kid obviously had a loose screw in that head.

Mary Theresa had barely entered the office when Sandra asked—no, *instructed*—her to close the door.

"I hope I didn't get anyone in too much trouble," Mary Theresa said as she let go of the door handle. "I only wanted to send a clear message that just because it is the holiday season, it doesn't mean—"

"Sit down, please," Sandra said bluntly. The woman's plus-size figure matched her plus-size attitude.

An odd feeling of displacement overtook Mary Theresa's nerves.

"How are things at home? You seem a little stretched these days."

Her sharp tone reminded Mary Theresa of the way she talked to the kids before an oncoming meltdown: slowly, calmly, and slightly high-pitched. She rushed to answer.

"Wonderful. The kids love first grade, Hadley is embracing the Mr. Mom role. We're extremely content."

"Glad to hear that." Sandra paused for half a second, then leaned forward, resting her chubby elbows on the wrinkled, coffee-stained desk blotter. "Mary Theresa, I discarded the yellow tickets."

"Excuse me?"

Sandra relaxed in her chair and slipped a pencil behind her ear. "I know you meant to save the company money, but with your salary rate, you actually cost us more by filling out each lengthy form. Technically, it would have been cheaper to let the staff members eat the Peanut Butter Kiss cookies."

"I suppose it cost more monetarily, but I wanted to make sure it wouldn't happen every holiday," Mary Theresa said in defense. Sandra launched into a lecture, but Mary Theresa's mind drifted. She thought about the last time she'd been in Sandra's office—to give a thirty-day probation review to an employee. Now Mary Theresa felt as though she were the one on trial. She almost wished she could be back at the record store. The stress from the fight with Hadley had taken its toll on her last nerve. She was blowing this meeting out of proportion. Sandra probably wanted her to lighten up for the holidays. But then she heard *it.*

"Can you repeat that, Sandra?"

"Mary Theresa, I said I put off this conversation, hoping things would change, especially after last month's managers retreat. But I've been instructed by Human Resources that I have to handle this today."

"Handle what?"

"Unfortunately I have a stack of *new* complaints. About you."

Mary Theresa gasped. "That can't be. I practice every guiding principle, every day. Number One: Do what is right. Number Two: To get results. Number Three: Do it as a team. Number—"

Sandra patted the air in front of her. "I know you have all the guiding principles memorized, which is admirable. The problem is, while your overall performance output is quite impressive, when it comes to leadership…"

"I *know* I'm a qualified team leader. A team leader must possess the following qualities—" Before she could count them off on her fingers, Sandra cut her off.

Sandra rubbed her thick neck and stared directly into Mary Theresa's eyes. "You're stressing everyone out. There, I said it. We don't use micromanagement methods here. I told you that when I promoted you. The work is tedious; we need to keep the employees loyal and stimulated. Sixty percent of your staff has either requested a transfer or resigned. We have to make adjustments."

"'Adjustments'?" Mary Theresa asked, holding back a choke. From the corner of her view, she noticed Trudy and Jay peering through Sandra's office window. Mary Theresa gave them stink eye until they scrammed.

"Am I fired?"

"We're not letting you go," Sandra assured her, "at this time. But as of tomorrow, we're moving you to the NorWest Mortgage project."

"NorWest?" Mary Theresa repeated, shocked. "That's part-time. And it's telecommuting...from home."

"Exactly," Sandra said. "Home."

*   *   *

With dinner completed, Mary Theresa volunteered to clean the kitchen so Hadley could relax for the night. She snapped the lid over the bowl of diced strawberries and tugged open the refrigerator door. As usual, the front had her family checklist taped to it (she didn't trust magnets).

As she wiped down the counters, Mary Theresa thought about Sandra's words. Did she really micromanage? She only wanted the best results, whether developing a banking software program or raising her children.

It occurred to her that she'd have to find a second job. Not only for the income, but also because the Cotorro household functioned more efficiently when she wasn't around. She had arranged the perfect blueprint for her family to follow, and despite all their differences, it worked. Plus, she didn't think Hadley could tolerate her day in and day out.

As soon as she polished the faucet and hung the dishtowels to dry, she'd tell him about her job and then present him with the make-up gift. She'd apologize for her inexcusable outburst, and the whole event would blow over like always. She was loading the last of the plates into the dishwasher when she felt a tap on her shoulder.

"Oh, honey, I didn't see you there. Do you need me to get you something?" she asked as sweetly as possible. She hoped he recognized that her edges had been softened a few grades.

"Let's talk, Mary Theresa."

"I'm going to one-up you—I have a gift for you!" she said, closing the dishwasher door and reaching across the counter for her bag. She retrieved the wrapped album and handed it to him as if it were on a platter. He didn't accept it fast enough, and that made her nervous, so she ripped it open for him to see.

"I thought it was my gift," he said. "Why did you open it?"

"It's that John Coltrane album. I know how much you liked it. I chased this copy down all over town." Her bottom lip began to quiver. It had been almost seven years since she'd felt nervous enough for that to happen. It was when she'd informed Hadley of her pregnancy. She had waited with bated breath for his response, and he had kissed her and told her he would move back in by dinnertime.

Now the lip quivers were for different reasons.

"I . . . I can't read you anymore," she said, standing against the kitchen aisle. "I don't know what you want me to do. Can't we please get past this? I'm trying really hard here."

"I've tried really hard too," he replied. "It's not working. We need a change."

Mary Theresa approached him. "I think so too. I know it is still November, but I'm starting my New Year's resolution now. I want to change, to be nicer. Remember when you used to think I looked like J. Lo in that *Wedding Planner* movie? Remember when you said you loved the color of my hair? I want us to be like that again." The trembles moved to her chin, and she fought back a sob. "Something happened at work today. . . ."

Hadley ran his wide fingers over her lips and then wiped a tear from his eye. "I'm leaving."

She may not have believed him, but certainly took his distress call seriously.

"What? Because of the album?" she asked. "Or...I know, the class! Honey, I signed up for a free-form stitching class today in Glendale. It's in this little record shop where I bought the album. They have lots of albums you would like. I'll take you there. We'll take the kids. Everything will go back to normal, I promise."

"Mary Theresa, we can't pretend anymore. We're settling for the bare minimum here. I love you, and I love our kids, but I don't know if I love *us*. I need to get away and feel like a man again instead of a single dad with a controlling roommate. I can't do anything without your permission, and it's driving me nuts. For once since our wedding day, I'm making my own decision. I'm moving to Palm Springs with my brother. He got me a temporary web-design job at the hotel he manages."

Mary Theresa imagined her husband chained to a desk in a tiny cubicle, banging away on the keyboard for twelve hours a day. How could he choose that over his wife and kids?

"I'll be back in February, and of course I'll stay in touch. I'll Skype the kids every night."

Desperation and disbelief crept way up her skin, and before she knew it, they invaded her every cell. "You're really leaving?"

"Don't worry, I'll send you money," he said as he ran his hands through his short black hair. "I put the debit and credit cards on your dresser."

"How am I supposed to run everything while you're in Palm Springs?"

"The same way I did while you worked," he said curtly. "All I want is for you to get to know your kids, and for you to know who you are as a parent."

Mary Theresa swallowed her pride. She closed her eyes and tried to rationalize what had just happened. He couldn't walk out. This was the most unreasonable time.

"Hadley, I was demoted at work today to part-time telecommuting. You can't do this to me now. It's too much for me to handle."

He placed a hand on each of her forearms. "You are a strong, intelligent woman. You'll be fine. You may even discover qualities you never knew existed."

She flicked his hands off, offended. "What do I tell our families? My boss? The neighbors? Oh my God—the kids?"

"I'm sure you'll make a plan, Mary Theresa. You always do." He left the room and walked to the stairs, where three packed suitcases waited for him. Mary Theresa put her hand over the handles of the largest one.

"Don't you at least want the John Coltrane album? I went through a lot to get it for you. To make up for the one I broke."

"Keep it as a gift to yourself," he said. "I have it on CD."

To Arizona people, the winter chill consisted of anything sixty-five degrees or lower. But to Joseph and Rosa, lifelong East Coast natives, it may as well have been spring. She watched as the old man grunted in frustration, sitting in front of the dashboard, searching the door panels for the button to lower the car window. He finally put the dang-blasted thing in park to inspect every crevice of the car's interior.

"What the heck kind of vehicle is this?" he grumbled. "How are the windows supposed to go down? I can't breathe."

Rosa giggled and let go of the purse straps that she clutched in her lap. She stretched up and pressed the switch that was an inch from Joseph's nose.

"It's called a PT Cruiser," she explained. "Isn't it so cute and sporty? It's like a little toy! Que bueno!"

Joseph slid back in his seat and gripped the steering wheel. "With all due respect, Ro, I don't understand this one. You know I'd go to the four corners of the earth for you, but there are numerable loose ends to tie up, before...you know...and we just arrived. We haven't even settled in, found a grocery store, or a pharmacy. Dr. Mercado called. We need to set up your treatments immediately. He's furious. You've had some crazy plans in your day, but this tops all of them. I'm worried this time. Really worried."

Rosa raised her hand to cup his cheek. "I told you before, doll, you didn't have to come, I planned to do this on my own. I hate to cause you distress, especially with that stubborn blood pressure of yours. But I love you for being here, I appreciate every ounce of attention. I'm unworthy. I hope you know of my undying gratitude. All I ask is that you have faith in me."

Joseph stroked her hand, knowing it would, indeed, be the last of a string of memorable world-traveling adventures. He proceeded, like always, and pulled out of the driveway to escort his longtime friend to her destination. One of the last items on her wish list.

They drove for twenty-five minutes down the diagonal stretch of Grand Avenue through Phoenix's arts district. Rosa didn't speak the entire ride. Instead she stared out the side window to capture the scenery with her eyes. If Rosa had been even five years younger, she would have stopped to visit each of the galleries, art houses, and diners they passed. When they reached downtown Glendale, she covered her mouth in delight. It appeared just as quaint and cozy as the pictures she had seen online and in tourist books—lots of red and brown brick buildings, and clean sidewalks lined with poplar trees trimmed in lights for the holiday season. She hoped to see them lit at night before she returned to New York City. In the meantime, Rosa begged Joseph to please drive her around the area, and he had no choice but to oblige.

They slowly rode up and down the 120-year-old streets of Glendale Avenue, taking in the neighborhoods of historic cottages that had been updated into contemporary homes. Many were transformed into boutiques, gift shops, craft stores, New Age centers, and even a Christmas store. Dozens of passersby strolled about the sidewalks to stop into one of the many eateries and pastry shops, while others lingered about the painted wood benches. Rosa admired the holiday decorations that had started several blocks back and traveled way farther than she could see.

She got a kick out of the fact that one could buy a six-dollar plate of jumbo shrimp at a greasy take-out called Pete's Fish and Chips, yet a few steps away explore the displays at a high-end doll museum.

After twenty minutes of passenger-seat sightseeing, Joseph pulled into a parking spot on Fifty-eighth Avenue, let out a sigh of relief, and turned to her. "We've arrived. I'll wait for you here until you're done."

"Joseph, I've survived natural disasters; my melodramatic, power-hungry family; and ghosts. This final detour is like stitching a button on a jacket: I could do it in my sleep," Rosa lectured as she popped open a crystal-covered compact and powdered her nose.

"Fine. Remind me, am I supposed to be your husband again?" he asked.

"Yes, if you don't mind. Now, go have fun. I'll call you when I'm ready. I won't be long. I just want an early peek at the classroom."

"I'm not leaving, so get used to it," he said. "I'll stay in this toy of a car and comb over paperwork. I must admit, it is a satisfactory Thursday. The weather is quite accommodating. I can't think of the last time we didn't wear overcoats on December first."

"Bangkok, 1990," Rosa said, licking her fingers to smooth down the sides of her silver hair that was cropped in a graduated bob. She ran her palms down the back of her neck, regretting the last-minute cut from her Manhattan stylist before leaving for Phoenix.

Joseph shook his head. "All this so you can meet some strange girl."

Rosa opened the door and carefully lifted her tired, swollen legs out, one by one. Before she slammed it, she bent down, ever so slightly. "She's not just *some strange girl*—her name is Scarlet Santana, and I think she might be the one."

Buttoning up her camelhair sweater, Rosa made her way up the busy sidewalk. Her veiny hand wobbled as she gripped the large metal handle of Vega's Vicious Vinyl and pulled.

The place reminded her of a bohemian gift shop in the East Village, except double the size. She was just about to peek outside and give an "OK, it's all good!" sign to Joseph, when she heard, "Can I help you?"

The tall young man who spoke was the spitting image of Rosa's childhood heartthrob, Montgomery Clift—a Latino version of him anyway. With facial hair. The thick head of charcoal hair, bushy brows, a strong jaw, and wide eyes, topped with a casing of silent suffering—something she recognized immediately because she had one of her own.

"I'm Rosa Garcia and I'm here to take the patternless sewing class with Miss Scarlet Santana."

"Oh, OK, great. For a second there I thought you were lost. Actually, the class starts Saturday," he said.

She laughed. "I know, dear. I wanted to come early to get the lay of the land. You need holiday decorations in here if you don't mind me saying."

He glanced around the store. "I'd say you're right. It's a pleasure to meet you, Rosa. I'm Marco Vega, the owner. On behalf of Scarlet, thanks for coming. Do you prefer Rosa or Ms. Garcia?"

"Rosa, thank you," she said as she began to wander about. "Where is your Latin section? I'm looking for a recording by a group called Mambo Estrella, released in the late fifties. Ever heard of it?"

"Ah, a mambo fan," Marco said. He rubbed his chin as if to summon the answer, then headed to a wall of bright purple shelves. "I have a pretty big selection from that era. But I don't think I've heard of that particular group."

Rosa made an indecipherable comment under her breath and nudged her elbow, as if to move someone out of her way. She then excitedly flipped through the records one by one. "I'd say you have the best collection I've seen." She put one hand on her hip, rested the other against the display case, and checked Marco out from top to bottom. "I bet you'd look dapper in a suit, young man. Do you dance?"

"Ha, not quite. My brother was a dancer," he said. "My job is to give people the tools to dance."

Rosa leaned forward and squinted at a blonde-wood shelf high on the back wall. She opened her purse and took out a chunky pair of black circular specs and put them on. Upon the shelf was a small photo in an acrylic frame of a teenager and, next to it, a stick of burning incense. Strawberry. She blinked softly and turned her head back to Marco. "Is that your brother up there?"

Marco cleared his throat and clapped his hands once. "Let me take you to the sewing room. I'm more than happy to give you a sneak peek. But I have to warn you—it's nothing fancy. Scarlet's original plan fell through, so I'm helping her make do. Come on, this way."

"I'm sure it is lovely. Yes, I'm excited to see it and get started," she said. "You have no idea what I've been through to get here."

DaisyForever.com
magical musings about love, beauty & fashion
inspired by the life of Daisy de la Flora
as told by Miss Scarlet Santana

Friday, December 2, 11:30 p.m.

Little Victories

Good tidings, my cupcakes—Merry Christmas!

Another Turkey Day down for the records! We are now up to our earrings in mistletoe and menorahs. I hope all of you are embracing the word "merry" by spending time with friends, cranking up the holiday classics, and sipping on peppermint mochas.

Tonight's lettered lecture is to help purify your spirit in order to start fresh for the New Year. I think it is doggone silly that people wait until January 1st to adjust the volume on their optimism. Now is the time to clear out the clutter, scrub the slate clean, and sweep up the icky cobwebs from high corners. Not just in your sitting room, but in your attitude.

At the start of the year, our minds and spirits are powerful and untouchable. But as the pages are torn off the calendar, the grumpity-grumps wear us down. Sometimes it is our boss, a coworker, or even our own family members who freak out when they see us happy. They chant us down, question our motives, or find fault in our actions. They distract us from noticing the nifty nuggets all around. By December, our psyches are tattered and frayed. I'm speaking from personal experience. I know what I want, but I feel like there are hurdles every inch of my way. Yes, with effort, practice, a good attitude, and a bit of visualization, I clear 95% of them. But why is it that stinky 5% messes with my mind?

No more! Chant with me! *No more!*

I saw a clip of an interview Daisy did on the *Dinah!* show in the early '70s. She talked about "Little Victories"—an exercise she practiced every December. I've adopted it, given it a Miss Scarlet makeover, and am now presenting it to you! It helps, really it does.

Take a stack of colored construction paper, colored markers (fruit-scented = yummy!), ribbons, stickers, glitter, glue, etc.

Think of twelve things you did in the past year that you loved and accomplished.

Write one on each of the papers and decorate them juicier than a triple-layered birthday cake. Now do something with them—sew them together in a book, hang them as a banner, make a hat out of them! Leave them up all month long and admire them as a way to appreciate all the good things you did.

But here is the catch: On New Year's Eve, take a lighted match to them. Oooh, you're thinking, "Whoa, Miss Scarlet is going all *Towering Inferno* on us!"

I'm serious! Set them aflame! Make a little ceremony out of the ritual. Toss them in your fireplace and send them off with blessings from your heart. This is how Daisy described it. She said it's wonderful to reflect on what we did in the past, but we must not dwell on them so much that they hold us back from accepting new trials. By burning them, you are releasing that good energy into the universe to make room for the new.

(I personally cut each paper into the shape of a heart before I toss it into the fireplace, but that's just me.)

Tomorrow is the first day of my patternless sewing class. You know, the one I've been planning for and bragging about since summer?

It didn't come together as I originally envisioned, but it all worked out thanks to a friend (hug). I hope Miss Scarlet's School of Patternless Sewing is as magical and wonderful as I envision it. I may not be using patterns, but I can feel that all our collective threads will find their way to our fates!

Scarlet's eyelids fluttered open Saturday like freshly minted butterfly wings to greet the morning. As she did every day, she wiggled her toes and fingers to ensure they were in working order, and thanked the universe. If all else failed in the forthcoming hours, at least she had a sharp mind and working limbs to be cheerful for.

She dedicated her morning ritual to her first class of Miss Scarlet's School of Patternless Sewing. She had left home at eight thirty a.m. and stopped by La Purisima Bakery on the way to Vega's Vicious Vinyl to choose a dozen of the finest Mexican pastries. Her students were more than credit-card-paying clients—they were her guests. Not only would she offer them an education of simplified sewing, but comfort and sweets too. If it weren't for their enrollment, she wouldn't have the funds to make it to New York come summer.

Her pulse doubled in speed when she pulled into the parking lot, right next to Marco's no-nonsense gold Pathfinder, and saw him climbing out of it. Like a true gentleman, he came around and helped her unload her luggage and a box of pine garland and tinsel.

"What's with the suitcase and decorations, you moving in?

Now I *will* have to charge you rent." His tone may have been drier than sandpaper, but his eyes gleamed.

"It's our class supplies," she replied in a flirty, singsong voice that took even herself off guard. "Rolling luggage sure beats schlepping around boxes. Hey, would you mind if I spruced up the room a little? It's bursting with personality the way it is, but I thought pretty embroidered tablecloths would give it a more homey feel. And it's December! We have to have Christmas cheer!"

Marco raised an eyebrow. "Follow me."

He unlocked the back door and they made their way to the new sewing room.

Before her toe even touched the concrete floor, she gasped.

Apparently Marco had done a bit of decorating too. He must have spent hours reenergizing the accommodations from the baseboards to the windowsills. The '80s music posters were replaced with mod fabric wall coverings from the '60s. Six chandeliers hung down from the ceiling to ensure proper lighting for the students, and in the center of the room were professional worktables. The front housed a giant metallic pink wall complete with a TV set, music console, and speaker system. All of it paled in comparison to the showpiece housed by the window—an eight-foot-tall Noble Fir Christmas tree trimmed in colored lightbulbs, silver tinsel, and antique glass ornaments.

"Marco, this is too much...," she said, still in shock at the makeover. She ran to the entryway and peeked out, and then semi-sprinted to the storefront window. "Is this for a hidden TV show? Are we on camera?" She spun around just as Marco handed her a sealed card.

"What's this?"

He stuffed his hands into the front pockets of his jeans and shrugged. "You have secret investor, I guess. All of this stuff arrived yesterday with a crew to set it up. I wish I could take credit, but..."

She threw her arms around him. "You've done so much already. You deserve more credit than anyone." The two of them then sat on the edge of the windowsill and read the card.

To Scarlet,
Your little victories are big inspirations to your fans.
Keep up the great work.

It had to be from her parents. They must have remembered about her class. Maybe they even read her blog! Scarlet excused herself from Marco and stepped outside the record store to phone them.

"Scarlet," her mom answered with a burst of relief. "Thank goodness, I just tried to call you at home. Eliza needs her dry cleaning picked up by noon. She has that big holiday shindig for work tonight and she's getting her hair straightened. The party is outside and you know what the open winter air does to our kind of curls—"

"Mom, slow down," Scarlet interrupted. "I can't. I have my first sewing class today, remember? By any chance, were you and Dad the ones who sent me—"

"Sewing class? Why are you taking a sewing class now? I thought you knew how to sew. Oh, Scarlet, what's happened to you? You're regressing."

Definitely not my folks, she thought.

"I'm *teaching* the class, Mom. I've been telling you about it for months. But I guess Eliza's dry cleaning is more important."

"Eliza has kids! Oh, here we go again," Jeane whined. "Nobody loves or understands you. Grow up, Scarlet!"

"Never mind. Mom, I have to go set up for my class. I'll come by later."

"Wait!" Jeane said. "So . . . are you getting the dry cleaning for your sister or not?"

Scarlet clenched her fist, kicked the redbrick wall, and chomped the air from frustration. "Fine. I'll pick it up for her."

"Thank you, mija. It's sixty dollars. Please bring it to her by three."

After Scarlet hung up, she thought maybe Carly felt guilty about the classroom situation and was the one to donate the goods. Only one way to find out.

Carly answered on the first ring. "You're late."

Bad idea to call her.

"Hi, Carly," Scarlet said, rushed. "I'm not late, I'm off. I put in a request to have Saturdays off for the next twelve weeks, remember? It's marked on the schedule."

"Well, then why are you calling? We're busy now that we're short a person."

"I, uh, just wanted to make sure you remembered I was off on Saturdays from now on."

"OK."

"OK, then! See you Monday, Carly!"

"Hold on, Scarlet—you need to come in this afternoon to fit Stevie Nicks's assistant for the Grammy Awards. I'm designing her dress. I guess she only trusts you and your goofy hugging method to measure her body. She'll be here at four thirty."

Scarlet kicked the wall again, but softer so she wouldn't wear down the velvet on the tip of her shoe. She wished so badly she had never called. Why in the world would she think Carly would do her a favor? Yet Scarlet had to be on call 24/7 because she had to stay in the woman's good graces for the pending promotion.

"Sure, I'll be there," Scarlet said, hiding her anger. "But I'm curious, what would you have done if I hadn't called?"

"Why does it matter, Scarlet? See you this afternoon."

Scarlet concluded that Marco was the secret investor, but would never admit it.

As angry as her mom and Carly made her, nothing would ruin this day. Scarlet soaked up her surroundings, from the adorable added accents, to the sewing machines on loan from her Auntie Linda's quinceañera shop, to the quirky, antique setting of downtown Glendale that topped it off.

For the most part, this is exactly how it was supposed to be.

But Scarlet still had the challenge of raising the funds for the Johnny Scissors tuition. Last week she had called the enrolled students about the location change, and all but four dropped out. Scarlet made the mistake of using Carly's switchboard to take the initial reservations, and suspected her fickle boss had something to do with her students' sudden mood change.

No worries, Scarlet thought. She made a batch of posters and fliers featuring vintage images of Daisy at her sewing machine and hung the signs around the neighborhood and in Marco's shop. She did get one bite—Mary Theresa, a shy but adorable mom of twins who had driven all the way across town on her lunch hour to Vega's Vicious Vinyl just to buy a John Coltrane album as a gift for her husband. Scarlet hoped maybe someday she would have that kind of love in her life.

Mary Theresa rounded out the group to five students.

If she let herself dwell on it, Scarlet would have panicked at the thought of losing out on $23,000. But $2,500 was better than nothing. The rest would come, just like the decorations did. In the meantime, she would present the best sewing workshop in the universe.

By the time ten a.m. arrived, every table had a student behind it. Scarlet stood on the tips of her pointy toes and opened her arms to the class.

"Hi-de-ho, my chicas, welcome! From the bottom of my heart, thank you for attending my first-ever workshop," she said. "By the time the curtains go down on this class, your lives will have changed for the better." She clasped her hands behind her waist, and paced about the concrete floor to continue her introductory pep talk.

She spent the next twenty minutes sharing her backstory of her love for her Mexican American culture, and how she was the only Santana in her family to inherit her great-grandfather's red hair. She expressed her admiration for Daisy de la Flora, giving up engineering, her job at Carly's, and her anticipation for the Johnny Scissors program.

"All right, let's talk patterns and why we are foregoing them," Scarlet said. "A pattern is comprised of elements that repeat in a predictable manner. The question I present is—why be predictable? Even though we are here for sewing, I believe there are deeper reasons the word "patternless" caught our attention. We all have a pattern we are working from to build the framework of our lives. But we can change it, enhance it, or skip it altogether."

"What is your pattern, Miss Scarlet?" one of the students asked.

Scarlet winked. "Great question, love. Well, my pattern was crafted for me long before I ever came into the world. It's the same pattern that all of my family used. I don't want to *totally* disregard it. I just want to put my own mark on it—you know, to make it one of a kind. Now it's your turn. Who wants to go next? Tell us your name and the story of your own pattern."

Two young girls in the front row exchanged looks as if to agree to go first. "We will," said a blonde in a black fedora and hoop earrings. "I'm Stephanie, I'm a junior at Apollo High. I'm here to check out my mom's pattern for me. She thinks I spend too much time playing softball, basketball, and tennis, so she made me take this class with my sister. You know, to help me be more . . . girly, I guess. I don't mind trying my mom's way as long as I can make gym shorts. Is that cool?"

"Of course," Scarlet said. "Tell your mom thanks! And who is your sister?"

"Jennifer. She's your stalker."

Jennifer, with black curly hair and a glittered rose behind her ear, scrunched her cheeks, squinted her eyes, and wagged her fist at Stephanie, then seamlessly morphed her expression into that of a teen angel. "I'm a sophomore at Apollo and I want to use whatever pattern *you* use, Miss Scarlet. I am a devoted follower of your blog. I pinkie swear we are so much alike. I love all the old movies like you do, and I love it when you talk like a retro girl. I'm ready to bebop if you are!"

"I am not related to you," Stephanie groaned as she tipped her hat to cover her face.

"Whatever," Jennifer said, gliding clear lip gloss across her lips.

A curvy black woman wearing a teal tracksuit, also with smoothed pin curls around her face, shoved her arm in the air. "Me next! I love your blog, Scarlet. I read it every night before I go to sleep. You're always so cheery. Now, I'll be honest, I've never stitched a thing; I've never even threaded a needle. I'm just here to meet you in person. If that means I get to learn how to sew something for this beautiful bod of mine, all the better!"

Scarlet immediately walked up to her new fan and put her arm around her shoulders. "Thank you, thank you, thank you. What's your name, doll?"

"Ohliveyah!"

"Olivia!" Scarlet repeated. "I love that name!"

The woman shook her finger. "Nuh-uh. Not *Olivia*. Ohliveyah!"

"My bad. I'm sorry! How do you spell it?" Scarlet asked with a mixture of confusion and embarrassment.

"O-L-I-V-I-A. Ohliveyah! Let me slow it down. *Oh*—as in Oh, my lord! And then *Live*—as in Lance Armstrong LIVE-strong. And then *Yah!*—as in YAH! Let's do this!"

"How 'bout we just call you Oli?" asked Mary Theresa.

Olivia turned in her direction. "In this life, every mood is a choice—or rather, a pattern. I don't know about you all, but I'd rather have more good moods—patterns, I mean—than bad." She swiveled back toward the rest of the room. "I dated and then married a bad *pattern* with two legs and a thick head. After ten years, my divorce is my Christmas present to myself. I didn't only change my last name, I turned my first name into an affirmation. There are lots and lots of Olivias, but there is only one Ohliveyah. I'm working on starting all over with a new pattern, and if that means no pattern at all, so be it."

"Right on, Olivia, my kind of chica," Scarlet said. "What are you interested in making in the class?"

"Anything you got," Olivia said. "Bring it on. In fact, I'll adopt the 'patternless' concept for other areas in my life as well. Loosen up that daily grind."

"Sounds good in theory, Olivia. But we can't function without rules."

This time everyone turned to face the condescending voice from the west side of the room.

"Mary!" Scarlet said, excited to see her again.

"Actually, it is all one name—Mary Theresa. Not Mary. Not Theresa. Together…Mary Theresa," she corrected.

"I see you had a strict Catholic mom too." Scarlet chuckled. "What kind of pattern do you have going on?"

Mary Theresa sucked her teeth. It took every ounce of energy not to walk out of the stupid, menial class and the crusty record shop. But Hadley had mentioned on the phone that he was proud of her for following through with the assignment.

"I have a pattern for my family, and it's worked fine so far," she said. "That's about it."

Scarlet walked over to Mary Theresa's table. "Did your husband like the record? That was so sweet of you to come out here and hunt it down for him."

"Yes, he did," Mary Theresa said. "I really don't want to discuss it, I just want to get the class over with."

Scarlet felt awful for obviously touching on a sore spot in front of everyone, and made a mental note to apologize in private. She examined Mary Theresa: the perfectly creased mom jeans, pressed navy golf shirt, and her pretty brown hair pulled in a too-tight ponytail. All visual indicators of a stressed lifestyle. If it were another time and place, Scarlet would kidnap her, send her to a spa, and give her a movie-star makeover.

Mary Theresa kept her hands—slim fingers, trimmed,

unpolished nails—clasped together. "When you said 'patternless sewing'—you didn't literally mean without patterns, correct?"

Scarlet sat on top of the table next to Mary Theresa and swung her short, shapely legs. "Sweets, why did you sign up? JoAnn Fabrics is about fifteen minutes away, and they have an excellent series of classes, lots of patterns. Don't get me wrong, I'm delighted you're here. But if you're less than thrilled with the free-form idea, maybe you should try there. I promise I won't be offended."

Mary Theresa bit her lip and nodded her head, obviously annoyed to the earth's end. "I have my reasons to stay. I just want to know if I should bring my self-healing mat and rotary cutting set."

Scarlet smiled affectionately. Mary Theresa would be her pet student, she could feel it. "We'll have some patterns, but not the traditional type you'd pull out of a Simplicity envelope. And no fancy tools. Miss Scarlet teaches old-school."

"That's insane," Mary Theresa blurted. "I used to be an A+ sewer in high school, and there is no way to make anything that fits or functions without double measurements, patterns developed by professionals, and proper pinning. Please tell me we are going to pin! What's next, are we going to use needles or pull the thread through with our teeth?"

The class broke out in a fit of giggles, even though Mary Theresa didn't mean it to be funny.

Scarlet put her hand on Mary Theresa's sewing machine. "Trust me, it will be fun. And yes, darling. Of course we will pin. And use needles. But no rulers."

Mary Theresa's mouth fell open in shock as Scarlet hopped off the desk and strolled down the center aisle between the two rows of tables.

"I'm going to teach all of you how to use your hands, arms, feet, and even the size of your head to measure. As for patterns, we'll use everyday objects and learn how to size them without tools. This is how I learned. Granted, I also know the traditional methods, but it's much more fun this way. Just wait and see, Mary Theresa. The best part is I'll share anecdotes about Daisy de la Flora's life that will inspire you so much!"

"Let me get this straight," Olivia said. "She's Johnny Scissors's mom, right?"

"Aunt," Scarlet corrected.

"I see you're wearing one of her brooches; it looks darling on you," said the final student, a woman who had to be a bit younger than Nana Eleanor.

Scarlet dipped her chin and rubbed the rhinestone Chihuahua pin with her fingers. "Thank you. It's my good-luck charm. I can't believe you recognized it. You must be a fan of hers too."

"I was at one time," she replied in a hoarse voice. She cleared her throat. "I'm Rosa Garcia, the granny of the group, I see. Miss Scarlet, do you think you could bring Daisy's lucky buttons next week to show us?"

"Hmmm," Scarlet said, thinking hard. "I have them locked in my Daisy display curio. I don't feel comfortable removing them. But I do have pictures of them on my blog."

"That's fine, I understand, dear," Rosa said as a raspy cough made its way out. She grabbed a tissue and covered her mouth. "Sorry. My throat is dry this morning. Didn't have time to take my usual teaspoon of honey."

Scarlet jogged to a table that had a pitcher of water, poured a glass for the woman, and took it back to her. "So what's your pattern, my fellow Daisy-phile?"

The woman nodded thanks, took a sip, and waited until it

passed through her throat. She scanned the room and acknowledged each person with a shy smile.

The room fell silent with a hint of enchantment.

"I have a pattern for a life that I love. My goal is to preserve it to the best of my ability. I lived a very adventuresome life—lots of traveling, meeting all kinds of eccentric and beautiful people. I'm too tired to continue all of that. I love to make things, always have. Miss Scarlet, I'm also impressed by your blog. It's such a gift to people everywhere. When I read that you were teaching this class, I immediately signed up. I'm thrilled to see what you have in store for us."

"Thank you, Rosa, I'll do my best," Scarlet said. She rubbed her Chihuahua pin again. "You said you were a fan of Daisy, too? She was so amazing and undervalued. She had to practically disappear in order to get any respect. Did she change your life like she did mine?"

"I guess you could say that. But not in the way you think. Scarlet, I know your online diary is dedicated to Daisy, but you really must know, she was...is...a human being like each and every one of us in this room. You know what you read, well, that is only half the story. She made many mistakes in her life, I'm sure."

Scarlet took one giant step back. "Rosa, do you know Daisy?"

Rosa took another sip from her cup and handed it back to Scarlet. "No, no. I apologize if I've disappointed you. But I did grow up in the same city as she did—Coconut Grove in Miami. After she became famous, the off-color stories came out of the woodwork about her. That she was a thief and a hussy, and even stole her best friend's husband. I know you adore her, Scarlet, but she was just as flawed as the rest of us."

By this time, all the students, even Mary Theresa, had turned their chairs toward Rosa, hoping for more juicy gossip about Daisy de la Flora.

Everyone except Scarlet, who felt somewhat off-put by such accusations. "Oh, Rosa, it's all chisme. Gossip. As soon as a girl becomes successful, old friends, cousins, and especially family will turn on her."

Rosa wagged her finger at Scarlet. "Don't be so quick to lump family in there. Sometimes when success runs out, family is all that's left."

The class stayed silent.

"Anyhoo," Scarlet sang out, clapping her hands twice, "let's get on with the lesson. Now comes the fun part. I have samples of all the things we are going to make in this workshop series, starting with today's fabric collage handbag made from place-mats. And...we're going to lie on the floor on top of butcher paper and trace our bodies with a marker."

"What?" Mary Theresa cracked.

Scarlet stepped next to her and gently gripped her elbow. "Hang on a sec," she whispered.

"Let's take a break first," Scarlet announced. "I brought some yummy pastries for us to enjoy, as well as coffee and juice."

The women took her advice and hovered over the treats. All except Mary Theresa.

"I'm so sorry for asking about the record in front of every-one," Scarlet said, pressing her hands on her own cheeks. "I take it that the gift didn't go over too well? How could he not like Coltrane?"

Just because Scarlet spilled her own life story to the world from her computer, didn't mean everyone else did too. Mary Theresa had no intention of sharing any of her personal details. Ever.

"Oh, he loved it," she replied, stiffer than a shot of gin. "Your question took me by surprise, that's all. Look, there's something you should know about me. I'm a very private person. I'm not really into the patterns-as-a-metaphor life lessons. I'm a busy mom with a lot of responsibilities. I just want to get through the twelve weeks."

"I read you loud and clear," Scarlet said, realizing she had stepped into a minefield. "But there's something *you* should know about *me*. If you ever need someone to talk to, or hang out with, or even sew with, I'm here for you."

9

Across the country in his Park Avenue penthouse, Johnny "Scissors" Tijeras lay sprawled in his black silk pajamas, belly down, across his Vera Wang sheets. He snored away the midnight hour, thanks to the Flexeril pill that had worked its magic on his ailing back.

"Mijo...," said a voice, floating through his dream.

His shoulder twitched.

"It's me, Mami. Mijo, the time has come."

"For what?" he grumbled in between a breath and a snort.

"Your auntie will be joining me soon... do you hear me, mijo? Mi hermana viene pronto..."

Johnny swatted the air several times, rolled to the edge of his bed, and clenched his pillow to his chest. "That's nice, Mami..."

Suddenly, the words rang clear in his head, jolting him awake. For years, he had prayed to his mother for a sign, and at last it had come.

A greedy grin spread from cheek to cheek because Christmas had arrived early. "It's time... *it's time!*" he chanted as he grabbed his iPhone from the white acrylic nightstand and made the call that would seal his financial fate.

"Emergency meeting. Inner circle only. Sixty minutes. My living room."

                    *   *   *

"It's one thirty in the morning. That snow was a bitch out there," one of Johnny's lawyers whispered to another while sliding his briefcase on the ceramic white coffee table. The last of the four executives trudged in and fell into the black leather couch. They began to murmur about what was important enough to pull them out of bed in the middle of the night.

"The old bat is finally going to kick the bucket," Johnny announced from the room entrance. A juice glass in one hand and an orange scone in the other, Johnny glided into the room, still sporting his silky ebony sleepwear.

The executives hushed. "How do you know?" asked Louisa, one of Johnny's top managers.

"My mother told me in a dream tonight."

The staff moaned.

"You've got to be kidding, Johnny," said Sam, his top accountant. "We fought our way here in the middle of the night, through a blizzard practically, because you had a dream about your mother? With all due respect, couldn't this have waited for the office?"

"Absolutely not. You know this is the opportunity we've been waiting for. We must trigger our action plan immediately. Today. The minutes are ticking!" Johnny popped the last bite of scone into his mouth.

Sam scooted to the front of his chair and placed his hands on his knees. "Johnny, we're a multimillion-dollar company. We can't change the entire strategic plan based on a dream. Don't you remember what happened last time? We almost filed for Chapter Eleven last year. We're lucky to have our heads above water. For all we know, your vision could have been triggered by your subconscious."

"Post-traumatic stress after they booted him from the judging panel on *Project Runway*," one exec discreetly added.

"Not to mention the meds," another whispered.

They all knew working with Johnny Scissors had its perks when his aunt Daisy was running the operation by proxy, but two years ago she handed him the reins, and it had all changed.

Daisy had taken him in as her own child, watching him grow as she grew her business into an internationally known brand.

From the runways of Paris to the department stores of middle America, Daisy de la Flora accessories could be seen everywhere. She may have kept a low profile, but her standards were higher than the Queen of England's. She kept all manufacturing in New York City's garment district, paid decent wages, and offered generous health benefits and retirement for her employees. She incorporated monthly birthday roundups, holiday parties, and day-care discounts into the budget, as well as tuition reimbursement. In return, Daisy's staff proved their loyalty through quality, timely work that garnered national press.

Daisy had paid Johnny's way through college, where he studied fashion design, of course. When he graduated, he requested his own label under Daisy's. She made him draw up a detailed business plan, complete with sketches, brand strategy, profit margins, manufacturing rates, and target market. When he presented it a month later, she granted his wish. But on one condition—that he honor her founding principles and offer annual scholarships and a mentor program for emerging designers as a way of paying his good fortune forward. At the same time, she stopped production of her famous award-winning Daisy line that had been around for decades. She felt it had run its course and it was time for her to tackle something new.

House of Tijeras was born.

Riding on the backs of Daisy's A-list Hollywood clients and the talent he farmed from the mentoring program, Johnny became one of New York City's elite faces. As the year's rolled by, his ego swelled. He despised that he still had to run every idea by his aunt, whom he could barely track down.

Daisy's life mission switched from running her company from her Manhattan office to visiting third-world countries to help the poor and suffering. Perhaps it was the guilt from mistakes she made in her younger years, or just a single woman trying to make a world a better place, but Daisy had found her calling in philanthropy. Yet no matter where she sat in the world, she always phoned Johnny every week at their regularly scheduled hour. She hoped Johnny would follow in her footsteps.

Every year for his birthday, he begged Daisy to let him run House of Tijeras his own way. He even offered to take over the entire Daisy de la Flora conglomerate so she could enjoy life. She declined, recognizing flaws in his character, though she never gave that as the reason.

But two years ago, Johnny had told Daisy about a vision he experienced while searching for a bottle of Dom Perignon in his wine cellar: His mother asked him to send a message to Daisy—that Johnny was ready.

The mention of her beloved sister brought back all Daisy's guilt. Swallowing her uneasy feelings, she stepped aside, eliciting a promise from her nephew that he would still adhere to her original conditions. She trusted him. She had to. She stopped the weekly calls and went about her journey.

Johnny reveled in his newfound freedom. The first night he threw himself a bash that cost more than a million dollars.

And the celebrating didn't stop there. He partied and let the company go on autopilot. His antics became so well known on gossip blog sites and in tabloids that he was even given his own reality show and book deal.

But what Johnny didn't realize until it was too late was that when his aunt removed herself from the picture, the perks exited with her. Without Daisy's infusion of spirit and sass, Johnny Scissors became a fool on the scene. All his former clients—from J. Lo to Julia Roberts—lost interest. A few copyright infringement lawsuits filtered in. His book and TV ratings plummeted. A major department store deal that Daisy had set up in her last days at the company fell through. Casa de la Flora needed cash flow desperately and, even worse, all the stress made him pack on twenty pounds.

A month ago he received grim news that the almost fifty-year-old business would go under by summer. If she wanted to, his aunt could save him. She could easily reignite her Daisy line with updated designs and captivate an entire new market, as many investors had asked her to. Not that she seemed inclined to do it. Besides, Johnny would still be dependent on her. The stacks of stocks, investments, and royalties from her accessory line . . . the thought of legally owning it all under his name alone made Johnny's mouth water.

As Daisy's only relative, he would take ownership of the empire when she died. Who else could she leave the company to? She'd always been a loner and a recluse. He'd hoped it would happen this year, for his fiftieth birthday. He wasn't creepy enough to plot a murder, although he did fantasize about it—something appropriately dramatic, like her spilling a tray of rhinestones and then slipping on the sparkly nuggets to her demise. Of course, that scenario wasn't likely—the woman wore sensible sneakers. If only he could find out the details of her heart rate and blood pressure. Every so often when Daisy called, he'd casually ask her about her health, but she always evaded the subject. She had to knock off sometime, and thanks to his mother's message, he knew the time had come.

Johnny took a long sip of his juice. "It's going to be soon," he said. "And when it happens we'll create buzz around Casa de la Flora to raise its value, sell it off, and focus on House of Tijeras. We'll move domestic manufacturing to Los Angeles and hire immigrant labor for cheap. Once we see the black in the books again, we'll dump it off to the highest bidder. Eternal 14 has already expressed interest."

Everyone took a moment to ponder his crazy plan.

"Could work," said Sam. "Daisy is an icon. We could play off her death as a way to introduce the line extension. We can dig up her original sketches and say she designed them from her deathbed. She's out of the limelight, no one will know."

Alex, Johnny's personal assistant, lunged toward the center of the group. "Don't forget the Young Designers Program. One of our selections was picked strictly for publicity reasons. She has a popular fan site—get this—it's called DaisyForever.com and it's dedicated to your aunt."

"And we're bringing her in?" Johnny shouted, sliding his glass on the table. "She is siphoning interest from our brands. Louisa, you're head of marketing, why haven't we filed a cease and desist? We should sue!"

"We have it under control," Louisa said. "Her name is Scarlet Santana. She's not doing anything illegal. In fact, she's largely responsible for keeping both Casa de la Flora and House of Tijeras in the indie press."

"Free publicity," the lawyer said. "We can use her to build more of the buzz you mentioned and sell off *both* brands to Eternal 14."

Louisa nodded in agreement. "Our interest is declining among the public, yet Miss Scarlet's—that's her moniker—is taking off like a firecracker. It would be in our best interest to capitalize on that. I'll take personal responsibility for this situation from this point on."

"Now you're talking," Johnny said, clapping his hands together. "Yes, let's use her to raise brand awareness. If we work it right, we can acquire the site from her and work it into the sale."

"What's your timeline for all this? What do you want us to do with this summer's designers program?" Sam asked.

Johnny grabbed his juice again and swallowed the last bit. "Move it up to mid-January; it'll be our last one, thank God."

"But the tuition . . . we have students paying on installments," Alex said.

"If they want it bad enough, they'll come up with the cash." Johnny shrugged. "Now, hop to it, people. Let's draw up a formal plan at the office. I'll meet all of you there at ten."

DaisyForever.com
magical musings about love, beauty & fashion
inspired by the life of Daisy de la Flora
as told by Miss Scarlet Santana

Friday, December 9, 11:59 p.m.

Chalk it up to being unique.

"Letter to myself:

If you have a head, shoulders, bust, waist, hips, legs and feet, you have a lot to be thankful for. Our bodies are the protective covering to a priceless treasure. Learn to love yours. I suggest lying on the sidewalk or carport and tracing every curve with a piece of chalk. Stand up and smile at it. There's not another one in the world like it. And then go on and wear those sexy heels. Pose for that spontaneous picture. Get up from your chair and do a cartwheel. Why? Because as each day closes, we lose a tiny bit of ourselves."

—Daisy de la Flora, journal entry, August 1971

Hola, my 100% cotton-loving chickadees! Today's post is a snapshot I took from Daisy's journal that was part of a fashion exhibit at the Metropolitan Museum of Art.

During this time in Daisy's life, she worked as a costume designer for many blockbuster Hollywood films. She spent all day and night fitting beautiful starlets and dancers, and doing so made her insecure about her apple-shaped body. Did I ever mention that one of Daisy's legs was shorter than the other? She refused to limp, and had special shoes made. But then she worried that the unevenness was obvious so she embellished the heels—that is what led to her designing footwear!

See? Instead of hitting the pity piñata, Daisy forced herself to appreciate her bod, and greatness followed. I hope these words inspire all of you to do the same. And if any of you happen to trace your bodies on the sidewalk, please send pictures—I'll post them in the gallery section.

I'm dedicating this post to my patternless sewing students, because tomorrow is duct-tape dress form day!

What's that? You've never heard of such a thing? Gather round, my beauties. A duct-tape dressform is just that—a dress form made from duct tape! Click on the Project Ideas link for instructions.

Why spend hundreds of dollars on a form that represents a standardized size when you can make your own? And when I say the word "form," I mean any kind of form in life. Be like Daisy and always strive to fine-tune your belongings and surroundings to your desire. That's what I do!

Ciao ciao, cinnamon buns!

Marco moved all the tables out of the way while Scarlet hauled in handfuls of bulky plastic shopping bags for the second week of her workshop. She swung the goods on top of the front table and began to remove the contents.

He chuckled as he watched her sort the rolls according to color. He couldn't believe that within the hour the room would be filled with women (voluntarily) bound in duct tape.

At first Marco decided to close the curtains on the room's front window, worried about cops passing by and getting the wrong idea. He changed his mind. Duct tape or not, ever since the room had been brightened up with chandeliers, wild fabric wall coverings, and that magnificent tree, passersby often stopped and pressed their noses to the glass to stare. Many times their curiosity led to their actually coming inside the store and buying records.

Marco's thoughts were interrupted by Nadine tapping on his shoulder. "Dude, I work for you, not Wilma Flintstone over there. I better get a raise for this shit. Last I recall, I was hired to sell music, not take grown women hostage. We're really going to wrap people in duct tape? Is this even legal?"

"Nadine! My new best friend!" Scarlet sang out when she

noticed the girl had entered. Actually, it was the glare off the silver spike in Nadine's nose that caught her attention. "Thank you for your help, precious. Do you remember all the details?" Scarlet asked, removing the gingham scarf from her head and tying it around her neck. "Just to be sure, want to review again?"

Marco set down the last of the music stands next to Nadine and whispered in her ear. "Twenty bucks."

"Twenty-five," she replied without moving her lips.

"Deal," he said.

"Yup. Wrap 'em and spin 'em," Nadine stated. "Got it."

Marco hadn't built up the nerve to ask Scarlet out yet, but he would soon. The trouble was that her free time revolved around raising cash for her Johnny Scissors tuition. Since the sewing class numbers fell short, she took on extra hours at Carly's as well as helping at her aunt's quinceañera shop. That took up half of her sixteen-hour workday. Scarlet spent her early-morning hours packing and shipping orders from her online store. During the middle of the night she designed and stitched her Mexibilly Frock dresses. Somewhere in there she managed to promote all of it online at various social networking sites. He *would* ask her out, but not until he was sure she'd have time for a date.

In the meantime, Marco stepped in wherever he could. Just the night before he had spent four hours at her place, taking pictures of all her dresses and uploading them to her online store.

No wonder Scarlet was so bubbly, he thought as he typed up the item descriptions. He didn't know anything about sewing, but he knew each outfit told a novel through vibrant layers and depth, as if she personally squeezed a drop of her soul into every pleat and sequin. No one deserved success more than her, and it bothered him that her family didn't see that.

He only wished she would relax a bit. With all she had going on in her life, she insisted on making him dinner for his help. He practically had to put up a block fence in front of the kitchen to stop her. Scarlet had more pride than anyone he'd known. She didn't like or want to accept favors. To her it was a sign of giving up control, and she didn't want to be in anyone's debt.

As Marco unscrewed the top from each music stand, he admired her from the corner of his eye. She wore red sneakers, tight Levi's rolled up at the ankles, and a black leotard that he couldn't stop staring at.

"Marco...How's it goin' over there, champ?" Scarlet called out right before she tipped her cup upside down to ensure she caught the last drop of her quad mocha. She stuck out her tongue and licked the foam off her bright red lips.

His face turned a soft shade of pink. "Just fine," he replied, as he accidentally stepped on the music stand and almost twisted his foot.

Scarlet giggled. "Take it slow mister, class hasn't even begun! Hey, do you mind if we have open sewing lab on Tuesday and Thursday nights, too—you know, so the students can get more practice?"

So much for asking her out on weeknights, he thought. "That's cool with me, but don't you already have enough on your plate? You don't want to get burned out."

"Ah, dontcha worry about me," she said. "Hey look, someone's coming!"

Olivia pranced in, twirling a huge white T-shirt around her chubby finger. "I'm here and I'm ready to rock! Oh my lord..." Olivia gasped and looked at all the body silhouettes they had made in last week's class. Scarlet had pasted them on the walls.

"Love it. Great job, Teach," Olivia said. "I read your blog this morning and cried my eyes out. No wonder you had us trace our bodies last week. What a beautiful post. I'm going to print it out. Ooh, Mexican pastries again!"

Scarlet set out napkins, pitchers of water, and a tray of pan dulce that Nana Eleanor had made for the class.

"Oh, chica, you read my mind," Olivia purred, and joined Scarlet in tasting one of the brightly powdered treats. "I'm gonna need more duct tape for my dress form after this! I'm telling you, Scarlet, being able to hang out with you like this has brightened up my life so much. Every time I feel like smacking someone, I think—'What would Scarlet do?'"

Scarlet laughed. "Every time I feel like smacking someone, I think, 'What would Daisy do?'"

As the rest of the students filtered in, Scarlet couldn't contain her excitement. She raced over to each one, hugged them, and welcomed them back to the class.

"I have an announcement," Scarlet hollered over the chatter. "In addition to Saturdays, Marco has offered the classroom every Tuesday and Thursday night for sewing lab."

"My, you're a live one today," Mary Theresa said as she backed away from her eager teacher. "Red Bull?"

"Four shots of espresso," Nadine blurted as she passed by to close the door.

Scarlet put her hands on her hips at the front of the class. "OK, everyone, scootch up close now. Did everyone bring long T-shirts? Go ahead and put them on over the shirt you're wearing now."

"How'd she get up there so fast?" Jennifer whispered to her sister while nodding in Scarlet's direction. "I swear she was standing right here half a second ago."

"I'm in Keds today, doll," Scarlet remarked while performing a mini-moonwalk. "Now, let me explain how this works. We're going to wrap your torso in duct tape from the bottom of your booty up to your neck and under your arms. We'll then snip the whole thing off, stuff it, and attach it to these adjustable music stands. What you'll have is a custom-made stuffed dress form tailored to your body's exact measurements. I'll demonstrate the first one, and then we can all help wrap each other. Who wants to be the first model? I have all different colors of duct tape."

"Hey, can we doodle all over it when we're done?" Jennifer asked.

"Ohhh, fashion graffiti! Sure, I love that," Scarlet said.

"I'm goin' Jill Scott all over mine," Olivia said as she recited her favorite lyrics from "Hate on Me."

"*'Cause in reality, I'm gon' be who I be*
And I don't feel no faults, for all the lies that you bought."

Mary Theresa stiffly glanced down at her invisible wrist-watch. "Come to think of it, I'm waiting for a very important call sometime today; I really should exit just in case . . ."

Rosa nudged her. "Hey, kid, I'm older than thread and I'm doing it, so you can too. Come on, we'll take care of each other."

"Well, this just doesn't seem . . . I don't know, healthy?" Mary Theresa said, obviously beyond concerned. "Doesn't duct tape have toxins? I have very sensitive skin. What if it comes in contact with it? And why do we want to see our bodies in true form anyway? Isn't the whole idea of clothing to conceal?"

"Think of it this way, Mary Theresa. Dress forms are very expensive. Once you complete the project, you'll see the value. Come on, I'd like you to be our first model," Scarlet said with affection. "I know it's not anything you are used to, but please give me a chance. Trust me. Please?"

Before Mary Theresa opened her mouth to refuse, Scarlet stepped in front of her and stared right into her pupils. "Instead of thinking of all the reasons why not to try this, think about how good it will feel to do something totally unexpected. What can it hurt to take a little risk?"

In that second, it wasn't Scarlet's voice or face Mary Theresa heard and saw, but Hadley's. It reminded her of why she was here and not at home working on the NorWest project. As much as she wanted to spurn the dress-form idea, she loved the irony of it . . . wrapping herself in duct tape in order to loosen up in life.

"Fine. Only because you are the expert." Mary Theresa slipped on her long T-shirt and braced herself as if she were going to be whipped with duct tape rather than wrapped in it. She tilted her head and weakly smiled at Rosa. "Pray for me."

Nadine turned up the music—a Portuguese samba station on Pandora.com—while Scarlet peeled away the first piece of silver tape from the thick roll and ripped it off with her teeth. Her eyes met Mary Theresa's. "Trust me," she whispered. She then applied it around the woman's petite waist. Seeing a collection of sweat beads along Mary Theresa's hairline, Rosa grabbed a second roll of tape and stepped over to assist. As Scarlet performed the specific directions, Nadine situated the other students so they could begin the process as well.

Scarlet and Rosa worked as fast as they could to cover Mary Theresa's entire body, while she stood stiff as a scarecrow with her arms out at her sides. In order to create the shell of the dress form, they had to press strips across her chest and around her hips, pelvis, and butt. They figured the sooner they finished, the sooner the tense, busy mom could relax.

"You're shivering. Are you OK?" asked Rosa.

"It's freezing in here. I'm holding my teeth back from chattering," Mary Theresa replied.

"Tell us about your twins," Scarlet said, hoping to lighten her mood. Nana Eleanor always said anytime you needed to butter someone up, ask them about their children, grandchildren, or pets.

It worked. "A boy and a girl," Mary Theresa said with her first hint of glee all day. "My mother is watching them today so I can be here."

"Twins? With this hourglass figure? No wonder your husband sticks with you! La verdad, no Scarlet?" Rosa laughed as she finished placing the final piece. She smoothed it down and exchanged a "Thank goodness, we are done!" glance with Scarlet. Rosa wondered why Mary Theresa had surrendered her Saturday morning when she obviously didn't want to be there.

"We're a very happy unit," Mary Theresa fired back, now resembling a mummy reaching for a snack. "I mean, sure, times get rough, especially around the holidays; arguments happen, people get hurt. But at the end of the day, all is calm and loving. It really is. We're very happy. We really, really are. We're far from dysfunctional." She blinked hard and held her breath.

Before Scarlet or Rosa could respond, a blaring, cringe-inducing siren went off in Mary Theresa's . . . pelvis.

Rrrrrrt!

Rrrrrrt!

Rrrrrrt!

The other women in the class stopped, then turned to look at the exact spot where the noise came from—Mary Theresa's bikini line. The teenagers broke out in giggles, but Olivia and Nadine froze, each with a perplexed expression.

Mary Theresa closed her eyes and counted to three to stay calm as the annoying alarm continued. "That's my husband calling. My phone is in my front pocket. I can't answer because I'm sealed in the tape."

"You use a Defcon-4 alarm ringtone for your husband?" Scarlet asked.

"I told you I was waiting for an important call!" Mary Theresa hollered over the repeating sound, embarrassed as she clawed at the hem of her thick silver bodysuit.

Scarlet quickly pulled out her scissors and was about to snip up the front of Mary Theresa's thigh. "I'm so sorry," she said. "I'll cut this off lickety-split so you can ring him back."

Mary Theresa thought about how she had left multiple messages for Hadley since Monday, and he hadn't had the decency to return the calls all week. What if Rocky or Lucy broke an arm? What if the kitchen caught on fire? What if she wanted to promise him again she would change her ways so he would come home? Well, now it would be his turn to wait and wonder. She tapped Scarlet's hand away. "No. I'll get back with him later. Let's continue."

Mary Theresa's sudden shift surprised Scarlet, but not enough to distract her from the day's mission. Still buzzing from her high-octane mocha, Scarlet finished wrapping Mary Theresa and the rest of her students. The next step would be slicing the back of the duct tape that was affixed to their bodies. But when she saw Marco poke his head in to see how things were going, a brilliant idea popped into her brain.

"Marco, take a picture of us, OK? I'll stand in the middle and hold up my nana's vintage shears." She reached into her back pocket. "Double darn! I think I left my iPhone at work yesterday. Can we use yours?"

"You read my mind," he said, pulling out his phone from his shirt pocket, which was well intact, Scarlet noticed.

All the women waddled their way to the center of the room, then they slowly zombie-walked their way over by the window upon Marco's suggestion. Scarlet was standing front and center when Marco decided she would look even better holding a roll of tape too, and impersonating a champion gladiator crafter.

"Scarlet, catch!" Nadine tossed a roll of duct tape to Scarlet.

"Noooo!" Scarlet shrieked, alarmed that it might hit one of the women—not to mention the six-inch blades she held in one hand. She almost toppled over just to catch the flying tape. She held out her arm and the roll slid down it like a ring toss at the state fair.

What she didn't notice was that she had caused Olivia to fall backward, which made Stephanie try to catch her—but she lost her balance and reached for Jennifer's arm, only managing to grab her hat instead. Jennifer then tried to move away from the commotion, but belly collided with Mary Theresa. All of them teetered back and forth as the Saturday foot traffic stopped on the sidewalk and crowded outside the window to gawk.

To Scarlet, the whole episode happened in slow motion. She scurried around, not knowing whom to catch first. Age before beauty, she thought, and she lunged for Rosa, but missed— all while witnessing the flapping arms, the shocked faces and squeals. One by one the ladies tipped to the floor in one brightly colored duct-tape massacre.

"Scarlet!"

"Oh, please no...," Scarlet mumbled. Standing in the middle of five fallen females bound in colored duct tape, and herself holding scissors in one hand over her head and a roll of duct tape in the other, Scarlet slowly pivoted to face...her mother.

"Hey, Mom! Oh. Carly...you're here too. Why?" Scarlet asked in a shaky voice.

Carly handed Scarlet her iPhone. "You left this at work yesterday. I was in the area, so I thought I'd be nice and drop it off. This is what you wanted to do at my design house? These poor women look like they've been held hostage by a bowl of Skittles."

"Mija, I came to bring you lunch," her mom, Jeane, said. "I

felt bad that we went out to eat for Charles's birthday and forgot to tell you. I brought you leftovers."

"You went out for Charles's birthday and didn't invite me?" Scarlet whined.

"You always say you can't go because you're too busy working, so we stopped asking," Jeane fired back. "Oh dear God. Look at this mess. This is why you gave up Cruz and a decent job? To play? Oh, Scarlet, when are you going to get serious with your life?"

After the duct-tape drama, long after Olivia, Stephanie, and Jennifer had finished constructing their dress forms and left, Rosa took her time and wandered about the room to pick up the last of the scraps. Mary Theresa hadn't yet finished but stuck around to see the project through to the end. Scarlet showed her how to secure her brand-new customized dress form to the top of the music stand. They both sighed with accomplishment, and set it next to the other forms along the wall.

The three women stood back and surveyed the array of stuffed torsos. Red, yellow, green, black, silver, hot pink, and one with multicolored swatches all over—of course belonging to Olivia. Some of the body shapes were sleek and lean, while others were lumpy and thick. All of them were breathtaking to Scarlet. She snapped pictures from different artful angles.

"This was a wonderful idea, Scarlet. I think Daisy would have been mighty impressed with this idea. They look like they could be in a magazine. They are like giant torso-shaped lollipops," Rosa joked. "I'm happy you made one too. Now we have a complete set."

Mary Theresa pulled the elastic band off her head and let her long dark hair fall to her shoulders. She massaged her scalp, stretched out her arms, and yawned so long she let out a tiny squeal.

Mary Theresa sighed as Nadine entered and handed out burritos Marco had ordered for them. "Marco ordered these from La Perla for you." "I cannot believe this day is already over," Mary Thearsa said. "I completely forgot about my task list. I've never done that before. I got lost in the project, I guess. Stuffing all that batting made my mind wander." She set down the food on the table and slid her hands down the sides of her taped masterpiece. "It's nice. I can't believe this is me. I pictured myself different."

"How's that?" Scarlet said, pulling up chairs for them to sit on.

Mary Theresa peeked around her dress form, raised a shoulder, and skimmed her chin. "It's embarrassing. I can't say it out loud," she answered with half a smile.

"An alarm went off in your pants today. I think you left embarrassed behind in the dust," Scarlet joked as she peeled back the wrapper from her food and took a bite.

Rosa, visually exhausted, limped to the chair and sat. She shook her finger at Mary Theresa. "Hey now, if anyone should be embarrassed it's me. I'm almost eighty; look at mine! My butt is flatter than a sketchbook, my waist is thicker than a tree trunk, and mis melones are bosom buddies with my navel. But everything is in working order, so I refuse to complain. I'm making it work—and for the record, I coined that phrase long before Tim Gunn ever did!"

Mary Theresa stood shoulder-to-shoulder with her duct-taped statue to compare the faux body to her fleshy one. "You're right...OK well...I've always been self-conscious about my chest. I'm so flat. If it weren't for having kids, I'd swear I had the body of a little boy. But now that I examine my silhouette on the wall, and this contraption I constructed for the past five hours, my chest isn't that horrible. I mean, I'm no pinup model like our teacher over there…" Mary Theresa wagged her thumb in Scarlet's direction.

Scarlet rolled her eyes and slouched back in the creaky metal chair. "Oh, stop! It's the clothes. I'm a sucker for the golden days when women wore bullet bras, girdles, and showed off their gams with class. Hey, I made this top and jeans—guess what movie it's from!"

"Marilyn Monroe in *The Misfits*. You told us three times this morning," Mary Theresa said.

"Oh, sorry," Scarlet said.

"Not that it isn't unique."

"Thanks," Scarlet said as she picked at the pink polish on her thumbnail.

"That didn't come out right…," Mary Theresa said. Scarlet's voice wasn't quite as chipper as before, and she thought she might have hurt the girl's feelings. "Your outfit is impressive. I mean, more than impressive. It's quite darling. You're very skilled at your craft, Scarlet."

"I agree," said Rosa. "And your mother was wrong to speak to you that way in front of all of us. Your boss, too. I feel guilty that I didn't vouch up for you."

"Aw, don't," Scarlet said. You barely know me. I'm used to my mom and Carly. One day I know my mom will be bragging about all the celebrities wearing my clothes, and Carly will boast about discovering me. I visualize the moment."

Mary Theresa sat on the edge of the folding chair and reached for her burrito. "I'm sure your mother didn't mean it. People often say, or even do, cruel things to loved ones and regret it later." She looked up at Scarlet. "I bet if you gave her the chance to apologize, she would."

"My mother won't relax until I'm spoken for, and earning

six figures," Scarlet said with a rough laugh. "Everything I do is a reflection on her. If I fail, she fails. And Carly? I think the woman has a catastrophe-seeking radar to locate me every time something goes wrong. I know what I want to do in my life, and I don't want to waste a minute trying to change what they think of me. I use their doubts to fuel my ambition. All I can do is prove them wrong. If that means going it alone, all the better."

"You're right," Rosa said. "I've always had family try to tell me what to do. Didn't listen to any of them, and they've deemed me nuts. Go with your gut and push through the pain to reach your goal. But there is one fact I learned, ladies. If they truly love you, they'll come around when you need them the most, so don't give up completely."

Mary Theresa couldn't comprehend their rationale. "But why make it so difficult? Every day is a struggle already. Why not go with what is proven to work to lessen the blow? Do the best you can with the tools presented and accept that there is no such thing as perfection."

Scarlet got up and knelt at Mary Theresa's side. "Have you ever heard the phrase 'Some people grin and bear it; others smile and do it'? Perfection is a state of mind, darling. Think back to the last time you felt truly happy. What were you doing? That should be your definition of perfection. Mine is when I'm sewing. And when someone responds to something I said, made, or shared. It makes me feel alive."

Rosa closed her eyes and smiled from ear to ear, recalling a multitude of those "perfection" moments. Like the time she swam between two dolphins in Hawaii or when she helped a team of women in Mexico open their own weaving businesses. Visiting a beach in Thailand just long enough to make love on a bed of diamond-colored sand. Yes, Rosa had had more than her fair share of perfection. And she hoped to pay it forward.

"Today was a perfection moment for me," Rosa said to her new friends.

"Oh really?" Mary Theresa said, slightly baffled. "Aside from the birth of my children, I don't know if I've ever had one." She dropped her head in her hands. "But after listening to you two, I really want to find out."

"We want cereal! We want cereal! We want cereal!"

So much for the eleven steps to preventing a headache. These days Mary Theresa knew of only one: three extra-strength Tylenol Gelcaps. Not that they'd work fast enough to take away the brain pain caused by the children pounding their spoons and chanting for their favorite sugar-coated breakfast cereal. Huddled over the beige granite countertops, the newly single stay-at-home mom ripped open two packets of Quaker Instant Organic Oatmeal, dumped the powder into plastic *Toy Story* bowls, and added hot tap water. Nearly two weeks had passed since Scarlet's lecture at sewing class, and Mary Theresa had yet to find a perfection moment.

She stirred the mixtures until creamy and added a mini-box of raisins to each dish. "There," she said aloud. "That ought to be sweet enough, and it is all natural."

Almost three weeks had passed since Hadley left, and she had yet to build a successful bridge between her part-time job and full-time motherhood. Each morning she awoke at six a.m. to a jumbled pile of duties for the day. She mapped plans on Excel spreadsheets, but in real life, her theories didn't translate. The kids were so darned unpredictable. She'd have better luck training wild horses to sip from teacups.

Her heart ached for Rocky and Lucy because she knew how much they missed their father, and no amount of hugs could reassure them that he would return soon. Hadley tried to help by videoconferencing with them every night. He read them stories, asked about the details of their day, and blew kisses through the screen.

Contrasting emotions flooded Mary Theresa's mind from hour to hour, swinging from one extreme to the next. The elation of making her children laugh to fear about the future of her marriage. To stay sane, she surrendered all her energy to being a mom. She cleaned the house while Rocky and Lucy were at school, and finished in time to pick them up and escort them to their various extracurricular activities. When they arrived home, she cooked dinner, helped with homework, argued and/or bribed them to bathe and go to bed. On a good night, she only spent twenty minutes begging them to fall asleep, but most nights it took an hour. By the time she settled in to work on the NorWest account, the clock hands had moved well past ten p.m. and she could barely stay awake.

Their relief came in the form of Margaret Anne, Mary Theresa's mom. At seven a.m. sharp on Saturdays, the chipper grandma didn't even have to walk up to the porch because Rocky and Lucy were already waiting on the patio bench, their little hands gripping their overnight bags. Mary Theresa sat next to them, excited to spend the day at Vega's Vicious Vinyl with her patternless friends. She had already made a purse and a basic skirt. Nothing out of the ordinary; she had made more impressive garments in high school, but she loved turning off her home life and tuning in to the antics of Olivia, the teenagers, and Scarlet's kamikaze work stories. Mary Theresa could hardly wait for the upcoming lessons, which included a mystery field trip next week, a wrap dress, and a simple shirtwaister.

She grabbed two bananas from the fruit bowl on the kitchen island, slung them under her arms, swooped up the bowls, and marched to the kitchen table.

Cooking for first-graders, Mary Theresa had learned these past few weeks, turned out to be more difficult than leading a team of snack-grubbing computer programmers. She blamed Hadley. She had specifically instructed him to feed the kids a healthy yet tasty morning meal consisting of his choice of either steel-cut oats, plain yogurt with granola, or turkey sausage and scrambled tofu. As a treat on Fridays, unsweetened Cheerios. Now that she wore the chef's apron, she was horrified to discover that he had tweaked her list: chocolate-chip pancakes, fried eggs, and pork sausage—and on Fridays, disgusting sugary cereal.

Mary Theresa did her best to lure the kids to the healthy side. Problem was, she had never cooked much in her life. Growing up, her mother ruled the kitchen, at college she ate in the cafeteria, and Hadley had handled the spatula spinning ever since. Last week, she'd made steel-cut oatmeal, but she didn't cook it long enough and both children spit it up. The next day she tried seasoned tofu with spinach and cheese, and grinned in delight when she noticed their plates were clean. But a few hours later, the school office called because her son had his meal in his backpack and the smell was disrupting class. So instant organic oatmeal it was. The kids were even picky about that....

"Look, Mommy, I can pick up this whole piece of oatmeal with my spoon! It's like Play-Doh!" Lucy shouted. "Can I make a flower out of it?"

"No, it's like peanut butter," Rocky said. "But Mommy, I think there are too many raisins. I can't see the oatmeal part very much. How do I only eat the oatmeal?"

Mary Theresa wiped her hands on her apron and pulled up

a chair in between her twins. "Mommy is still getting used to cooking. It doesn't look pretty, but it still tastes yummy!" She lifted a big spoonful of Rocky's raisinfied oatmeal and *Choo-choo*-ed it to his mouth.

Lucy broke out in a fit of giggles. "He's not a baby! We don't do choo-choo anymore. You're funny, Mommy!"

"OK, then. Open your mouth and eat your breakfast," Mary Theresa ordered.

"But Mommy, I can't…"

"Yes, you can. Open."

Lucy jumped off her chair and tugged at her mom's arm. "He can't!"

Mary Theresa gave her a scolding stare strong enough to send little Lucy back to her chair. Her chocolate eyes welled up with tears.

"Rocky Javier Cotorro you *will* open tu boca. Now."

Tears streamed down little Rocky's face as he let his frowning jaw fall. Mary Theresa shoveled in the full spoon and he began to slowly chew and shake his head in sorrow.

"Why are you crying? See, it's good!" She said proudly, wondering if Hadley went through this every morning.

"I'm…cryin' 'cause I'm—"

"Chew!" she said.

"I'm allergic…to…raisins," he said as he was just about to swallow. Lucy handed her mom the phone and covered her eyes with her hands. "You hafta call 911, like Daddy did."

Suddenly Mary Theresa remembered Hadley warning her about Rocky's raisin allergy. Oh gosh, she had even taped a sign on the refrigerator door. How could she forget?

"SPIT IT OUT!" Mary Theresa yelled, lunging for him. She cradled him in her arms, tipped his head down, and scraped the offending oatmeal from his tongue into the bowl. She rushed him to the kitchen sink, heaved him up, and washed out his mouth under the faucet, even though he swore he didn't swallow any of it. Without even turning off the water, Mary Theresa clenched him to her and kissed his head and apologized repeatedly to both him and Lucy. Full-time parenting sure wasn't what she thought. It's like *Nanny 911* meets *COPS* meets the Dalai Lama meets Rachael Ray, all on steroids.

Once the commotion subsided, Mary Theresa let the children choose whatever they wanted to eat, and they both pointed at the Nilla Wafers in the pantry. She handed them the box.

"Go for it, sweeties," she said as they all filed back to the table as if nothing had happened. Lucy and Rocky devoured the cookies with both hands. One day off schedule won't hurt them, she decided, especially after the unnecessary trauma she'd just put them through.

"So, my angelitos, tell me what you're learning in school."

"Kwanzaa!" Lucy said. "It starts the day after Christmas, but we're doing it now."

"That's wonderful," Mary Theresa said, relieved that the raisin situation seemed to have disappeared from their minds. "Tell me what you're making to celebrate."

Rocky stopped chewing. "Mommy, me and Lucy are proud to be African American. You know that? I'm very proud. Kwanzaa is really cool." He shoved another cookie in his mouth and nodded.

"Oh, sweetie." Mary Theresa laughed. "You're not African American, you're Mexican American."

Lucy shook her head no. "No, Mommy, we are African American. Our teacher told us!"

This wasn't the first time Mary Theresa had dealt with this issue. Both she and Hadley had the complexion of tamarind, she with wavy hair, and he with micro curls, which he often kept cropped close to his head. Many thought she was Italian and he was black. But this was a first for Lucy and Rocky.

Mary Theresa motioned for them to sit on her lap. "You are not African American, so please don't say that. It is incorrect. I'm Mexican American, so is Daddy. All right?"

Lucy began to cry. "No, Mommy. Just like with the raisins, you don't know. We are African American!"

Hadley's words rang in Mary Theresa's mind: "I want you to get to know your children." How could she not know all this time that her kids weren't aware of their own culture? Was this their fault as parents, or the school's? She honestly didn't have a clue how to resolve the wreckage.

Noticing the clock, Mary Theresa quickly put their coats on, handed them their backpacks—but not before checking them for oatmeal—and guided the kids out the door to make it to school.

When she returned, she would surrender her pride and seek reinforcement. And she knew exactly whom to call.

Thank you for coming, Rosa. You must think this is very odd," Mary Theresa said as she invited her new friend inside her home. "Did you have any trouble punching in the code? A lot of people who don't live in gated communities get flustered right away...."

"No trouble at all. Joseph had a business matter to tend to, so I asked Scarlet to bring me. I hope you don't mind."

Scarlet came up from behind Rosa and hugged Mary Theresa. "Hi, chickie, you OK?"

Mary Theresa groaned. "Oh no, I didn't mean to turn this into a big production. It's really no big deal. Scarlet, shouldn't you be at Carly's right now? I don't want you to fall behind on your work because of me. I know you stay up late sewing, and you were late to class last night helping with your aunt's dress order, you don't have time for this."

"I took the morning off. No biggie," she replied, removing her winter-white overcoat. "Rosa said you needed help; I'm happy to oblige. We're here. Let's make the most of it."

"Well, then—thanks. Come on in and have a seat in the family room," said Mary Theresa as she held out her arm to guide them. "I called about um...a...um...sewing project." She had made a sudden executive decision *not* to discuss her personal marital issues with these women. Even if she did feel awful about them driving across town on her behalf. She would whip up a quick lunch and send them on their way.

"You called about a sewing project. OK," Rosa said, semiconvinced, noticing the clutter of plastic game pieces, chunky kids' books, and the random pint-size shoes strewn throughout the two-level house. They brought back memories of when she had a child in her life.

Mary Theresa didn't have any makeup on, but wore her usual creased jeans and pressed polo shirt. As Rosa and Scarlet trailed behind her, they wondered if the mom knew that she had a chunk of oatmeal hanging from her ponytail. Scarlet, in a black pencil skirt and emerald cardigan, unsnapped the hinge on her black patent-leather handbag, whipped out a tissue, and removed the clump when Mary Theresa wasn't looking.

"Wow, this is a lovely casa," Scarlet said, admiring the vaulted ceilings and wide hallways that stretched in two directions. The walls were tall but bare, except for a solo framed southwestern print on each one. She took a quick gander around to find the entry wall decorated with stick figures in crayon and said "Awwww..."

"The kids did that," Mary Theresa said in a flustered but controlled tone. "My husband is working in Palm Springs until February and they miss him a little...so they draw pictures of him. On the walls. I apologize for the mess; I haven't had much time to clean up today. It doesn't usually look like this. It's always very orderly."

Rosa let out a polite chuckle. "It's nice to see a house where children play," she said. She felt so weak, she almost didn't make it over. She had wrestled through the night with an upset stomach after her doctor's appointment. In the morning, Joseph had tried to make her stay in bed, but she refused. She sensed an all-too-familiar hint of desperation in Mary Theresa's tone.

"So where is that sewing project?" Rosa asked.

"What sewing project?" Mary Theresa replied, nervously spinning the wedding ring on her finger. And then she remembered. "Oh, *that* sewing project.... Hmm, let's see."

Just then, the sound of sizzling water came from the kitchen. Mary Theresa jokingly smacked her head. "I forgot I put water to boil for our tea. I'll be right back; please make yourself at home," she said, leaving Rosa and Scarlet alone in the family room.

"Mary Theresa...," Rosa sang out. "Your computer is ringing like a telephone. I'd answer, but I don't know how."

Mary Theresa hustled over and hunched over the screen. "It's a video phone call. It's my kids' teacher calling. This is very efficient because we can converse face-to-face at any time. I called the school and filed a complaint this morning; wait until I tell you what happened!"

"Answer it, dear," Rosa said. "I'll go finish making the tea." Scarlet joined Rosa in the kitchen and they both winced when they overheard the gruesome conversation in the other room. The teacher explained, quite loudly, that Rocky told the entire class that "Mommy made his daddy live at a place called Skype in the computer and his daddy can't get out."

Still eavesdropping, Rosa gasped while Scarlet poured the water into the teal ceramic mugs. They heard Mary Theresa argue back that her children were Mexican American, not African American. Whatever that meant. The women waited until Mary Theresa hung up and then they proceeded to join her back into the room with the tea.

Rosa placed her hands gently on Mary Theresa's shoulders.

"Take a breather, dear. Let's go sit down and drink our tea and talk," Rosa suggested.

Mary Theresa blew air out of her mouth and reached for the cup—but then the telephone rang. She held up a finger, mouthed "school principal," and then picked up the handset.

"Just because my husband is dark complected and wears a cowry-shell necklace does not mean he is from the islands!" she scolded to the person on the other line. "He's Mexican American and so are our children!"

Scarlet could tell by the instant shock on Mary Theresa's face that it was not the principal she expected.

"Oh . . . Sandra, it's you, heh-heh," Mary Theresa said, collapsing into the padded office chair. "Please excuse that outburst . . . what do you mean I sent you my life-goal list last night? Noooo, it should have been the NorWest PowerPoint presentation. . . . Yes, everything is fine here. . . . I'll e-mail it right away . . . um-hm . . . OK, sorry . . . bye."

Enough of the charade, Rosa thought. She set down the mugs and folded her arms across her chest. "What is going on, Mary Theresa?"

Mary Theresa's hands trembled as she raised them and covered her nose. She closed her eyes, opened them, counted to three, and sat up tall. "I'm fine. I'm just attempting to adjust to a few small changes in my life, that's all."

Rosa, angry, stomped to the family room and picked up her purse. Her only reason for moving to Phoenix was to take the patternless sewing class, not to play games with unstable mothers. She should have listened to Joseph and stayed home. "When you are ready to tell the truth, call me and I'll just have Joseph drive me all the way back over here. Scarlet, will you take me home please?"

Mary Theresa stood up to stop her, but didn't know what

to say. It was a defining moment in her life. Would she allow herself to open up or continue holding her problems inside and praying they would be resolved without anyone ever knowing? A tear rolled down each cheek, which Mary Theresa quickly wiped away. She stopped analyzing the situation and opened her mouth to hear what would come out. "It's so hard to say it out loud.... I need a moment...."

Her intensity made Scarlet uneasy, so she reached out and rubbed Mary Theresa's arm. "Hey, there. Whatever it is, we're on your side. There is nothing to be ashamed of. Let it out."

They all paused to give Mary Theresa time to take a breath.

"My husband left me," she finally admitted through a weary but polite smile. "And—I've been demoted at my job. And—I almost poisoned my son this morning. And—both my kids think they are African American because I haven't paid enough attention to them to even teach them their own culture."

"Oh, dear, let's go sit." Rosa sighed as she put her arm around Mary Theresa's back. They made their way to the monstrous tan sectional couches and sat, where Mary Theresa broke down and continued to share her recent shortcomings while sobbing.

"Basically, after a lifetime of devotion and hard work, the only task I've been able to accomplish with any degree of success is assembling a synthetic replica of my torso made from duct tape and a fifteen-dollar bag of Poly-Fil. I'm a horrible wife and mother. I don't know if Hadley is going to come back; I pushed him to his limit. And my family or neighbors or coworkers can't know about any of this. I'm so tired of living a lie; it's depressing. And crippling."

The women sat down on either side of her and let Mary Theresa cry it out.

"We have all day to talk, right Scarlet?" Rosa asked. Scarlet agreed and picked up the stack of child-rearing manuals, worksheets, and DVDs that were on the coffee and end tables and set them on the floor, out of sight. Rosa found the DVD of Pixar's *Up* and put it in the machine while Scarlet headed to the kitchen for snacks. Ten minutes later she emerged with a heavy tray overflowing with treats.

"Forget the tea; we need the hard stuff. I made popcorn and root beer floats," Scarlet said, handing a tall, frosty mug to Mary Theresa and then one to Rosa. "We'll go with you to pick up the kids and we'll smooth this business all out."

"I don't even know where to start," Mary Theresa said, breathing heavily, holding her chest. She paused when she spotted a gleam on the wall. She traced where it came from to find a black sparkly cocktail ring on the carpet.

"Oh my God, I knew it. He's cheating on me. He had a woman over here," Mary Theresa said as she bent down to pick up the bejeweled evidence. She held it up like a trophy. "It figures his mistress would be tacky enough to wear this cheap piece of tin!"

Rosa politely pried the ring from Mary Theresa's angry grasp and slipped it in the pocket of her chunky red sweater. "It's mine. I've lost a few pounds recently and it must have slipped off."

"Oh, Rosa, I'm sorry. See? I'm a lost cause. I'm despicable."

"That ring is gorgeous," Scarlet whispered to Rosa. "Anyway, Mary Theresa, I know where to start. And your answer will decide where you go from here. But you have to be honest with yourself. Can do you that?"

"I think so."

Scarlet cleared her throat. "Do you *love* Hadley? I mean deep in your heart, stomach-tingles-when-you-bump-into-him-by-accident kind of love? Or are you in love with the convenience of having a domestic partner?"

"The first one," Mary Theresa said confidently. "But I never showed him that side of me, because I didn't know it was there. I got so wrapped up in work and the bills. I took him for granted. I'd trade all of it to bring him home."

Mary Theresa spent the next hour sharing the play-by-play about her marriage history, while Rosa and Scarlet offered words of support. They all agreed she needed to have faith in her husband and give him space, but at the same time, work on building a new *happy* life for herself and the kids—with or without him.

After all that intense discussion, Mary Theresa began to clear the dishes from their comfort snacks, leaving only the root beer floats. Scarlet used the break to answer a text on her iPhone, and then giggled, her face beaming. Scarlet told them Marco had sent her a link to a funny YouTube video featuring a group of East Indian teens from the '50s dancing the mambo. Rosa smiled to herself. Whether that boy liked it or not, she was going to school him on some dance moves.

"Scarlet," Mary Theresa asked. "Do you have a boyfriend? How do you know so much about relationships?"

"Ha! Glad I fooled you!" she replied, putting away her phone. "You know the part I said about being in love with the convenience? That was my former fiancé. He was more interested in my potential tax bracket than me as a person. I thought I was in love with him, but once it ended, that's when I really came into my own."

"I think you and Marco would make a cute couple," Rosa said, suddenly feeling like a matchmaker and clasping her hands on her lap.

"Me too," Mary Theresa added. "You're so opposite of each other, yet you seem like a natural fit."

"I love Marco—as my pal," Scarlet said. "I don't know what I'd have done for my sewing class if it weren't for him. But on a personal level, we would never work. Plus I overshare on every topic and he hardly says anything. I can never tell what he's thinking. Besides, the last thing I have time for is dating. But today is about you, Mary Theresa. Just know that you are in control. It's all how you see it. You can fix all of it."

Mary Theresa sniffled, lifted a tablespoon of foam from her float, and stared at it. "But how?"

"Let's start with the African American thing," Rosa said. "It's a kicker of a story. The kids will be fine, and it'll make great table talk years down the road, trust me. Think about what Scarlet said about the patterns in our lives. Nothing is working because you are forcing your life into something it's not. It's time to start a fresh pattern that represents right *now*, even if you have to make it up as you go."

"That's such a broad statement. I need specifics. Unless it is laid out in list form, I don't get it," Mary Theresa said, frustrated.

Scarlet pulled out her iPhone again and tapped on the screen. A moment later, she turned it around to show a website to Mary Theresa. "It's family night at the Latino Cultural Center. Take the kids so they can see the beauty of their own heritage. Maybe you can enroll Lucy and Rocky in folklórico dancing."

"And stop putting everything on hold for Hadley," Rosa added. "Think about your favorite stories when you were their age; share them. Take the kids to the park, find a grassy hill, and take turns rolling down it. Get on their level. Read a book with them. Being a mother isn't about how clean the house is, it's about the little moments that make a big impact."

"Daisy called them Little Victories!" Scarlet said. "I wrote about it on my blog!"

"I get it," Mary Theresa said hopefully. "You know, I just picked up the latest children's dictionary. We can work on improving their vocabulary."

Rosa felt the passion and sincerity in her friend's intention, but knew she still had a long way to go.

"Why don't you let *them* choose the book and go along with it?" she suggested.

By now, Mary Theresa had finished the float. It had been years since she had indulged in a frothy, sweet treat. "You know," she said, setting down the glass on the coffee table, "I have no idea why I felt compelled to call you over, Rosa. Please don't take offense, but I think it is the wise grandma syndrome. How many grandkids do you have anyway?"

Now it was Rosa's turn to be taken off guard. "None."

"None?" Scarlet and Mary Theresa repeated in unison.

"But I've helped raise many children as if they were my own. I'll tell you about it sometime, but not today. I'm feeling a little winded. I think I need to get back home."

"Of course, Rosa, thank you for coming over and cheering me up. I feel empowered," Mary Theresa said. "My instincts were correct. You certainly were the right one to call. And I'm happy you brought Scarlet. For the first time in my life, I feel like I have friends."

❧ ❧ ❧

To: missscarlet@daisyforever.com
From: ohliveyah@tox.net
Date: Tuesday, December 20 at 8:25 PM
Subject: Class

Hello Scarlet!

I know you are working your little tushy off to raise your tuition money and I'm sorry to interrupt, but I have a quick question about our Tues-Thurs and Saturday class start time. Do you know if it will begin on time, or will it start 15 minutes later like the last five sessions? My daughter, Missy, is in fourth grade and I don't like to leave her alone. It's OK if you need to change the time, I just need to know so I won't have to leave class early like last week and fall behind on my project. I can just let my sitter know to come 15 minutes later. Again, sorry to impose. Excited for Thursday's field trip to the Phoenix Art Museum!

O.

ᔕ ᔕ ᔕ

To: ohliveyah@tox.net
From: missscarlet@daisyforever.com
Date: Wednesday, December 21 at 2:25 AM
Subject: RE: Class

Olivia—I am personally slapping my wrist. Please excuse my tardiness! I've taken up extra shifts at my auntie's quinceanera shop. It seems like every day, one of her customers has a lace emergency that only I can fix, so I'm always late. I apologize for imposing on your time and promise it won't happen again. How about we meet up later this afternoon at Vega's and I'll help you get caught up on your project? 5 p.m.? I'll order takeout from La Perla. Bring Missy along too. I'd love to meet her and give her a quick lesson, too!

Hearts and rhinestone-trimmed buttons,
Scarlet

❧ ❧ ❧

To: missscarlet@daisyforever.com
From: ohliveyah@tox.net
Date: Wednesday, December 21 at 7:15 AM
Subject: RE: RE: Class

Dang, girl, you are still sewing at 2:30 in the morning? So we are sticking with the scheduled time, thank you. Yowza, a personal sewing session with THE Miss Scarlet? Um, YES, I will take you up on your offer. I'm supposed to cover for my coworker at the bookstore tonight, but I'll get out of it (don't blog this!), LOL. See you at five! Here is my cell if anything changes. 555-978-0126.

O.

P.S. You haven't blogged lately. Don't forget about your readers!

❧ ❧ ❧

To: missscarlet@daisyforever.com
From: ohliveyah@tox.net
Date: Wednesday, December 21 at 9:00 PM
Subject: Where were you?

Went to the record store at five to find an anime drawing class going on in our classroom. We waited for twenty minutes. Marco didn't know anything about our meeting, but he allowed me to stay with Missy and let her take the class for free so I guess it worked out. Wish you had called. Hope everything is OK and nothing happened. Guess I'll see you tomorrow at our field trip to the art museum. At 4 p.m.

O.

🐜 🐜 🐜

To: ohliveyah@tox.net
From: missscarlet@daisyforever.com
Date: Wednesday, December 21 at 11:47 PM
Subject: RE: Where were you?

Olivia—I am SO sorry! I didn't enter our meeting in my iPhone calendar and I spaced it. Carly offered me a double shift today (time-and-a-half!). I just barely got home. Would have called right now but I thought you might be in bed. I'll make it up to you, promise. We'll work it out tomorrow. Please accept my apology! And yes, tomorrow's class is at 4 p.m. at the museum. I promise to be on time!

Scarlet

P.S. Hope to blog soon!

E ver since Scarlet came up with the idea for the patternless sewing class, she knew it would include a sketching lesson at her favorite inspiration spot—the Phoenix Art Museum's Ellman Fashion Design Gallery.

Scarlet had plenty of motivation, but any time she needed to conceptualize, she zipped over to the gallery. Located in the heart of the city's landmark museum, the collection showcased more than 4,500 garments dating back as far as the eighteenth century.

She visited at least twice a month to inspect each outfit on display. She discreetly snapped pictures and took notes. Her mind wandered through clouds of cream-colored taffeta, skipped along highways paved with chiffon, and got lost in a sea of buttons and brocade.

The ultimate highlight came at the end of the exhibit: the display of an original Daisy de la Flora gown. Scarlet had seen it more than a hundred times, and it always took her breath away. The masterpiece consisted of a floor-length, asymmetrical fishtail gown covered in muted black sequins and trimmed in rows of black crystals around the bodice. Created in 1967 and sold to Sophia Loren in the mid-1990s, the monochromatic piece stood out because it was the only time in Daisy's career that she didn't use her usual rainbow palette. According to Wikipedia, when Daisy's husband, Sebastian Garcia-Ybarra, unexpectedly died from appendicitis, she created the outfit to wear to his funeral, and designed it around her favorite bejeweled ring.

Scarlet couldn't wait to surprise the class. She knew the up-close-and-personal Daisy experience would increase their passion for fashion.

The only setback: her schedule. For the past two weeks Scarlet had shown up late to class, each time promising not to let it happen again. Yet today she was already nearly an hour late, thanks to the holiday traffic on Central Avenue. With less than a week to go until Christmas, everyone's nerves were on edge. So the second she realized she'd be tardy, she phoned Rosa and asked her to lead the tour at the museum.

Rosa didn't mind; in fact, she enjoyed feeling valued simply for her personality and expertise, no strings attached. But Scarlet's recent behavior concerned her. The girl was so bent on raising her Johnny Scissors tuition that she was beginning to stretch herself too thin. She had doubled her workload and she'd become a bit too loose with the term "patternless" in class, encouraging the ladies to "wing it" on their garments. Olivia, Stephanie, and Jennifer's projects were a complete failure, and Scarlet didn't even offer to help, because she had to leave at three p.m. for a freelance alteration.

There was an expression that Joseph had once told Rosa: "The bigger the wall, the thinner the paint." It reminded her of Daisy de la Flora in her early days, when she put work before her relationships. And there were hints that the usually put-together Scarlet might be headed in the same direction. Rosa planned to pay close attention to see how Scarlet would handle herself under these stressful conditions.

Ten minutes before class was to start, Joseph dropped Rosa off in front of the Phoenix Art Museum. Rosa climbed out of the PT Cruiser and buttoned the collar of her lime overcoat. And like she did every time before a big event, she popped a piece of spearmint Trident in her mouth. She made her way up the museum's shallow staircase to the entrance, holding tight to the railing.

When she reached the top, she stopped to appreciate the artful reflecting pool and the ripples of water cascading down its tiered black tiles. She did a double-take when she caught sight of her reflection in the liquid mirror. The image she saw wasn't her as an old woman, but rather as she had been in her prime—shiny curls, a silky red dress, and a flower behind her ear. The scene made Rosa giggle and turn to the side to pose. But when she glanced again, there were two other transparent-like women at her side. She shivered and hurried to enter the museum, where she found Mary Theresa, Jennifer, Stephanie, and Olivia, with her daughter, Missy, buying their admission tickets.

"Scarlet's going to be a bit late today," Rosa said, collecting her nerves. "I'll cover and do my best to fill her stilettos. It will be you, me, and two hundred and three thousand square feet of museum goodness to explore!"

The group breezed through a few of the museum's exhibitions before they finally reached the Fashion Design Gallery.

"I love Scarlet, and I know she's hustlin' these days, but she can't keep showing up late especially during Christmas week," Olivia commented as the class meandered through the first half of the displays. "The only reason I'm here is because I'm a fan. I don't want to look at old clothes. I appreciate her struggle, but I have a life too."

No one acknowledged the gripes out loud, but Rosa witnessed the other women nod in agreement. She tried to change the subject.

"If you truly want to learn the art of sewing, you need to become educated on the masters," Rosa lectured in a professional manner.

"Hi-dee-ho, my lovelies!" Scarlet sang out as she hot-stepped it into the gallery. She inhaled the sweet smell of vintage fashion and met the hard stares of her students. With her hands crossed over her chest, she apologized. "This is the last time I'll be tardy, swear on my pinking shears. Carly's most loyal customer had a last-minute seam emergency. Can you believe the little minx ordered her dress a size too small? I had to take the whole thing apart and stitch it back together this afternoon!"

"We don't care about the Carly's customer, Scarlet," Olivia said. "We care about you. Have you seen a mirror lately? You have bags under those peepers of yours. You better slow down before you lose your head. Or your fans."

"Aside from being embarrassed for being late and missing our appointment the other night, I'm swell," Scarlet said as she opened the front clasp of her chunky gold Lucite purse and retrieved a small rectangular packet. She ripped it open with her teeth and tapped the coarse black powder onto her tongue. "Whoo! Now, that's what I'm talkin' about. Now let's get this soiree a snappin'!"

"What did you just eat?" Mary Theresa asked with a cringe.

"Instant coffee! It works faster, lasts longer, plus saves me money and time."

Mary Theresa didn't go for it. "Wrong, Scarlet. That's very dangerous. When was the last time you had a good night's sleep?"

"Every night. And it's just like eating chocolate-covered espresso beans, without the chocolate. It helps me keep the pep in my step," she said with dilated pupils. She raised her hand in a grand gesture and waved her class along. "This way, my chickadees."

They made their way to Daisy's display, and everyone crowded around to see. Everyone except Rosa, who stood at the back of the group, speechless.

A large framed paparazzi photo of Daisy rested on a black lacquer easel next to the mannequin. The shot was of her wearing the glamorous dress as she exited the church of her husband's funeral service in Miami, Florida.

Jennifer hovered for a closer view. "She looks like a movie star."

Rosa's blood pressure rose and she rubbed her wrinkly neck with her hands. "Let's go outside now; I'm feeling a little clammy."

"Wow, get a load of that honking ring!" Stephanie exclaimed, pointing at Daisy's hand in the photo. Jennifer and Olivia leaned in to admire it too. "You girls are missing out; look at this!" they told the others.

Rosa took a brief glance at the photo and almost swallowed her gum. She didn't have the strength in her bones for this kind of surprise today. She needed fresh air—and to clear these women out of the room, quick. Right then, a knight in shining armor arrived....

"Marco!" Rosa said, suddenly uplifted. Scarlet's eyes lit up too.

"This is a surprise," Scarlet said. "What brings you here? Did you miss us?"

He handed her two heavy Vega's Vicious Vinyl plastic bags and whispered in her ear. "You left the sketchbooks in the sewing room and I knew you needed them today."

"Oh, thank you! Seriously," Scarlet said softly back to him. "You always save the day, don't you?"

He shrugged and smiled. "It's cool."

All of a sudden, the concentrated caffeine lost its magic.

Scarlet felt zapped of all her energy and spirit. Maybe she did need a nap. "We're going to grab a snack from the cafe. Do you have time to stick around?" she asked Marco.

Rosa slipped her arm through his, relieved that the attention had moved away from the Daisy dress. "Of course he does!"

They all migrated through the museum to the cafe while Marco found them a cozy spot in the sculpture garden seating area. For the next hour, Scarlet sat with each student and instructed her how to sketch a body and limbs. The exhaustion slowed her down, but she pushed herself. She wanted to give 100 percent attention to everyone—especially Olivia, who seemed to have chilled out. When Scarlet finished with Mary Theresa, she noticed Rosa was nowhere to be found. She mentioned it to Marco and the pair excused themselves from the group to go look for her.

Backtracking through the coffee-bar area, they assumed Rosa used the bathroom and got lost. When they didn't find her, Scarlet asked the barista. He squirted whipped cream on a mocha and tilted his head in the direction of the fashion gallery.

They found her.

Leaning over the red velvet ropes in front of Daisy's display, Rosa lovingly traced her fragile hand down the front of the gown while an elderly man rested his palms on her waist. They must have felt Scarlet and Marco's presence because they both turned their heads to face them. Scarlet ran over with Marco right behind.

"Hey, kids," Rosa said. "If you don't mind, we're heading out. I'm not feeling too well tonight."

15

"Your home makes my place look like a boring sheet of graphing paper," Mary Theresa joked as she stepped into Scarlet's house. "It's cute, and fits you perfectly. I feel like I'm at my nana's."

"That's because you're at *my* nana's; this is her house. I rent it. Glad you like it," Scarlet proudly replied. She tugged a long gold silk scarf from her coatrack and handed it to Mary Theresa. "Here at La Casa Santana, glamour rules. Tie this baby around your neck and come on in!"

Rocky and Lucy let go of their mother's hands and bolted a few steps across the wood floors to Scarlet's vintage sofa.

"It smells yummy in here," Rocky announced, letting his head fall back and sniffing as hard as he could.

Scarlet picked him up and playfully plopped him on the couch, and then Lucy. "It is yummy, little dude. You're smelling my nana's tamales, and my personal favorite, pumpkin chocolate-chip loaf. I popped it in the oven especially for you and Lucy. It'll be ready in a little bit."

The kids tickled each other and tossed their jackets on the floor before pulling out their Nintendo DSs. From one second to the next, silence. Scarlet raised her brows at Mary Theresa in impressed astonishment.

"This is the first time I've let them have those game devices since their father left," Mary Theresa whispered while she fluffed the scarf. "It'll keep them busy for a while."

Right after the museum excursion, Mary Theresa had begged Scarlet until she agreed to let her come over and streamline Scarlet's operation process. Mary Theresa might not have been managing her marriage at the moment, but she still excelled at organizational skills.

Scarlet gave in and invited her and the kids over at seven that night.

The house resembled a sweatshop. Stacks of fabric swatches and measuring tapes littered the chairs, tangled balls of trim covered the end tables, and paper sketches were thumbtacked all over the walls. Mary Theresa became secretly excited at the thought of clearing Scarlet's mess. Mary Theresa whistled a tune as she cleared the kitchen table of stacks of paperwork and marched them into the sewing room. She hadn't whistled since childhood. Life was breezy when she could forget her drama and focus on someone else's. And she loved being in charge again. Scarlet did her best to keep up with Mary Theresa's aggressive directions of "Take this and set it over there, group these by date, rubberband these and stack them in this box."

They eventually made it to Scarlet's busiest spot in the house—the sewing palace (formerly a cozy guest room). Scarlet had managed to squeeze in two dress forms, a changing area, a chaise longue, a sketch table and light table, plus racks of fabric, trims, and buttons. And her sewing area, of course. The only open space was a skinny walkway that led to the center of the room. The rest was overtaken with see-through boxes of material.

While the room appeared very artsy and overflowing with creativity, Mary Theresa knew it could be more efficient. Scarlet approved, and they worked nonstop, breaking only for dinner and to check on Rocky and Lucy.

Mary Theresa marveled at a dress rack in the corner as she filed the final box of papers. "These are gorgeous dresses. Whose are they?"

"Mine. I made them. I have a fashion show every month for First Fridays," Scarlet boasted as she lifted two dresses to show them off. "They're made from blank silk scarves. I prep them one at a time, so no two are ever alike. I draw on each one with wax resist, then dye it and stamp all over it with my own carved graphics of Aztec icons. Once the fabric is washed and pressed, I close my eyes and skim it up and down my cheek until I see the dress it wants me to make. I call them my Mexibilly Frocks."

Mary Theresa took one dress from Scarlet's hand and held it up against her body. "Gorgeous. I don't know too much about fashion, obviously," Mary Theresa said, pinching her cream-colored sweater vest, "but you could go really far with these. Has your family seen these? I think they would change their perception of what you do and why you do it."

"Yup," Scarlet replied, hanging the dress back on the rack. "They came to my first few runway shows. But I guess they weren't impressed, because they haven't been back since. I can hardly wait until I make it big and they *have* to give me props."

"But you have made it big!" Mary Theresa handed the dress to Scarlet, circled the center of the room, and raised her hands to the air. "Consider the success of your blog and the clothes you make. I wish Rosa were here; she'd say something wise and profound."

Scarlet put the second dress away and adjusted the copper lampshade on top of her sewing table. Something had been pricking at her curiosity since the last class and she wanted to run it by Mary Theresa.

"Speaking of Rosa," Scarlet baited, "something she did gave me the chills. It happened the other day at the museum in front of Daisy's dress. It got me thinking."

The tone of her voice piqued Mary Theresa's interest. "What are the details? I'm good at connecting the dots."

"I think our fabric *vetrana* is hiding something," Scarlet said, tapping her finger on her cheek. "And I'm going to get to the bottom of it tomorrow, even if it costs me a day of work."

"I've always found her to be very mysterious. Tell me what you know."

Rocky's and Lucy's footsteps pounded across the hallway until they reached the sewing room and screeched to a halt. "Can we have our chocolate pumpkin pies now, Scarlet?" Rocky asked.

Lucy clenched her head. "Chocolate-*chip* pumpkin pie, Rocky!"

"Pumpkin chocolate-chip *loaf*. It's like dessert bread," Mary Theresa explained, glancing at Scarlet.

"Let's go eat," Scarlet said, leading the way out of the room. "The story will sound better with a cup of decaf French Roast. And by the way, *mujer*, you're taking a Mexibilly Frock home with you. I don't care if you never wear it, I just want you to have one. Consider it my Christmas gift."

DaisyForever.com
magical musings about love, beauty & fashion
inspired by the life of Daisy de la Flora
as told by Miss Scarlet Santana

Friday, December 23, 11:05 p.m.

Embrace mystery!

Hola, my darling Daisy-inspired divas!

Today's passage is dripping with mystery. Yes, the spirit of Agatha Christie has crept through the lace that lines my brain. As I type this, my mind is stacked with odd-shaped nuggets of clues that don't fit. But I *know* they are meant to fit together. Therefore, in the middle of working three jobs in my quest to raise my Johnny Scissors tuition, I've retrieved my proverbial magnifying glass. I glued crystals around its frame, and am determined to discover a big reveal. I do believe, my dear Watson, I'm on to something GRANDE! Sorry, dixies, these lips are sealed.

In the meantime, let's chat about the concept of mystery: secrets...the unexplained...the unknown...

Intrigue!

As the high-strutting glamorpusses that we are, we each have a mystery within us. Mysteries are alluring.

Think Greta Garbo, Grace Kelly, Bettie Page, and of course—Daisy.

Did you know in her early years, Daisy encountered some kind of tragic incident that changed the course of not only her life and career, but also personality? I don't have actual verification, but I read about it on several message boards. Some say a car crash, others a bicycle accident. Different people from different backgrounds have shared similar specific details, yet no one knows for sure. Believe me, I've searched. I've read every single biography and article on Daisy only to find nada. Some industry experts claim the stories are untrue, just made-up tales by the suits at House of Tijeras to ring up extra sales.

I believe the stories. I've never met Daisy, but I feel connected to her. If it weren't that I look like a walking clone of my mother's younger self, I'd swear I was Daisy's long-lost daughter.

Many say the above-mentioned calamity is what shaped Daisy's design and business direction. Certain loyal historians even claim it is what triggered her into early stages of secrecy, which ultimately led to her life in hiding.

Now, here is my challenge to all of you. I want you to discover the mystery within you and put it out there right under everyone's schnozzolas. Maybe it is not as tragic as our beloved Daisy's, but think about a secret that resides in your soul. Create something based on it. Maybe it already exists, like a pair of earrings you wore the night your boyfriend broke your heart, or a gift your secret crush gave you. Perhaps it's the silky drawers you're wearing under your 501s. If you have no mysteries, then at least sport a fashionable floppy hat to hide half your face!

Something.

Anything.

Keep them guessing.

As for me, I have to mail off two of my Mexibilly Frocks to a customer and then I'm off to solve a mystery! Nancy Drew has nothing on me!

16

Scarlet didn't mean to sneak up on Rosa, she really didn't. She also didn't mean to spill homemade chicken soup all over the pristine marble floor of the woman's swanky loft. Daisy made her do it.

The night before, Daisy fluttered into Scarlet's subconscious and practically ordered her to drop in on Rosa. So, whipping up a batch of Nana's healing chicken caldo, Scarlet looked up Rosa's registration form and copied the address—a fancy block of million-dollar lofts in central Phoenix called Châteaux on Central. When the housing market collapsed, the property owners went bankrupt.

How in the world did Rosa end up there? Scarlet speculated as she climbed the redbrick staircase and reached Rosa's extravagant front door.

She rang the bell and waited. No answer.

She rang it again, twice. Nothing.

After two more rings with no response, she turned to leave.

Open the door.

Scarlet would never do such a thing, but the voice in her head convinced her to. Her cold hand had barely touched the long brass handle and before she could stop herself, she clenched it and it opened.

Armed with the plastic container of soup, Scarlet held her breath and entered. The crisp smell of new carpet and the gleam of sleek, chrome appliances greeted her. Very unlike Rosa. Scarlet peeked around a wall and gasped so hard, she dropped the soup and it splattered all over the floor.

Before her stood Rosa, also shocked, in a violet-and-teal checkered bathrobe and matching slippers. Both accented with tiny rhinestones and gems.

"Scarlet!" Rosa shouted angrily, holding her hand over her chest and panting. "What are you doing here? How did you get in?"

"Rosa, I'm so sorry! You scared me last night, the way you left. You didn't answer my calls and I was worried. I just came to check on you, and I made you chicken caldo. I rang the bell, but no one came so I tried the door. I'm sorry."

"You can't just enter an old woman's home unannounced, dear. I know you meant well, but you just about gave me a heart attack. How the hell did you find me?" Rosa asked as she pressed the stainless-steel wall intercom and politely asked for clean-up help in the entryway. Within seconds a housekeeper arrived and mopped up the spilled soup.

"I got your address from the registration form...."

Rosa rubbed her eyes. "Joseph," she mumbled. "He's slipping in his old age...." She straightened up, put her hands on her hips, and eyed Scarlet from head to toe.

"You're wearing an original."

Scarlet paused, opened her coat, and half-modeled it. "Oh, my outfit? It is. It's one of my Mexibilly Frocks. I see you're wearing an original as well. That's a Daisy bathrobe, circa 1969, Macy's holiday exclusive."

Rosa skimmed her waist with her fingertips and acknowledged the robe. "You certainly know your Daisy wear. Sit down, dear. Let me change my clothes and I'll be right out."

Before Rosa could leave, the sound of another unexpected guest caused both women to jump.

"Good morning, ladies," Mary Theresa said nervously. "I hope you don't mind; the door was open. Rosa, I heard you were ill, so I brought you chicken soup."

"Aye, you girls are going to wear me out," Rosa said with a dash of playfulness. "I'm fine, I just had a touch of the flu, but I'm over it." She shook her head in disbelief as she took the elevator upstairs to change. Yet at the same time she laughed. These kooky women reminded her of two other chicas she once knew.

Making their way into a small seating area, Scarlet squinted at Mary Theresa. "What are you doing here?"

"I read your blog post this morning and followed you, my dear Watson," Mary Theresa said. "Don't worry, I'll just sit here quietly."

Used to her nana's time schedule, Scarlet estimated it would take Rosa at least fifteen minutes to return from changing her clothes. After removing her coat and setting it on a chair, Scarlet approached the tall media center and picked up a stack of decorated pieces of construction paper.

" 'Little Victories.' I read it on your blog," Rosa said as she entered only a few minutes later, surprising Scarlet. The mysterious matron had brightened up her face with rose lipstick and changed into black velour pants and a knitted teal sweater. She reached across Scarlet and turned on the iPod stereo just enough for the infectious salsa sounds of Héctor Lavoe to softly fill the room.

Scarlet scooted next to Mary Theresa on the slate gray mod

couch while Rosa situated herself in a large maroon recliner. "I know you have questions after my episode at the museum."

"I don't mean to be nosy, but would you mind if I pried an eensy bit?" Scarlet asked.

"Go ahead, Nancy Drew. I read your blog this morning, by the way. I should have expected you."

"All righty—are you the one responsible for decorating our workroom with all those fancy wares, and the tree?" Scarlet asked.

Rosa lifted her hands as if to surrender. "Guilty. I scoped out the room two days early and noticed it was in dire need of holiday cheer. Why? Don't you like it?"

"Why yes. I do, thank you!" Scarlet said before leaning closer to Rosa. "Next question: How did you get that robe?"

Rosa swallowed hard and tapped her fingers together. "It was given to me many years ago by a dear friend. In fact, Miss Scarlet, you remind me so much of her. Your happy spirit and the message you send out into the world. The first time I read your blog, I was struck by how similar you seemed."

Mary Theresa kept her promise and didn't say a word.

"Is that why you signed up for my class, because I reminded you of your friend?" Scarlet asked, considering the crazy thought that Rosa's friend might be...Daisy.

"Yes, in a way, I suppose," Rosa confessed. "Like most of your fans, I was curious to meet you firsthand." Her lips turned up at the corners, but the smile didn't quite reach her eyes.

"Do you mind if I ask about what happened at the museum?" If, as Scarlet suspected, the friend in question *was* Daisy, shouldn't Rosa have been happy about seeing the dress in the collection?

Rosa stared into the distance. "All the memories flooded back as if I were right there at that funeral. Those of us who grew up with Daisy remember when her husband passed so unexpectedly. She loved him so much. Heartbreaking," Rosa said sadly.

Scarlet knew the time had come for the burning question.

"Rosa," Scarlet whispered, "about Daisy...and you..."

Mary Theresa tightened her ponytail and bit her nails in anticipation.

Rosa picked at the hem of her sweater. "I had...friends who knew her quite well. I heard all the stories. She was an incredible woman back then, so smart and creative. She wanted to make everyone proud of her. Kind of like you, Scarlet. She wanted that dream of hers to happen so fast; she pushed it so hard that she made mistakes. And then fame hit and she could never turn back."

Scarlet couldn't believe the conversation. She couldn't believe Rosa knew all this golden, exclusive information and was willing to divulge it. "What kind of mistakes?" she asked.

"I'll tell you if you promise never to repeat it—for Daisy's sake. And for my sake, I don't want to get involved in any trouble. I lead a quiet life, and I want to keep it that way."

"Of course," Scarlet assured. "My lips are sealed."

Over the next hour, Rosa recalled so many specific details about Daisy de la Flora that Scarlet could barely sit still. According to Rosa, the articles Scarlet had read and took at face value were only half correct.

For example, her uncle's purse factory: Daisy didn't bring home damaged and leftover supplies. She smuggled out goods every night and used them to make her pieces that she then sold. When her uncle caught on, Daisy convinced him that two new female employees committed the crime. He fired the workers solely on Daisy's claim.

"The truth came out when Daisy left with Saide for New York to meet Carmen Miranda," Rosa said. "She not only stole money from her aunt's savings jar the day before her trip, she also swiped the factory's weekly deposit. Daisy left Coconut Grove without even saying good-bye to her sisters, because she thought they were against her. Those girls were devastated."

Rosa continued, taking a break now and then to sip from a glass of water that Joseph had brought her. "A few years later, Daisy's career had finally built momentum in Manhattan, thanks to her handmade line at Her Madgesty's Closet. But then the unexpected happened—she fell in love with Saide's husband, Javier, the owner of the business. Neither one meant for the affair to happen. They started with the common goal of using Daisy's designs to make a living, and the relationship settled deeper as the days passed. Poor Saide was too busy running the store; she had no idea. But all those hours of Daisy and Javier working together, the late nights, the talks about their dreams and fears, laughing over silly fashion disasters, all of it solidified a bond that could not be stopped. Or so they thought."

"Oh no, what happened?" Scarlet asked, rubbing her own shoulders. The wintry air seemed to have seeped into the house.

"I heard from a direct source that one afternoon Saide, who spent all her time manning the shop, went upstairs to find a new receipt book," Rosa said. "And instead found them making love in the storeroom. She raced back downstairs, grabbed a hat stand, and smashed the window display the three of them had made in Carmen's honor. The shrine to Carmen that had become a tourist hot spot was demolished forever. Daisy tried to stop her and explain. Saide wouldn't hear any of it and accused Daisy of stealing Javier to further her career, and that the two of them would then cut her out of the business. That night Saide left for good."

Scarlet drew a breath and tried to put the pieces together.

"So then, why didn't Saide call them out in her big *Vanity Fair* interview?"

"Daisy felt so guilty that once she hit the big-time, she paid her off," Rosa said. "Saide accepted and never told the real story, but she also never forgave her. She died a very rich and resentful woman."

"And what about Javier?" asked Mary Theresa, her vow of silence forgotten.

"Daisy broke up with him, even though he asked her to marry him after his divorce. He adored her and begged her to spend her life with him. He did so much to help her. Daisy pretended to be over him, but she still loved him. She probably lied to prove her loyalty to Saide. She never saw him again.

"Daisy returned home after the disaster. She visited her uncle's factory to settle up, but he had passed away, and her aunt had sold the business and moved. All that remained were Daisy's sisters, and even they wanted nothing to do with her."

"I've always wanted to talk to Daisy's sisters," Scarlet said excitedly. "Do you know how to reach them?"

"They're unreachable," Rosa said.

"Oh." Scarlet sat still for a moment, then shook her head. She couldn't bring herself to accept all this new information so easily. "Do you have any proof of any of this? If not, it's just gossip. Daisy's work is so buoyant and full of light. The Daisy you are talking about sounds like a desperate, scamming lunatic."

Rosa cocked up an eyebrow and folded her arms. "Hey, missy, I never once said she was crazy! I'm only telling you because those of us from Coconut Grove who knew Daisy back then... well, it was plain pitiful to see her search and sweat so hard for her dream. And to lose herself in the process. Her wishes came true, but at the expense of everyone who loved her."

A loud crash of thunder came from outside. Rosa leveraged

herself up from the couch and, trying her best not to limp, walked over to the window.

"A winter rainstorm in the desert," she said softly as she held the black curtain and peeked out. "I've never experienced that. I thought I smelled wetness in the air this morning." Rosa let go of the drape, carefully bent down to lift a crocheted blanket from an emerald green loveseat, and swung it around her drooping shoulders. "Have I answered all your questions, Scarlet?"

Scarlet sighed, rubbed her thighs, and nodded. "Yes, thank you for taking the time to share all of this. It gives me a lot to think about."

"It's a little chilly," Mary Theresa said, rubbing her hands together. "Let's go eat our soup in the kitchen."

"Good idea," Rosa said, turning to leave the room. "Enough about Daisy's past. It's time to focus on the present."

17

Taking Rosa's advice, Scarlet tried to push Daisy from the forefront of her mind.

The women sat in Rosa's sleekly designed kitchen, ate their chicken soup, and sipped on cups of Earl Grey. They exchanged jokes that it was a good thing that both Scarlet and Mary Theresa were gracious stalkers—each bringing a meal for their target. While Scarlet had made her soup from scratch, Mary Theresa had picked up three large bowls from the Duck and Decanter sandwich shop on the way over.

"Rosa, do you own this condo? I thought the owners went bankrupt," Scarlet asked as she blew on the hot liquid in her spoon and let her eyes roam around.

"It was recently purchased by an acquaintance of Joseph's," Rosa said, dropping two sugar cubes in her tea. "We're only here for a while. I hate contemporary décor, but it works for us."

Mary Theresa exchanged glances with Rosa and they both looked at Scarlet. "So, Scarlet," asked Mary Theresa, "how do you feel about all that Rosa told us? Does it change your perception of Daisy?"

Scarlet put down her spoon and thought for a moment. "Actually, it makes me feel closer to her than ever. If the stories are true, she wasn't a saint, but she made those mistakes to further her business. She didn't set out to steal money or Saide's man; she was on her own and did what she had to do. I'm not saying it's right, but if she hadn't taken those risks, there would be no Casa de la Flora or House of Tijeras—or DaisyForever. com, for that matter. Right, Rosa?"

"I suppose," she replied.

After all the revelations about Daisy, Rosa still remained a mystery to Scarlet. She felt like the woman had refrained from sharing a bigger part of the story.

"What was your life like after Coconut Grove, Rosa? You never really told us," Scarlet asked.

Rosa fidgeted. "My life? Ha! We don't have enough time for that story."

"You know all about us, Rosa," Mary Theresa said. "Please? A condensed version?"

"Back in the day, I had my own career. After high school, I earned a scholarship to a Paris university and received my bachelor's degree in textile science. I traveled a lot. Got married once. Sewing and making clothes has been my life's calling. It's the one passion I share with Daisy. But I decided long ago I didn't want the glamour. I volunteered for the American Heart Association and made hundreds of heart-shaped pillows for bypass-surgery patients. And, of course, all throughout my life I've made hundreds of quilts and things for our servicemen overseas. I also taught sewing classes for a women's shelter."

Both Mary Theresa's and Scarlet's eyes lit up in admiration. "Which are you most proud of?" Mary Theresa asked.

"Easy. The time I went undercover for NBC to expose the crimes taking place in the Mexican maquiladoras."

"You did all that?" Mary Theresa said. "No wonder you know

so much about everything, Rosa. I can't believe you never told us this. Wow, I'm honored to know you."

Rosa rested her chin in her hands. "I don't speak of it because I didn't do any of it for recognition, I just wanted to help. Those factories and the way they treat their employees are atrocious."

"I've heard horror stories," Scarlet said, thinking back to a special she watched on PBS about the subject. "It happens here in the United States, with those fast fashion chains like Eternal 14. That's why I love House of Tijeras. Daisy makes sure everything is produced right here in the U.S. to ensure proper and ethical business practices. She is why I tell my blog readers if they don't have time to make their own clothes, then they can research their favorite stores online to find out how that company handles production."

"Good girl, Scarlet," Rosa said. "That set of ethics will take you very far, not only in your career, but in life. I'm confident of that."

"I agree," Mary Theresa said to Scarlet. "All this time you've made it seem like you're lucky to be accepted into that Johnny Scissors program, but have you ever thought maybe they are the ones who will benefit from having *you*?"

"I never thought of it that way. Thank you," Scarlet said. "I want to show them I'm more than just a designer and a blogger. I'm also a product developer! I even invented a killer duel-action fabric adhesive called EmergiSew. I'm saving it for when I get out there."

Scarlet noticed a defensive look come over Rosa.

"Don't give up all your pearls just yet. Read up on Johnny Scissors," Rosa advised. "House of Tijeras isn't the same as it used to be. I heard that Johnny isn't quite holding true to his aunt's standards. Their stock is down, he hasn't designed anything worthy in ages, he has that whole copyright infringement trial going on—people are noticing. Be careful, always guard your goods, especially around successful business people!"

Scarlet tapped her knuckles on the table and eyed Rosa suspiciously. "You sure know a lot about the trade."

"I'm just an old woman who loves the garment industry," she muttered, taking another sip of tea.

Scarlet still had many questions for Rosa, but what she didn't have was time.

"Well, ladies, I better be off. I have a long shift today and then orders to fill tonight, and then a six-to-eight-a.m. shift at my aunt's shop in the morning. Oh gosh, and I have to prep for tomorrow's class."

"Tomorrow's class?" Mary Theresa asked. "Scarlet, it's Christmas Eve! No one expects you to work. Besides, we all want to be with our families, don't you?"

"They won't even notice if I'm there or not," Scarlet said. "Maybe I'll use the day to make some new dresses to earn more tuition money."

"Escúchame, mija," Rosa said. "Listen. You're working these crazy hours, hurting your body, all to pay for the Johnny Scissors school, right? What is your goal, Scarlet?" Rosa asked, staring deep into her eyes. "Is it to be near Johnny Scissors because he is related to Daisy, or for the accreditation, or to launch your career as a designer?"

"All of it," Scarlet answered.

"Do you have your collection together yet? Which designs will you show Johnny Scissors?"

"My movie gowns, of course! There's *nothing* like them on the market. I even have a name: Cinema Couture by Scarlet Santana. I have about sixty of them."

Rosa nodded calmly, evaluating the concept. "Have you marketed the line anywhere?"

"No way. I don't want anyone to steal my idea," Scarlet said.

Rosa reached across the table and clasped Scarlet's hands. "I hate to break it to you, but my dear, *you* are stealing designs… from all those films you say inspire you."

"What? No, it's not that way at all," Scarlet argued. "I change them just enough by adding Daisy-like accents to them. That is my signature."

Rosa groaned. Scarlet swallowed and crossed her brows. She was beginning to feel offended. "What's wrong?"

"Mary Theresa, you're a critical thinker. Tell her." Rosa said.

Mary Theresa responded by gritting her teeth and reluctantly nodding. "Your Cinema Couture line is divine, but to market it… well, it goes against everything you preach. You are an originator, Scarlet, not an imitator."

Scarlet didn't want to admit that her friends were right. How could she not have realized such a huge oversight? She didn't know if it was her caffeine intake or the bluntness of reality making her heart race and her head feel dizzy. She fell back in her chair and stared at the crystal light fixture above.

"It's too late for me to change anything; it took so long to come to this point. How am I supposed to scrap Cinema Couture and start all over? Plus raise the tuition money?"

"Mexibilly Frocks," Mary Theresa said.

"These?" Scarlet asked, taken aback as she stood up and moved her hands down her dress. "But Carly said they'd never cut it—"

"Carly is wrong," Mary Theresa said. "And likely jealous."

Rosa got up from her chair, shuffled to the counter, and put on her big, round black eyeglasses. She wiggled her finger for Scarlet to come near. Rosa lifted the girl's chin with two fingers. "Close your eyes. I want you to forget all that crap about proving yourself, or Carly Fontaine, or earning a quickie degree from Johnny Scissors."

Rosa pretended to claw at the air with her age-spotted hands. "Strip it all away.... It's gone."

Scarlet squeezed her eyes shut and hoped her false-eyelash adhesive stayed put. "It's all gone."

Rosa folded her arms and strutted around Scarlet like a drill sergeant. "Why do you want this, Miss Scarlet?"

"Because I love to sew?" she replied, peeking out of one eye.

"So does your aunt who owns the quince shop. What separates you from her?"

Both lids flipped up. Scarlet was beginning to feel empowered. "I have a talent all my own and I deserve to put it out there!"

Rosa waved her hands in the air, as if to erase what Scarlet just said. "Who do you want this for?"

Scarlet stared deep into Rosa's enchanting and wrinkled face and together they shared a moment of glory. "I want it for me," Scarlet said.

"Well, then—it's right under your nose, young lady!" Rosa cheered while tugging at Scarlet's Mexibilly Frock.

Maybe Rosa wasn't exactly Daisy de la Flora, but she had spent her life in the world of women's wear. Rosa proved to be a better mentor than Carly ever could be. "You really think so?" Scarlet wondered aloud, grasping the fabric from her top.

Mary Theresa leaped from her chair and put her arm around Scarlet. "We don't *think* so Scarlet, we *know* so. Mexibilly Frocks are all *you*. I think you should proceed with them as your signature collection."

Rosa held her hand out like a serving platter. "I couldn't have said it better."

All of a sudden, their words sank in. Scarlet raised her hands to her forehead. "I do already have buzz around my Mexibilly Frocks from my First Friday shows. I make the dresses so fast, I didn't think they were all that big of a deal. They're not exactly high fashion. I need to simmer on this for a while to see if I can pull it off. Do you really think?..."

Rosa closed one eye, bit her lip, and held out her thumb in the center of Scarlet's body. "With a little editing and fine-tuning...absolutely. Scarlet, you are on your way!"

House of Tijeras
Johnny Scissors Emerging Designers Program
New York, New York

December 22

Ms. Scarlet Santana
5839 W. Flores Lane
Glendale, AZ 85304

Dear Ms. Santana:

We are writing to inform you of a change to the upcoming
Johnny Scissors Emerging Designers Program. After twenty
years of nurturing, educating, and launching the careers of
talented artists such as you, it is with great regret that we
will be terminating the program.

   Your class will be the grand finale to a long, successful run.
However, due to changes within our corporation, we must
move the season up from June 15 to January 16. Enclosed
is an invoice for your remaining balance, which is due upon
receipt. If you cannot pay the balance, please contact our
office immediately so we may make other arrangements.

   We hope you are as excited as we are that you will be
participating the 20th Annual Johnny Scissors Emerging
Designers Program!

Sincerely,

Louisa Brandt
Johnny Scissors Emerging Designers Program Coordinator

From: Carly Fontaine
To: Scarlet Santana
Date: December 24 9:30 AM
Subject: Your inventory

What is your current inventory for your Mexibilly Frocks? I have a client from Santa Fe who would like to purchase 40 pieces (size 2) for an event she has coming up. If you have these in stock, please bring them to the studio Thursday morning, as she is driving through town and can only pick them up at that time.

I took the liberty of referring to your online store for pricing and quoted $80 each, totaling $3,200, less 20% commission. If this order transpires, I'll cut you a check for $2,560.

Please keep in mind that this is a non-related work agreement, so please bring the dresses in before the start of your shift Monday so it does not interfere with your CFS responsibilities.

C.F.

18

Rosa opened the curtains of the workroom so the downtown Glendale passersby could catch of peek of the class hard at work. Because all the students were off from work and school between Christmas and New Year's, Scarlet and Marco kept the sewing room open all day. Everyone took advantage of the extra hours to work on spring shirtdresses.

After nearly three lessons a week on draping, pinning, sketching, and hand-stitching, almost all the students were finally pushing the pedals to the floor with confidence. The machines hummed at a steady pace, except Olivia's, the sound of which could be likened to a new driver learning to use a stick shift.

With the island grooves of Celia Cruz piping through the sound system, Mary Theresa wadded up her light cotton poppy-hued dress-in-progress and threw it across the room. "When is Scarlet getting here?" She sneered. "The neckline is too low, the chest area is too big, the waist is unbalanced. It's all wrong. I've tried so hard to embrace patternless sewing, but it is impossible."

Stephanie and Jennifer ignored Mary Theresa's hissy fit; they were too busy slaving away on their own projects. But Olivia walked over and picked up the dress. "You sweated over it; respect it and give yourself some credit," she said before handing it back to

Mary Theresa. "Plus, it's way better than mine. It doesn't seem right to you because you're used to wearing jeans and polo shirts."

Rosa took the dress from Mary Theresa and tugged it down the dress form.

Mary Theresa propped her rimless glasses on her nose. The dress didn't look half bad. In fact, it looked quite . . . pretty.

"I did it," she said, her voice more astonished than excited. The surprise success of it reminded her that she needed to have faith, instead of always expecting disaster. She may not have been a superstar sewer—or mom—but she wasn't a loser, either. This dress served as tangible proof of that.

Olivia stood up and put her hand on her hip. "That slinky number is damn sexy. Wear that for your man with a swish of matching lipstick and he'll be biting your ankles." Olivia playfully bumped Mary Theresa's hip, laughing hysterically at her own joke.

Mary Theresa flashed Rosa a glare as if she had been betrayed.

Rosa responded with an innocent "I didn't say anything!" shrug of the shoulders and returned to her sewing machine.

Olivia sat back down at her sewing machine too, and continued with her dress. "Girlfriend," she said without looking away from her work, "we've been stuck in this room for weeks. I don't need to know the details to smell trouble in the home. When you're ready to spill it, I'll gladly offer my two cents. Lord knows I've been through the worst of it."

Mary Theresa tightened her already cinched ponytail. "Thank you for the offer, Olivia, but I don't want to burden all of you with my marital issues." She sighed, picked up a stray needle from her work area, and inserted it into her apple pincushion.

"It's not a burden," Stephanie chimed over her machine. "Dang, our parents argue all the time about money. But my mom says their secret to happiness is they always go to bed with a kiss and a snuggle."

Mary Theresa wished it were that easy.

"I wasted years married to a gambler," Olivia blurted. "He secretly blew all my parents' estate money. I had a feeling all along, but ignored it. We had a luxury custom home in Laveen. Six months ago, I came home from work and the electricity was off, my daughter, Missy, was crying at the kitchen table, and the house was empty. You know where he was? Sitting on a damn rickety folding chair in the living room, playing solitaire. That was the last straw for me, boy. I was at the lowest of the lows. I packed a suitcase and me and Missy left for my sister's. I couldn't sleep, so I went online and stumbled onto DaisyForever.com. It was the Word-to-Life Transformer blog post Scarlet wrote. Have you seen it? You jot down your biggest fear and then add empowering words to it make it an affirmation. The point is to show that you can take any negative situation and with some heavy thinking you can turn it around to be empowering."

"What were you afraid of?" Mary Theresa asked before she could stop herself.

Olivia bent over, grabbed a couple sheets of scrapbook paper and a Sharpie from her craft caddy, and wrote for a minute. She lifted up one sheet of paper in front of her buxom chest and it read:

I AM AFRAID TO BE ALONE.

She then wiped a tear from her eye, blinked away the others that threatened to fall, and held up the second paper:

I AM A STRONG WOMAN AND A GOOD MOTHER. I WILL NOT BE **AFRAID TO BE ALONE** IF IT MEANS SHOWING MY DAUGHTER A LIFE OF HOPE.

Mary Theresa sniffled, as did everyone else.

"The next day I learned we had lost our home. Our cars. Our credit. All. Of. It. We started fresh with a twenty-dollar Starbucks card and five dollars cash. But Missy and I held our heads high. At least I still had my job and we had our health. I divorced his ass and I've since dedicated my life to showing my daughter the art of starting over. There is always room for a second chance—sometimes a third or fourth, too. And even though Scarlet's late again for class, I'm forever grateful for her words of inspiration."

"Wow," Mary Theresa said, moved by Olivia's honesty and courage. "I would have never known you've been through so much. You are always so upbeat."

Olivia folded the papers and put them back in her caddy. "That's why I told you on the first day, you can choose your mood. I choose an Oh-LIVE-yah state of mind!"

Stephanie began to clap slowly and chant, *"Oh! Live! Yah!... Oh! Live! Yah!"* By the second round, the rest of the class joined in and Olivia broke down in tears. They took turns hugging her until Olivia wiped her eyes on the inside of her plus-size sweatshirt and looked up at Mary Theresa. "No more about me. Now, what's up with your man? Is he good to you? Do you love him?"

In that moment, Mary Theresa decided that if Olivia could go through all that and still be such a positive force, she could certainly lighten up too and share with the class.

"We're having a trial separation until February," she said. "I guess I bossed him right out of the house. But I do love him; he's a good guy."

Olivia strutted over to Mary Theresa. "Don't go blaming yourself. Did he need bossing around? Come on, be honest."

Mary Theresa cracked a smile. It felt good to have someone as strong as Olivia stand up for her. "We both did, and we could have handled it in a different way. We're working on it. I miss him, I took a lot for granted." She took the dress off the form, held it up, and admired it.

"If you wear that dress, he'll work on it harder!" Olivia giggled.

Mary Theresa had a sudden flash of genius. "I'm going to surprise him with it," she said. She was just about to describe the fantasy scene when Marco appeared.

"Anyone heard from Scarlet?" Marco asked, looking around as he ran his hand down the center of his fitted red T-shirt. Jennifer stared at his chiseled upper arms and elbowed Stephanie to check them out too. She slapped her sister's leg and ordered her to get back to work.

"Want us to give her a message?" Stephanie asked, practically flirting.

"Nah, it's cool. I just wanted to let all of you know that there is nothing scheduled for this room for all of January, so feel free to come in and work whenever you want."

Stephanie and Jennifer pursed their lips and winked at each other. Olivia noticed and raised her head and blew kisses to the air. "Marco, we all know you're—how would Scarlet say it—drooly for her. When are you going to ask her out?"

Marco brushed off the comment by offering a courtesy chuckle. Scarlet had pretty much become a slave to earning any kind of income she could. A date would be out of the question until that changed. Hopefully she'd have time to mend a pocket here and there, if he was lucky.

As if they felt a cool breeze swirl into the room, the group turned to the doorway to find a petite, slouchy woman carrying a thick load of laundry, which she dumped on the floor. "I have an announcement to make, could everyone please take a break and listen up?"

"Scarlet?" Rosa and Mary Theresa said in unison.

Between her disheveled look and slurred speech, they almost didn't recognize her. She walked over to the refreshment table and poured herself a cup of black coffee. Marco ran up behind her and removed it from her hand, replacing it with a bottled water. She didn't even notice. Her hair hung limp like cooked red spaghetti under a red trucker hat. She peeled off a lumpy flannel jacket to reveal baggy track pants and an oversized Cardinals T-shirt. She didn't even have on a lick of makeup, but she did have dark shadows under her eyes.

Olivia tossed down her pinking shears. "I knew this would happen. She went over the edge. Scarlet, what have you done to yourself?"

"I'm sorry I'm late," Scarlet grumbled. "I was so deep in thought, I got lost driving here."

"It's not about being late, it's about your health. You can't go on like this," Olivia lectured. "You didn't sleep last night, did you?"

Instead of responding to Olivia, Scarlet dragged a chair away from the wall and fell into it like a limp sandbag. "I have good news, bad news, and more bad news and good news...." She pointed up as if to draw a diagram in the air. "Or maybe it's bad news, good news, bad news, and then good news—depending on how you look at it...."

"Just tell us," everyone snapped.

Scarlet capped the top of her hat with her palms. "I received a letter from House of Tijeras the other day. The Emerging Designers Program has been moved up to mid-January...and the remaining balance is due *now*." Scarlet's voice quivered somewhere between laughing and crying.

"What?" Rosa said, standing up. "That can't be. Ew, that Johnny!"

"It's true. And I still have several thousand dollars to go. I called and they told me if I don't pay it by January 5, they'll give my spot to someone else. And the letter also said this is the last year of the program. This is the end of the road."

Scarlet moved her hat brim away from her face. "I'm going to have to cancel the rest of this class after the New Year. Either I'll be going to New York for Johnny Scissors—or, if I don't raise the money, I'm taking a break from fashion and taking a full-time gig in engineering. Look, guys…I'm sorry I dragged all of you into this. The engineering job will allow me to refund your money."

Mary Theresa ran to Scarlet's side. "Oh no. I'm so sad to hear this, Scarlet. You wanted it so bad. How much do you need? Maybe we can hold a car wash or something. If I had the money, I would invest in you."

"Thanks, but there's no time," Scarlet said. "I do have a last-minute wholesale order for forty of my Mexibilly Frocks. They're almost done. I've been working on them for the past twenty hours. Would you guys mind if I finished the hems here today? They're due Thursday morning. It's not enough to cover my balance, but it's a nice chunk. I have to finish them."

Jennifer and Stephanie scooped up the dresses from the doorway, carried them to the front worktable, and set them down. They each held one up and made a stink-eye face at it. The dresses were lopsided, with loose threads dangling, and some of them were smeared with stamp ink. Not Scarlet's usual pristine craftsmanship.

"Were you blindfolded when you made these?" Stephanie asked.

Rosa pushed her jumbo black glasses up her nose and inspected the dresses. The ladies and Marco awaited her verdict. "I hate to tell you this, dear, but these dresses are not saleable. As your friend, confidente, fan, and student—I can't let you send them out. You'll need to buy new fabric. I suppose if we help, we could remake them all by tomorrow night. But we would need a pattern. Do you have a pattern, Scarlet?"

Scarlet shook her head slowly. "No. Patternless sewing, remember?"

"I guess we'll have to make one, then. Do you have an extra Mexibilly Frock that we can use?" Rosa asked.

Scarlet's lip quivered. "No. I sold them all."

"Scarlet, it's OK, I have the dress you gave me. We can use that as the pattern!" Mary Theresa said with enthusiasm. "I'll race home and get it and bring it back."

"I can't sew for shit," Olivia said, pulling her chin into her chest. "But I'll call Scarlet's Auntie Linda from the quince shop and bring her down here to help. Jennifer, Stephanie, you think your mom can come? I have to pick up my daughter, but I'll bring back food for the night."

Scarlet dragged off her hat. "No, Olivia. I don't want you all to do this. This is *my* mess. I don't deserve your help. You guys should be hopping mad with me for taking your money and then not even showing up on time for class. I'll figure it out."

With her sunglasses already on her face and her keys in her hand, Olivia strolled out with a chuckle. "Oh, we'll find a way for you to make it up to us, don't worry. But today we're making your dresses. So you can get some rest. So you can get back to blogging. Adios for now!"

"Thanks for the help, everyone...," Scarlet said dazed. She stood up and rubbed her forehead with the back of her palm and teetered a bit.

Thinking she was about to fall, Marco darted over to help her. She finally caught her balance and pulled out two small bottles from her pockets. She unscrewed the top from one of them and began to drink the contents, but Marco snatched it from her weak fingers.

"Instant energy drink?" he said, alarmed. His eyes skimmed down the label. "These are like two cups of strong coffee each. It says not to exceed more than two a day. How many bottles have you had today?"

"I don't know. I've been making dresses since yesterday, I haven't gone to bed yet. I think a double cappuccino will perk me up." Scarlet released a stretchy ten-second yawn and tried to sit down, but wobbled until her eyes crossed and she fell to the floor, unconscious.

19

Scarlet used all her might to lift her eyelids. At first, everything appeared blurry and gray. It took a moment for her vision to adjust, but when it did, Marco stared back her.

"I feel so... comfortable, this bed is awesome," she said groggily, licking her lips. Her tongue felt bloated and drier than crusty sandpaper. She carefully raised her arm to find an IV attached. "Where am I?"

"You're at Glendale Samaritan Urgent Care," Marco answered, holding a cup of water to her mouth. "Drink. You've been asleep for two hours. That's an IV with some much-needed fluid. You're dehydrated and exhausted. You fainted."

She leaned her head against the pillow and softly combed her fingers through her hair. The dresses... the tuition, her mind clicked back into place. "I have so much to get done. I feel a lot better, did they say when I can leave?"

Marco leaned over and stroked her cheek, making Scarlet's heart race in a much better way than caffeine ever did. She placed her hand on top of his to trace the shape of his fingers, feeling the roughness of his skin and taking in his scent. That single moment of bliss helped alleviate the pressure from her mind.

"We can go whenever you feel ready," he assured her.

"Can you drop me off at the shop so I can help make the dresses?" she asked, already knowing his answer.

He used his foot to tug the wheeled stool to the bedside, and sat. "No, I cannot," he said without any room for negotiation on her part. "The class has it under control. They made an executive decision for you to go home and sleep. I'm your designated watchdog. If you want to be on your best game to get that tuition money together, you need your rest. Maybe it's time you try a more traditional method, like a bank loan?"

"No, I still have my school loans."

"What about your parents or your brother or sister? They must know you're good for it."

"I would rather eat burnt polyester than ask them. I'll figure something out. It's meant to be. I can feel Manhattan in my system already. I see myself stepping onto the subway train. I can smell the roasted nuts they sell on the street corners. I'm ready."

Poking his head out of the room to look for the nurse, Marco playfully tapped her feet on top of the blanket. "Let's get you home. I bet after a long nap you'll have some ideas."

For once, Scarlet gave in. At that moment, nothing topped the peace she felt of closing her eyelids and letting her mind drift away like a balloon among the clouds. That is, until her parents busted into the room.

Jeane caught one glimpse of her youngest daughter in a hospital bed and threw her hands up in shock. "What happened, mijita? What did they do to you?"

Scarlet gave Marco a disparaging look, scooted up in her bed. "Mom, I'm fine. I've been working overtime and it caught up with me."

"The doctor said she'll be fine," Marco assured them. "I'm taking her home in a little while."

"Who are you?" Manny asked.

"I'm the one who called. I found your number on Scar's phone. She fainted in her sewing class this morning and I brought her here. I didn't know how serious it was, so I dialed."

"Thanks," Manny replied. "We can take it from here. Scarlet, you're coming home with us. I don't care if you're thirteen or thirty, you're still our daughter and we're getting your life back on track. We'll get your résumé together this weekend and send it out to Charles's boss first thing Monday. Accept it: The sewing thing didn't work, and it's perfectly fine to give up sometimes. It happens to the best of us. At least you can say you gave it your all."

"You're not getting any younger, mija," Jeane said.

Standing between the IV rack and the blood-pressure machine, Marco began to rock on his shoes. He watched silently as Scarlet gently removed the IV from her hand and swung around to the edge of the bed.

"I'm going to New York next month for my fashion internship. I'm committed to it; I already signed the papers."

"Oh, great, you signed papers." Manny sighed as he pulled out his phone and quickly scrolled to find a number. "I'm calling my lawyer. We'll get you out of it. I heard from your aunt Linda that you don't even have money to get out there."

"Dad, no. I'll get the money." Scarlet reached for his phone. "Please—"

"Get a grip, girl," her father boomed. "You're acting desperate. Have some respect for yourself."

Marco couldn't bite his tongue any longer. "Why are you so hard on her? You should be proud of her. Do you even realize who your daughter is and what she does? She's an Internet star with thousands of fans who hang on her every word, because she writes articles that inspire people. She's a gifted artist on the brink of a successful career. I've watched her from afar for the past few years; haven't you seen any of what she's doing? Do you know she has been working three jobs to raise her own tuition money for her internship? Anyone else would give up. She's not asking for anything except maybe for you to say 'I believe in you' or maybe 'What can we do to help?' or even an old-fashioned 'Buena suerte.'"

Angry and offended, Manny fired back. "Of course I know my daughter. I raised her! And I know she is meant for a better life than what she has right now. My daughter is teaching her class in a rundown record shop because her slave of a boss doesn't think she is good enough to teach on his property. Scarlet is thirty and doesn't even own a home or a car. Everything is secondhand. Yet she works three seamstress jobs. She doesn't have time to visit her grandmother anymore, much less call us to let us know how she is. We love her no matter what. But she has two college degrees and the brain of a genius and turns her nose up at good jobs and her family that loves her because she wants to make clothes? Do you know the odds of making it in the fashion industry? Slim to none."

Scarlet snatched her purse from the room's guest chair and when she stood, her eyes pooled with tears. She couldn't believe Marco had the guts to stand up to her parents and say the words she had always wanted to express but never had the courage. Until now.

"I'm sorry I haven't been around," she said, stepping toward her parents, "but it's not like I'm out partying. It's been over two years since I made this decision yet all of you ignore it. You want me to fail. I feel like I'm running a marathon, and all along the sidelines are strangers I've never even met. They're holding up glittery signs that say 'You can do it!' or 'Don't give up!'"

She swallowed hard and looked into her father's eyes.

"And then I see you and Mom and Charles and Eliza on the sidelines too, right by the finish line. I'm going as fast as I can, dreaming about making you proud. As I get closer, I assume that you guys, out of everyone, will have the biggest signs and the loudest megaphones to support me—because you're my family. But as I run by, I see your signs. And you know what they say, Dad? 'Give up' or 'you're wasting your time.'

"Every time we're at family events, no one ever asks me about my work, yet they drag out every detail of theirs. And when I do try to toot my horn, I'm made fun of. So I clam up. You guys make me feel disconnected and unworthy. Imagine how that would feel. It hurts, Dad. I'm sorry that my vision of a happy life is different from the rest of the Santanas'. But I'm doing this. I'm going to New York to have a career I love. If you can't give me your blessing, please don't chant me down."

Jeane bowed her head and left the room swiftly without saying good-bye. Scarlet knew her words hit her hard, but she couldn't hold back.

"That's what you think of us?" her father said, his voice cracking. "Sorry to have disappointed you. Good luck, Scarlet. I really hope you get what you want. And no matter what you think, I *am* proud of you." He pulled her head toward him and planted a light kiss on her forehead. Before he walked through the blue curtain of the room, he tipped his head to say good-bye to Marco.

Her deadlines, the money, the class, now her parents. For a fleeting moment Scarlet wondered if the stupid Johnny Scissors program was really worth it. She didn't know anymore. She didn't mean some of those things she'd said but had no idea how to take them back. The more she thought about it, the more she felt her emotions overtake her. She turned to Marco and hugged him as tightly as she could. He held her close and rubbed her back as she unleashed two years' worth of sobs, frustration, and guilt.

Around lunchtime, they pulled into Scarlet's concrete driveway alongside two rows of potted petunias. The entire ride
home she tried calling her parents' house but was only met by
the answering machine. She wanted to see them, even though
she had no idea what to say. If she backed down and apologized,
her words would have meant nothing. Yet if she showed up and
stood her ground, another argument would ensue. When she
entered her house, she saw the blinking light on the answering
machine and pressed the playback button.

"Hey. It's Eliza. What the hell did you say to Mom and Dad?
They're really upset. I've never seen them so mad. My advice is
to stay away for a while until they cool off. Good job. Later."

Scarlet erased the message and took a running dive onto her
couch and curled up in the corner. "I envisioned that scene with
my parents on a regular basis. I thought I'd feel great afterward,
but I feel like shit. Why is that?"

"Because the truth is hard to digest sometimes," Marco
said. "They're mad because you painted a picture and put it up
to their face. But I can tell they really love you. They'll come
around when you least expect it. For now, you should go get
some sleep. Doctor's orders, remember?"

Scarlet grabbed the tapestry toss pillow from the corner of
the couch and squeezed it. "I have so much adrenaline rushing
in me right now, I need to be shot with a tranquilizer gun in
order to sleep. I feel like getting out of here and doing something to take my mind off everything."

"Like what?"

"It's stupid and totally inappropriate after all that's happened
today. Never mind. You'll think I'm bipolar if I mention it," she
said as she twisted the tassel on the pillow.

"After a day like this, anything goes. What?"

"Can we go on a date tonight?"

"A date?" He expected her to say a movie or a bite to eat, but not "a date."

Sensing what she read as hesitation, she flipped her hand at him. "See, never mind. I just better go have a conference with my Sealy Posturepedic."

"No, let's go," he said. "But take a nap first. I'll be back to get you at seven."

Mary Theresa spent seven long hours at the record store helping the ladies work on Scarlet's dress order before returning home. For a class of beginners only a month ago, they proved they could operate as a competent production team— or at least a moderate one. Rosa gave Olivia and her daughter, Missy, cash to buy the fabric while she stayed and drew the master pattern off of Mary Theresa's Mexibilly Frock. Because of the time crunch, Rosa had to alter the design a bit, but after hearing purrs of praise from the class, she knew the first prototype came out flawless. Rosa then gave Jennifer and Stephanie the go-ahead to trace and cut the fabric, while their mother pinned the pieces. Mary Theresa helped Scarlet's aunt Linda sew like the wind. There were still dresses to be constructed, but Auntie Linda promised to finish them at home and bring them in the morning so Rosa could show everyone how to add the trims and embellishments. Their reward was when Marco returned from Scarlet's with the good news about her health. He said she'd be well enough to come in the morning to help finish the order.

Mary Theresa thought of the day's events as she cleaned up her kitchen and tossed the paper plates after dinner. Tonight's special: a take-and-bake ultimate pizza from Zecchini's Italian

Restaurant. Hadley often bought the sixteen-inch pie because the kids considered it "the goommyest food in the world!" "Goommy," as Mary Theresa had learned, was the twins' word for something that was both good and yummy. For months, Hadley, Rocky, and Lucy had attempted to persuade Mary Theresa to try a nibble, but she refused. She'd dismissed it as empty-calorie junk food, just like she did with all of Hadley's meals. However, tonight she indulged. It took a single swallow for her to agree that her kiddos knew goommy.

It wasn't the food that made her feel satisfied inside, but rather the feeling of enjoying a meal with her children. She, Rocky, and Lucy were finally bonding—and all it took was her tuning in to their little world instead of always trying to drag them into hers. As with any set of first-grade twins, there were moments of mayhem each day, especially when Mary Theresa tried to meet her work deadlines. But she worked through each situation without the aid of books, manuals, or printed lists. Well, at least not as many as usual.

Mary Theresa shut off the kitchen light, jogged upstairs, and checked on Rocky and Lucy. When she confirmed they were still happily playing in their room, she strolled into her bedroom and turned on her iPod. John Coltrane.

Hadley still called every night for the kids, and he now chatted with her, too, once a week. At first just small talk about Rocky and Lucy, but as more time passed, their conversations stretched. Sometimes Mary Theresa forgot she was married to him; he became more of a friend she could open up to about anything...except her marriage. Any time she hinted about their counseling or even her sewing class, he changed the subject. She didn't push it. Mary Theresa took Scarlet's advice and visualized the actions she wanted in her life. She imagined her and Hadley embracing. In love, this time showing it.

Mary Theresa stepped in front of the orangey-red dress she had finished in class that hung from the top of her closet door. She lingered for a moment, removed it from the velvet hanger, and slipped into it. She even ripped off the elastic band around her ponytail and let her long, dark hair fall on her petite shoulders. It had been a decade since she had showed off her body, much less inspected it in front of a mirror. After having two kids, Mary Theresa appreciated how well-toned she was.

She pranced around in the dress and tried on various layers of jewelry with it. If only Hadley could see her now. She thought back to the crazy idea that had popped into her head during class. She raced downstairs for her smartphone before she changed her mind.

"Mommy, don't run down the stairs, you'll fall and knock your teeth out," Lucy hollered from the entranceway of her room.

By then Mary Theresa had already retrieved her phone from the kitchen counter and raced back up the stairs, two at a time, until she reached the top. Both her children cheered and pumped their fists in the air as if she had just won a relay race. The image of Rocky and Lucy trying to copy her moves shot into her mind.

"Just because I did that doesn't mean you can, you hear me, sweeties? It only works for grown-ups."

Both kids nodded their heads dutifully. "You look pretty, Mommy," Rocky said. "You should send Daddy a picture in the computer."

Mary Theresa kneeled down and scrunched Rocky's face with her hands. "That's a swell idea. I'll be right back. Go back and play, OK?"

She went back in her room, took a deep breath, and sat in front of her vanity. After teasing the hair at the crown of her head and then smoothing it down, she opened her makeup bag and applied a heavy coat of mascara and liner. She dabbed some gloss on her pinkie and ran it over her lips. Hadley would either appreciate her efforts or think she had popped a wire in her brain. After slipping on her black strappy sandals that she'd worn only once (to a funeral), she posed in the mirror and snapped two photos. Before she could second-guess her instinct, she sent them to Hadley with the subject line: "My latest creation from my patternless sewing class."

Mary Theresa decided to treat herself to a shopping spree soon and ask Scarlet to guide her. The idea reminded her of something she had meant to do—check out DaisyForever.com.

Mary Theresa carried her laptop to the kids' room, crawled onto Rocky's bed, and read Scarlet's entire blog while the kids worked on their USA floor-map puzzle.

She learned even more about Scarlet. The girl could launch her own beauty magazine or style column. There on the site, Mary Theresa watched makeup application tutorials, how to smile for photographs, how to keep positive during hard times, how to open a Roth IRA, how to clean vintage shoes, and so much more. Scarlet was a media natural.

When she finished reading every article and even commenting on a few, Mary Theresa felt invigorated. She wanted more! So she Googled Daisy de la Flora and followed a new cyber wormhole that led her to numerous photo galleries, movie pages on IMDB.com, and video footage from the infamous funeral. She even found a thirty-second clip of Daisy chatting about her muse, Carmen Miranda.

The last link carried Mary Theresa to eBay, where 107 auctions were listed for Daisy originals: purses with outlines of animals and flowers and filled in with gems, crystals, beads, and rhinestones; gaudy belts; triple-stitched cloaks; stoles dripping with dangling trims; and beaded gloves with hats and shoes to match. Growing up, Mary Theresa had heard of Daisy de la Flora, but only realized now what she had missed out on. Between Scarlet and Daisy, Mary Theresa wanted to reinvent herself inside and out.

She almost closed out her browser when her eye caught a photo that stood out from the rest—a pair of sleek suede black boots dotted with diamond-shaped crystals. She moved her mouse over the Bid Now button, but then clicked Buy It Now instead. Before today, she wouldn't have dreamed of spending $425 on such a frivolous splurge—especially with her current salary reduction.

But Mary Theresa didn't only *want* the boots, she needed them to step foot into the soon-to-come adventure of her life.

She powered off the computer and decided to check her smartphone for a response from Hadley. Who knew if he even received her silly pictures? As she waited for new messages to load, she held her breath.

He answered: "Daddy like!"

DaisyForever.com
magical musings about love, beauty & fashion
inspired by the life of Daisy de la Flora
as told by Miss Scarlet Santana

Tuesday, December 27, 5:25 p.m.

You are worthy.

Salut, my soulsearchers!

Are you still with me? I promise I haven't ignored you. I've had a series of exciting/time-consuming events march their little sticky feet into my life and take up residence on my schedule. They're here to stay for a while, so let's all be friends, shall we?

I just finished reading more than 300 comments on the Little Victories post, by far the most DaisyForever.com has ever seen. Mil gracias for all the kudos. I'm delighted to my crystal core that you got all goosepimply about the idea. Pretty please, send me pictures of what you make so I can share them here.

As far as my mystery...did I solve it? Yes. Someday I'll share it with you. Who knows, maybe I'll write a book about it!

Now on to today's topic: self-worth.

Last week a little birdie flew in my window and delivered a sealed envelope to my bed pillow. (OK, it was an e-mail, but I like drama!) In the envelope was a letter informing me that the Johnny Scissors Emerging Designers Program has not only been moved up six months, but will be discontinued after this season! And this was the twentieth year, too! Well, you know I'm kissing my lucky stars that I made it in on the tippy top of the final tailfeather.

An odd thing happened when I initially announced the news of my trip to my family. They weren't as excited as me. In fact, they didn't dig the idea at all. And with the recent developments, they suggested I throw in the embroidered towel. With a little encouragement from a friend, I cranked up my moxie meter to level ten and spoke my mind. I stood up for myself to people I had been intimidated by for years. We're currently not on speaking terms because of it.

At the same time this happened, my dear friends in my sewing class helped me complete an enormous order that I would have never been able to finish on my own. I owe them so much gratitude, and love them so much. You know who you are.

They motivated me to never let anyone make me feel unworthy again, or settle for anything less than what makes my heart sing. Remember Daisy's trip to New York when she was seventeen that I wrote about? My situation is hauntingly familiar to hers. She had a meeting with Carmen Miranda; I have one with Johnny Scissors. Except in my case—I will have the honor to shake his hand, and I'll do it on behalf of Daisy for Carmen.

I've been inspired by Daisy's adventure and want to pay it forward. This is my gift to you:

Miss Scarlet's Tips for Standing Up for Yourself

1. **Be proud of your skills and successes.** Acknowledge them and appreciate them; these are your own personal superhero tools for fighting off mediocrity.

2. **Be firm, honest, and choose your words wisely.** Yelling, name calling, crying...none of it will work in your favor. Come from love in your heart and respect who you are talking with.

3. **Don't hide and sulk. Toot your horn, darn it!** I don't mean to overdo it—love is a two-way street, you know. If you deserve credit for something, and everyone pretends otherwise, remind them!

4. **Don't let the Negative Nellies/Downer Dans steal your joy.** They can only get away with it if you let them. Chances are they are unhappy and it makes their eyebrows twitch to see you smile. Shock them and say something nice to them to lighten their day!

5. **Show appreciation.** Once you have said your piece, end the conversation with kindness. Be the one to set the example.

P.S. I have a date tonight (my first in over two years!!) with a dear friend. Pray for me that I don't act like a spaz!

P.P.S. Daisy, if you are out there, Merry Christmas to you!

Until next time, kiss kiss, bang, bang!

21

Scarlet had three minutes before Marco was to arrive for their date. She quickly sprayed on one final coat of AquaNet and grabbed her purse—a tiny drawstring velvet bag.

Dressed in a simple olive green cocktail dress and her favorite black patent-leather heels, Scarlet stripped away layers of her vintage-loving lifestyle. Her shiny red hair that she normally pressed into finger waves now rested flat down one side and behind her ear on the other. She finished her toned-down look with medium gold hoop earrings, a light layer of foundation, and sleek black eyeliner. Scarlet compared her look to that of a secretary on an afternoon soap opera. She hoped it would balance her out with Marco, who was known for his simple trousers and button-up shirts.

Just as he said, the clock struck seven and the doorbell rang, sending a new kind of zing into Scarlet's stomach. She licked her finger and slicked the edge of her hair and opened the door. She took one look at Marco and heaved a sigh of delight.

The normally conservative Marco had transformed himself into the spitting image of a '50s-era Rock Hudson. His tall, muscular frame showed off a shiny black suit with narrow lapels on the cardigan-style blazer, a skinny tie with a gold tie bar, a hankie peeking out from his front pocket, and glossy black hair parted sharp on the side. In his hand, Marco spun a fedora around his finger.

"Hey, kitten, ready for a spin around the city?" he cooed.

Scarlet admired every feature of his ensemble. "Que rico, hombre! Que rico! I love it! What brought this on?" she asked, tracing her finger around his shoulders as she circled him.

Marco blushed a bit, slid his hands in his pockets, and leaned against the doorframe. "After I left your house earlier, I went back to the shop. I didn't breathe a word about tonight, but Rosa got hyped up when she saw me, like she knew.... She dragged it out of me. Next thing I know, we're at Second City Resale and I'm trying on fedoras. But if it's too much for you, I can change. I have my other clothes in the car."

"Are you kidding? If I had punched in an order in a wishing machine for the perfect date. You are what would have come out."

*   *   *

Marco had made reservations at Sangria, an upscale Latin restaurant, gallery, and nightclub. It had been decorated for the holidays with hundreds of silver glittered balls, hanging at different lengths from the ceiling. But even as beautiful as the restaurant looked, the first thing Scarlet noticed was how much of a true gentleman Marco was. He went all out, opening every door for her, taking her hand, making her feel like the night was all about her.

Ever since Scarlet took a break from working, her body—inside and out—felt recharged and hungry. She and Marco ordered an appetizer platter, two entrees, desserts, and various cocktails and shared all of them. They discussed funny pranks they played in high school and compared notes on new galleries in downtown Phoenix. Both agreed they loved downtown Glendale more because of its small-town charm. They then moved on to affectionately analyzing the lives of all of Scarlet's students, especially Rosa. Scarlet recounted the entire Daisy drama that Rosa had told her and Mary Theresa, and then made Marco swear on his lease not to repeat it.

The lights dimmed above the dance floor across the restaurant, and a Brazilian samba showered down from the overhead speakers. Sangria nightlife had begun. Scarlet tugged Marco up and forced him to the dance floor, which was already packed.

For the next forty-five minutes, the handsome couple freestyled through mambos, merengues, cha-chas, rumbas, and tangos until they could barely catch their breath. Marco led Scarlet to a tall black-lacquered cocktail table in a private corner. After requesting two Picasso Punches from the waitress, he moved in close and adjusted Scarlet's hair back behind her ear. She, in turn, scrambled her fingers through his hair to mess it up.

"You're a brat," he said, fan-folding the white cocktail napkin.

"A crazy brat at that!" She laughed, taking the napkin from his hands and blotting her nose. Still panting from the spontaneous dance session, Scarlet made up names to go with their one-of-a-kind moves: the Santeria Shimmy, the Beyoncé Bossa Nova Booty Bounce, and the Tango Tackle. She chattered on and on about the outfits Carmen Miranda used to wear during her dance numbers and the way she posed her hands around her chin while singing. Marco just smiled and watched until the waitress appeared with their order.

Scarlet removed the drinking straw from his glass and inserted it in hers. Seductively scooting the fancy drink between them, she motioned with her eyebrows for them to share. They both went in for their respective straws at the same second and conked heads. Scarlet, laughing, massaged her forehead and Marco lifted the icy glass to soothe it.

"Round two," she said. This time they succeeded. With their faces barely three inches apart they sucked down as much as they could of the first drink.

Scarlet stood back, winced from the alcohol a bit, and fanned her face before nuzzling up under Marco's neck. She liked him—*really* liked him. And she knew he wanted her to.

Marco gently gripped her neck and gave her a short, simple kiss. Soft, sweet, and as delicious as a strawberry tart from La Purisima Bakery. He pulled away to gauge her reaction, and she responded by anchoring her fingers on his lapels and reeling him in for another. The waiter came by and dropped a package of mistletoe on the table.

"It's on the house," he said with a smirk.

Embarrassed—but only a little—Scarlet slipped it into her purse and then put her arms around the back of Marco's neck. "Thanks for having my back today . . . and every day."

He kissed her cheek and whispered in her ear, "Always."

*   *   *

"What are you in the mood for?" Marco asked, sitting on the edge of his wood-framed sofa, scrolling through the large silver laptop on the coffee table. "Adele? Shakira? AC/DC? The world of Internet radio awaits us."

"Keep trying," Scarlet sang out as she unbuttoned her red wrap coat and tossed it across a set of black fiberglass bar stools. They, like everything else she noticed in Marco's living room, were nothing like the feel of his record store. Aside from two wireless speakers that hung from the corners of his ceiling, no trace of music adoration could be found. Otherwise, the atmosphere was that of a well-disciplined bachelor with eclectic taste: blue/gray tones, modern vintage accessories, packed bookshelves, *National Geographic* and *Oceanography* magazines, two laptops, random dishes and cups, and your typical fish aquarium. Her favorite accent was a shark-themed paint-by-numbers lampshade on the recycled-wood end table that he'd colored in with black marker.

"Earth, Wind & Fire?" he offered.

Scarlet's eyes narrowed and she winced. "Not even close. You were kidding about Internet radio, right? I want to hear the at-home version of Vega's Vicious Vinyl."

"Prince?" he ribbed, still searching. "Miley Cyrus?"

"You're scaring me," she said as she ran over and pretended to wrestle him out of the way of his comfy command center. He held his hands up to surrender and went to the kitchen. "Let me do this," she said, as if she were the expert. "Sweet niblets, you were serious. You seriously don't have any albums or CDs here?"

"I have a few in my room."

"Well, sorry, Mr. Vega, but we're not doing Internet radio tonight. I'm breaking into your playlists. I love my LPs, but I'm a downloading diva too." Scarlet opened his iTunes program and scratched her head. "You have one playlist and it's called Miss Scarlet's Revue?"

"You're so nosy, I knew you were going to find that," he said, leaving the kitchen with two icy Coronas. He used his shoulder to turn off the lights, leaving only the glow from the hallway lamp.

"It's just some tracks I put together. I was going to burn them on a CD as your Christmas present. I chickened out."

"Awwww. You were going to give me a gift?" she asked, punching the keyboard mouse with an exaggerated click. "Let's see whatcha got."

One of Scarlet's faves, Pérez Prado's 1955 classic "Cherry Pink (And Apple Blossom White"), began to play. Marco set the beers on the table and reluctantly summoned her to the center of the flagstone floor for a dance. He blamed his recent interest in dancing on Rosa and her love of Latin music that she often pushed on him.

One beer swig later, Scarlet joined him. He slid his hand around her waist, tucked her in close, and they swayed to every note, groove, and beat of the song. At one point, he even dipped her.

When the song ended, he lifted her chin and searched her eyes, as if he didn't know if he would ever have the chance again. Eartha Kitt's "Santa Baby" came on, and the swanky sound inspired Scarlet to pull away and twirl.

"I can't figure you out," she said, finishing a complete circle and then coming back in so they could continue their moves. "You own the coolest record store in the world, but you don't have any music in your house?"

"That's because it's not my store."

"Not your store. What do you mean?"

Marco sighed and stared down at Scarlet as they paused from dancing to hold hands. "It's my little brother's store.... He died a week before he could open it."

Scarlet pulled back and paused. She thought of the picture Marco kept on his office desk. "Oh, Marco, I'm so sorry. You're running the shop in his honor, is that what you mean?" All her questions about him clicked into place. He could pass as a walking encyclopedia of music of every era, not because it was his passion but because he wanted to sell records to keep his brother's dream alive. "Do you mind if I ask what happened?"

They began to dance again, in place, and much slower than before as Marco told her the story, nary a hint of emotion.

"Where to start? OK, well his name was Michael and he was a drummer in a punk band when he was in high school. Had the Mohawk and the tattoos—all of it. He dropped out and fell into a bad crowd. Drugs, stealing, all that. He even spent time in jail at Tent City. My parents were livid. They disowned him when he stole their car and wrecked it. I talked him into going into rehab. While he was in there, he met this girl, and she gave him hope, you know? Like . . . he had a whole new spirit to start over. Their dream was to open Vega's Vicious Vinyl. He got out and got a decent job, he saved up enough to make a down payment for the store. He took all kinds of jobs to save money. My parents still didn't want anything to do with him, even when he showed them the paperwork to his bank loan. They didn't believe in him. By that time, I was almost done with college and dating this yuppie chick, and all I wanted to do was impress her. She didn't like his tattoos; she didn't want me to help him. I chose her over him. So anyway, one night we're at a party for her work and I get a call. He needed me to pick him up in Tucson. His car broke down, and he needed a ride back to town to make it to work on time in the morning. I . . . didn't call him back."

A thick lump formed in Scarlet's throat as she saw Marco's eyes fill with tears. She knew he didn't want the tears to escape, but then he blinked. Hard. And two streams that had been pent up for who knows how long poured down the sides of his cheeks.

Scarlet cradled his face between her hands. "He didn't make it home?"

"He hitchhiked. The driver fell asleep on the long drive back . . . they crashed into a semi in front of them."

At that moment, "Santa Baby" ended, leaving the air empty and silent. Scarlet still held Marco's face as more tears raced down over the tops of her hands. She realized his quiet demeanor all along wasn't from shyness or arrogance, it was sadness. They both held their breath until the tender serenade of Sam Cooke's "Nothing Can Change This Love" floated down from the speakers. She had never heard the song but fell instantly in love with it. And Marco.

She stood on the tips of her toes and kissed his dry lips with every last drop of energy inside her. Still holding on, she pulled him down to the floor with her and didn't let go. He curled his strong arms around her petite body and accepted her warmth. She knew no words could heal his wounds or even console him, but perhaps being his friend and lover would.

*   *   *

Eight hours later, Scarlet's eyelids flickered open as she woke up snuggled against Marco's back on the futon in his bedroom. She doodled with her finger across his toned shoulder blades and then kissed them one at a time. Any other time, she would be up sewing by now, but as long as she made it by nine to meet her class to finish the dresses, she'd be fine.

Marco rolled over and ran his fingers up her abdomen, between her breasts, and to her lips. "Thank you," he said, then kissed her good morning.

"Whatever happened to your brother's girlfriend?" Scarlet asked, resting her hands on his chest.

"She's Nadine."

At that moment Scarlet's clutch began to beep on the barstool. Marco slipped on his boxers and sprinted out, grabbed her bag, and handed it to her.

"I missed a lot of messages yesterday," she said, tapping through the screen, holding the sheet over her chest. "Six! And they're all from the same number—212 area code; that's New York. Oh no, what if it's House of Tijeras asking for the money?"

She pressed the speakerphone button and set the phone on the nightstand while she crawled into a Changing Hands Bookstore T-shirt that Marco set out for her.

"Hello, my name is Nexa Shinenfeld from Fashion Faire Weekly. This call is for Scarlet Santana, the author of DaisyForever.com. I'm contacting you because the Met Costume Institute is planning a celebration in honor of fifty years of Daisy de la Flora's career. We'd like to discuss the idea of possibly hiring you as a consultant for a cover feature to coincide with this high-profile event. Please return my call at 212-555-6382, as soon as possible. Thank you."

Scarlet snatched the phone and then fumbled it so much it bounced back and forth between her shaky hands. Marco caught it, dialed the number, and handed it back to her. He sat back and listened as Scarlet presented a polished, business-like attitude throughout the conversation. Good thing Nexa couldn't see Scarlet's foot shaking more than Charo's booty on a Las Vegas stage.

After a series of "uh-huh, I see, hmmm," Scarlet politely said good-bye and disconnected the call.

"They want to hire me for a fee of five thousand dollars, fifty percent upon agreement," she said dryly. "Between that and the dress order, I'll have more than enough for my tuition." She tossed the phone onto the sheet in front of her as if she didn't want to be near it.

Marco slid over and put his arm around her stiff shoulders. "Talk about the Law of Attraction...problem solved," he said.

Scarlet didn't move or even change her expression.

"What's wrong? This is what you've wanted, and you got it."

Scarlet raised her knees, hugged them, and examined the grooves in the floor. "They want the dirt on Daisy," she said.

"They're calling her the original bad girl of fashion. They have this horrible info on her and they want me to piece it all together with timelines. And there's a bonus if I can gather information on her early—quote, unquote—troubled days at Coconut Grove."

"Oh," Marco said, falling back on the bed. "Coconut Grove...that would mean..."

Scarlet turned to face him. "I'd have to sell out Rosa."

22

In the far corner in the busy production room of Carly Fontaine Studio the next day, Scarlet wiped the sweat from her neck, reached across the cutting table, and raised the volume on her iPod. Her new playlist consisted of nothing but Sam Cooke. She ever so carefully removed a turquoise crepe de chine silk gown from the petite dress form and held it up to admire Carly's design work.

Nice, she thought. But if Scarlet had created the gown, she would have dropped the neckline and added a row of flat-back crystals to each layer of vertical ruffles. Scarlet knew that was why Carly kept her hidden in production and not design—Carly hated sparkle, like salt to a snail, even in eveningwear! Scarlet slipped the billowy dress over a velvet hanger and hung it on the rack for steaming. From the corner of her eye, she watched Carly cruise in her direction.

Carly slowed her pace when she reached Scarlet, giving her outfit a complete once-over. "Let me guess—today you are Natalie Wood in *Rebel Without a Cause*?"

Putting her hands on her hips, Scarlet smiled and smirked at the same time. "Nope. I put an end to Cinema Couture. This is one hundred percent Scarlet Santana."

Thanks to Scarlet's sisterfriends, as Olivia would say, forty fantastic Mexibilly Frocks were delivered to Carly Fontaine Studio that morning. Ready to be bought and paid for. Scarlet planned a party to thank her class as soon as she cashed the check. Maybe this order would garner her a bobbin's worth of respect from Carly, and she'd be invited too.

"Good for you," Carly said in lowercase emotion, removing her chunky white eyeglasses and gliding them to the top of her head. "Why did you bring the dresses?"

"Excuse me?" Scarlet asked. "Your e-mail about your client from Santa Fe. I have it in my inbox. You said—"

"She canceled. I texted you Monday. Did you not receive it?"

Scarlet whipped out her iPhone. She had been in a caffeine-induced trance all week, but she would never miss even a sneeze from Carly. She scanned all her incoming texts, but Carly's didn't exist.

"There's no text," Scarlet said, her voice going up a bit.

"Whoops, sorry about that. I could have sworn I sent it. At least you can sell them in your Internet store. Anyway, can you remove the items from the showroom on your lunch break?"

If Scarlet could confront her father, she thought, Carly would be like frosting on a cupcake.

"No. I can't do that."

The sound of a sea of sewing machines came to a halt as the production workers paused to listen.

"Carly," Scarlet said, "I had a team of dedicated women help make those dresses in two days. They're perfect. Better than perfect. You placed the order. I'm a designer and business-woman just like you. You owe me the money for the invoice I left on your desk. I need it for my tuition payment for Johnny Scissors."

"You've got to be kidding me," Carly snipped, confronting

Scarlet. "You were serious about Johnny Scissors? Why didn't they call me as a reference?"

Scarlet moved the garment so it wouldn't burn from being too close to the steamer. That poor dress didn't deserve any further harm. "They did. Several times, but you didn't call back."

"How could they accept you without *my* recommendation?" Carly said, propping her elbow against an overstuffed fabric-supply cabinet. "You have zero notable experience. I run the biggest fashion house in Arizona, I should have some say in the decision. It's just...ridiculous. We both know at least a dozen designers who deserve this more. They are properly educated and have invested years in their craft. I don't mean to be rude, Scarlet, but I have to wonder about the motivation of the jury."

"Maybe they saw something in me that you don't," Scarlet replied coolly as she finished the hem of the dress. "Not every person has to follow your formula in order to succeed."

Carly let her head rest against the stacks of folded fabrics. "Ahhh, I know what's up...the fifty-year anniversary of Daisy de la Flora. They chose you for the novelty of that shrine of a blog you have," Carly replied.

"You would say that. Whatever the reason, I leave next month and I need payment for the dresses. Today."

"I'm not buying your tacky crafty couture. If you were a sharp so-called businesswoman, you'd see that I didn't place an order. I asked *if* you had them on hand. I said I'd cut you a check *if* the transaction went through. It did not, therefore I don't owe you anything. And you're lucky I don't fire you after this confrontation. I'll grant your time off for Johnny Scissors, but don't come back expecting a promotion," Carly said firmly. "Miss Scarlet may have scored a lucky pass from Johnny Scissors, but with me you'll always be Scarlet Santana, the woman hustling for a short cut. I guarantee you won't last a week in New York. Those designers will outshine you ten-to-one in talent and expertise alone. You should save yourself, me as your boss, and Arizona from the humiliation and stay home. Let someone else who deserves it have a shot."

In a moment of rage-infused self-empowerment, Scarlet turned off the steamer, covered the dress in a plastic bag, and handed it to Carly.

"I'm done here. This is my last shift. Forever," Scarlet said.

"Smartest decision you've made in two years," Carly said in her usual high-handed way. "I'll send security to help you clean out your things. And the dresses as well. Think I'm tough? I dare you to take those frocks to Johnny Scissors and see what he has to say."

Carly glanced at the gawking production team. She swung around on her black pointy heels, raised her chin like a queen who had just ordered a beheading, and high-stepped it out of the room.

Scarlet had always aimed to play fair, and gave things her best shot. *To hell with it,* she thought. If she wanted to get ahead in life, she had to take drastic measures. Just like Daisy. There would be explaining to Rosa, but she had to understand Scarlet's predicament. Rosa lived her life and accomplished all her dreams; Scarlet deserved the chance to do the same.

Scarlet's nostrils and nerves flared as she pressed Call Back on Nexa Shinenfeld's entry on her phone list. She plugged one finger into her ear so she could hear over the hum of the sewing machines.

"Hi, Nexa, this is Scarlet Santana. I've had time to think about your offer. I'm ready to negotiate. I'll divulge everything I know, plus I can find out more. I'll even write the article if you want me to. Payment in full by this week or no deal. If you're interested, here are the numbers you can reach me at…"

23

No one wanted to see Scarlet go. As she packed up the last of her items from the desk, her former coworkers gathered around to send her off with smiles and hugs, despite the tears many of them shed.

"It's time, Miss Scarlet," Barney, the normally frumpy security guard informed her as he lifted her box of unwanted Mexibilly Frocks and carried it out to her car for her. "Late-fifties-model Mercedes. This is one sweet ride. You've sure taken good care of it."

Polishing the roof with the sleeve of her overcoat, Scarlet nodded in agreement. "Yes, sir. Mint condition. My nana gave it to me when she stopped driving. You know my tata used to take her out on dates in this car? After days like this, that happy energy sure comes in handy."

"Always seeing the bright side," Barney said as he watched her get in the driver's seat. "We're sure gonna miss you around here, but you're gonna be just fine."

"Thank you." She went to close the door, but he blocked her.

"Like I said, this is one sweet ride. You ever decide you want to sell it, you let me know."

Scarlet waved good-bye to Barney and the Carly Fontaine

Studio parking lot for the last time. As soon as her tires hit the asphalt of Roosevelt Street, Scarlet knew there were only two ways to calm her soul: sewing...or Marco. Scarlet intended to reach Vega's Vicious Vinyl without any interruptions.

Fighting against the sharp, windy chill outside, she parked Nana's Mercedes and hoofed it down the sidewalk in her 1930s T-strap pumps and ivory trenchcoat. She used all her strength to swing open the glass door to the sewing room. Then she paused, pleasantly puzzled at the scene before her: Rosa and Mary Theresa giving Marco a sewing lesson while loud mambo music blared from the stereo. If she didn't know better, she'd think they were having a party without her.

Their faces lit up when she entered, excited to hear about the big dress sale. Scarlet didn't have the heart to tell them right away. So she kept the secret inside and snuggled her way onto Marco's lap, gripped his neck, and gave him a long kiss.

"No wonder his eyes are sparkling today," Rosa said proudly, as if he were her son.

Mary Theresa appeared pleased for them as well. A part of her wished it were she and Hadley.

Scarlet kissed Marco's nose and swung her legs cheerily, as if life were swell. As if she hadn't just lost her job, her shot at paying for Johnny Scissors, and possibly a career in fashion.

"What brings you all here on a Wednesday night?" she asked, genuinely curious.

"My mom took the kids shopping," Mary Theresa explained. "I couldn't handle being cooped up alone, so I thought I'd change my scenery. Apparently this is where the action happens. I walked in on Rosa *dancing* with Marco."

"Oh, really? You're already trying to make me jealous, are you?" Scarlet said, poking Marco in the chest. She winked at Rosa.

"Did Carly pay you?" Rosa asked, steering the conversation to a serious direction.

Scarlet cautiously stepped down from Marco's lap and removed her coat. "I have a bit of bad news about that...."

After Scarlet gave them the scoop, the women and Marco were furious at Carly. Mary Theresa suggested Scarlet call her out on her blog. Rosa was tempted to ask Joseph to drive her over there to tell the woman off. But neither suggestion was Scarlet's way of doing things.

"I'm not dwelling on Carly anymore. What's done is done," Scarlet said. "I have some other ideas up these sleeves."

Marco crouched forward in his chair like a military strategist. "We'll find another way. I'll come by tonight and put the dresses up for sale on your Etsy page. We can also put some for sale in the shop. You can blast it out on your blog."

"Even if they did sell, I'm still short by a mile," Scarlet muttered, thinking about the phone message she left for the *Fashion Faire Weekly* writer. Scarlet currently had an unopened voice mail from the woman, plus two e-mails she refused to look at. Her biggest fear was that Nexa would give the go-ahead to Scarlet's demands. At the time Scarlet left the message, she couldn't control her anger. But now that she had cooled down, she was having second thoughts about selling little old Rosa down the river.

Scarlet softly kicked the floor with her shoe. "On the drive over here I decided that I'm going to sell my nana's car. And possibly have an estate sale to declutter my house. I could do it this weekend and probably make enough to cover all my expenses."

"No," Marco moaned. "Bad decision."

Mary Theresa agreed. "That's extremely drastic, Scarlet. All those beautiful memories, you can't just sell them off. Did you at least talk to your nana about it?"

"I know if I asked, she would give me her blessing because she knows I have no other way to get to New York. She's the only one in my family who wants to see me succeed."

Marco stared down at the sewing machine and flicked a scrap of material off the table. "Funny way you have of showing her thanks. Just last night you were saying how guilty you felt that you haven't taken her for a ride in it all month, you know—the Sunday lunch thing?"

"I know it sounds awful, but they are just material things," Scarlet said. "Daisy once said—"

"Sell your Daisy collectibles or, at least, the jar of lucky buttons," Rosa interjected. "There are enough Daisy de la Flora antiquaries out there who will pay more than what you need."

It figures Rosa would say that, Scarlet thought. Sometimes she swore the woman thought of Daisy as a rival.

Mary Theresa clapped her hands once. "She's correct. We can write up a press release, send it out to build buzz, and then post them on eBay. You might even get some good publicity for your website."

"No way! I wouldn't sell those buttons if I was dying of starvation. They were Carmen Miranda's and she gave them to Daisy as a gift. I'm taking them to Johnny Scissors."

Rosa huffed, propped herself up from the seat next to Marco, and shook her hands at the sides of her head. The usually calm and reasonable senior citizen had transformed into an angry tigress.

"They were important to *Daisy*—not you," she pointed and shouted at Scarlet. "You're willing to sell all your grandmother's personal things—the woman who taught you to sew, the woman who stands by your side—instead of a jar of cheap wood buttons from a vieja you never even met? If you do it Scarlet, you will not be the woman I thought you were."

Rosa swung her coat around her shoulders. "Marco, will you please walk me outside? Joseph is waiting for me in the car."

Scarlet ran to stop her. "Please don't go, Rosa, you don't understand. It's my last resort. You don't know my nana; she won't mind."

All of them were shocked to see Rosa break down in tears. They didn't understand why Scarlet's words struck such a nerve.

"You really are just like her or no. Even worse. You are just like *Johnny*! Selling out!" she cried. "I thought you were stronger, but no. You're making the wrong choices, forgetting about what is really important."

"I am strong," Scarlet said, holding on to Rosa's elbow. "I'm going after what I've always wanted. Why is that wrong?"

Rosa pulled an embroidered hanky from her jacket pocket and dabbed her eyes. "If you don't get it after all this time, Scarlet, you never will."

Marco patted the air with his hand to suggest that Scarlet back down, and then guided a still-sniffling Rosa out the door.

Scarlet let her head drop back and paced around the door a moment before running outside after them. She caught a quick glimpse of Rosa and Joseph pulling out into the street. She chased after their car and hollered, "I'm sorry! I love you, Rosa!"

Marco put his arms around her and led her back toward the shop. "It'll be all right. She looked really tired. I don't think she meant to get so emotional. We'll see her later after she gets some rest. Let's go inside, it's freezing."

They stepped back into the record store, still huddling from the cold, just as Mary Theresa was leaving. "I'm going to get home too," she said with a sigh. "Please sleep on this decision, Scarlet. To be honest, I'm jealous that you still *have* a nana, much less her mementos. I'd give anything to have something from mine. Promise you won't do anything yet, OK?"

Scarlet nodded in agreement, "I promise." When Marco excused himself to help Nadine with a customer, she added quietly, "I'm worried about Rosa."

"She'll be fine once she rests up this week. By the way, I'm happy for you and Marco."

"Thanks...I'm so happy I met you, Mary Theresa. You're a good friend," Scarlet said before giving her a hug. "When Hadley comes back, all four of us will go out dancing. You'll love it, trust me."

"It won't be any time soon, but I'll take you up on that—maybe for Valentine's Day," Mary Theresa said. "I forgot to tell you—I bought a pair of original Daisy boots on eBay! That will be the perfect time to wear them"

They said their good-byes and Marco returned to check on Scarlet. Seeing the worried expression still on her face, he took her hand and led her back into the sewing room.

"Here, sit down and sew. Forget about everything that's happened today."

Scarlet dropped her head in her hands. "For the first time I can think of, the last thing I want to do is sew. Can we go to your house and just...talk?"

It had been a Cotorro tradition ever since the birth of Rocky and Lucy: both Mary Theresa's and Hadley's families descended upon the Cotorros' otherwise quiet house on the first Saturday evening of the new year.

To Hadley's credit she supposed, he factored in the stress of Mary Theresa's workload and knew she wouldn't be up for entertaining a group of eight nitpicky relatives. If it were up to Mary Theresa, she'd make reservations at the Cheesecake Factory and be done with it. But no, every year, Hadley insisted on cooking an extensive five-course meal to show off his culinary skills. Before the soup even reached the lips of his mother and sisters, they purred as if it were liquid gold that Hadley created. Mary Theresa played along. She appreciated the free meal, and the fact that her mother stayed to dry and put away every last dish while Mary Theresa went back to work in the home office.

However, the situation changed this year. Hadley bailed, and neither he nor Mary Theresa had the courage to inform their parents of the truth about why he was in Palm Springs. Their lives were stressful enough without lectures, cross-examinations, and speculation. Of course Rocky and Lucy made keeping the secret a little more challenging. The first time Mary Theresa's mother picked them up to babysit, the precocious twins announced, "Daddy left us." Their grandmother screeched the wheels of her Nissan Maxima, made a sharp U-turn, and interrogated her daughter on the front lawn. It took a whole two weeks for Mary Theresa to convince her that Hadley's brother needed him at the hotel.

And now, a week into the new year and still no Hadley. How would she explain that a father of twins could not find a way to come home for the holidays? Mary Theresa attempted to cancel the annual event, but neither set of parents would hear of it. As a buffer, she invited all the sewing class to join in the celebration.

Mary Theresa manned up and prepared to cook, even though all the family, neighbors, the kids' schoolteachers, and even grocery-store clerks knew kitchen work was not her strong suit. She knew Hadley's folks likely expected her to serve Oscar Meyer mini-weenies on Ritz crackers . . . with spray cheese in a can.

She'd show them. Mary Theresa would channel her inner Scarlet and impress them to tears.

Mary Theresa ordered menudo from Sylvia's La Canasta, lasagna from Streets of New York, and seafood salad from the Fish Market. She also picked up a tray of icebox cookies from AJ's Pastry Palace. She'd transfer them to her dishware; no one would know the difference.

To make sure the next day's operation would be error-free, Mary Theresa decided to conduct a trial run twenty-four hours before the official event. She had picked up small portions of her menu choices—and even added her own special touch to each dish. That way she wouldn't be lying when she'd say, "I made it myself!" She also figured she'd score extra brownie points from Hadley and their marriage therapist for her "free-styling" efforts.

First, she added a bag of frozen Swedish meatballs to the menudo. Next she coated the top of the lasagna with cubed French bread and tomato sauce. The seafood salad came last— she mixed in red seedless grapes. Her only trouble spot? The darn vinaigrette.

She printed off a recipe online, but it tasted a bit bland, therefore she added a splash of apple vinegar and tasted it. The tartness made her wince. Rachael Ray loved olive oil, so Mary Theresa would love it too! She turned the bottle upside down over the mixture.

"This is going great, actually. I definitely can see the benefits of freestyling," she said aloud. She dipped her pinkie in for a taste. Her entire body shuddered. It needed one more topper....

Seasoning! She thought.

Mary Theresa stepped in front of Hadley's prized six-level spice rack and analyzed it as if she were trying to defuse a bomb. She didn't know how to begin. She didn't want one taste to overpower the dressing. Maybe they had an "all-in-one" kind of spice that delivered every "must-have" flavor sensation. She searched through all the cabinets until...

"Aha! Creole seasoning!" she said with confidence and read the ingredients. "Salt, red pepper, garlic. Perfect!"

She shook the can a good ten times to provide the dressing with much-needed zip. She dragged her fingertip through the thick liquid and felt one eye squint uncontrollably. Without wasting an instant, she opened the refrigerator, grabbed a hand-ful of shredded cheddar from a plastic Ziploc bag and mixed it in.

She added the dressing to the salad and served three plates.

"Lucy . . . Rocky . . . ," she shouted from the bottom of the stairs. "Come downstairs for breakfast!"

*   *   *

Three hours later, damage control had arrived to clean up Mary Theresa's mess.

"Now, what in the *hell* did that woman put in this food?" Olivia asked, disgusted as she poked the lasagna with a spatula. "What is that on top of this? Soggy tomato-soaked garlic bread? And she put grapes in the seafood salad! No wonder they all got the runs!"

"Dump it all," Scarlet said, rushing back into the kitchen with a bottle of Pepto-Bismol in one hand and a box of Imodium AD in the other. "Thank God the kids only nibbled, but Mary Theresa is down for the count. I need to clean this kitchen and get cooking. Her parents and in-laws are coming."

Olivia scraped the lasagna into the trash, followed by everything else. Scarlet scribbled out a shopping list and slapped it and a hundred-dollar bill in Olivia's hand so she could race to the store for fresh groceries.

Scarlet knew how much the gathering meant to Mary Theresa. She had told her all about it earlier in the week when they got together for a spontaneous sewing therapy session. When Mary Theresa mentioned her lack of culinary skills, Scarlet thought she was joking. She should have taken it at face value; Mary Theresa rarely exercised her funny bone.

Sure enough, the inedible concoctions Scarlet and Olivia witnessed that afternoon were proof—for the sake of her children, marriage, and mankind, Mary Theresa should order out.

When Mary Theresa had called an hour earlier and explained her dilemma, Scarlet immediately rang the other members of the group to help clean the house, tend to the kids, and remake the next day's meals. It would be the first time the group would be together since the fainting fiasco.

Doom lingered on Scarlet's spirit. She had tried to call Rosa several times over the past week and a half but had only gotten through to Joseph, who told her Rosa had the flu. Scarlet had whipped up a batch of homemade chicken soup yesterday and tried to deliver it. When no one answered, she tried the door, but this time it was locked. And then today when Scarlet called again, the line had been disconnected. It wasn't like Rosa to disappear like that. Even Mary Theresa hadn't heard from her. Scarlet worried that Nexa from *Fashion Faire Weekly* had called Rosa before Scarlet had a chance to explain, which she fully intended to do.

Marco had a mystery game going on as well. He hadn't returned Scarlet's calls for a couple of days, which threw her off guard because up until then, they had become joined at the hip. Literally. In his bedroom, his living room, kitchen. And her house too—even in her sacred sewing room that she had been neglecting. She had no idea why he would avoid her now. She hadn't mentioned the topic of the car or sale. In fact, she was going to share some exciting news with everyone.

But until then she needed to forget about her own issues and focus on helping Mary Theresa. The doorbell rang, and she knew it had to be Stephanie, Jennifer, and hopefully their mom. She opened the door to find Marco.

"Hey. I brought the girls."

Before Scarlet had a chance to respond, Stephanie and Jennifer raced up the Cotorros' wavy concrete walkway and busted through the front door, elbowing each other, as if to win a race to hug Scarlet first.

"Happy New Year! It feels like ages since we saw you. You look great—back to your fabulous self!" Stephanie said, hugging her sewing teacher tight before removing her pink Japanese souvenir jacket and hanging it on a steel coatrack. "Look—I made a new shirtdress, no pattern!"

Scarlet spun her around, checked the seam and waistband, and held up an "OK" sign. "You're a natural, doll!"

Jennifer rolled her eyes at her giddy sibling and wandered into Mary Theresa's home, stopping to inspect every open doorway. Marco held up his keys to signal good-bye. "I'll see you ladies back at the shop."

Stephanie leaned in and whispered to Scarlet. "Something's up with him; every time we mentioned your name in the car, he changed the subject to something stupid. You guys did it, didn't you? You went all the way. I know that kind of tension—you should have stayed friends. Sex ruins everything."

Scarlet recoiled in shock. "Aren't you still in high school?" she asked over her shoulder as she slipped into Stephanie's souvenir jacket and followed Marco outside.

"Chick flicks!" Jennifer shouted.

Scarlet kicked off her cherry stilettos and raced barefooted past Marco to his gold Pathfinder parked in front of Mary Theresa's house. Her teeth chattered from sprinting across the chilly winter lawn. "Can we talk?" Scarlet asked, trying to catch her breath. Mary Theresa sure had a big front lawn. "Where have you been? I miss you. Did I do something wrong?"

He walked around and opened the door for her to get in his car. "Come on, get in. I'll turn the heater on."

Scarlet scooted down the upholstered seat and kissed him, but he just sort of nudged into her.

"Well, that was a like a flat tire," she said. "What's up?"

He rubbed his fingers up and down his Levi's and gazed out the windshield. "I've just been thinking about a lot of things."

Oh, God, he was going to break up with her already. Years of being innocuous acquaintances singed after a week and a half of steamy romance. But he seemed to enjoy it as much as she did. Had going from zero to sixty made him uneasy? Could he read her mind to know she wanted him as a permanent fixture in her life, and had that freaked him out? She gulped. When she and Cruz had sat in his vehicle having the same type of discussion, she had felt relieved. But now, quite the opposite.

"What kind of things?" she asked.

"You're not going to like what I have to say. . . . I bumped into your dad at Copper Star Coffee the other day at lunch."

"Oh, no," Scarlet said. "This can't be good."

"Your family was really hurt that you didn't come over for Christmas or New Year's. He said your mom cried all day. You used to take your nana shopping every weekend; your dad said you haven't gone over there in weeks. And you haven't returned his calls."

Scarlet shrugged. "I don't know what to say to them after what happened at the hospital."

"When I first met you, all you talked about was your family and your nana. Once I got to know you, you made them seem like they didn't want anything to do with you. Scarlet, they are worried about you. They want to help you. Ever since this whole Johnny Scissors thing, you've cut them off."

"They cut *me* off."

Marco raised his voice a notch out of frustration. "Sometimes love isn't about blindly agreeing, Scarlet. When they offer ideas, they aren't discounting you, they're trying to help. They see you worshipping Daisy above all of them, even over your nana, and they're hurt—jealous, even. Your dad is reaching out, but you won't give him a chance."

"I love them too, but I don't have time to deal with it right now. You know what I'm up against these days. I'll settle up with them soon and everything will be fine. That's how it goes with my parents. We argue, we cool off, all is well."

"Not buying it. You've lost sight of why you started that website in the first place. And when was the last time you even sewed anything?"

"This is why you've been avoiding me all of a sudden, because I haven't been sewing?"

"All of it. I needed to step away in order to look at the big picture."

"And now that you let it out, do you feel better?"

He sighed and ran his fingers through his hair. "I'll feel better if you rethink the Johnny Scissors thing."

Scarlet cocked her head back. "Are you kidding? Oh my God, you guys act like I'm going to Afghanistan. It's a short-term fashion program in the Garment District of Manhattan!"

He turned to face her and slouched in his seat. "Everything has been working against it. You're forcing your will. I'm telling you because . . . I love you. I've always loved you. And I don't want you to get hurt. I'm trying to protect you. Rosa was right. I see it now. You're letting Daisy de la Flora and Johnny Scissors get in the way of what really matters."

Scarlet glanced down at the black rubber floor mats and sucked on her bottom lip to let his words marinate in her head. "My dad brainwashed you."

"Scarlet . . . ," he moaned, tapping the back of his head against the window. "You're such a pill. Stop and listen to me, OK? They love you and want to be a part of your life but don't know how, so they try to lure you into theirs. That's why they push the engineering thing. You have to find the happy medium before it's too late."

"Before I follow through with my fashion career, become a success, and prove them wrong?"

"All I know is, if only my folks had been like that with my brother, he would be behind that record counter with Nadine, not me. You've never lost someone, so you don't understand. It's like going through life carrying your roots over your shoulder, searching and hoping and wondering if you'll ever find a place to anchor them into the ground. I thought I found that place with you, until..."

"Let me deal with my family in my own way, please. And I'm sorry about what happened to your family—you know I am. But—I'm not your brother. I'm not calling you in the middle of the night to come rescue me. I have everything under control."

"I did rescue you. Without my brother's record store, you wouldn't have had a place to run your sewing class."

Scarlet began to breathe faster. This was the price for taking his free offer of the room. "I would have had that class anyway, at my house or somewhere else. I wouldn't have given up. Besides, a lot of good it did; I only had five students. That's enough to cover my meals for a week."

"You sure aren't like my brother. Michael would have never sold out his friends like you did. I can't believe you went through with it."

Rubbing her temples in disbelief Scarlet tried one of Mary Theresa's tricks and counted to three in her mind. "Went through with what?"

"I know about *Fashion Faire Weekly*. They called the shop yesterday afternoon looking for you to fact-check the article. You actually sold out Rosa for your tuition money."

"I didn't sell them anything! I told you I had a weak moment the day I quit Carly's. I called Nexa, but it only took a second to come to my senses. I passed on her offer. She's been hounding me ever since. She nailed down my parents' house and Carly's and I guess the record store too. I finally volunteered to fact-check

Daisy's career timeline, but only to make sure they had it right. And I did it for free. You know I love Rosa, how could you even think—"

"I didn't know what to think," he said, flicking his hands in the air. "Every time I hear you mention Johnny Scissors or New York, I have the same feeling in my gut as I did the night my brother called me. I couldn't prevent what happened to him, but I can with you. I just wish you would trust me on this."

Scarlet took his hands, lifted them to her lips, and began to kiss them. She closed her eyes and held them to her cheek. "I'm going to be all right." She lowered his hands and took a deep breath. "You see my challenges as bad signs from the universe. I see them as opportunities. If it hadn't been for Carly canceling my class, I wouldn't be here with you right now."

Marco pulled his hands back into his lap and shook his head, unconvinced. "You're sacrificing too much for this. Something's not right."

Now Scarlet became agitated. She thought Marco knew her better and began to second-guess her relationship with him. Maybe they were opposites after all. Two single people who came together during a lonely, stressful holiday season. Nothing more.

"You're asking me to give up when you've never even tried to do something for yourself," she said coldly. "At the hospital, you agreed with me that I shouldn't live for my parents, yet you live your life for your brother. You think he is proud of you? I doubt it. You're chained there, lonely, playing Michael's favorite music day after day. There is no love or cariños within those walls. Michael is probably sitting up in heaven, holding his drumsticks, screaming for you to follow your own life plan. If he hadn't died, what would you be doing with your life? He worked his ass off to open that store because he loved music the same way I love sewing. Michael gave it his all. The same way Daisy did. You need to stop using us as an excuse to put off your own life."

Marco started the engine and clenched the top of the steering wheel. "You'd better go," he said. "Here come Jennifer and Stephanie."

Scarlet reached over to kiss him, but he turned his head. She bowed her head and chipped at the pale pink polish on her pinkie. "You need a break, don't you?"

"Yeah, that would be best for both of us. Call me when you get back from New York."

*   *   *

"Now, *this* is what I call a meal!" Olivia said with wholehearted approval after her first taste of Scarlet's red chili flautas and Spanish rice. "OK, missy, if you ever decide you don't like fashion design, cooking is your next calling!"

Stephanie, Jennifer, Rocky, and Lucy, all with their mouths full, raised their forks in agreement. Mary Theresa even felt better. She didn't want to eat any food, in order to protect her sensitive stomach, but she sat by and admired the packed table of smiling faces. Her sewing buddies had whisked through her abode like a professional cleaning crew and didn't stop until it could pass for a model home.

Around nine p.m., Mary Theresa tucked the kids into bed and read them a story while Scarlet and her team cleaned up the kitchen. Once the crew had settled down after their long day, Olivia removed a sweet surprise from the refrigerator. A tall red velvet cake that she and Missy had baked. As soon as the ladies spotted it, they scrambled to the dining table for a seat.

"I miss Rosa," Mary Theresa said. "It's just not the same without her. I can't believe she left without saying good-bye."

"Have faith in her; she'll be back," Olivia said, passing out small paper cake plates and plastic spoons. "That flu had been messing with her. I bet she went someplace relaxing to get some rest."

"I hope so," Scarlet said, cutting a hunk of the cake and dropping it onto her plate. "Mary Theresa, will you do me a favor tomorrow?" she asked cautiously. "Will you come clean with your family about you and Hadley? Unleash the truth, no matter what they think."

Jennifer slapped her hand on the heavy table. "Amen to that. John 8:32—the truth shall set you free! Heh, heh, I've always wanted to do that!"

Mary Theresa pushed her chair away from the table. "Oh, noooo, I can't. That's impossible; please don't apply this kind of pressure after the morning I've been through. You don't know our families."

"Oh, please," Scarlet argued. "All our families have unrealistic expectations of us. No matter how hard we try, we can never please them. The least we can do is be honest with them."

"She's right," Olivia said. "When I left my husband, it was hard to tell my sister. I hid our problems for years. She fought me at first, but then she saw the light. My light. And now? She is still around. He isn't."

"You have it all wrong." Mary Theresa laughed nervously. "The reason we're keeping it a secret is because the separation is temporary. We'll be back to normal soon enough."

Olivia laughed. "Did he say he was comin' back? Did you ask?"

"He said he needed a break until after the New Year," Mary Theresa replied. "He'll be back."

"You need to fess up to your folks for the sake of your kids," Jennifer said, picking the lint from her baseball cap. "You're setting a bad example by teaching them to lie to their grand-parents. Next time, they'll lie to you."

Stephanie cut a thin slice of cake and ate it with her hands and glanced at Jennifer. "We know, trust us."

"Don't be afraid," Olivia said to Mary Theresa. "We'll all be here if anything gets weird. We'll come up with hand signals for you to give us in case you need a bailout. You know, like wipe your eye if you want someone to change the subject. We got your back."

Mary Theresa cocked her head to the side and knew her friends were correct. She couldn't go on with the lie any longer. "OK. You're all right. Tomorrow, I'll tell them. I have to."

"Now that we have that settled," Scarlet said, "Marco accused me of selling out. Do I still seem like the same Miss Scarlet from DaisyForever.com?"

Mary Theresa took a bite from her cake. "Why, because you almost hawked your grandmother's prized vintage car to score cold cash?"

Scarlet stopped chewing to stare at her.

"I'm kidding. I hadn't read your blog until recently, but I know you've changed since the beginning of class. You were excited before. Now, aside from being happy around Marco, you appear more stressed and worried because the stakes are higher with the tuition and all."

"I'll give it to you straight," Olivia said. "You haven't blogged since forever. I used to look forward to your chirpy words of wisdom every morning but now they're dried up like a day-old chicken bone. But I know it's because you're so close to making it to New York. I'm still pissed at that Carly for turning away those dresses. Not a day goes by that I don't think of going down there and—"

"You hardly talk about sewing anymore," Jennifer said.

Scarlet threw her hands up in surrender. "Got it, thanks." She reached into her bag, grabbed a small jar, and set it on the table.

"I'm going to put Daisy's jar of buttons up for sale on eBay."

"These are them?" Mary Theresa gasped, peering through the thick glass.

"Yes. But first I want each of us to have one in honor of our class, our friendship, and all that patternless sewing has taught us." Scarlet twisted off the lid and passed the jar around so each woman could choose a button.

"If this jar sells for as much as Rosa said, it was meant for me to go on my trip."

"And if it doesn't?" Jennifer asked.

"In honor of Marco—who, by the way, wants nothing to do with me anymore—I'll take it as a sign that the pairing of Johnny Scissors and Scarlet Santana was not meant to be and . . . I'll give up."

The New Year has come and gone, Rosa. It's time to go back to New York, per our agreement," Joseph said. "Don't even consider trying to talk us out of it."

Rosa's first instinct was to smack his arm, but she didn't have the energy so she stuck out her tongue instead. "I'm aware of that. Can I finish this meeting first?"

Joseph and the two other men in the room chuckled. "Of course."

"All right, Rosa. Let's get down to business. I understand that terminal cancer takes its toll on the body and mind," Rosa's lawyer, Brandon Jarvis, said. "But I seriously recommend you take time to really examine your reasoning for this request—and the consequences it will bring to your family."

"My family is dead as far as I'm concerned," Rosa chided, tightening her emerald taffeta robe across her chest.

Mr. Jarvis looked toward Joseph and Rosa's doctor, Marvin Mercado, for help. They shrugged. They both knew once Rosa made up her mind, no one could change it.

"Technically, not," Mr. Jarvis said, scratching his ear, the same way he did with all his difficult clients.

"It doesn't make a difference," Rosa replied, raising her sore voice. "I didn't want it to happen like this, but I have to preserve this company so it will carry on for at least five more decades. My contracts are sealed like cement. This is my life, my death, my will. Not yours or anyone else's. Joseph has the amended paperwork, and I want it implemented today. If you refuse, you're fired."

Joseph placed his hand on Rosa's shoulders and handed the papers to Mr. Jarvis, who took them and speed-read them page by page. "Your wish is my command, Ms. Garcia, you know that. You've made me sprout many a gray hair over the years, but I always come through in your best interest." He flipped to the last page and staggered a bit. "Wow. This is like a plot twist in a film, but I'll follow through. If you change your mind, I'm on your speed dial."

"I appreciate that, thank you, Mr. Jarvis. The pleasure is all mine," Rosa said. "And please note the embargo date and the details surrounding it."

"Noted," Mr. Jarvis said, already highlighting various areas of the packet.

"Rosa, we need to increase your treatments immediately. We need to get you back home to New York," said Dr. Mercado.

Rosa swallowed hard and nodded. "I know. I'll need a few days to settle things here, say my good-byes, you know."

Joseph sat at the edge of her bed and took her hand. "We have a car out front to take you now; it can't wait. Especially if you want to fulfill—"

"OK! OK! Joseph, will you stay behind and stitch up the loose ends?" she said, motioning her hands in circles above her head. "Please tell them I'll be in touch."

*   *   *

At the same time, in another part of the city, clustered in front of Mary Theresa's small laptop, Scarlet and her patternless sewing class—minus Rosa but plus Rocky and Lucy—chewed their nails in suspense.

Last Monday night, Scarlet had scripted a press release to announce the upcoming one-day eBay auction of "Authentic Jar of Buttons Owned by Carmen Miranda and Daisy de la Flora."

Reserve bid, $8,000, per Olivia's instruction.

That's too much! Scarlet worried. But it was a tad more than what she needed to cover her expenses—and refund her students' money, even though they said they wouldn't take it. All five women had helped Scarlet craft the description and choose the best photos for the auction. After completing the online forms, they all placed their hands on the mouse to click Confirm.

"Wait!" Scarlet said. Her ruffled teal scarf framed her chin as she looked upward. "Daisy, wherever you are right now in the world, if you can hear or feel me—I'm handing this over to you. If it is meant to be, the reserve will be met, if not, I'll let it go. I'll still love you."

"OK, now!" Scarlet said to the group.

"Wait!" Olivia hollered, holding up her hands. She looked up too. "Dear Lord, work your will for Scarlet."

Scarlet giggled. "Anyone else?" When no one replied, she pointed her finger. "Now!"

They all clicked the button and then sat back to watch. After a few minutes of no action, Mary Theresa went into her kitchen and prepared a big bowl of popcorn.

Jennifer and Stephanie clicked on the Refresh button every minute, and when they became bored, they taught Rocky and Lucy how to take over. A few minutes later they came back in the room with a game system. Jennifer plugged it into the TV.

"Do you mind if we set up Guitar Hero?" Stephanie asked Mary Theresa.

"Go right ahead; my home is your home. Have fun," she replied.

Scarlet sucked in a deep breath and plopped down on Mary Theresa's giant couch, ignoring the action around her. In the same dress that she wore on her first date with Marco, she crossed her legs and let her mind take a tour through their relationship. Not just the last few weeks, but all the way back to the first day she discovered Vega's Vicious Vinyl and bought a 45 of Pérez Prado's "Cherry Pink (And Apple Blossom White)" for one dollar. Marco told her it was the first sale, so she kissed the bill and handed it over and introduced herself. She thought about the conversation he had with her father.

"Why don't you call him?" Mary Theresa said. "You can go in the other room if you like."

Scarlet stood up. "I think I'll do that." She walked to the kitchen, picked up the phone on the counter, and dialed. Two rings passed and she tapped the plastic on the handset, tempted to hang up.

And then the ringing ceased. Her breath stopped and her eyes filled with tears that had been waiting for weeks to come out. Right as she was about to say "Hi, Dad," she heard: "You've reached the Santana residence. We can't take your call right now, but please leave a message at the beep."

"Mom, Dad, it's me. Just calling to let you guys know I love you. Talk to you soon...."

Scarlet didn't have a chance to say much else. The shouts and hollers coming from the other room distracted her. She hung up and raced out to see what all the commotion was about.

"We got a bidder!" Olivia said, throwing her hands up in the air. "Scarlet—Daisy answered you! You're going to the Big Apple!"

26

Scarlet nervously hummed as she sat in her Mercedes and checked her hair in the rearview mirror. After spending three hours morphing it from a side part with Veronica Lake finger waves to a Natalie Wood '60s flip bob, she finally settled on a four-inch-high curly updo, complete with a fresh daisy behind her ear.

She never expected a send-off party, much less that her jar of buttons would end up selling for $24,000 dollars to an anonymous collector. By the end of the online auction, three bidders had waged a sniping war until the last second. Hoping the good news would break the ice with Marco, she sent him two texts. The first one about the auction, he replied to with a polite "Congrats!" and the second, to invite him to the party, he didn't reply to at all.

Mary Theresa and Olivia spent the week after the auction organizing the shebang. Stephanie wrote a snappy press release as extra credit in her marketing class and blanketed the local media. Scarlet didn't expect any reporters to bite, but the coupling of the auction with being the first Arizonan to break into the Johnny Scissors program qualified as a top local news story.

Scarlet made the rounds all week on local morning shows

and afternoon radio to share her story about her roller-coaster ride to triumph. Carly even called and offered to sit in on interviews with Scarlet to talk about how wonderful she was at her former job. Scarlet didn't bother to reply to her message.

Despite the publicity, Scarlet only expected a small crowd of her local followers and, of course, her family. She tossed her lipstick into her purse and climbed out of the car. She shut the door with a swing of her hip and used one hand to tighten her coat's patent-leather belt and the other hand to lift her cell and thumb-dial her sister, Eliza.

Between the voice-mail apology Scarlet left on her parents' answering machine and another message about the good news of the auction, she knew they'd come. If anything, her dad had to be impressed at the $24,000 she made in one night from the buttons. Tonight they would all hug it out and wipe the slate clean.

"Hi, Sis!"' Scarlet said cheerfully when Eliza answered. "I saved tickets for all of you; they're at the will-call window. I hope you guys are ready to dance. There's a super groovy blues band performing!"

A thick pause followed.

"Oh, hey Scar," Eliza replied.

Scarlet curled in her lips. She knew what would come next.

"But, uh, sorry, we won't be able to make it tonight."

"Eliza, you guys *have* to come, this is a *big* deal for me, I was even on the news promoting it. Didn't anyone see?"

"Charles is in Seattle for his job this week. And Mom has been so stressed out that Dad took her to Hawaii for a New Year's vacation. They'll be back tomorrow. Not that you would know, since you haven't talked to them in weeks."

Eliza and her guilt trips, Scarlet thought as she began to pace in the empty parking space next to her.

"You're the one who told me to stay away! Plus, I've been a

little busy over here," she said. "Not that you would know, since you nor any other Santana have ever taken an interest in my life. I thought maybe this one time…"

"The rest of us work regular jobs, Scar. I only see the evening news. Sorry I missed it. You should have called to let me know the exact details, I would have recorded it. Congratulations, though. Glad to see it all worked out."

Scarlet walked around to the front of her car and rested her backside against the hood. "What are you doing tonight that you can't come? The club is only fifteen minutes from your house. You don't have to stay all night. I'll feel stupid if not even one of my family members is here."

"There's no way," said Eliza. "Damon's boss is a finalist at his work's sumo wrestling challenge. We're going to cheer him on because Damon's up for the head of the East Coast division next month. We're trying to get on management's good side. We really need the money from the promotion."

"Let me get this straight," Scarlet said, scratching her head with her gloved hand. "You're missing your only sister's going-away party to watch your husband's boss fight in a fat suit? What do you need the money for? Another Escalade? I leave for New York in two days. I won't be back for months."

"God, Scarlet, you should have been the middle child," Eliza snipped. "Mom and Dad plan to visit you there. Do you know I'm about to get fired? I can't afford to lose another job. Things are hard. We sold the SUVs; now we're looking to sell the house."

Scarlet stood up. "Oh, shit, Eliza, I had no idea. I'm sorry. Does anyone know?"

"I've been keeping it a secret, hoping for a miracle," she said, trying not to cry. "You think you're the only one who has wanted to make Mom and Dad proud? At least you have a talent. Math and design come easy to you and Charles, but not to me. All I've ever wanted was to be like you two. But today my boss told me I don't have what it takes to be an engineer, and I know she's right."

"You should have asked us for help," said Scarlet.

"I've tried, but no one takes me seriously. Dad spends all his time worrying about you. Do you know every night he is Googling Johnny Scissors to get more information?"

"Really, he does? Well...if he overlooks you, it's because you make your life seem perfect," Scarlet said. "They're only concerned about me because they think I'm a flake."

"I'm going to come clean," Eliza said. "I do read your blog. Mom does too. And it hurts us that you devote more time to helping strangers than you do to your own family. And if we dare say anything, you get defensive and think we are bringing you down."

Marco's words rang in Scarlet's mind. Was he right about her cutting them off, instead of the other way around?

"I'm sorry, Eliza, really. Is there anything I can do to help? Just tell me; I'll do whatever I can."

"You already are helping...by leaving," said Eliza. "I don't mean to sound rude, but maybe now Dad will have more time for me. I was going to wait until next week after you're settled in over there, to talk to him. He's so good at stuff like this. If anyone can help me figure it out, it's him."

So many scrambled thoughts filled Scarlet's head. She didn't have a clue what to say. After a moment, Eliza cleared her throat. "By the way," she said. "Dad asked me to tell you that he and Mom want to take you to the airport tomorrow."

"OK, cool..."

"You still there, Scarlet?"

"Yeah...I'm here, just taking all this in. I wish we could have talked about it sooner."

"You never had the time."

"I know, I'm sorry I haven't been there. I wish I could give you a big bear hug of support right now." Childhood memories popped up of when the girls used to share a double bed. They often chattered so loud, their mom would holler from the hallway for them to stop. "Hey, remember when we were kids and used to tell each other everything? We still can. Call me, OK? I promise to drop what I'm doing and talk. Like old times. And I have extra money if you need it!"

"Thanks," said Eliza. "I'll be fine. We all want you to focus on the Johnny Scissors school. Whether you know it or not, we're all cheering for you with glittery signs...."

The women said their good-byes and hung up. Even though her family had valid reasons for not being there and it felt good to have a mini-breakthrough with Eliza, Scarlet couldn't chase away the disappointment that lingered inside. It wasn't even about the party or her trip anymore. She missed her family.

As she started walking across the parking lot toward the club entrance, she heard the large squeaky brakes of a minibus. No... a van. Dial-A-Ride.

Scarlet wasn't the only person outside the club to stop and stare at the van. The creaky doors slid open as the driver hopped out and ran around to set out a footstool.

"Rosa?" Scarlet said under her breath, hoping for a miracle. Joseph had called the other day to say thank you for the cards and treats she and the other sewing group members had left on their doorstep. He also informed Scarlet that Rosa had to leave town indefinitely due to a family matter back home. Could Rosa have heard about the button auction and decided to surprise them?

From the side of the doors of the van, Scarlet watched as two chunky wheels, attached to a shiny red walker dotted with crystals, emerged. Scarlet gasped. She knew that walker—she was the one who'd blinged it out!

"Nana Eleanor!" Scarlet squealed as she darted to the van to help her grandmother climb safely down from the vehicle. Behind her were five other friends, all in walkers as well. "You took Dial-A-Ride all the way from Glendale, Nana? Why didn't you call me?"

Nana Eleanor stepped to the ground and stuffed a folded dollar in the driver's pocket. Her friends repeated the gesture. "Thank you, young man, there'll be more of that if you pick us up in an hour."

"No, don't worry," Scarlet assured him, "I'll make sure they get home. Thank you for bringing her!"

Scarlet hugged and kissed her nana and then swung around to wave good-bye to the driver. When she looked back, Nana Eleanor and her elderly entourage had already wheeled their way to the club's concrete entrance. Scarlet caught up. "I feel so awful that no one drove you here!"

"Oh, mija, I called you this week but when I didn't hear back, I figured you were busy getting ready."

Scarlet's stomach flipped from a lightning bolt of guilt. All this time she had been whining about her family not supporting her, when Nana Eleanor had been her number-one cheerleader since Scarlet had picked up her first spool of thread. As Scarlet's gaze made contact with her nana's deep-set, espresso eyes, Scarlet thanked God she did not sell any of her grandmother's precious belongings, including the car.

"I saw you on the news, mija!" Nana Eleanor said, gripping the black rubber handles to her walker. "There I was, holding the winning hand of gin rummy when all of a sudden I heard the beautiful voice of my youngest granddaughter shoot down from the TV set into my hearing aids. I got right up from my chair and pointed at the screen for everyone to see. 'That's my granddaughter!' I shouted. And it just so happened I was wearing the pretty sweater you made me for my birthday...."

Scarlet covered her hand with her mouth as tears welled up in her eyes. "Nana, I love you...."

"Hold on, permítame terminar...let me finish. Well, everyone found out. I haven't seen news travel that fast since Mr. Cuttlebug was caught in the sack with those cleaning-lady twins. From the rec room to the beauty shop and then the coffee area...we all gathered around to watch you. Mija, I'd like you to meet my friends from the resort: Mundo, Tencha, Reymundo, Isabel, and Gordo...we're your biggest fans!"

Scarlet doubled over with laughter and introduced herself to each of her nana's friends and hugged them. She graciously welcomed them to her party, then led them up to the ticket window to retrieve the family passes. The ticket clerk handed them over and Scarlet approached the front door to the club, her nana and friends in tow. The buff African American bouncer in the tight black T-shirt winked at Scarlet. "We've been waiting for you, Scarlet. Welcome to your send-off."

He opened the tall black-leather-covered double doors to reveal scores of women and men from all backgrounds and ages cheering as Scarlet passed the threshold. Mary Theresa and Olivia were there to greet her first.

Scarlet's nerves finally subsided.

"People came!" Scarlet shouted to her nana.

"Of course," Nana Eleanor hollered back. "To hell with Daisy de la Flora; here comes my granddaughter, Scarlet Santana!"

*   *   *

Two hours later, Scarlet returned to the club after dropping Nana Eleanor and her friends off at the retirement resort. For having silver hair and false teeth, they sure knew how to party. Her nana's friend Thencha even brought a batch of bubble wands and handed them out to the other guests. And Gordo fell in love with the velvety voice and plus-size juiciness of lead singer Candye Kane—so much that he even stalked her during the break and flirted with her until she signed his walker.

For the next hour, Scarlet cut loose on the dance floor with Olivia and Mary Theresa.

What a way to end the night! This is how a girl goes out in style! Scarlet thought. By midnight the crowd had thinned out, but the dance floor remained packed thanks to Candye Kane's finger-snapping, shoulder-shimmeying, hip-swiveling swing and blues tunes.

By one a.m., Candye finished up her last song of the third set, "Superhero," and Olivia and Mary Theresa twirled off the dance floor and dropped their achy bodies next to Scarlet, who relaxed in a red padded banquet chair.

"I haven't danced since high school!" Mary Theresa blurted, slightly tipsy from a recent margarita on the rocks.

Olivia squished the side of her sweaty face in disbelief. "You've got to be kidding. That's wrong, Maresa—wrong, wrong... incorrect with a capital *I*."

Mary Theresa let her body fall back limp on the seat next to Scarlet, her arms and legs sprawled to each corner. She blinked a few times, chuckled, and then unleashed rolls of uncontrollable laughs. "You called me Maresa—get it? Mary Theresa... Maresa! Ha! My mother would flip!" Mary Theresa sat up straight and imitated a robot. "I am. Mary. Theresa. Or... I am Maresa!" she said, snapping her fingers across her face like a diva. "I like Maresa. She'll be my sneaky alter ego. Olivia, gracias!"

"De nada!" Olivia said.

Scarlet held out her hand and read off the list. "It's the giggle water, the sexy red dress you made—and Daisy's boots, of course. You're transforming from the tame Mary Theresa into rowdy Maresa before our eyes!"

Mary Theresa patted her red face with a damp cocktail napkin, called the waitress over, and asked for a club soda with lime and a glass of water. "Oh, I needed tonight. Great party, Miss Scarlet. I had *fun*. F-U-N... fun. This is the first time I rose from the sidelines and actually partook in what I normally dismissed as silly and impractical."

Scarlet straightened up in her chair. "You need to do it more often. Dancing and cutting loose, they are stress busters. You should bring Hadley! They have the best live bands—blues, swing, R&B, reggae, rockabilly, even jazz. Surprise him."

The corner of Mary Theresa's mouth curved up in a bashful way. "I don't know. Yesterday he told me that he can't return home for a visit until the week after next. We've been talking for two hours before we go to bed. I feel like we're dating, not married. I don't know if he's being a tease or if he truly is stuck at work. It would be fine if I didn't... oh, I don't know what I'm saying. I'm not my clear-thinking self tonight."

"If you didn't miss him?" Scarlet asked, dragging her chair next to hers.

"Yeah," Mary Theresa replied. "And I hate that. All of this would be so much easier if I didn't still love him. We could make a clean split, share the kids, and go on with our lives. Sometimes I wonder if I'd be doing him and the kids a favor if I asked for a divorce."

"No way. Listen, little bird, I've witnessed you cry your soul out over him. This has nothing to do with your marriage or your kids or your family. It has to do with reigniting the flame."

"Oh, I don't know...," Mary Theresa replied. "I feel like I'm being graded; I'm on thin ice. I feel like if I stay perfectly still, he'll come back, and our lives will continue as if this glitch never happened. I don't want to rock the boat."

Olivia and Scarlet exchanged negative head nods and said in unison, "Rock the boat!"

"Mary Theresa," Olivia started, "do you want for your relationship to continue the way it was? We'll never forget the first day of class when you were stiffer than a broomstick. Life is too short to live like that, believe me. Plus, you're glowin' tonight. You could pass for Sandra Bullock right now in that dress and the bod you got. You've come a long way from that woman with the siren cell phone in her pants."

Mary Theresa couldn't argue; she thought about that day often. "I really have. Hey, not to change the subject, but you'll never believe what I've been doing these past two weeks—sewing! I bought a stack of vintage patterns at a new antiques shop in my neighborhood. I've made all kinds of spring ensembles for Lucy and Rocky, except I followed Miss Scarlet's rule of thumb and added a special signature touch that is all mine...."

Scarlet whistled. "Meanwhile, back at the ranch..."

Mary Theresa crossed her leg and bounced it up and down, clearly uncomfortable that her marriage was back to being the focus of the discussion. "So, what do you suppose I do?"

"Surprise him with a visit in Palm Springs," Scarlet said. "Show up in this dress you're wearing—get it dry cleaned first— and the boots. Tell him you want to make him custom clothing and measure him around the chest, waist, and hips using your arms and hands. Let *Maresa* do the steering."

Mary Theresa slouched and tried to hold back a naughty grin. It would be the craziest trick she ever pulled, but she couldn't wait to try. "I'll do it."

"Now we're talkin'," Olivia cheered. "Go get your hombre and bring him home!"

DaisyForever.com
magical musings about love, beauty & fashion
inspired by the life of Daisy de la Flora
as told by Miss Scarlet Santana

Saturday, January 14, 6:49 p.m.

Scarlet does New York

Hola, you vintage-loving vixens...three guesses what is on the front burner today. Oh, let's just get to the headline; my heels are on fire over here! Tomorrow at 6:45 a.m., I'm hopping on a plane to New York City for three glorious months of the Johnny Scissors Emerging Designers Program!

In my new life, I'll be living among twelve of America's most promising emerging designers in the penthouse of House of Tijeras.

And even more exiting, I'll be sewing in the famous student sewing center that Daisy designed many decades ago. Honestly, they could put me in an upright cot in the broom closet and I'd give thanks. I've waited so long for this!

Well, my lovey-lovelies, my blog posts for the next three months will be slimmer than Spanx, as all of my energy will be aimed like a can of whipped cream at the delicious sundae that is my program. But I do have my iPhone and you know I'll be doing the snap 'n post thing.

I'm wishing all of you love and prosperity for this New Year—I wish you many little victories!

Yours in sequins,

Miss Scarlet

P.S. Kamikaze kudos to those of you who donated to mi causa, but I'll be returning all your $$$.

27

Scarlet ended her first day as a temporary New Yorker by cuddling in bed and saying an earnest prayer for her family and her patternless sewing students—most of all, Rosa, wherever she was. Scarlet then fell back in bed and blinked several times before reaching for her iPhone. She took a deep breath and punched in a message to Marco.

Are we OK? I miss you. A lot. Thinking of that Sam Cooke song you put on my playlist...
Nothin' can ever change this love I have for you...
—XO, Scar

*   *   *

The next morning when her alarm rang, Scarlet's eyelids opened and she searched for her iPhone to see if Marco had answered. She had waited several minutes, but must have drifted to sleep. Pressing the phone to her chest, she gulped and peeked at the screen.

miss you too. thought about what you said to me in the car. time for me to rip some seams too. wishing you the best because you deserve it. love, m.

Scarlet sighed as she read it and sat up on the lumpy mattress that would be her bed for the next few months. Setting the phone on the chipped gray nightstand, her body shivered from the cold. The overbearing scent of Lysol dominated her tiny matchbox of a room. Scarlet hadn't lived in conditions like these since her early college days.

She hated to admit it, but so far Marco's gut feeling had been correct. When she'd arrived yesterday and met with the other interns in the main entrance of House of Tijeras, they were greeted by Louisa, the program coordinator. After a round of informal introductions, Louisa politely explained that the date wasn't the only change made to the program.

"Due to budget cuts beyond our control," she said, "we've had to rent out the penthouse and move the student quarters to a nearby facility."

Louisa instructed them to gather up their luggage and follow her all the way through the giant complex. The twelve up-and-coming designers were then led across the street to the subway terminal where they were given maps to take the train to Harlem to a YMCA dormitory.

Little did they know that that dormitory was only the beginning of the disappointments to come.

*   *   *

On the first official day, the group sat through a two-hour orientation about the history of Casa de la Flora. Scarlet appreciated the slideshow, but it took all her might not to raise her hand and "fill in" some of the spotty history about Daisy's career. It also bothered her that only fifteen minutes of the orientation focused on Daisy, the rest on Johnny Scissors.

After the orientation, the students grabbed a quick lunch in the cafeteria. Scarlet scanned the offerings behind the smudged buffet glass and searched for the best of the worst. Just as she reached for a soggy salad, someone tapped her arm.

"Leave it," said the guy standing behind her in line. "Don't eat anything here that isn't prepackaged." Scarlet ducked and wormed her way out of line and bought a cup of Yoplait.

All she wanted was to get on with the day, because a tour of the 15,000-square-foot building was to come after their meal. At least that didn't disappoint. The place made Carly's look like a Circle K. Scarlet felt like little Charlie Bucket wandering through Willy Wonka's chocolate factory. She watched every step to ensure she didn't fall into any chenille rivers or eat any candy-colored ribbons. She kept her hands to herself and processed every morsel of detail.

They paraded through the fabrication shop, then wandered about the materials center, as well as the sketch lab, design studio, and fitting room. When they reached the Johnny Scissors runway on the tenth floor, everyone took turns impersonating his or her favorite supermodel. Except Scarlet. She had already started to think of new dress ideas. It had been a while since her mechanical pencil touched her sketchpad, and before she knew it, she had cranked out two gowns and a pantsuit.

Still sketching, she pressed on, last in the group. Her favorite floors had to be those with the libraries and galleries—thousands of books, magazines, slides, picture files, and even Daisy collectibles. Their first assignment involved a research and essay project about each student's muse, the specific inspiration, and how they applied it in a tangible form to their own work.

*   *   *

The next days were all about production; very similar to the work she performed at Carly's. Some students were downright divas about sweeping up the loose threads or winding dozens and dozens of bobbins. Scarlet, however, considered it a way of paying her dues. Johnny Scissors likely wanted his students to appreciate all levels of fashion design.

At the end of Friday's class, Scarlet felt more drained than if she'd worked a sixteen-hour shift at Auntie Linda's quince shop. Completely exhausted, Scarlet rolled over on her bed, aimed the remote at the twelve-inch plasma screen TV, and pressed the On button. When the remote refused to cooperate, she crawled off the mattress and tripped on a box on the floor.

"My box!" Scarlet forgot that her mother had sent a gift box of her famous "Juicy Jeane" handmade sachets. The mail clerk had delivered it Thursday, but Scarlet didn't have time to open it. She used the tip of her pinkie nail and sliced open the tape to find a set of pretty fabric pillows that smelled of fresh gardenias, roses, and cherry blossoms. A little bit of home—just what Scarlet needed. At the bottom of the box sat a book and card sealed inside a Ziploc bag. She opened the bag and slid out the tattered pink book—her first fashion sketchpad. She thought it had been tossed out years ago.

A picture reel of past events played in her mind as she lovingly traced her hands over the ink-drawn figures on the cover. She then flipped through page after page of sketches. Scarlet could see the raw shape of what would later become her Mexibilly Frock collection.

Scarlet grabbed the card and read it.

Honey,

After we dropped you off at the airport, I went home and rummaged through my memory chest. I hope you are as pleased as I am that I found your first sketchbook. I think back to your days in grade school and the colorful outfits you

used to put together. I remember every Halloween, how we searched through patterns at the fabric store so you could make your own costume. And prom and homecoming... you didn't only make your dress, you made all your friends' dresses as well! I only wish I had noticed and respected your talents back then. Your father and I stayed up late talking last night and we agree you were right. We should have enrolled you in fashion club instead of math camp!

I hope the designs within these pages bring you joy, success, and empowerment (as if you don't already have enough!).

Nana Eleanor told all of us about your wonderful party. I'm so sad we were not there to celebrate with you. When you come home, be ready for a fiesta here at the house. Eliza and Charles send their love. Your father set up that video conferencing thing on our computer, just like you have, so we can see you when you call us.

Sweetie, I apologize if I ever lent the impression that I doubted your vision and life plan. The shine and confidence on your face as you said good-bye to us at the airport assured me that you are a compassionate and creative woman who isn't afraid to go after her dream.

I am proud to be your mother, Scarlet.

Love,
Mom

P.S. Gracias mija for the heads-up on Eliza.
P.P.S. Guess what? Mary Theresa is giving me sewing lessons and Nana Eleanor is very jealous!
P.P.P.S. Please send pictures of that pretty penthouse you are living in!

Scarlet inserted the card back in the envelope and decided she wanted to sew. Five days had passed, and she hadn't pricked a stitch. The more she thought about it, the more she wanted to check out the famed student sewing center, so she rushed to apply a fresh coat of makeup, changed into a pair of tight cuffed jeans and a lilac ribbed-front cardigan blouse she'd knitted last summer, and smoothed down her forties war-time updo. Right before she left her room, she kicked off her white Keds and slipped into four-inch-high Daisy-inspired painted platform sandals and secured a matching comb in her hair.

Scarlet scooped up her decorated sewing basket and jumped in a cab downtown. When she arrived at House of Tijeras, she headed to the front office to ask about driving an official Johnny Scissors sewing machine. The receptionist rang an assistant, who led Scarlet to the elevators.

"Hey, you're the one who warned me about the cafeteria food the other day. Hi, I'm Scarlet Santana. How long have you worked here?" Scarlet asked as they stepped in.

"I'm Ronnie. Couple of years," he replied. "They moved the sewing room to the eighth floor. Budget cuts."

"Darn," Scarlet said. "That's fine. So, how do you like your job? It must be exciting!"

"Not really." He shrugged. "I'm an assistant to the reception-ist. My job is to escort guests to their proper floor. Been doing it for three years now, hoping to move up someday. Are you a new employee?"

Scarlet straightened her posture. "I'm here for the final Johnny Scissors Emerging Designer Program."

"Good luck with *that*," he mumbled.

"You're lighting up the tilt sign there, mister man. Stop feeding me a fib, and spill," Scarlet said forcefully.

Bing! The elevator doors opened. Scarlet lunged for the Close Door button.

"Fine. I went through the program too," said Ronnie. "I used to have it made in Austin before I came here. I had my own studio and line, models. The whole Texas-sized waffle. But I had to stay here to pay off my debt."

"Your tuition?"

"No, I'm talking about the bill they hand you on your last day." Ronnie stepped closer to Scarlet, lowered his voice to a whisper, and pretended to check the time on his watch. "I hope you read the fine print on your contract. You get charged for wear and tear on the supplies, the machinery—all of it. And you know that business about him mentoring the students? I heard that for this class it's by DVD, and you'll get charged for it."

Scarlet clenched the handles of her sewing basket. "That's not right. Maybe I'll request an appointment with Johnny; if he is anything like Daisy, the happiness of his employees is crucial to the success of the operation," she said.

"That must be why this company is going down. I hear a big overhaul is coming this summer. Johnny Scissors is supposedly waiting for his aunt to keel over so he can cash all this in. I've said too much already; this place has cameras and microphones everywhere."

Ronnie pressed the Open button to find the one and only Johnny Scissors standing outside the elevator doors. Both Scarlet and Ronnie recoiled in fear and darted their eyes to opposite directions, as if Medusa and her head of hissing snakes had just materialized in front of them. Scarlet squirmed and slowly scanned Johnny from the feet up: Hermès black leather cap-toe Oxford shoes, Canali black striped wool two-button suit jacket and trousers, a thick head of black hair slicked back. Johnny Scissors lived up to his flashy reputation.

"What? Is there a problem with the lift?" Johnny asked.

"No, sir, just showing her around, she's one of the new students in the JSED program," Ronnie replied, staring only at Johnny's silver dotted necktie. "Here you go, Miss Santana, eighth floor, the student sewing center."

Scarlet stepped out of the elevator and Ronnie the assistant gestured for Johnny to enter. Johnny clasped his palms in front of his waist, intensely eyeing Scarlet up and down and side-to-side.

"Go without me," Johnny said. "I'm going to chat with our new flame-haired Dita Von Teese in training."

Scarlet inhaled and wished she had dressed up instead of tossing on the lazy jeans. Of all clothing to meet *the* Johnny Scissors in!

He motioned with his finger for her to follow him down a long, ceramic-tiled hallway lined with oversized framed pictures of Johnny posing stiffly with celebrities throughout the years: Tom Cruise, Drew Barrymore, Heidi Klum, and dozens of others. More images hung on the walls of all the other floors too.

"Interesting shoes. Did you paint those yourself?" he asked.

Scarlet posed sideways and lightly kicked one up behind her back. "I did, and the matching hair comb, see?" She lowered her head as she tried to keep up with his fast stride.

"Are they a one-time project, special for the occasion?"

"No, I'm Daisy's long lost granddaughter; I inherited all her talent!" Scarlet joked.

Johnny came to a halt. "What did you say?"

"Um...in spirit! I'm a huge devotee of Daisy's. I collect her pieces. She's the reason I want to become a fashion designer."

"What's your name?"

"Scarlet."

"To be honest, Scarlet, we hear that a lot around here. Students pimp out my aunt because they think it will win me over."

"Not me! I mean, yes I'd like to win you over, but with my work, not because of my passion for Daisy. I'm as serious as grease on silk when it comes to my love for Daisy de la Flora. I even have a website dedicated to her."

"Oooh, so you're the one with the website... nice to meet you, Scarlet," Johnny said, holding out his hand to shake. "Funny we should connect this way. My team is going to be calling you in soon; we have an event we want to use you for."

"The fiftieth-anniversary celebration of Daisy's career at the Met's Costume Institute?" Scarlet asked. "I helped fact-check Daisy's life for the *Fashion Faire Weekly* article that just came out."

"You really are on top of the news, aren't you? Yes, that's the event. Well, Scarlet, here is the student sewing center; enjoy it. I look forward to talking again, checking out your designs and such."

"Thank you, Mr. Tijeras, I swear I won't disappoint."

Johnny Scissors waved good-bye to Scarlet as she raised her shoulder and winked at him and entered the sewing room. She chose the first machine that she spotted, right in the center of the room, unpacked her supplies, and worked on a dress project she hadn't touched in a month.

She popped in her earbuds and stitched away, never noticing that Johnny lingered just outside the door. He then punched the button on the Bluetooth device in his ear.

"Bring me up to speed on Scarlet Santana first thing tomorrow morning."

28

On the other side of the country, the taxi driver slammed the car's trunk after he unloaded Mary Theresa's black overnight bag and set it on the entryway of the Palm Springs Sanctuary Hotel & Spa.

He's cute and he's checking me out, she thought as she combed a piece of her flat-ironed hair behind her ear and held out a folded twenty-dollar bill between her freshly manicured nails. She raised an eyebrow and flirted with her eyes, just like Tyra Banks.

In the spirit of Olivia, Mary Theresa considered herself quite the hottie today. She had set up a sewing area in the family room and used her dress form to stitch a new outfit for her romantic getaway: a beige jersey knit wrap dress that hugged and draped the most flattering points of her trim figure. She'd never sported a plunging neckline in daylight before...or ever, for that matter, but today she worked it. The flowy hem hit just above her knee and she capped the ensemble with a tall set of zebra striped peep-toe platforms Scarlet had given her for good luck.

Me, Mary Theresa, in zebra-striped peep-toes? If only my employees could see this! So this is what beautiful, smart, healthy, and adventurous feels like, Mary Theresa thought with a laugh on the taxi ride to the hotel.

Maybe winning the affection of a random stranger was a sign she could win back the heart of her husband. That was her mission. Hadley wasn't supposed to return home for a few weeks, but on the advice of Olivia and Scarlet, Mary Theresa planned to "drop in." What better way to prove how spontaneous she'd become than to surprise Hadley with a Saturday brunch?

Before she left for the trip, Mary Theresa practiced Scarlet's—or rather, Daisy's—Little Victories exercise. No fancy paper or embellishments, just accomplishments scribbled on index cards:

1. Quality time with her children. She recently discovered this meant eating the icing before the cake has been frosted; pillow fights after bedtime, mismatched socks to save time. And her all-time favorite: kisses on her cheeks while she read Rocky and Lucy their bedtime story.

2. Eating realistically. She now focused on the experience of family meals rather than the entrees. But she did plan to take a cooking class.

3. Being honest with those she loved and, most important, with herself. No more covering the truth for appearance's sake.

4. Work. She still worked for DelTran Computronics part-time from home, but serendipitously fell into the world of sewing. After making play clothes for Rocky and Lucy from vintage patterns she bought at the antiques store, she graduated to designing her own versions and even ventured into pattern-making. Mary Theresa was so sure of her new calling, she applied for a business license so she could sell at art fairs, co-ops, and in online stores.

5. Lastly—her marriage. Mary Theresa would learn to elongate the best moments to appreciate her husband. After

all, he shaped her children into loving, adorable little
people she adored.

Those were her five little victories, and they all had taken
place in the past two months. After Mary Theresa penned her
cards, she decided to deviate from Scarlet's plan. Instead of
burning them, she would read them to Hadley.

She prayed her next little victory would happen tonight.
Mary Theresa had wished on Rocky's lucky rabbit foot keychain
earlier that morning that she would reconcile with her husband
and bring him home. Not by force or guilt, but by the power of
100 percent unconditional love.

The taxi pulled away down the resort's cobbled driveway.
Mary Theresa gripped her rolling overnight bag and boldly
crossed the entrance of the Sanctuary Hotel & Spa.

*   *   *

That same Saturday, Johnny Scissors ordered his maid to fix
him a double bourbon in a rock glass. He finished reading the
new issue of *Entertainment Weekly* and slowly made his way to
the office at the other end of his 2,000-square-foot penthouse.

"Sorry to keep you all waiting, I think best after a good
sweat," he said to the roomful of managers, lawyers, creative
directors, and his marketing and public relations staff. He could
smell the stench of annoyance, but didn't let it affect his mood.
Not one bit. "I met Scarlet Santana yesterday. Before I take her
to the Met event next week, I need to know more. What does
she have to offer us?"

The lights dimmed, and at the front of the room the walls
parted to reveal a large projection screen. Johnny had asked his
staff to compile a complete profile and they did not fail.

Lousia Brandt, director of the Johnny Scissors Emerging

Designers Program, stood at the front of the room, holding a remote. She clicked it and Scarlet's website appeared from one side of the screen to the other.

The slideshow included pictures of Scarlet, her dresses, quotes, and sample posts from her blog. Every post was followed by a multitude of comments cheering her on.

"When our staff initially found out about Scarlet and DaisyForever.com, we were amused and thought it would be great publicity for JSED," Louisa said. "But once we measured how valuable her online presence is for the eighteen-to-thirty-six female target market, we knew we had to act fast. Our initial plan was to contact her and invite her to host the site on our servers and through contract negotiations—"

The staff members chuckled as Louisa mimed finger quotes.

"And make her an employee of ours, and thus her blog our property. We drafted an entry-level position to lure her in, but then she applied for JSED and it solved our problem. Now we can say we discovered her."

"Did you charge her tuition?" Johnny asked.

"Of course," Louisa said through a crooked smile.

"Give Louisa a raise for that one." Johnny laughed as he slapped the table. "Scarlet Santana is paying *us* to steal *her* blog. That's how business is done, my friends."

Louisa sped through a few more slides until she came to one showing Scarlet's online store.

"She is also a designer; would you care to see her work?" Louisa asked.

"Not interested," Johnny said. "I think we should take it up a notch and make her the face of our Daisy de la Flora line extension. She's pretty enough to appeal to Eternal 14's demographic. That will seal the deal for us."

"I'll get on that." Louisa nodded.

"And then sell it, so I can be done with it once and for all," Johnny said. "Before I escort her to the Met, I want to take her on a test run. Suit her up for the premiere of that new Eva Alegria flick. I'll take her as my plus-one."

*   *   *

Mary Theresa didn't know whether or not to book a room at the hotel. She hoped to stay in Hadley's, but she didn't want to assume the game would go the way she planned. So she reserved a suite. Regardless of what happened she wanted to indulge in the serene setting of the hotel. And her suite would give her a home base to escape to if things went bad.

No wonder Hadley wasn't in a rush to come home, she thought as she admired the row of tall trees that stretched to the high lobby ceiling. While the front desk clerk checked her in, she picked up a spa brochure and ran her hands over the counter-top's art deco mosaics.

Her suite turned out to be in a private bungalow section away from the main hotel. Her plan was to drop off her suitcase, freshen up, and go to the bar for a drink before calling Hadley's cell. *Why rush?* she thought. After what she had been through in the past months, she deserved pampering.

A massage, pedicure, and shower later, Mary Theresa glided through the main atrium and noticed several businessmen turn to gawk. One of them rose his glass to her, and she let out half a sneaky smile before slipping into the lounge. She spotted a booth framed by two tall marble pillars, offset from the main thoroughfare, and took a seat. Mary Theresa had never been much of a drinker, but the rum punch that a group of college girls was sipping with their dinner salads made her mouth water. So she ordered two, knowing she'd only get through half of one. And with each sip, she felt her face flush. She slowed down because she didn't want to be drunk when she phoned Hadley—just a little breezy.

The first drink went down like Kool-Aid on a summer day. Mary Theresa dried her clammy hands on her dress and exhaled as if to blow on a whistle. She looked out the window of the lounge to see a happy couple and their two children, about the same age as Rocky and Lucy, taking turns going down a giant waterslide, two-by-two, in the indoor pool. She stared until the faces on the gleeful couple morphed into hers and Hadley's. She liked that vision. Without realizing exactly how "breezy" she had become, she stretched out her long, toned arms across the booth and rolled her head along the top of the cushion and let out a "Mmmmm…"

A rash of goosebumps flooded up her legs and arms as she felt someone staring at her. She slowly opened her eyelids to see Hadley, holding a drink in his hand, admiring her from across the room. When their eyes met, he fumbled his glass and almost dropped it.

Mary Theresa sat up straight and stretched her lips into a smile and waved hard at her husband. He picked up his drink and went to the bar to tell the waitress something. Mary Theresa used the spare moment to bend down and check her breath.

"Hi, honey," she said, popping back up to see the businessman from the atrium standing at her table.

"Hi."

Right then, Hadley slid next to her in the booth, so close she could count the stubble on his face. He wrapped his arm around her and pulled her close.

"She's taken, buddy," Hadley said.

Embarrassed, the gentleman apologized to Mary Theresa and then to Hadley. "All the good ones are taken," he joked.

"That's right, they are," Hadley said, turning to his wife.

Mary Theresa reached for her rum punch and took a long sip while she gathered her thoughts. The entire flight over, she worried about what mood she might find Hadley in. Laid back in his usual style, or uptight now that he had a full-time job? And what would he think of her visit? Would he think she was checking in on him—which she wasn't, but she did want to check on *them*. She had to admit, the flirting executive certainly put her in a desirable light.

"Let's try this again—Hi, honey!" she said. "My mom has the kids all weekend, so I thought I'd pop in and surprise you."

For being married to this man for almost ten years, she felt as nervous as a teenager on her first date.

"I'm surprised," he said. "Pleasantly surprised."

She placed her hand on top of his and felt the cold silver of his wedding band. He may have been away in presence, but he had never really left her in spirit.

Hadley's eyes roamed over her from forehead to chin, across her shoulders, and down her long neck to her cleavage. He moved in closer and brushed his nose against hers, first on one side and then the other.

Mary Theresa licked her lips and stared at his. She had forgotten how beautiful and red they were, but she did remember how good they tasted. She almost couldn't catch her breath, but her instincts picked up where her insecurities left off and she opened her mouth next to his. He smiled and stroked her neck before meeting her for a long, loving kiss.

Mary Theresa didn't pull away or make an excuse to stop like she used to. She didn't care that they were sitting in a public place, or whether Hadley was on the clock. She had his full, undivided attention and was not about to cut it short. Hadley was the first to separate his lips from hers.

"Does this mean you missed me?" he asked.

"It's been a long nine weeks," she whispered, skimming her fingers around his ear and then his hairline. "Love the buzz cut. It's sexy."

"I love seeing your long hair again."

"I like my long hair too," she said. "I've been wearing it down lately."

He kissed her again, longer, until she squirmed from anticipation. "Come on, let's go. I have a bungalow suite, you'll love it."

She downed the last of her second rum punch, bit the pineapple slice, and stuffed it inside the tall hurricane glass. "You'll have to show me more than that; I rented a bungalow suite on my own."

"I think that can be arranged," Hadley said, sliding out of the booth and holding out his hand for Mary Theresa. She took it, stood up, and straightened her dress while he lifted her hand above her head and guided her around in a circle.

"Welcome to Mary Theresa, version two-point-oh," she said.

Hadley bit his lip and smiled. "No, this is the original. This is the woman I remember."

Scarlet didn't need to poke her finger with an embroidery needle to know she had been thrust into the middle of every wannabe fashion designer's fantasy. *Funny how fate happens,* she thought.

Only yesterday she met Johnny Scissors face to face, and tonight she would be his date at the movie premiere of *Work What You Got*, a *Thelma & Louise*–inspired comedy starring Oscar-winner Eva Alegria. Scarlet loved her some Eva. She read in an interview that Eva loved to sew. Scarlet would be sure to bring along a gift pack of goodies in case, by chance, she met the star. If she could meet Johnny Scissors, practically get hired by him, show up to a red carpet event—on his arm—during her first week of living in New York, anything was possible!

Scarlet stepped out of the shower and snuggled into her sunshine-colored terrycloth robe. She wiped the steam from the mirror and ran a comb through her long red hair. She had to be downstairs in the lobby in four hours and she still hadn't decided on what gown to wear. The pressure loomed—her first big event in the Big Apple—she couldn't afford to end up on the worst-dressed list standing next to Johnny Scissors. He'd send her cactus booty all the way back to Arizona. She narrowed her choices to three but had yet to choose. Just then, Scarlet heard a knock on her door.

She peered through the peephole. Ronnie! She opened the door and he handed her a garment bag with a card hanging from it. Scarlet flashed him a quizzical glance and he shrugged his shoulders in an "I'm just the messenger" way.

"Have fun tonight," he said before leaving.

Scarlet set the bag carefully on her bed, opened the card, and froze.

> *Here's an original Daisy for tonight. Good luck, Miss Scarlet.*
> *—Louisa*

Scarlet held her breath, unzipped the padded vinyl bag, and slowly removed the dress from its protective cocoon.

"Well, razz my berries, Louisa, you know how to pick 'em!" Scarlet said aloud as she held the dress up and inspected it from neckline to hem. She had only seen this gown in old magazine pictures. Daisy had created it for the famous Italian actress Gina Lollabrigida. A low-cut, red satin asymmetrical mermaid gown that twinkled with miniature diamond clusters sewn all around the bodice. Scarlet had never been this close to a Daisy dress. She skimmed it across her face to feel the texture of the silky fabric on her cheek. She closed her eyes and imagined Daisy, circa 1971, her hair propped up in a ponytail, in Capri pants and an art smock, conversing with the masterpiece-in-the-making as she brought it to life. And now, decades later, Scarlet cradled it in her arms.

*   *   *

When Scarlet climbed into the Hummer limo, Johnny took one gander at her outfit and had a hissy fit.

"You can't be seen in that garment," Johnny fumed. "Where did you get it?"

Scarlet's heart dropped about a thousand gears. "Louisa sent it to me. Am I not supposed to wear it because it is a treasured antique?"

Johnny punched his Bluetooth headset, asked for Louisa, and scolded her. Scarlet couldn't make out the full scoop, but it seemed he worried that Scarlet's dress would upstage the one he'd designed for Eva Alegria. He insisted that Louisa deliver a replacement gown for Scarlet ASAP.

Scarlet pretended not to notice the meat of the conversation. Security guards would have to tackle, shackle, and tase her before she would take off Daisy's dress.

"There has been a misunderstanding. You must change when we arrive at the theater. Louisa is bringing you a new dress."

This man had access to fashion history gold, yet refused to flaunt it. If Scarlet didn't know better, she'd think he was jealous of his aunt's work.

"Oh, OK, sure," Scarlet agreed. She let a moment of silence pass. "I thought Louisa wanted me to show off this little number to build buzz for Daisy's fiftieth-anniversary gala next week," she said as she admired her outfit. "You know, like House of Tijeras is ahead of the curve with the hoopla?"

Johnny folded his hands across his round belly and simmered on Scarlet's words. Apparently deciding she made a good point, he pressed his Bluetooth button again. "Cancel that last request. Over."

Scarlet's eyes twinkled with satisfaction.

Johnny cleared his throat. "We're lucky there is no snow this week. Tell me, Scarlet, have you ever attended a red-carpet event?" he asked as they rode across Manhattan to the Ziegfeld Theatre.

"Not unless First Fridays in downtown Phoenix counts," Scarlet joked as she straightened the long cream velvet shawl around her shoulders.

"The reason we've brought you tonight is to practice for the Met event next week, which will be five times as big as this. I want to see how you handle yourself and how the press takes to you. As long as you stick with me, we'll make it a night you will never forget."

She nodded and stroked the chunky multistrand, red-and-pink Daisy-made Lucite necklace she'd brought from home. She bought it at an estate auction for $750 a year ago. She had been saving it to wear for a once-in-a-lifetime adventure, and this certainly qualified.

"I heard Eva is wearing one of your dresses for the premiere tonight," Scarlet said.

Johnny lowered his brows. "How did that get out?"

Not wanting to throw Ronnie under the catwalk, she improvised. "I thought I heard it on the radio today. Everyone was looking forward to seeing it," Scarlet said just as her gaze latched onto the monstrous marquee that was mounted to the top of the Ziegfeld Theatre. Framing the flashy movie house was a gigantic woven copper arch that sparkled with strands of blinking white lights from one end of the structure to the other. Scarlet whipped her iPhone from her silk pouch, snapped a photo, and uploaded it to her blog with the headline: "Wearing a Daisy gown, going to a movie premiere at THIS theatre!"

Johnny clapped his hands and asked Scarlet to concentrate so he could repeat the etiquette rules to her three times.

1. She was to stay on his arm and was forbidden to speak, no matter what.
2. If he tapped her arm once, she was to break away and stand approximately two steps behind him.

3. To pose for pictures, she needed to balance on her back
   leg, lower one hip, and put her hands on her hips.

She knew the rundown but didn't want to show disrespect,
so she politely agreed.

Scarlet would tell her future grandkids about the experience
of the next moment. The driver opened the limo door, Johnny
Scissors popped out, grandstanded for the hundreds of fans and
press, and waved his arms in the air like a champion. He then
turned to help Scarlet out of the vehicle.

The movie fans and paparazzi were captivated from the
first glance. They screamed, cheered, and whistled at the
mysterious woman who stepped onto the red carpet and waved
to them. Her sleek, bright auburn hair gracefully lay in finger
waves across one side of her head, topped off by a small feathered
headpiece. Someone in the crowd noticed right away that the
dress was a Daisy de la Flora original, and from that point on the
cameras popped and flashed from every direction. Scarlet thought
she even heard a group of people talking about DaisyForever
.com

Johnny reveled in the attention as he led Scarlet down the
long walkway, stopping every few seconds to wave. He clenched
her close to ensure he would be in every shot. Scarlet held her
face poised and polished, and modeled all her favorite poses she
had practiced in the mirror ever since childhood.

At one point, Johnny let go of Scarlet to kiss the cheek
of a young starlet on the other side of the carpet. Doing as
instructed, Scarlet didn't move or talk. Even when a reporter
shoved a microphone into her face and asked her name, she
paused. Johnny's hand appeared out of nowhere and shoved the
mike away, then signaled for security to guide them to the front
of the theater. Two uniformed men tugged open the heavy cop-

per gates. Scarlet and Johnny passed through and waited until the theater's doors closed behind them.

"Stay here, Scarlet," Johnny ordered. "I'm going to the men's room. Don't move."

"Sure. Wow, that was nutsola!" She laughed. She inhaled to catch her breath and watched as the theater doors opened again. Her stomach tightened when she saw Eva Alegria and her crew enter.

"That goddamn Johnny Scissors made me another piece-of-shit dress!" she shouted from inside her entourage circle. "Where the hell is he? My gown ripped in the same spot as last time."

Scarlet moved left and then right to try to sneak a peek of the little woman with the big voice. "He's in the bathroom, but maybe I can help?" she offered. Eva's main bodyguard blocked Scarlet, and another just about pounced on her. "Seriously, I can help. I even brought my sewing kit!" Scarlet opened her mini drawstring bag and held up a mini satin pouch.

"But some of these little beads came off too," Eva said, scratching the bodice of her gown. Scarlet eyeballed the hole in Eva's waistband.

"Easy. I have my EmergiSew fast-bonding adhesive! I can fix it right here, or we can meet in the ladies' room," Scarlet said. "That is, if your guards will allow it."

Eva signaled for her crew to stay put, and she followed Scarlet.

*   *   *

Scarlet stayed calm as the petite Eva Alegria shouted obscenities about Johnny and paced in the bathroom in her black body shaper, diamonds, and skinny slide-on stilettos. "Johnny sucks, his designs are outdated, and he must have blind monkeys stitching his stuff because every time I wear something of his, it fails. I only wear it because he's related to Daisy. This is the

last time!" She paused in her pacing. "So what do you do for
Johnny?" she asked as Scarlet stitched the dress on the copper
bathroom counter.

"I'm a new student in his Emerging Designers Program."

"And for that you got your dress? I've been begging Johnny
to let me wear a Daisy gown!"

"It was kind of a fluke," Scarlet said humbly, trying to focus
on her handiwork. "I run a website called DaisyForever.com,
and the head of the program thought it would be cute for me to
wear the gown to create buzz for the Met gala next week."

Eva covered her cheeks with her long hands and practically
floated to Scarlet. "You are Scarlet Santana? Oh my God, I love
your site. I read it all the time with my staff! I'm a big Daisy fan
too, a collector. I have a whole wall filled with her bags. I sure
hope she comes to the event. I heard she is really ill, though."

Scarlet paused and gulped. "What do you mean ill?"

Eva hopped up on the sink counter. "Aw, probably nothing.
In this industry people say stuff like that to get out of a public obligation. She's such a private person. I don't think she'd
want to come out in the crowd. They say her whole demeanor
changed when her sisters died in that crash. Plus, what is she,
like a hundred years old now?"

Scarlet trembled as she turned to get back to work.

"Hey, I loved your recent post about Little Victories. Except I
didn't want to burn them, so I made them into papier-mâché,"
Eva said, dangling her legs over the counter.

"That's great, thanks! But business first," Scarlet said calmly.
"Come here and step into your dress; let me button it up and then
tell me what you think. If you don't like it, I'll change it back."

Eva put it on, faced the full-length mirror, raised one arm up
like a flapper, twirled, and kicked up her spiky heel. "Wow, it
looks like a new dress! What did you do?"

"I reworked the sash, see? I brought it up and draped it over your shoulder, stitched it in place at your hip at a forty-five-degree angle. Now it elongates your torso, adds curvature to your chest, and makes your waist appear even smaller. I repaired the hole, but I couldn't resist the makeover. I'll probably get fired for it."

"Oh, I'll make sure you don't get fired. I feel like I got a boob job! Gorgeous work. But what about the beads?"

"Easy. This is my special EmergiSew adhesive I developed back in Arizona." Scarlet uncapped a small tube and got to work affixing the beads. "I'll have it fixed in a jiffy."

Eva stood still as a statue while Scarlet worked. "I loved your patternless sewing idea. I'm a sassy stitcher myself."

Scarlet still couldn't fathom she was discussing sewing, glue, and Daisy de la Flora with a million-dollar movie star. "I know. I read it in *Latina* magazine. I'd love to see what you make."

"Nothing like this." Eva laughed. "But I do want to make one of those duct-tape dress forms."

"You know who to call," Scarlet said, patting the beads to make sure the glue worked. "OK, the beads are secured."

Eva squeezed her waist. "I'm astonished. Scarlet, you saved my night. Johnny is very fortunate to have found you. But girl-friend to girlfriend—be careful. He's a cheater and a stealer."

Scarlet flinched. "Oh, no... I'm not involved with him; I kind of have a boyfriend back home."

Eva playfully slapped her arm. "No, comadre, Johnny's gayer than faux fur on hiking boots. I mean businesswise. Don't tell him any of your secrets. I've seen what you can do from your site, and now meeting you in person—you're the entire pack-age. Don't sell out to Johnny, Daisy wouldn't want you to."

Someone opened the bathroom door. "Everything OK in there?"

"Everything is perfect." Eva snapped her fingers on either

side of her head and slid her arm in Scarlet's. "Now—time to get back out there. Thanks, girl."

Right before they turned the corner to the dimly lit ladies' room seating area, the women hugged. Eva no longer felt like a movie star to Scarlet. She felt like a new friend.

Scarlet exited the room first to clear space for Eva's grand re-entrance. The paparazzi had made their way inside and bombarded her with photos. Scarlet stepped aside and watched adoringly until she felt an iron grip on her elbow. She turned to see Johnny, flames of fury dancing in his eyes as he tugged Scarlet away to a quiet corner.

"You broke *every* rule. The car is waiting for you out back. Leave immediately." He shut up when he heard Eva Alegria talking about House of Tijeras to TV cameras.

"And I owe it all to Scarlet Santana, founder of the site Daisy-Forever.com and new student from the Johnny Scissors Emerging Designers Program!" Eva announced to the press. She rose to her tiptoes and waved for Scarlet to come over. Scarlet looked to Johnny as to what to do.

Johnny blew a kiss to Eva and then placed his hand on Scarlet's back and whisked her in Eva's direction.

"Smile, but don't speak," he whisper-shouted as they breezed across the theater's atrium.

Eva elbowed herself away from her bodyguard and pulled Scarlet into the frenzied circle.

"I accidentally ripped my Johnny Scissors dress crawling out of my limo—I'm a klutz!" Eva lied. "Scarlet repaired it and made it even better using her mad design skills and her EmergiSew adhesive! Visit her website, it's fabulous—DaisyForever.com!"

The reporters then turned to Scarlet for a response. There was only one thing she could think of to say.

"Hi, Mom and Dad!" She waved. "I love you!"

30

Johnny's eye twitched in anger at the Sunday-morning fashion headlines.

MISS SCARLET SHALL NEVER GO HUNGRY AGAIN: Arizona designer becomes a fashion hero to Eva Alegria at NYC movie premiere.

He immediately called upon an escort to pick Scarlet up from her dorm and bring her to his place for a business breakfast. The man could not contain himself. The morning papers had arrived on his desk, all of them with photos of Scarlet and Eva, arm in arm, heads tossed back, laughing and posing. Every image lacked the most important aspect to Johnny. Him.

How dare they crop him out! Not only in the picture, but in the copy of the articles. Even worse, some fashion pages showed the before and after photos of Eva's dress. Damn that Scarlet! If he didn't need her, he would have paid her to go hide in Siberia right about now.

Instead he sent his fleet of worker bees out in full force. He had the publicity department call all the fashion reporters to spin the story. Scarlet didn't design the makeover—he did in a previous dress; Scarlet just used the design and took credit. It sounded good to him.

He had to rein Scarlet in before she did any more damage. He needed to get her locked under contract. Not just her website, but the stupid glue, the dresses she sold online—which he learned were completely sold out since yesterday morning's presentation—the unspeakable duct-tape dress form, the patternless workshop, and, most of all, the girl herself as a media personality and spokesperson.

Johnny's lawyers worked all night drawing up the papers. At breakfast he would make her a golden offer she would be stupid to refuse.

*   *   *

Scarlet woke up shocked that she had fallen asleep still wearing Daisy's dress. The night's events exhausted her, and all her rational thinking. She ever so carefully climbed out of the gown, replaced it on the hanger, and zipped it back up in its cozy home.

A series of knocks came from her door. *Ronnie . . .* she thought. She guessed correctly, except that next to Ronnie stood a man in a dark suit. Forget the fashion police; this guy looked like he belonged to the fashion FBI. They informed Scarlet that Johnny wanted to meet with her and didn't even give her a chance to dress appropriately. After all of the excitement from the previous night, the only appetite Scarlet had was for researching Daisy's car crash. But it would have to wait if she wanted to keep her potential career with House of Tijeras. Eva had certainly upped her value with the media.

Scarlet itched to check her web stats after the awesome plug Eva had given the site. Maybe somewhere out there, Daisy in her hidden bungalow, or wherever she lived, read the papers and found Scarlet's site.

Scarlet tugged on a pair of sweats and a T-shirt, twisted her hair in a bun, and transferred her wallet from last evening's drawstring bag into a large Daisy-decorated burlap tote sporting a parrot across the front. When she grabbed the bag, she noticed an overlooked stack of mail. On top was a small package with Vega's Vicious Vinyl as the return address. Scarlet shoved it in her bag too, and went to leave.

"The dress?" Suit Man asked before Scarlet closed the door. She removed the dress from her closet and gingerly handed it to him.

Fifteen minutes later she was sitting with eight members of the Tijeras team, sipping coffee and making polite conversation about Arizona weather. Yes, Scarlet told them, it does sometimes reach 122 degrees in the summer. Thankfully the maid interrupted to let them know Johnny would be out in a few minutes.

Scarlet used the time to pull Marco's package from her purse and open it. It was a CD with the handwritten title "Miss Scarlet's Revue" across the top. Along the bottom it read *"Listen to this to know I'll always be nearby. Nothing can change this love. Love, M."*

Johnny clapped his hands twice when he entered the room and sat at the lacquered dining table.

The maid set out a tray of scrambled eggs laced with strips of cheddar cheese, a bowl of cubed sausage (Johnny liked them that way), a pastry tray, and fresh-squeezed orange juice.

"Scarlet, what would you say if I told you we want to make your dreams come true?" Johnny said.

"You already have," she said, wondering if they were about to offer her a job in production, or maybe even as a design assistant!

"Scarlet," Johnny's manager said, "we're highly impressed with all you've done to keep Daisy's brand relevant in today's competitive industry. You achieved a status with a target market that House of Tijeras has strived to hit, but has not been able to."

"Uh-huh." Scarlet listened, taking a sip from her champagne glass filled with juice.

"Daisy is about to sign her complete empire over to Johnny, any time now; we're waiting for the final word."

Scarlet gulped and remembered what Eva had mentioned about Daisy being ill. "Why?"

"Well, she's at a point in her life where the business has become a burden to her," the man said in a flat lawyerly voice. "Anyway, we have a plan to relaunch her famous de la Flora line of accessories and handbags in her honor—for the now generation."

Scarlet almost choked on her eggs. "The *now* generation?"

"Yes, the cool crowd—people who read your blog," Johnny stated as his phone buzzed with a text. He read it and grinned. "We would like to hire you as the new face of Casa de la Flora."

One of the men at the desk retrieved a heavy stack of contracts and heaved them on top of the table. He opened a thin velvet box, removed a shiny pen, and set it on top of the stack. "I can go over all the details with you, and by this afternoon it will all be official. Photo shoots and fittings begin Tuesday; we'll have a press conference on Wednesday."

Scarlet lost her breath and couldn't speak. She placed her hand over her belly and inhaled slowly. She couldn't believe her ears. Scarlet imagined holding Nana Eleanor's hand and walking through Times Square to see her own picture across one of those lighted billboards. Scenes played in Scarlet's mind of her mother proudly flipping open a copy of *InStyle* magazine and showing the new ad campaign to all her friends. Oooh, and Carly! *Yeah, Carly,* Scarlet thought. She would probably ask

Scarlet to sign the broom that she used to use to sweep the floor. Which she would do, but only after charging Carly a large stack of green to be donated to charity. *Sweet revenge,* Scarlet thought. *Sweet, sweet revenge.*

Just as she was about to answer *Yes! Yes! Yes!*—a cold gust of wind blew throughout the room, causing the drapes to flutter and the napkins to drift across the table. Everyone's heads turned to search the room for a reasonable explanation, but couldn't find one.

Except Scarlet.

Out of nowhere a strong spirit came over her, as if it were sitting right next to her in the chair, reminding her to stay grounded and think smart. It reminded her of Rosa, or Nana Eleanor. It forced her to set aside her silly fantasies about showing off. This...energy...pushed Scarlet to ask questions. Important questions.

"I'm honored to be considered for this opportunity," she said. "But I have questions, if you don't mind. What designs are you rereleasing?"

And so began her long round of rapid-fire questions about design copyrights, domestic manufacturing, importing, and so on. She recalled her conversation with Rosa about their shared business ethics—practices Johnny and his team had no interest in.

To anyone else, the deal would sound promising. But the more Scarlet listened, the more she felt sorry for Daisy.

Johnny wanted Scarlet to be the face of the relaunch, yet he wanted his own creative team to create cheap knock-offs of Daisy's work and have them mass produced overseas. He wanted to close down the New York production plant in the Garment District and move it to Los Angeles to take advantage of immigrant labor. Of course, neither he nor his staff worded it this way. They delivered the package in such a way as to make it sound like a win/win situation for everyone involved, even the underpaid immigrant seamstresses they planned to exploit.

Another issue troubled her, but she would wait for proper timing to ask about it. Johnny and his hifalutin team forgot that pretty little Miss Scarlet had two college degrees behind her silk stockings—but she wasn't about to let on to that. The more she played the naïve ingénue, the more they answered her questions in extensive detail, thinking it would all float over her fluffy, pinned-up hair.

After Johnny's maid cleaned up their dishes, the men became restless and one of them nudged Johnny as if to seal the deal. Scarlet wiped her face with her napkin and took a drink from her water glass.

"To be honest, coming here is not at all what I expected," Scarlet said. "If it weren't for Daisy, none of us would be here, yet you've erased all trace of her. She was about creativity, quality, edginess, and self-empowerment. I thought I would come here and feel connected to her more than ever, but I don't. I feel closer to her when I'm blogging about her. I feel like she is peeking over my shoulder telling me what to type."

Johnny put his hand up for her to stop. "Scarlet, we are in this business to make money, and times are not what they used to be. Trends change much faster than they did during my aunt's era. Now consumers want affordable, disposable fashion. That's what we deliver. You'll be the Daisy de la Flora of your time, and you won't have to do anything except pose for photo shoots, attend parties, and make public appearances. Our team will handle the rest. You'll earn plenty of money to help your family in Arizona, travel, or whatever else you want to do. Trust me, this is a deal of a lifetime. Right now you are a thirty-year-old nobody. We will make you a somebody."

Scarlet stared up at the black chandelier hanging over the table.

"Ready to kick-start your new life, Scarlet? We want to debut you and the campaign this Friday at the Met's gala for my aunt."

"Do you know if Daisy will be there?" Scarlet asked. "Is there a chance in all of this... that I could meet her, maybe have tea with her?"

Johnny let out rolls of laughter and gave a roaming glance to his staff. "What is it about that old woman that people are attracted to? Here's the truth: My aunt is batshit loca, a recluse who is only popular now because back in her time she had a loud mouth, a bad reputation, and a tacky sense of design. House of Tijeras is about the future. Come on board, Scarlet."

Johnny's lawyer removed the top contract and walked it over to Scarlet. She set it in front of her, and he placed the pen in her hand.

It didn't matter what the contract said; she had to take this job. How could she not? She came to New York hoping to learn more about Daisy de la Flora, and now she could carry on her legacy.

She took a deep breath and closed her eyes. Memories and images flooded her mind: ten years of heartfelt blog posts; preaching to her sewing class about letting go of rules; little victories; the fight with her father at the hospital; Rosa and her work in the sewing factories; her sister's confession; the texture of Marco's skin; dancing to Sam Cooke; making love. She could hear Marco's voice telling her about his brother and the bad feeling he had about her trip. And she remembered the hurtful things she'd said back to him.

Most of all she heard Rosa's haunting words from the night at the record shop: *If you do it, Scarlet, you will not be the woman I thought you were.*

Scarlet cleared her throat.

"I'll need time to review this with my family and my attorney. There will be changes, because I don't want to just be a face; I want to be involved in the business. I'll need two weeks," she said. "I'll give you my answer then."

"Sorry, Scarlet." Johnny chuckled. "This offer expires the moment you leave the room. If you don't sign, we'll find someone else who will."

Scarlet used both her hands to push the contract away from her. "I'm very sorry, Mr. Tijeras, but I decline. In fact, I'm withdrawing myself from the Emerging Designers Program as well. I'm flattered at your interest, but Casa de la Flora is not for me."

The men grumbled and Johnny pressed his hands on the table so hard, Scarlet could see his brown knuckles turn white. "You signed the contract for the program, which states we own everything you produced and/or used of your own creation while under our terms. That means your blog, your glue, your design career, your relationship with Eva—"

"That is incorrect," Scarlet said, summoning her inner Mary Theresa. Scarlet had read the JSED contract several times with a magnifying glass, and there was no such clause. "My lawyers will be in touch to close this out. Thank you for your time, Mr. Tijeras." She scooted her seat away from the table.

"Not so fast," Johnny said snidely. "You have a debt to repay."

"What?" Scarlet asked. "For the thread I used in the student sewing center?"

"For ruining an original Daisy de la Flora gown," he said. "The entire inner lining is ripped beyond repair. That dress is valued at fifty thousand dollars."

"Fine, send me the bill—and the dress," Scarlet said, standing up to leave.

"You need to be out of your room and off the premises by four p.m. today," Johnny ordered coldly before stomping out of the room.

He stomped back in.

"Louisa, you too."

*　　*　　*

Around the same time that Scarlet hot-tailed it out of Johnny's breakfast meeting, Mary Theresa lay curled up in heavy white sheets next to her husband.

Last night was a complete, magical, blissful blur.

It must have been Scarlet's zebra-toed platform shoes that had cast a spell on Mary Theresa strong enough to turn her into *Maresa*.

After leaving the bar, she and Hadley flirted all the way to his room—a luxurious deluxe two-bedroom suite with a roomy terrace and fireplace. They had barely made it into the suite when Hadley unwrapped Mary Theresa's dress, swooped her up, and carried her to his bed.

One two-hour Sade playlist later, they emerged smiling and satisfied, arm-in-arm, draped in tan microfiber bathrobes. Hadley called room service to deliver champagne and a decadent dinner. He lit the fireplace and the couple spent the rest of the evening holding each other, sharing stories about how the last two months had changed their lives.

When Mary Theresa awoke in the morning she found a note on the dresser: He was at the gym and would be back by lunchtime. He signed it with a heart and a P.S. "Change into your new outfit; it's time for golf practice at 2!"

She kissed the note, reset the Sade playlist, and went to the TV room to find breakfast. After searching through the compact fridge, she came across a half-eaten sub and decided it would do.

Mary Theresa picked at it as she wandered around the seating area, fighting a battle between critical thinking and blind faith.

On one hand, it elated her that she and Hadley had reconnected without terms or agreements. No mention of home, therapists, work, stress, bills, parenting, or in-laws. She didn't have a single guarantee, but she had hope they both wanted to bring what they shared last night back home.

And on the other hand was Hadley's current living situation. Every other week he sent her $800 from his paycheck, which came from a job she knew nothing about. Sure he called the kids every night, but never once had he invited her to bring them for a visit. As much as she loved last night, she had to ask some questions today. She showered, got dressed, and spread out across the couch to watch television until Hadley returned.

Twenty minutes later, Hadley punched his card in the slot and entered. "I'm back," he sang out. He sauntered over, bent down, and gave her a juicy kiss. "How about massages after golf today?"

Mary Theresa glanced down.

"Uh-oh, I know that look."

She rubbed his arm and looked up into his eyes. "I wish the kids could be here today. Wouldn't that be nice? All four of us together again?"

Hadley stared across the room at the framed photos of Rocky, Lucy, and Mary Theresa. "Yeah, that would have been cool."

"Hadley," Mary Theresa said, "what would have happened if I didn't show up yesterday?"

Hadley rubbed his hand around his head, sat down next to his wife, and held her hand. "I'd be here by myself, like always."

Mary Theresa scooted closer, practically on his lap. "Let's go home today, surprise the kids, shack up in our own bed... want to?"

"Oh, honey, I can't. I have a big workload this week; the drive would drain me," he said.

She crossed her legs and slouched into him. "Have you thought about coming home? We miss you so much. I want to show you something. . . ." She hopped off the couch and pulled out her Little Victories papers from her purse and handed them to him.

After reading them one at a time, he smiled and nodded. "These are great, Mare. I can tell you put a lot of thought and heart into them. And I love that. I miss all you too," he said, still staring at the papers.

"Last night was amazing," she said, "but honestly right now all I can think about is why you've never invited us here. Yesterday I sat at the bar and watched the families splashing around in the indoor pool. Doesn't being around that make you miss us?"

"Well, I'm working. This is not playtime for me; you remember what it's like."

"Hmmm . . . OK," she said, pulling strands of her hair behind her back. "At least your assignment is over next month. We can hang on until then."

Hadley fell back on the couch's armrest and scrubbed his face with the backs of his hands, as if he had bad news and wanted to postpone the delivery. "They really like my work, the site has increased sales by a mile, and . . . they've offered me a full-time position."

"What?" Mary Theresa said as she sprang from the sofa.

"Mare, think of the pay. And look at the fringe benefits: medical, dental, 401(k). Our whole family will stay free at any hotel in the chain!"

"What did you tell them?" she asked.

"Nothing yet. I didn't expect it, honest. They gave me until the end of the month," he said. "I was going to call you this week. I had my speech prepared and everything. But when you showed up looking like a Brazilian bombshell and strutting around here in your flesh-colored skivvies, it made me rethink it all. I miss you. I miss my family."

Mary Theresa knew this play. He wanted to butter her up as a diversion. "And what do you think now that I'm dressed? Do I have to strip naked to get you follow me home to your children?"

"It wouldn't hurt," he kidded. "Look," he said, crouching forward, "work is everything to me now. It feels good to be appreciated for something other than stirring Spaghetti-Os and chauffeuring kids to school. Being here gives me time to focus on meeting all my deadlines without a zillion distractions."

"When I talked like that, you left me," she said.

He rose and put his arms around her. "We don't have to be traditional; we can have the best of both worlds. You and the kids can come down on weekends, just like today. The bills are covered, and so are our careers. You have your space, I have mine. We meet in the middle with the kids. A lot of families are doing this these days. And think about it: It'll add to the excitement of when we see each other. Man, last night—when have we ever had sex like that?"

Mary Theresa shook her head. "That's not my kind of family," she said. "We may as well be boyfriend and girlfriend, not husband and wife."

All of Mary Theresa's hope for a reconciliation faded. Rocky's and Lucy's faces were all she could think of, and she couldn't get home fast enough to hold them and kiss them.

"I'm going home," she said, walking toward the bedroom to gather her things. "I know where I want to be, and it's home with my kids, with or without you. I took them for granted before, and I never want to do that again. I'm leaving it up to you to decide about your job. It's your choice, not mine."

Mary Theresa came out of the bedroom and gave Hadley a tight hug, gripping his chest near hers. She breathed heavy and knew what she had to do. She looked up at him and gave him the wettest, sexiest kiss of her life. Pulling away from him proved difficult, like separating duct tape from fabric. But she succeeded, knowing it might the last time their bodies would be that close.

A hhhh, nothing like home," Rosa purred as she snuggled up in her favorite poodle-pattern flannel pajamas atop her queen-size four-poster bed. She carefully adjusted her tired body to sit back and pull up the pink-and-red-beaded quilt she'd bought at a Mumbai flea market many years ago. The bed covering wouldn't budge because of the dozen worn, cracked scrapbooks and collage-covered photo albums that were strewn across her bed. Rosa had spent the day soaking up a Doris Day marathon on cable while examining old photos and letters from her life. She had always planned to have the pictures scanned before they aged any further, but neither Rosa nor her staff ever followed through. Perhaps some pictures were meant to have a specific life cycle, just like people.

Three weeks had passed since Rosa returned home to New York, her symptoms growing stronger each day. The weakness, the fevers, the reactions to her medications, the crankiness. She'd made her peace with God and was ready to leave this Earth with grace. She had just one last order of business to tend to.

She blew her nose in a tissue and called out for the maid to come remove the books. Reyna, her longtime housekeeper, jogged in and quickly stacked the albums, returning them to Rosa's bookcase.

Reyna jogged back and asked if Rosa wanted her to untie the curtains around her bed.

"Not yet," Rosa said.

Rosa had always despised bare walls and ordinary furniture. So during her more limber years, she'd tacked a large sheet of lattice across the tops of her bedposts. She then used thin, waxed twine and strung hundreds of glass beads she'd collected from all around the world, and hung them from the edges. Rosa did the same with trims, except those she fed through the outer edge holes of the lattice all the way around. Over the years, they became heavy, stringy curtains in a wild array of colors and textures—pompom fringe, lace, chunky yarn, leather straps.

Rosa was never one to waste fabric. If she didn't use it within a year, she found a way to incorporate it into her bedroom. Therefore her walls, from the ceiling to the floor, resembled a never-ending hobo quilt. When it came to buttons, Rosa poured them into ice-cream dishes and flowerpots and used them for decorations throughout her living quarters.

As the credits of *Calamity Jane* scrolled up the TV screen, Rosa slowly scooted herself up to reach for the table-sized remote. Next on deck, HBO's *True Blood*.

Rosa's thin, veiny fingers tap-danced across the jumbo remote as she increased the volume to almost maximum, then altered the color and shape of the screen. She'd finally tweaked it just right when Joseph buzzed her on the intercom.

"Rosa, you decent?" he said.

Frustrated by the interruption, she switched off the set. "Come on in! Can you be a darling when you get here and move my flowers a bit closer? I can barely notice their scent."

Joseph wheeled in a dress rack with six gowns swinging from the center while another maid hustled in and closed the tall green velvet curtains around two of the room's walls.

"It's always so chilly in here, ma'am," the maid said, rubbing her arms up and down. "Would you like the heater turned up?"

"I know, it's cold in here, but turning up the heater won't help. I'm fine, thank you," Rosa assured.

"Well, the plan didn't turn out exactly as we expected," Joseph said, sitting on the edge of Rosa's bed. "That slimy Johnny pulled a fast one, but our girl persevered. We're ready for Friday."

"Delightful!" Rosa said in her weakened voice as she tried to stretch a few inches to peek at the dresses. "They're as lovely as I remember. I knew she was the one. I knew it! Poor thing, I hope she isn't too shaken up. It wouldn't have mattered if she signed those papers or not. Um, the flowers, dear?"

"Oh!" Joseph remembered, looking up and around distractedly. "Sorry about that."

He shuffled across the bedroom, past the vanity table, beyond the double walk-in closet, and three steps to the left of the wall of dress closets. He gripped the vase of that day's batch of fresh-cut lilies, daisies, and roses from the brick fireplace mantel and slowly trekked his way back to Rosa's bed, where he set it at her side atop the cherrywood nightstand. Rosa lovingly plucked out a daisy, and passed it under her nose, inhaling the beauty of its scent.

"Joseph, it's time to book the flights," Rosa said. She flattened the flowers against her chest and whispered, "Please, Lord, give me the strength to make it through this week. I've come so far, please let me finish."

*   *   *

By Wednesday, Mary Theresa had yet to receive a call, e-mail, or even a text from Hadley. The glow that had lit up her face from the weekend faded to a look of disappointment—but only at night when the house was quiet and she slept alone in her bed.

The rest of the hours were divvied up between the kids, work, chores, meals, exercise, and sewing.

"Mommy, can I wear this dress to gymnastics tomorrow, please, Mommy, please?" Lucy begged as she paraded around the family room in her new hot-pink-and-purple springtime dress. "I like that the flowers are bumpy when I touch them. You make pretty dresses, Mommy."

Pleased that her daughter appreciated her mother's domestic talents, Mary Theresa spread out a long piece of vintage drapery across her worktable.

"Thank you, sweetie! Let's save that dress for a super-special occasion, OK? But Mommy will make you a sweatsuit for gymnastics. How about that?"

"OK! But put bumpy flowers on it like this one, you promise?" Lucy replied.

Mary Theresa reached behind her, grabbed a large basket of embroidery thread, and presented it to her daughter. "Here, mija, pick out the colors you want and I'll make the bumpy flowers just the way you want."

Mary Theresa's need to be a micromanager had been replaced with fashionitis. Creating clothing from scratch had become a healthy antidote to corporate stress.

Taking a cue from Scarlet—Santana *and* O'Hara—Mary Theresa came up with the idea to use unwanted drapes, tablecloths, sheets, scarfs, napkins, and dishtowels and cut them into square and rectangular quadrants to make her own bolts of fabric. She then used vintage sewing patterns on that fabric to make a collection of tops, pants, jackets, skirts, and dresses for kids.

Scarlet's patternless sewing class had unfurled Mary Theresa's tightly wound imagination. And now with the workshop over, she put her newfound creativity to work. She loved that her memories and skills of pattern- and dressmaking from high school bobbed to the top of her brain, anxious for action. Therefore, every morning after she dropped the kids off at school, Mary Theresa stopped at a downtown café, sketched until nine a.m., went home, clocked in her time for DelTran, and then hopped on the sewing machine until the kids' school day ended.

While Mary Theresa could blueprint bloomers in the dark, she tripped at coordinating colors and patterned fabrics. It took Rocky to point that out. One afternoon after school, he nibbled on Goldfish crackers and watched as she pinned a marigold and yellow batik fabric pocket to a sagey mud-colored jumper. He stopped chewing to say, "Ewww, Mommy, that material looks like someone pee-peed on it, and the other one looks like... *poop!*"

Rocky fell to the carpeted floor, covered his face, and rolled around, laughing and shouting, "Poop, poop, poop, poop!" Lucy stared at him while innocently sipping her apple juice.

"Ugh. Boys," Lucy said, as if his actions nauseated her. She peeked over her mother's shoulder, and Mary Theresa held up the pocket and jumper combo for her opinion.

"Poop and pee?" she asked Lucy.

Her daughter scrunched her face. "Yeah." Lucy then set down her juice box, sorted through her mommy's fabric bin, and wrestled and tugged with two pieces from the very bottom—orange gingham and lime green polka dots. "I like these," she said.

Ever since then, Mary Theresa let Lucy and Rocky serve as the certified Cotorro committee for fabric matching.

This afternoon, the three of them snacked on chicken fingers and apple slices, watched reruns of *Hannah Montana*, and took turns choosing fabrics for a quilt donation project. Rocky tossed down a fat quarter of black-and-white stripes, and Lucy set a roll of purple satin trim on top of it.

"Wow, you two make a great team!" Mary Theresa said, clutching her kids close to her and kissing their foreheads. The kids sharply pushed themselves off of her and scrambled across the long distance of the family room through the foyer and to the front door.

"Daddy!" they hailed at the top of their lungs. "Daddy's home!"

Mary Theresa's heart shivered. *Those poor kids,* she thought. She hated that Hadley's ghost lurked around every corner of their home. Just then she heard the doorknob turn and, thinking it was a home invasion, she sprinted with all her force across the room to grab the children. She threw her arms around them and glanced up slowly to see Hadley on the doorstep.

*   *   *

Four hours later, Hadley joined Mary Theresa as she read the kids their bedtime story and put them to sleep. Their faces beamed with a mixture of excitement, relief, and comfort as they both tightly held their father's hand. Mary Theresa did her best to pretend the night was like any other, but in reality she could barely think straight. She could tell by the look on Hadley's face that he had given his answer about the job offer.

Once they put the kids to sleep, Mary Theresa made her way downstairs to clean up the dinner dishes while Hadley turned one of the couches to face the big-screen TV and plopped down like a floppy rag doll. He grabbed the remote, hit the button, and grabbed an apple empanada from a dessert plate Mary Theresa had set out earlier. She finished cleaning the kitchen, shut off the lights, checked her hair in the glass of the oven door, and proceeded to the family room. She didn't know what to say or how to act or even where to sit. Before he left her, she felt like his boss. In Palm Springs, his equal. Now? A former girlfriend.

Trying to look at ease, she offered him a napkin and a bottle of water and then curled up at the end of the couch, ready to bring up the topic.

"Wow, I can't believe how much the house has changed; I didn't even recognize it," Hadley said, glancing around, chewing his empanada, sounding just as uncomfortable as she felt.

"Yes! My friends from the patternless sewing class came over and helped me redecorate. You like it?"

"Yes, it looks great. The kids look happy. You? Gorgeous."

Mary Theresa's cheeks heated up from flattery. She wanted to leap across the sofa and hold him, but couldn't get the image of him leaving out of her head. Or his announcement about the job extension. She may have evolved from her former nit-picky, drill-sergeant style, but that didn't mean she'd become a pushover.

"I noticed you didn't bring a suitcase. Is this only a visit?" she asked, reaching across the couch for an empanada. He wrapped his arms around her waist, pulled her close, and nudged her head up with his chin so he could kiss her neck. She went with the moment and then blew out a mouthful of air and climbed back to her corner of the couch.

"What do you want it to be?" he asked.

"Well, we're happy without you. I mean, we miss you, but whatever you decide, we can handle it," she said. "If you want to pop in and out for the kids' sake, we should set up a schedule."

"I don't want to pop in and out. I would never be the kind of husband or father who only pops in and out," he said. "My family always comes first." Hadley leaped to the floor and knelt at Mary Theresa's knees. "I'm sorry I went away on such short notice like that. My brother had been dangling this gig in front of my nose for months; I guess I was waiting for a reason to take it. I snapped like you did with the Coltrane record, just in a different way."

Mary Theresa didn't know what to think. "If you were serious about the job, you should have told me when he brought it up, and we could have discussed it further. I would have had an open mind."

Hadley rolled his head on her knees. "Sweetheart, I did bring it up. You wouldn't even hear me out."

Mary Theresa's mind raced back in time. Sure enough, she remembered the times he had mentioned it, and how he said he missed working. If only she had taken it seriously.

"Stop those negative thoughts," he said. "They're so strong, they're bouncing off my forehead. We're both at fault. What is that saying? 'A good marriage is the union of two good forgivers'?"

"Ruth Bell Graham," Mary Theresa whispered through a short smile. "So...did you accept the full-time job?" It was the question stenciled in her mind ever since he'd arrived. No matter what the answer was, she would cope with it. If he turned it down, she could finally let her mind and spirit relax. If not, well, at least they would be civil with each other for the sake of the children.

"Yes. I accepted."

Mary Theresa bit down on her back teeth and gripped the piping on the couch for support. For a second there, she actually thought—

"Is it time, Daddy?" Lucy asked sneakily, peeking through the space between the staircase rails.

"Shhhh, not yet, Lucy! You'll spoil it!" Rocky said, shoving his hand over her mouth.

Mary Theresa sniffled and slowly turned her head toward the stairs. "You two should be asleep already. Hadley, I'm going to go tuck them in. You're more than welcome to sleep on the couch tonight."

Hadley sat on the floor between the couch and the coffee table, and waved the children over.

"No, they have school tomorrow," said Mary Theresa, frustrated and somber. "Plus, I don't want them to see us like this."

By that time the kids had scrambled across the room and fallen into Hadley's lap, giggling. Lucy was wearing the cotton dress with the embroidered flowers from that afternoon. Rocky chose wrinkly black slacks, a Lucha Libre kids' T-shirt, and a clip-on tie. Hadley gave both children a thin stare and then a nod.

Rocky and Lucy stood side-by-side and handed Mary Theresa a small velvet box. "It's for you, from Daddy, and it's not a gift card!" Lucy said, presenting the gift on the palm of her hand.

Taken aback, Mary Theresa stared at the box. *He's trying to buy me off?*

"Daddy told Uncle Mike he wouldn't take the job home so he wouldn't have to take the palm to the spring anymore. Uncle Mike said, You don't want to take the palm to the spring? And Daddy said, I want to take the palm to a continental at my home—"

"No, Rocky!" Lucy said angrily, crossing her arms over her chest. "You're getting it all wrong!"

Hadley switched places with Lucy so he would be in the middle of the kids. "Mare, I told them I'd accept if they let me work from a local Continental Comfort Hotel here in town. They agreed. It's nowhere as fancy as Palm Springs, but I don't care. I'd rather be home."

Mary Theresa parted her lips and lifted her shoulders in anticipation—and then she went for it and popped up the lid on the box to find a beautiful gold locket. Definitely vintage, trimmed in the tiniest diamonds she had ever seen. She flipped it over and read the engraved label: DE LA FLORA.

"How do you know about Daisy de la Flora?" Mary Theresa asked. Now she really felt blown away.

"My mom read your friend's blog about how you've recently become a fan. Would you believe that locket used to be my grandma's? My mom had it in her safe because she said it is worth a lot of money. Now it's yours. I had it engraved."

Mary Theresa shyly giggled and used her fingernail to unlock the clasp of the locket. One side showcased a family portrait from last Christmas, and the other read, A HAPPY WEDLOCK IS A LONG FALLING IN LOVE.

Hadley removed the necklace from the box, put it around Mary Theresa's neck, and kissed her nose. "That's us, a long falling in love."

32

Just because Johnny Scissors had ripped all her dreams out from under her feet on Sunday morning, it didn't mean Scarlet would leave New York City on a low note. As soon as she left Johnny's penthouse, she went uptown to collect her things and then checked herself into a posh hotel. She made a quick call home to tell her mom and dad the gory details. They wanted to fly to New York immediately to collect their little girl, but settled for buying her a ticket home instead. Then Scarlet hit the streets for a marathon of sightseeing, eating, and shopping.

By the time her plane touched down in Phoenix early Tuesday morning, Scarlet couldn't wait to toss her suitcases in her house, shower, and visit Marco at the record store.

When she finally crossed the shop's threshold, she paused. Vega's Vicious Vinyl looked as though it had been gutted. One wall had a row of paint splotches in blues and greens. All of the album bins were now black and clustered at one end of the shop. Even the concrete floor had changed—stenciled with different shapes of gold stars.

"We're closed until mid-February," she heard Nadine yell out.

"Nadine, it's Scarlet. Oh my gosh, what happened here?" she asked Nadine, who was hunched under the empty storefront window, wearing rubber gloves and scrubbing away at the wood frame with a rag.

"A face-lift," she said. "Check out the sewing room, you won't recognize it either."

"Hi to you, too," Scarlet mumbled as she walked through to the other room, which now had crimson walls and marigold borders; it also had gold stars stenciled on the floor to tie it in with the record shop. The chandeliers remained, otherwise the space was a work-in-progress, too. She bent over one of the many boxes on the floor and opened it to find stacks of blank journals that had covers of trimmed LPs. Still baffled, she glanced around and noticed a rectangular glass box that appeared to be the register counter. She stepped over to see that it showcased colorful jewelry made from cut up record pieces.

Scarlet pointed to the earrings. "Those look like..."

"Yup." Nadine said, tugging off her cleaning gloves as she looked down at them too. "Your David Bowie picture discs that you dropped here on Black Friday. A local trash-to-treasure artist used them. Clever, huh?"

"Wow," Scarlet said as she stepped into the middle of the store, remembering where each of the worktables had been set. "Why did Marco do this?"

Nadine snorted. "Marco? He didn't do it. I did. Didn't he tell you?"

"What?"

"He's selling me his half of the business."

Scarlet felt her chest tighten. "His half? I thought he owned all of it."

Nadine sighed and pulled out two black vinyl chairs trimmed in silver sequins. "Come on, sit. I'll fill you in." She went on to explain how she and Michael had planned to open Vega's Vicious Vinyl as half record store, half gallery of local artists. When he died, Marco came in as co-owner and they made it work, except that they never got the gallery portion going. Hence the available space for Scarlet's class.

"It wasn't until you came with your sewing group that I really saw the potential," Nadine said. "I asked Marco if I could do this, I gave him a business plan and everything. The next day he came in and told me he was taking a break from the store."

Scarlet eyes dulled as she searched around the air for answers. All of this information came so unexpectedly. "I'm sorry you lost Michael."

"Thanks," Nadine replied, hanging over the back of the chair and fingering the bright orange gauge in her earlobe. "Marco told me a little about what happened between you two. Whatever you said shook him up. He went to spend time with his parents in San Diego for a few days. It was good for him, for me, and for the store. He wasn't ever really into this place. The only time he ever livened up was when you'd come in. He was too shy to talk to you; I used to rip his shirt pockets."

Scarlet covered her mouth and laughed. "I can't resist a repair waiting to happen."

"I know. Anyway, when he came back, he told me he wanted to sell me his half so he could move on with his life. Not only that, he got his parents to co-sign on a business loan for me so I could remodel it and really give it a shot to be successful. I'd say Marco Vega is my hero."

"He's my hero too. Where is he now?" Scarlet asked.

"You'll find him at his house. He's showing it to some renters today because he leaves for San Diego next week."

*   *   *

Within minutes, Scarlet raced to Marco's. The tears flowed nonstop. She had to convince him to stay. She needed to let him know he had been right, apologize for putting her obsession for Daisy de la Flora before everything and everybody, and tell him she loved him. She pulled into his driveway, ran up to the door, and knocked as hard and as fast as she could. He finally opened the door, wearing only a pair of faded jeans.

His face lit up instantly. "You're back! Come on—"

Scarlet couldn't wait for him to finish. She pressed her hands up to his chest, stood up on her tiptoes, and kissed him. Without breaking away, he pulled her into the house and shut the door behind them. She grabbed his arms and dragged him to the bedroom to find only a futon on the floor. They tumbled down, pausing only for Scarlet to prop up her iPhone and set it to the playlist Marco made for her at Christmas. Within seconds they had peeled off their clothes and made up for lost time.

When they finished, tears streamed down Scarlet's face. This time, Marco was the one to hold her face in his hands and wipe them away.

"I just came from the shop," Scarlet said. "Nadine told me. Please don't move. I'm sorry for what I said. I know Michael is so proud of you. You loved him so much. I was an idiot."

Marco, still holding her face, kissed her neck. "Whoa, slow down. I want to hear everything about what happened to you."

"None of that matters," she said, shaking her head and kissing his hands. "I love you, Marco. I've known it ever since that day I stitched your pocket. If you move, I want to go with you. I have nothing going for me here anymore."

He scooted up against the wall and ran his fingers through

her long hair. "It's time for me to get on with my original plans before my brother died . . . and I need to do it on my own."

She rolled over to face him. "What was that?"

He had never told her about life before Michael, only after.

"I was going to the University of San Diego to be an oceanographer. I was almost done when I dropped out to move to Glendale and help Nadine with the record store. I'm going back to find work and finish my degree."

"Oceanography?" Scarlet repeated. It made sense. She glanced around his house. She had always been so busy searching for music-related items, she didn't really think about why he had a seashell shadowbox on the wall, a big aquarium in his bedroom, or framed beach art in his bathroom. Even his office at the record store had a shelf with different kinds of starfish.

"What you told me in the car that day," he said, stroking her neck with the backs of his fingers, "it made so much sense. That night I came home, depressed. But as the hours went on, I could feel the release of the guilt I'd been carrying around with me. After living in that grungy cave of a record store for so long, I'm ready to go back to the light of the beach."

Scarlet dropped her face in her hands and sobbed. The past few months had presented the lowest of the lows and the highest of the highs and by this point she was too exhausted to keep her cool. Marco hugged her to his chest and rubbed her back. "It's good, Scarlet. Don't cry. You have helped me figure out something really important for my life, and I'll always love you for that."

"I'm crying because I'm happy *and* sad. Remember when you said I never knew the feeling of losing someone? I do. I feel it right now. But at the same time, I'm happy for you. As much as I want to stop you from leaving, I want you to go, because I know what it's like to go after a goal, a dream, whatever you want to call it…and try to conquer it. I just came off of that, and as much of a catastrophe as it was, I wouldn't trade it for anything."

"Thank you," he said. "I love you, Scarlet. Let's try our best to make it work. Who knows what will happen in the future. Maybe our lives will line up again. I'll always be there for you, and wherever I am you are always welcome. Don't think of it as losing a boyfriend, think of it as gaining a vacation."

She sniffled and snuggled as close to him as she could. "And if you should ever need me, remember, I'm only one ripped pocket away."

*　　*　　*

Scarlet sat relaxed, eyes shut, and let her body melt into the curve of her backyard's garden swing. She tuned in to the sound of chirping birds, the clean scent of citrus trees, and lightly pushed her feet against the dry winter grass to keep the movement going.

Scarlet had plucked every petal she could from the life of Daisy de la Flora, and like Rosa had told her, and like Marco did with Michael, it was time to let go. She still wondered about Daisy's mysterious car crash. Maybe someday after she felt settled into her new life, she would research it. Until then, she would just have to live with the mystery.

Tuesday night after she returned from Marco's, Scarlet's brother, Charles, helped her tidy up her house. She didn't talk much, but she asked him to pack everything up in her sewing room and donate it to a local women's shelter. Charles, convinced she would eventually change her mind, simply straightened up the room, replaced the cover on her sewing machine, shut the light, and closed the door. She cooked him a late dinner and they talked about job opportunities. Charles hadn't been kidding when he said his boss would hire her as long as she submitted an official résumé. She opened her Mac laptop and finished it right there.

CAREER OBJECTIVE: To obtain a position as a civil engineer with the opportunity to apply my knowledge of physics, project management, mathematics, and design.

She printed the résumé and handed it to Charles so he could turn it over to Human Resources at Metropolitan Advanced Systems in Tempe—$70,000 with benefits and a cubicle. Sure, she had sworn off sewing of any kind, but it wouldn't hurt to whip up a few custom suits for the new journey in her life. *At least a thread of positivity still remained,* she thought.

By Wednesday afternoon Scarlet was called in for an interview and aced it. Her new boss, Franklin Reynolds—who reminded her of a younger Alec Baldwin—walked her around the office and introduced her to the staff. Wearing her hair in a simple updo and sporting a basic gray suit, Scarlet made the rounds and met her new coworkers.

*   *   *

Later that afternoon, Scarlet's feet came to a halt and gripped the ground when she heard the lock open on her side gate and the screeching sound of metal on concrete.

"How ya doing, over there, Scar?" her dad asked as he cruised into her yard on his shiny orange touring bicycle.

"Fine, Dad, just soaking up the warmth of the sunshine. Feels good. I missed it last week. How are you? Enjoying your week off from the office?"

"Oh, yeah," Manny said, nudging down the kickstand. "But it's better when I can hang out with my daughter. Scoot over, kid."

Scarlet slid to the end of the swing, and her dad moaned for his back and then sat too.

"Monday's the big day, huh? You ready?"

Scarlet let her head fall on her father's shoulder. "Yes, more than ever. I'm finally a bona fide civil engineer—er, Monday I will be. I'm actually looking forward to it. I feel like my slate has been scrubbed clean and I'm ready to get it all messy again."

"Good for you," he said, rubbing her head like a champ. "But who are you trying to convince? It's your dad you're talking to. It's OK, Scarlet, not to know what is going to happen in your future, and it's OK not to always be in control."

"Why are you being so understanding now? I could have used this pep talk way back when."

"It wasn't the fashion career that turned us off, it was the fact that you excluded everything and everyone who loved you. Everything was one-sided, and you wouldn't listen to any of our advice. What have I always told you?"

" 'To achieve success, we must strive for balance in all we do,' " she recited. "You know, it wasn't really about the fashion career for me, either. I was just tired of being babied. I wanted to prove to all of you that I didn't need to follow a pattern that was already cut for me."

"I get it," Manny said as the swing slowly swayed. "You proved it over and over, Scarlet. We all noticed your skills and talents ever since you were a toddler. Do you remember that Fisher Price dollhouse you got for Christmas when you were five? You got mad because no one would assemble it for you?"

Scarlet chuckled and nodded. "Yes! I put it together myself! You guys were too busy watching the football game. I was so mad."

"Exactly," he said. "Everyone in this family is left-brained, except my mother, who came out very creative and artistic. But you? You are both. You can design a house and decorate it too. Your brother and sister can't even use a felt pen without freaking out. You're capable of anything."

"Anything?" Scarlet offered. She poked her finger into his arm. "I have always wanted to learn the ukulele."

"We'll learn together, mija, how's that?" Manny said as he demonstrated the Rosie the Riveter fist-pump. "And don't worry about that Johnny Scissors slimeball; my lawyer will take care of it."

Scarlet shrugged. "Whatever happens, happens. I set my goal, I reached it, and I have a whopper of a story to tell to my grandkids someday."

Scarlet and her father swung in silence for a moment, then she let out a small laugh. "Funny how in the end, it was the same. They had a pattern cut out for me too, and I didn't want to do it *their* way either.

"At least I can say I tried. I just couldn't go along with their plans, Dad. I could have been an overnight sensation. It took all my might not to sign those contracts. Fashion is even more cutthroat than it is in the movies. One week aged me ten years. I bought my first jar of Oil of Olay this morning!"

A few more moments of silence passed between them, broken only by an annoying mockingbird. At least, at first.

"Scarlet! *Scarrrlet* . . ." Olivia's robust, husky voice floated over the fence and into the yard.

"I'm back here!" Scarlet yelled. "She's a friend from my patternless sewing class," she told her dad. They heard the gate screech open, and watched Olivia, Mary Theresa, Stephanie, and Jennifer hustle down the pathway toward Scarlet.

"Where the hell have you been? You haven't returned any of our calls!" Olivia scolded.

Scarlet jumped up from the swing, altered by the anguish on all their faces and the emergency inflection in Olivia's voice.

"I'm sorry, I turned off my cell phone. Everything went haywire in New York, I just needed some time to decompress. . . ."

Mary Theresa pushed herself up front and gripped Scarlet's arms. "Joseph called. Rosa is sick, *really* sick. She's in New York City, that's where she lives. He booked us flights to get out there to say our good-byes. We're all going tonight. You have to come with us, Scarlet!"

Scarlet twisted around to face her dad. "I promise I'll be back in time for work on Monday."

He leaped up and headed to the house. "Come on, I'll help you pack."

33

Twelve hours later, the women were riding in the back of a black Town Car that Joseph had waiting for them at John F. Kennedy Airport. Between the long plane flight and the ride into the city, Scarlet told the group all that had happened at House of Tijeras.

"House of Terror is more like it," Olivia snapped. "Johnny Scissors needs to go down. He can't take all your good work away just because Daisy is his aunt."

"Don't worry, he won't. My dad's lawyer is looking into it to make sure. At least it feels good to catch my breath; I've made it to bed by ten p.m. almost every night this week. Sleeping is underrated. Except now that Rosa is sick, I don't know if I'll sleep until she gets better. As it is, I go to bed praying for her every night."

Jennifer, who had never traveled beyond Arizona, perched her forehead against the window and admired the East Coast scenery as it flew by during the ride. Stephanie worked on her new hobby, knitting.

"I'm glad my mom let us come. I miss Rosa. It's weird how she didn't even tell us good-bye," Stephanie said, all of a sudden frustrated with her stitches. Olivia stretched across the seat to help her.

"When a woman is sick...terminally sick, she doesn't want to see anyone except her family," Mary Theresa said. "It was mandatory for her to get away immediately to receive the medical attention required. I'm in awe that Joseph went out of his way to bring us here. I offered to pay, but he refused. He sounded pretty grim."

Scarlet put her hand over her heart. "Please don't say anything like that. We'll know how bad it is when we see her." Scarlet moved to the driver's window. "Do you know how much longer?"

"Ladies, we're here," he said, pulling into a charming neighborhood. Old-growth trees loomed over antique buildings, casting shadows on the cars lined up on the streets. The driver opened the door, and Scarlet descended from the vehicle, taking note of the surroundings. Two brownstone buildings that sat side-by-side had been converted into one large mansion.

"I knew I should have worn pantyhose under these dress pants," Olivia mumbled, right on Scarlet's heels. "This is a fancy area, isn't it?"

Within several minutes, a petite maid named Enid escorted the ladies inside the building. They were so astonished at the magnitude of the property that none of them noticed the DE LA FLORA name plaque nailed above the entrance.

The women huddled close together, feeling small as they walked through a series of hallways in the monstrous-sized house.

A mixture of striped and patterned wallpaper lined the main entryway, which spilled into a room of wall shelves and curios cluttered with worldly knickknacks, paintings, and photos. Scarlet's favorite was a room they passed that thumped with an old-time burlesque theme with feathered-boa lampshades, shimmering sequin pillows, and flocked window treatments.

Stephanie loved that a white cockatiel graced the corner of

the entrance to the grand room, like a feathery guardian ready to squawk at any unsuspecting visitor. She sniffed to capture the sweet aroma of flowers that danced through the air.

"Well, hey there," Rosa said, waving both her hands. "You made it. Welcome to my home."

"Rosa!" they all squealed, happy to see her on her feet, boiling water for tea and not in a hospital bed on life support. After a few minutes of hugs and small talk, the elderly woman guided them into the eccentric palace that she called her bedroom.

Enid helped Rosa climb into bed while Reyna fluffed and propped up the pillows by the headboard so Rosa could rest on them. Enid then suggested that the ladies have a seat on the sofas next to Rosa's bed.

"I had the staff bring these over so we can catch up," Rosa said, motioning to the cozy set of black velvet couches and a coffee table that appeared freshly arranged. "I'm conserving my energy; I hope you don't mind if we hang out here."

The women graciously agreed and switched places on the couches until they felt comfortable. Joseph came in with a tray of coffee and cookies and offered them one at a time.

Stephanie recoiled. "Those look mighty yummy, but to be honest, I'm a little freaked out by all of this. Rosa, are you a millionaire or something? And how are you feeling?"

"I've seen better days," Rosa said, ignoring the first half of the question. "Thank you for coming. It means so much to me."

Scarlet, who hadn't taken a seat yet, froze behind the couches, bit her thumbnail, and thought hard. She had whizzed through all her statistics classes; she should have solved this puzzle long ago, but all the chiffon and rhinestones of her Daisy obsession smogged her noggin.

Scarlet began to slowly pace about the room, as if she were

searching for something. She ran to the foot of the bed and picked up Rosa's shoes from the floor and examined the soles to find one thicker than the other. Scarlet dropped her arms to her side, stepped over slowly to Rosa's bedside, and barely touched the skin on Rosa's hand.

"You're her," Scarlet said softly. "You're Daisy."

Rosa patted Scarlet's hand and met her gaze. "Oh, dear, we have so much to talk about. I've been planning this for ages, and I never thought where or how to tell this story."

"At the beginning," Scarlet said gently, sitting at the edge of Rosa's bed for a front-row seat.

"All right. The beginning," Rosa said, clearing her throat and then motioning repeatedly to signal Enid for a glass of water.

"I'd have to say it started the night of the accident. It was a beautiful spring night in Miami, barely cold enough to warrant a shawl. I was only twenty-two. My sisters and I had the magic touch for sewing. Let me tell you—we could create clothing and embellish it so gallantly; one seam could turn a head. One of us made the patterns, the other the sketches, another sewed and added the final details. Our skills were equal.

"One of us happened to be a mile more ambitious than the others. She moved away for a while and started to make a name for herself, but got caught in the middle of a marriage scandal. She came home broken and desperate. She came so close to hitting it big but let love get in the way. And then she got wind of an opportunity and promised she could take all of us to the next level of business with her.

"After much deliberation, we decided to crash the biggest Florida fashion event of the year. We snuck in wearing our gowns, purses, shoes, and belts that we had just finished that morning. We partied like we belonged there; no one even questioned us. We had a plan—to locate Walter Reese."

"I've heard of him," Scarlet said. "He created innovative garments for both men and women during the 1960s. He's the guy who did those thigh-high boots and short-waisted jackets; he was known for using neon colors."

"Yes," Rosa said. "We knew he'd be attending the event to sign new designers to his expanding label. He had a direct connection to department stores and wanted to bring artful glamour to the everyday woman. We gathered all the details ahead of time of what he wanted and created a presentation on our line. We knew he'd bite—if only we could pin him down long enough to hear the pitch."

Rosa took another sip of water and continued. "The banquet-room setting is still fresh in my mind. The waiters with their white gloves and silver trays buzzed around the guests like busy bees in a flower field. I remember noticing that the glass and silverware clinked in time with the Mambo Estrella playing "Que Rico El Mambo" at the front of the ballroom. The horn section gave me chills. Do you know that Marco found me an original recording of Mambo Estrella while I was taking the patternless sewing class?"

"Who cares about Marco right now! Did you get to meet Walter Reese?" Stephanie asked, eating her fourth cookie, totally intrigued.

"Oh, yes, we did," Rosa said joyfully. "We were right; he gobbled up everything we had and signed a temporary contract that night. He came by our table, kissed our hands, and welcomed us to his fashion family. He invited us to an afterparty to celebrate and even offered to put us up in a hotel so we wouldn't have to take a cab home so late at night."

Sadness washed over Rosa's wrinkled face, tugging it down into a frown.

"One of my sisters had too much to drink," she said. "She'd

just had a baby, the father skipped town; she wasn't thinking clearly that night. All the excitement, I suppose. I knew she needed to get home to her son. So . . . I talked everyone into leaving. I didn't want to cause a scene with my sister, so I pretended to have a headache. They were angry with me at first. They followed me outside and tried to lure me back in. I threatened to leave on my own; I knew they would join me. I stepped into the street and waved down the first cab that swooshed by. He wasn't happy—I think he was off duty but he saw us all dressed up and waved us in."

Rosa turned to reach for the embroidered hanky on her nightstand. She sniffled, took a sip of water, and continued.

Scarlet crawled closer to her on the bed. "You don't have to tell us now, Rosa. We can wait until morning. Right?" Scarlet said to the group.

"If she's cool, I want to hear more," Jennifer said. Stephanie scolded her with a flash of her eyes.

"Anyway, we forgot about the business of the afterparty and celebrated the contract," Rosa said. "That yellow cab may as well have been a VIP party lounge. All three of us held hands and cheered as loud as we could. We were so happy; we knew our lives would change forever. Our hard work paid off. Even our driver cheered for us.

"They say your life can change in an instant. Ours did. The driver didn't pay attention to the road . . . and hit an oncoming car. He overcorrected . . . and sent us flying over the embankment."

Scarlet felt her heart stop; so did the other women in the room, including Reyna and Enid, who had never heard the story until now. Scarlet cupped her hand over her mouth and felt her eyes flood with tears.

"All I remember is closing my eyes and feeling the car crash, bump, and roll over and over and over again. I didn't think we would ever stop. When we did, I tasted oil and dirt on my lips. I opened my eyes and saw the quilted tan upholstery fabric that lined the roof of the car. The windows were at the bottom and the doors at the top. We landed upside down. I could barely move my head, but I counted to three and gently turned it until I saw my shoulder...and then my arm...and then my hand that my twin sister was still holding. She squeezed it so tight, her giant black rhinestone ring on her finger sliced the skin on my knuckle."

"You're a twin?" Mary Theresa asked, lifting her head from crying. "And the ring...the one that slid off your finger in my house."

"Yes, that one," Rosa said. "My sister designed it—it was her favorite because she modeled it after one that Carmen Miranda always wore. My sister must have pressed it into my skin to get my attention. It worked. I bent down and was able to hold her head in my arms. She could barely speak.

" 'Rosa, I signed the contract in my name on our behalf; if I die tonight, it will be void,' she said to me. 'If any of us make it out alive, please carry it through...for me?'

"If my hermanas weren't bleeding to death, I would have smacked the girl. I thought she was going to ask me if I was OK, or tell me she loved me as her last words. But instead she wanted to make sure I knew about the contract. That little cabrona. She wanted more than anything to be a famous designer.

"I told her not to worry about the contract, that we'd all be fine. I didn't let her see me cry when she coughed up blood and finally told me she loved me. And then she squeezed my hand as hard as her weak body could and...and...then it went soft the exact moment I saw the life leave her eyes. I lost my two sisters that night. All because I wanted to go home early."

Mary Theresa, Olivia, Stephanie, and Jennifer ran to Rosa's side to console her.

Everyone but Scarlet, who sat up, her face motionless. "Who was your twin sister, Rosa?" she asked, staring at a vintage photo that hung on the wall of two twin girls sitting at a sewing machine.

Rosa gulped and took Scarlet's hand. "Daisy."

Scarlet jumped from the bed and ran across the hardwood floor of the bedroom until she reached Rosa's bathroom. *Daisy couldn't have died,* she thought over and over. *No way.* Scarlet turned the ceramic faucet handles on the copper sink and splashed her face with water. A cool, calming breeze passed through, and Scarlet reached for the bathtowel to dry her cheeks and eyes. She paced up and down the corridor of the bathroom and sat on a red chaise longue in the corner to think.

She didn't understand any of Rosa's actions. Why did she come all the way to Arizona to torture Scarlet by taking the class? Why did she hold back the truth? Were *all* her stories lies? Daisy couldn't be dead, Scarlet had seen newsreels and articles. She collected them, for God's sake. Unless, they were all of . . .

"Rosa," Scarlet said coldly as she exited the bathroom. "Have you been impersonating Daisy?"

"Scarlet, if I didn't heart you so much, I'd slap you for being so rude," Olivia said.

Rosa held up her hand to quiet Olivia. "Yes, I did. I did it to carry on my sister's dream," she said in a strict, grandmotherly tone. "And I do not feel guilty. She was so talented and worked harder than anyone I have ever known—well, until I met you, Scarlet. You remind me a lot of Daisy. It happened so quickly. The ambulance came and I kept hearing her last words in my head. I passed myself off as her. No one figured it out. I've been living somewhat of a double life ever since. Back in the eighties we had everything settled with the lawyers, for the safety of the business. Very few people know. Not even Johnny knows. I expect all of you to take this to the grave. I'll deny it if anyone asks."

The women nodded in agreement. Rosa knew she could trust them.

Joseph brought in another tray of cookies just in time. The women took a short break to eat. Scarlet sat in a large wooden chair at the opposite side of the room. She didn't feel mad anymore, just flustered.

"Scarlet come here," Rosa said. "I want to explain how you fit into this."

Scarlet rose from her chair and made a stop at the cookie tray for a cup of hot tea. She needed something soothing to pass through her veins. "I think you should write a book, Rosa," she said as she sat on the bed. "You have quite a page-turner here."

Rosa rubbed her hands together like the master storyteller she was. "Oh, it gets better," she said. "Not only did I pretend to be Daisy, I raised Lily's son, too. John."

Rosa grinned. "That boy was trouble from day one. Daisy told me that Lily made him that way as my payback."

"What do you mean, Daisy told you?" Mary Theresa said. "I thought she died."

"Oh, her body passed, but her spirit is alive and well. How else do you think I could design all those fabulous clothes?"

"Daisy haunts you?" Scarlet asked.

Rosa elbowed the pillows against the headboard to make

them fluffy again. "I wouldn't call it haunting; she's just a nag. I don't necessarily hear or see her. I feel her. It's the twin thing."

"She needs to cross over," Olivia said. "You need to tell her to cross over and go with the good Lord!"

"She can't, or rather…she won't," Rosa explained. "I raised little Johnny the best I could, with good ethics and business sense, with the plan of turning over the Casa de la Flora empire to him. But the kid is still a brat. He's greedy and doesn't care about fashion one bit. All he wants is his picture in the magazines, and money. I've given him so many chances. He deserves to be demoted to Johnny "Hand Me the" Scissors.

"Daisy and I even decided we would set him up with a test and find a Plan B. As we expected, he failed miserably. So we put Plan B into action." Rosa reached for her intercom. "Bring in Louisa now, please."

The clock struck one a.m., yet Louisa from the Johnny Scissors Nightmare Experience strolled in, wearing jeans and a tie-dye T-shirt.

Scarlet gasped. "I thought you worked for Johnny!"

"I work for *Rosa,* Scarlet," Louisa said. "I processed your tuition, and reworked your contract so Johnny has nothing on you. I'm sorry for being rude last Sunday, but I had to play along with Johnny so he wouldn't find out."

"You mean the entire time, my tuition was paid?" Scarlet asked.

"No. Not in the way you think," Rosa said. "I don't believe in shortcuts! I believe in hard work and proving oneself. You had so many obstacles to overcome, but you never let them stop you. However, we wanted Daisy's buttons back something fierce."

Scarlet dropped her hand on the top of her head. "You won the buttons? Oh, Rosa, how awful that I had them the whole time. You asked me to show them to you and I said no. I feel so stupid."

Rosa flipped her hand at Scarlet. "It wasn't me asking, dear. It was Daisy nagging in my ear. We're happy to have them back. And thankful to Louisa for bidding on them. She's our spy. She gives us a live feed of everything Johnny is purposely doing to ruin our company. I'm cutting him off tomorrow."

Scarlet perked up. "What do you mean, 'cutting him off'?"

"He owns a portion of House of Tijeras, but other than that, he is a salaried employee," Louisa said. "He's assuming when Daisy, err...I mean Rosa, dies, she is going to leave everything to him. However, that is far from the case.

"Ladies, remember the first day of class when we talked about the patterns in our lives? I said I wanted to preserve mine. If I leave it to Johnny, he'll shred it to pieces," said Rosa. I came to this conclusion a few years ago, and have been in search of a replacement for me—and Daisy. Not just any replacement, the *perfect* replacement. And it's you, Scarlet."

"What?" Scarlet asked, spreading her hand out on her chest. "Me?"

"Yes, dear," Rosa said. "I took your class to see if you were as smart and kindhearted in real life as you are on your blog."

"What does it all mean? I start my new civil engineering job on Monday."

"Well, if you accept, you'd have to cancel that. We want you to take over as CEO of Casa de la Flora Enterprises. Louisa will be your senior vice president and will handle the daily operations so you can focus on the long-term vision. You'd have to fly out here and stay while we set everything up. We have a team in place to guide you."

"I am so honored to keep Daisy's designs alive. I'll make you proud, Rosa," Scarlet said.

"Good. But we also want you to launch your own Scarlet Santana brand too. Mexibilly Frocks and accessories to match. And because we want your own brand to thrive, I'm also handing over the property on Central Avenue in Phoenix. Use it as a remote location, maybe for your Scarlet Santana headquarters idea, whatever you want. You'll want to appoint someone in charge of that."

"I can hire my sister!" Scarlet said. "Yay, Scarlet can blog again!" Olivia cheered.

Scarlet laced her fingers in front of her face and ducked behind them. She paced a few times and spun around. "This is huge. You really have that much faith in me?"

"Of course. Daisy and I see you as our long-lost granddaughter; we trust you. Do you accept?" Rosa asked.

"Yes!" Scarlet said. "Yes!"

"Great," Rosa said. "We'll announce it at the fiftieth-anniversary party at the Met tomorrow night. There's going to be a fashion show of Daisy's and my dresses, so I bought some of your dresses from your online store for us to wear. It will be a nice way to introduce you. We already called Eva Alegria; she'll be wearing a Scarlet original as well."

Joseph pulled a red cloth off of a rack of clothing. Scarlet gasped. "My Mexibilly Frocks are going to the Met?"

"They sure are," Louisa said. "They're gorgeous, Scarlet. We do fittings in the morning."

Scarlet and the other women exchanged glances and approached Rosa's bedside. "Was pretending to be sick part of the plan?" Scarlet asked, hoping for Rosa to answer yes.

"My illness is what triggered the plan," she replied. "I have stage-four cancer. In early November, my doctor gave me a month to live."

"Oh, Rosa, *nooo,*" they all said in unison.

"No, it's beautiful," she said. "I'm seventy-four. I've lived my life to the fullest and accomplished everything I wanted. And of all the places I've traveled and the sights I've seen and the people I've known...nothing touched my heart more than meeting all of you. Scarlet, your class was one of my most favorite experiences. After my diagnosis, I came home and spent days in bed, waiting to die. But Daisy wouldn't let me. I'd pass my office on the way to the kitchen and I'd see your blog about your class on the laptop screen. I talked Joseph into joining me on an excursion to Glendale, Arizona."

Mary Theresa had always wondered about the odd relationship between Joseph and Rosa. With so many juicy details swimming around the room, she couldn't help but ask him.

"It's another story for another time," he said, glancing at Rosa.

Rosa threw her hands in the air. "There is no more time, dear," she told him. "Joseph used to be married to Saide, but he left her for Daisy."

"He's Javier! Her Madgesty's Closet," Stephanie said. "Scarlet wrote about him in her blog. You were the owner that flirted with Saide. You fell in love with Daisy too?"

"Yes, he sure did. To make a long story short—she nags him, too. He has stayed on as my confidant and house manager. But he'll be retiring soon. Now it's time for us to get some sleep. Reyna has arranged all your rooms. We have a big day tomorrow."

35

Johnny Scissors cursed before punching the button on his Bluetooth. He listened to the first few words and talk-shouted to the public-relations director of the Met.

"For the last time, my aunt cannot make it tonight; she asked me to represent her at the anniversary celebration. I'm going to need her reserved seats, but thirty more in the front row for my entourage. I'll be backstage to follow the models when they finish the runway show."

He held his finger to the earpiece and shook his head. "What do you mean she already collected the tickets? She's supposed to be on her deathbed somewhere. Cancel her seats. Actually, never mind, I'll take care of it myself."

Johnny removed the earpiece and tossed it on the desk in front of him. "Always last-minute drama," he said with a pout. "Tonight is my night, not hers. She steals everything from me."

"Hello, Johnny," Rosa said from the other end of his grand living room. Behind her stood a fleet of well-suited lawyers, as well as a few of Johnny's inner-circle executives.

"Auntie Daisy!" he said, perking up like a mischievous school-boy who had just been caught red-handed. "You came! Thank goodness you made it!" he said, gushing as he swiftly weaved his way through his faux-fur-covered chairs and end tables. Johnny, like his aunt, loved excess.

"No thanks to you," she said. "We're here to discuss your future at Casa de la Flora."

He slapped his arms on his legs. "Now? I have a big event in about two hours. Can't it wait until morning? Louisa, what is going on here?"

"You're fired," Louisa said.

Johnny turned and walked over to his bar and poured himself two fingers of gin. "Ha! I own this place. I run it while my loca aunt over there goes to work the sewing machines in China. She lost sight of the company a long time ago."

"Actually," Louisa said, "she traveled there as part of the International Council of Garment and Fashion. Your aunt's firsthand experience of working conditions has helped improve the lives of seamstresses and factories across the world. And throughout all that time, Johnny, she's been correcting, sometimes preventing, all your costly mistakes here at House of Tijeras."

Johnny threw back his gin. "Auntie, I love your old-school Cubana drama. Is all this because you want to come back on board? I guess we can add an extra chair to the conference table. Will that make you happy?"

Rosa slowly approached him and glared into his eyes. "I'm sorry your mother died, and you never were able to bond with her. I miss her too. But I did everything in my power to raise you and teach you right. I wanted to hand all this over to you, but mijo, you are not meant for this." She raised her crooked finger and tapped his chest. "There is something else inside you that you need to discover and nurture. Your time here has run its course."

"You're mad because my line is more popular than yours; you

think I'm stealing your limelight," he said, slamming his glass back onto the bar.

Out of nowhere, Scarlet popped out from behind Louisa. "Don't try to give her the royal shaft," Scarlet snapped. "It's the other way around, mister. Daisy's good name and history are the lifeboat that keeps you afloat. Instead of coming up with your own signature style, you copy and steal. Don't you dare disrespect her!"

Scarlet slipped her arm in Rosa's. "Come on, let's go. You need to rest up."

"We'll handle it from here, Ms. de la Flora," Louisa said, putting her arm around Rosa and patting her back.

"I love you, little John," Rosa said. "I tried to make it work, I really did, but we want this company to last well into the next century. We feel there is only one person who can lead the way. The paperwork has been completed; security is here to escort you out."

"What the hell?" Johnny sputtered.

"Johnny," Rosa said, "I'd like you to meet the new CEO of Casa de la Flora, Miss Scarlet Santana."

*   *   *

The changes at Casa de la Flora were the buzz of the night at the Met gala. Rumors bounced from one cluster of gossipers to the next. Eva Alegria indeed arrived and kissed Scarlet's cheek to congratulate her. Turns out, Eva had been singing Scarlet's praises to the press ever since the material makeover in the ladies' room.

The only person missing from the big night? Johnny Scissors, who supposedly went crying to his lawyers, only to learn he didn't have a dress form to stand on.

Scarlet couldn't wait to get started on her new career. She

hadn't quite wrapped her head around how big of a challenge awaited her. But she didn't intend to worry about it now. The weekend was all about celebrating friendship and fashion—and most of all Daisy and Rosa.

When they returned to Rosa's house, the women changed into silk pajamas that Reyna and Enid had set out for them. "This is so cool. It's like a slumber party," Jennifer said. Joseph promised to take them on a sightseeing tour of New York for the rest of the weekend, but before they retreated to their rooms for the night, they all met in the large seating room to wind down.

"That was the most grand diva entrance I've ever heard of, even better than the movies," Mary Theresa said to Rosa. "The way they piped in the mambo music and then those two hunky guys slowly opened those mile-high golden parlour doors..."

"And the twinkling light show and all the exotic feathers they dropped from the ceiling on us when they carried you out on that big crystal-covered chair!" Stephanie dreamily recalled as she crossed her skinny legs and rested her chin on her hand.

"I got goosebumps when they held those huge feather fans over your face and then lifted them so everyone could see you," said Olivia. "Did you hear how loud everyone gasped and then whistled? It was like you were a queen."

"She is a queen," Scarlet said. "Rosa, I don't know what I would have done if I never met you. Next to my Nana Eleanor, you changed my life. And I'm not talking about all this, or Daisy. I'm talking about you, Rosa. Right here, you from the class. Thank you. I'll spend every day doing right for the sake of Casa de la Flora."

"For the sake of fashion!" Rosa corrected. "And please, take care of that nana of yours. We are thankful to her for priming you for us."

Mary Theresa, Olivia, Jennifer, and Stephanie gathered around to be with Rosa. No one spoke of the invisible giant in the room—her illness. They listened in awe as she shared even more stories about her childhood with Daisy. She made them giggle until their sides hurt and made them cry until Jennifer had to sprint to the other room for tissue. When they finally decided to go to bed, they escorted Rosa to her room and hugged her good night.

"Tomorrow, we'll go to the former home of Her Madgesty's Closet!" Rosa promised. "That's where my sister made her window display and got her big break!"

After the girls left Rosa's room and turned out the lights, the surviving de la Flora sister sighed and rested in her canopy bed. It had never felt more cushiony and comfy. She tugged the coverings under her chin and looked to the dresser by the window. The small flame of a lone white prayer candle waved and flickered, casting a warm glow against the wall and ceiling.

Content and fulfilled at last, Rosa silently made her peace with God, creation, and her sisters. Her gaze followed the beads that hung from the top of her bed and blurred into a kaleidoscope of memories: emotions, images, and sounds she loved and cherished. They swirled through her mind as she began to doze off to sleep.

"I did it. I feel so free now," she mumbled just before she slipped off to neverland with a petite grin of accomplishment and pride.

The vibe of the mansion shifted, as if the house felt relief from the tension of the past few years. A heavy silence permeated the property, and with a sudden gust of wind, the prayer candle on Rosa's dresser went out, plummeting her room into darkness.

Rosa opened her eyes to an exceptionally bright morning light that filled her room with a warm yellow glow. If she didn't know better, she'd swear it was the bedroom she'd once shared with her sisters at Coconut Grove. She then heard familiar voices chatting and giggling at the vanity dresser next to her closet door.

"Daisy? Lily?" Rosa asked.

"Aye, don't hog the mirror, hermana!" Daisy said. "Have you seen my earring? I just made them last night and I already lost one!"

Rosa watched two young women bustle in front of the mirror and she flinched when they stared at her in its reflection.

"Get off the bed. Andale, Rosa, we're going to be late for the party!" her sister, Lily, scolded. As a time marshal, she considered an hour early to be an hour late.

The two girls ran up to Rosa, who sat speechless on the edge of her bed, and pulled her upright. "Come on, they're waiting for us outside! Mom and Dad are going to be there, too. And you'll never believe who is driving us!" Daisy said.

Rosa tilted her head down to find herself wearing a thin gold sparkly halter dress. She gasped when she examined her slender legs and creamy brown skin. Just to make sure she wasn't dreaming, she jumped up to take a gander in the mirror, but almost tripped in her stilettos. It took only a second to get used to them. She checked herself out in the mirror and ran her long, svelte hands down the front of her gown. She last wore this dress for her and Daisy's twenty-first birthday party.

"We make a great team, don't we?" Daisy said, joining her sister in front of the full-length mirror. The sisters held hands and admired their handmade outfits. Daisy wore a dress similar to Rosa's, except red with mini-pieces of crystal-accented fruit sewn into the neckline.

"Yes, we do," Rosa replied. "Lily, about little John..."

"He's going to be just fine, Rosa," she said. "He's going to become a stronger person because of you."

"I hope I served you both well," Rosa said, her eyes filling with tears.

Daisy and Lily slipped their skinny arms around Rosa's waist. "More than we could ever ask for. Thank you, Rosa."

Outside, a car horn honked.

The girls squealed and ran as fast as they could without tripping out the front door of their former home.

Daisy and Rosa ran arm in arm across the front porch and down the walkway of their aunt and uncle's lawn.

"All aboard for the Cha-Cha Express, my chickadees!" sang a strange lady at the driver's side of the old-fashioned limo. Rosa squinted for a better look...Carmen Miranda!

"It's time to come home, baby sister," Daisy said to Rosa as she climbed into the car, where Lily waited for them.

Rosa looked back at the house, and then at her dress, at Carmen, and then her sisters.

"Am...I...dead?" Rosa asked nervously.

"No, baby, this party's for the living!" Daisy proclaimed, shoving her fists in the air.

"Come on, get in," Carmen said, honking the horn. "We'll be late for the first dance! I'm due to sing onstage anytime now. You know those mambo heads, they don't like to wait."

Rosa climbed into the car and smiled down the row at her sisters. Each with a flower behind her ear—a rose, a daisy, and a lily.

All of them holding hands.

EPILOGUE

A teenage girl walked with her grandmother along the streets of downtown Glendale. Their only mission was to stop at the Mexican pastry shop for a treat. But first they had to pass Vega's Vicious Vinyl.

"Grandma, stop, I want to see this window display. Whoa!" the teenage girl said. "It's so sparkly, look at those dresses hanging up . . . and all the photos on the floor."

"Beautiful," the grandmother said. "It looks like a tribute to the woman in the picture. She must have liked fashion and travel and dancing. Look at those big black round eyeglasses; they're so mod. What does that record album say? Mambo Estrella? I've never heard of them."

The girl pointed up at the hanging strings of blinking bulbs. "I want to hang up lights like that in my bedroom; they look like twinkling stars. And check out the buttons in that jar. That's the shade of green I want for my bedroom. Hey, I wonder what kind of store this is."

The teenager ran around her grandmother, pulled open the glass door, looked inside, and then stepped out and waved for her grandmother to come in.

"Hurry, Grandma!" she said. "This store is so cool; the inside looks even better! It's like a party in here!"

The woman paused so she could read the framed letter at the bottom of the display that was covered in handwritten salutations.

This window is dedicated to our dear friend, Rosa de la Flora
Garcia. November 1, 1937–January 29, 2011.
Rosa—Thanks for the secret mambo dance lessons & for
teaching me the art of proper thrift shopping.—Marco
Rosa, You will always be dear to my heart for helping
me through my "patternless" transition. You may not have
had any children, but you were a mother to us all.—
MTC
To my Rosa: May your sparkle shine forever.—Olivia
Hi, Rosa! We love you and we hope you are dancing the night
away with your sisters and making lots of sparkly clothes!—
Jennifer and Stephanie
Rosa, my dear. All I can say is mil gracias for believing in me
and helping me become the woman I am today. May you
find the perfect sewing machine in heaven. Please give
Daisy and Lily a smooch for me. Love, SS

Overhearing the conversation, Scarlet and Nana Eleanor grinned at each other as they passed by, having just left the Mexican bakery next door. They strode peacefully down the sidewalk like they did every Sunday afternoon, munching on warm apple empanadas.

When they reached Nana's black Mercedes, Scarlet opened the passenger door and helped Nana in. She then went around the other side, climbed in, opened the glove box, and pulled out two Scarlet Santana prototype scarves dotted with micro crystals. Nana Eleanor took one, and both women tied them around their heads and slipped on big tortoiseshell sunglasses.

"Well, Nana, where to?" Scarlet asked, revving up the engine.

Nana Eleanor raised her finger as she stopped to think, and then dug through her purse and pulled out a piece of paper. "The fabric store," she said. "There is a pattern I want to buy."

Scarlet couldn't help but laugh. "Anything you want, Nana. A pattern it is!"

Spanish Glossary

Miss Scarlet's School of Patternless Sewing has Spanish (and Spanglish) terms sprinkled throughout. Many of these words have multiple meanings according to region. However, this glossary features the translations as presented by the characters in this book.

andale: hurry up!
angelitos: little angels
cabrona: stubborn female
cafe con leche: coffee with milk
caldo: soup
casa: house
cascaron: an empty eggshell filled with confetti
casita: little house
chisme: gossip
comadre: a dear friend, female
De nada: "It's nothing." Used as a reply when someone says "Thank you."
empanadas: Mexican pastries that are similar to turnovers
escúchame: "listen to me"
estrella: star
folklórico: Mexican folk dance

grande: large

hermana: sister

hombre: man

la verdad: the truth

loca: crazy female

los niños: the kids

menudo: soup made of beef tripe

mi causa: my cause

Mi hermana viena pronto: My sister is coming soon

mija: "my daughter" or an affectionate term an elder says to a
  younger woman

mijo: "my son" or an affectionate term an elder says to a
  younger man

mil gracias: a million thanks

mis melones: my melons

pan dulce: sweet bread

Permitame terminar: "Allow me to finish."

Que rico, hombre!: "How rich, man!" or "Looking good, man!"

quinceañera: celebration of a girl's fifteenth birthday

red chili flautas: small corn tortillas filled with red chili meat,
  rolled into "flutes" and deep fried

tu boca: your mouth

vetrana: seasoned, experienced (female)

vieja: old lady

HOW TO: Make a Duct-Tape Dress Form

The key to making custom clothing is to have a personalized dress form like Scarlet and her class made. You can make your own too! Not only is it completely functional, low-cost, and tailored to your every curve, it also makes a great conversation or art piece. Gather your friends together and have a duct-tape-dress-form-making fiesta!

Materials Needed:

Long T-shirt
2–3 rolls of duct tape
10 lb bag of polyester stuffing
nonstick scissors
Adjustable music stand (remove the sheet tray)
A friend to help you!

Instructions:

1. Put on the T-shirt and stretch it down over your bottom so it hits at the top of your thighs.
2. Tear off two long pieces of tape and place them in an "X" across your chest, followed by a piece underneath that so

it begins to look like a swimsuit top. Continue to add tape tightly in long crisscrosses across all four sides of your torso, and then your bottom and pelvis area.

3. Add a tight layer of tape to your upper chest, shoulder area, and underarms. The back as well.

4. Add a third tight layer of tape, all vertical, over the entire torso.

5. Add a last layer of tape, horizontal, over the entire torso.

6. Look and feel around your torso to make sure it is evenly layered and covered.

7. Remove the form from your body by having a friend snip up the back from behind all the way up.

8. Slide out of the form. Cut away excess T-shirt material from the bottom and from the sleeves.

9. Tear off several 6- to 8-inch strips of duct tape and have them ready. With the backside facing up, slide your arm inside the form and carefully place the tape to seal the back seam. Keep adding tape until the structure is uniform thickness and strong.

10. Add tape to cover the neck and arm holes.

11. Turn the form upside-down and fill with stuffing until sturdy.

12. Tape off the bottom, leaving a small area to insert the stand.

13. Insert the stand so the bar goes up the center and to the top of the form. Tape in place.

TIP: For a sturdier base, you can cut a thin piece of wood or thick cardboard and tape it onto the stand, then insert the form and tape it together.

HOW TO: MAKE "LITTLE VICTORIES" PAGES

We all have little victories in daily life, and like Scarlet preached to her blog readers, we need to acknowledge and appreciate them. Sometimes when life is a challenge, those mini-accomplishments are all we have to hold on to—so embrace and celebrate them!

Materials Needed:

12 pieces of art paper in assorted colors and textures
Assorted sizes of markers or paints
Rubber stamps, ink pads
Stencils
Stickers, magazine photos, drawings, etc.
Piece of writing paper

Instructions:

1. On a piece of paper, write down each month of the year with space underneath. If you have a calendar from that year, flip through it and make a list of the special events you had. Mark them under the appropriate month. Also,

do your best to think back to milestones you reached, big or small. Maybe you discovered a new flavor you liked.

2. Now dedicate one month to each of the twelve sheets of art paper. Write down the little victory from your list in colorful, fun lettering so it stands out.

3. Embellish all around the page and text using glitter, markers, stickers, pictures.

4. When all twelve are done, hang them up, make them into a book, and share them.

5. You don't have to burn them at the end of the year like Daisy and Scarlet did, but you can tuck them away in your treasure chest to make room for more little victories to come!

HOW TO: Make Your Own Mexibilly Frock

Scarlet Santana had her own method to whipping up a one-of-a-kind patternless dress made from scarves. Here is a simplified version for you to make on your own.

Materials Needed for a Size Medium:

3 square vintage silk scarves, 24 x 24 inches (4 for a large, 5 for XL)
1 tube top
Straight pins
Sewing machine
1 long, thin silk vintage scarf, or two sewn together

Instructions:

Line up the square silk scarves and sew them together. Press the seams. You will have one long piece of fabric. Hold the fabric lengthwise, grab a corner, and begin to pleat and pin at the back of the bottom hem of the tube top. Make sure the scarf fabric is pinned from underneath. Continue all the way around. The pleats should be even; if they aren't, remove the pins and adjust. Try the dress on to make sure it is to your liking. Sew the skirt of the dress in place on the machine. After you put on your dress, tie the thin scarf around as a sash at the waist seam.

READING GROUP GUIDE

1. When you first heard the term "patternless sewing," what did it make you think of?
2. What type of "pattern" do you have for your life?
3. Can you think of a time when a traditional pattern, either literally or metaphorically, didn't work and you had to make adjustments?
4. Scarlet had issues with her family. She thought it was because they didn't respect her; they thought it was because she was too busy for them. Have you ever been in a situation like that? How did you resolve it?
5. Olivia looked to DaisyForever.com as her daily dose of inspiration. After reading Scarlet's postings, can you see why? Did her words have an effect on how you see the world?
6. Scarlet was almost obsessed with Daisy de la Flora. Do you think this helped her or held her back from her fashion career?
7. If you were Mary Theresa, how would you have handled the situation with Hadley? Do you think he had valid reasons for leaving?
8. Rosa had to share her life with Daisy's because of the guilt from the car crash. Do you think she did the right thing?

9. How important do you think Scarlet was to Marco's life? If he hadn't allowed the class to work at the shop, do you think he would have ever come to terms with his brother's death?

10. Though teenagers, Jennifer and Stephanie connected with older women in the class. Do you think these relationships will help shape what kind of women they will grow up to be?

11. Olivia took a bad experience and transformed it into something positive. What is a recent downfall you had where you had the opportunity to do the same?

12. Rosa, Marco, and the sewing class had to deal with the death of a loved one. How did their grief differ?

Author Q&A

Q: What inspired this book?

A: I have always loved to sew. I think I get it from my Nana Eleanor, who was a master seamstress, a perfectionist. However, I've never been able to successfully use a pattern. For some reason, it never works out and I end up taking the project in a whole new direction. I thought it would make a fun story to see these different types of women tackle a patternless sewing class.

Q: How different is the final book from your original idea?

A: Oh, wow. Very different. Once I started writing it, it became clear that "patternless sewing" doubled as a metaphor for our lives. We are all born into this world with some kind of pattern or tradition to follow. Some of us want a fresh pattern, some want to alter theirs, others want to stay exactly on the lines. Once I realized that, it allowed me to take my characters to a deeper level.

Q: This seems to be a lighthearted book at first, but there are several instances of death. Why did you feel that was important to include?

A: It might have to do with my father passing away around the time that I wrote this book. I had so many issues to work through. I learned that it is important to celebrate the lives of our loved ones who died, but at the same time, we have to let them go. It was also important for me to present their crossing over in a positive light.

Q: Were any of the characters based on real people?

A: Texas purse designer Enid Collins is my inspiration for Daisy. Not so much Enid's life story, but her crazy purse designs. I wondered what kind of woman in the '60s would be so bold to make such awesomely kooky handbags dripping with gems and stones in the shapes of animals and flowers and cars. However, I took it to the next level and added costumes, gowns, and accessories to her résumé. Also, by the time I finished the book, I saw a lot of my father in Rosa. The way she was so smart and calm and talented and loved to travel. She knew about so many issues and always put love first. That is 100 percent my dad! Nana Eleanor is a blend of both my nanas.

Q: Why Carmen Miranda?

A: I love Carmen! A lot of people don't know that she used to be a hat and purse designer before she was discovered. When she became famous she sketched and sewed all her costumes. I felt that, given the era and sparkle factor I had going on with Daisy de la Flora, Carmen would totally be her inspiration.

Q: You live in Phoenix, Arizona, yet this book takes place in Glendale, Arizona. Why is that?

A: I was raised close to Glendale, so I've spent a lot of time there. I also set the book during the holidays, because I love the season of Glendale Glitters when all the downtown streets are lined with lights and decorations. The area is so charming and old-fashioned. Lots of thrift stores, Mexican bakeries, candy shops. Marco's record store is fictional, but I could totally see it on Fifty-eighth Avenue and Glendale!

Q: Did you listen to any music while writing the book?

A: Oh, yes! Every time I worked on Mary Theresa and Hadley, I listened to John Coltrane, because that is what triggered everything. With Scarlet, I always listened to Glenn Miller or other Big Band groups when she was happy, and when she was confused and frustrated I listened to an English band called Marina and the Diamonds. Daisy and Rosa—mambo all the way, as well as Carmen Miranda albums. For Marco, he was so dark and deep, I played Fleet Foxes over and over. My favorite song for this book is Sam Cooke's, "Nothing Can Change This Love." It reminds me of Scarlet and Marco!

Q: What is the main takeaway you want readers to close the cover with?

A: To step outside their normal boundaries, or in some cases, step inside boundaries. Basically just try something new to mix up your lifestyle. And to stay true to your family, and they will stay true to you!

Acknowledgments

Thank you to my husband, Patrick Murillo, and my kids, DeAngelo and Maya, for always having my back! Lots of love to my family: Theresa, Davy, and Michelle. My mom, Norma, for listening to my book updates and even offering tips when I called on them! Much love to my mother-in-law, Susie Murillo, for coming over to cook dinners while I was in deadline lockdown! Blessings to my dad, David, for watching over me from heaven.

Three golden dress forms for Arizona designer Angela Johnson, and fashionista Marytza Rubio, and Brini Maxwell for the education and inspiration for all things fashionable. Love to Robrt Pela for inviting me to join his writing group.

Mucho appreciation to my coworkers at iLoveToCreate, and my former coworkers at the *Arizona Republic* for cheering me on! Hugs to my agents, Erin Malone and Scott Wachs. Double hugs to the staff at Grand Central Publishing—my editor, Selina McLemore, for helping me shape this book into a story I love; and to Latoya Smith for all the support.

Mil gracias to all my online friends from my blog, Twitter, Facebook, MySpace, Flickr, and YouTube. And all my crafty friends in the industry, may your scissors never dull: Thank you for all the sequin love. Most of all I'd love to thank *you,* for supporting authors and reading books!

ABOUT THE AUTHOR

Crafts! Drama! Glitter!

Kathy Cano-Murillo leads an artful life and her mission is to inspire others to do the same. A Chicana pop artist and writer, she is the founder of CraftyChica.com, a lifestyle site for creative women. Kathy has authored seven craft books and her work has been spotlighted in Bloomingdale's, Target.com, and Michaels, and featured by NPR, the *New York Times,* HGTV, and SiTV. Her debut novel, *Waking Up in the Land of Glitter,* was chosen by *Latina* magazine as a "Top 10 Latina Summer Beach Read," and by Publishers.org as a selection for Latino Book Month. Kathy lives in Phoenix, Arizona, with her husband, two kids, and five Chihuahuas.

**Did you miss the hilarious
first novel in the Crafty Chica series?**

A group of unlikely allies teams up to compete in the world's biggest craft competition, and discovers that fostering a friendship is truly an art.

"A fun read about stumbling into love, honoring friendship, and celebrating the power of craft. Full of good cheer!"
—Kate Jacobs, *New York Times* bestselling author of
The Friday Night Knitting Club

"Every word in this hilarious, fun read sparkles. Kathy Cano-Murillo is certainly an author to watch. I woke up in the land of happy reading!"

—*Debbie Macomber,*
#1 *New York Times* bestselling author

"*Waking Up in the Land of Glitter* is wildly addictive! Funny, sweet, and slyly wicked, it draws you in so deeply that you're not even remotely mad you've spent the night on the couch, reading, and missed all of your shows on Bravo."
—Laurie Notaro, *New York Times* bestselling author

If you enjoyed the Crafty Chica series, then you'll love the Quinceañera Club—a new series exploring the relationships between mothers and daughters during the most important time in their daughters' lives.

Now available from Grand Central Publishing

DAMAS, DRAMAS, AND ANA RUIZ

A QUINCEAÑERA CLUB NOVEL

BELINDA ACOSTA

A mother does the best she can to hold her family together while teaching her daughter what it means to be a strong and powerful woman in this first installment in the Quinceañera Club series.

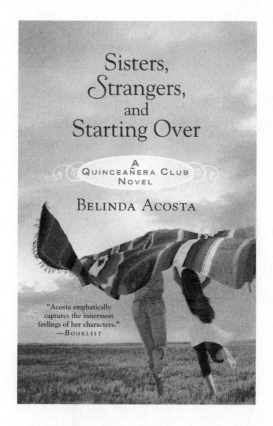

Sisters,
Strangers,
and
Starting Over

A Quinceañera Club
Novel

Belinda Acosta

"Acosta emphatically
captures the innermost
feelings of her characters."
—Booklist

A woman must come to terms with the death of her estranged
sister while learning to become a mother to her orphaned niece,
in this second novel of the Quinceañera Club series.